NATALYA L

Natalya Lowndes is an English university teacher who lives with her husband and two children in the south of England. Her first novel, *Chekago*, was published to great critical acclaim in 1988, followed by *Angel in the Sun* in 1989, both revealing her close personal knowledge of the Soviet Union, derived from family ties and friendships. She is now at work on her fourth novel which, like *Snow Red*, is set in England and Russia.

Also by Natalya Lowndes and available from Sceptre Books:

ANGEL IN THE SUN
CHEKAGO

Natalya Lowndes

SNOW RED

British Library C.I.P.

Lowndes, Natalya
    Snow red.
    I. Title
    823 [F]

ISBN 0-340-57981-1

Printed and bound in Great Britain for Hodder and Stoughton Paperbacks, a division of Hodder and Stoughton Ltd., Mill Road, Dunton Green, Sevenoaks, Kent TN13 2YA. (Editorial Office: 47 Bedford Square, London WC1B 3DP) by Clays Ltd., St Ives plc.

МОЕМУ ОТЦУ
ОДНОМУ ИЗ ПЕРВЫХ БЛАГОРОДНЫХ АФГ
АНЦЕВ

To my father, one of the first
noble *Afgantsi*

Contents

I

VEROCHKA'S

Moscow, November

1

It was Slater's last night. He had wanted to leave early but the little brunette with the squint swept her arms round his neck and kissed him on the mouth, and he allowed her to lead him back into the sitting-room.

After more sweet champagne he sat down at the piano and sang "The Snowy-Breasted Pearl" to his own accompaniment while the brunette caressed his hair from behind, whispering endearments. When a woman's voice called his name from the next room he did not immediately rise but let the girl continue to caress him until the last note was struck, because he knew she was unhappy and thought that the words of the song were for her.

In the bedroom Vera was leaning against the huge painted side-board, a glass of port in her hand, above her head a hanging cabinet full of china dogs, picture-hatted ladies and boys with bird-cages. The bedroom always reminded Slater of a fifties Ideal Home Exhibition, everything cream and green, even the bulky telephone which had never been connected and was there only for show.

As he came in Vera put down her glass and went over to the bed.

"She thinks she is too big."

Obedient to the pressure of the woman's hands on the small of her back the girl on the bed canted her head downwards into the single pillow and stared past the man to the wall.

At the beginning he was usually given a few facts: age, upbringing, background, that kind of thing. But this last time Slater preferred to know very little.

"Here," Vera said, flinging back the half-bustle of the frock so that the deeper magenta of the doubled hem fell nearly to the girl's slant eyes, darkening her gaze within the spread of her hair.

As interested, for the moment, in watching Vera's quick, unprim touches to the body of the girl, as in the exposure of the thick, muscular thighs which held her so high before him, Slater took a stand at the foot of the bed and watched while the elderly woman showed out the defects of the blonde beneath her fingers.

"Here," she said again, one hand drawing up the stiff, embroidered

3

underskirt, the other peeling away what was beneath – skimpy, Slater noted, seen before, Prussian blue, artificial, cheap. She was beautiful, there, this girl, heavy-framed, the way she held herself taut against the woman. Flagrant. An actress? Acrobat, artist? He didn't care. It was too late now, much too late.

The blonde thrust against the sweep of Vera's nails, unparted, and looked back at him imperturbably, seeming not to care that she was uncovered, whether or not he cared or did not care, unsure whether to weep or smile, sure of nothing except her resistance to the woman who bent over, intent on exploring her for the man.

"Do you have to be quite so rough?" Slater said.

Vera let him remove the girl's shoes and stockings. That was not enough. Vera knew it would not be enough.

"And here," she said, her hand between the pillow and the long warm throat, scooping out the breasts. The girl burst into tears, but Vera ignored her as she had ignored Slater, and rolled back the straps of the *décolleté*, pinning the blonde's arms to her sides. "Savlyevich the Orientalist, his youngest daughter, twenty-five and already *kandidat nauk* . . ."

"Be quiet," said Slater. He was not ready. He must have drunk too much. Or was the girl to blame? Too stylish perhaps, intimidating in her languor. And tears had never been on the menu before. And tonight bloody Vera was even more of a caricature: too much lipstick in that dead white face, too high a sheen on her dyed Bloomsbury bob, and a voice half an octave higher than could possibly be natural.

"My dear, you don't mean to tell me you are at last feeling your age?"

She had always been old. Some women were. Not precocious, knowing, pert, as little girls could be, but simply old.

Then she touched him. For the first time in his life Vera touched him, and although tonight she looked older than she had ever looked before, quite horribly old, he allowed her to touch him as she had touched the girl because now, above all, he wanted the girl.

"Think of it, Professor," murmured Vera. "How can you permit this in an Englishwoman of my class . . . ?"

Over and over. Quicker and quicker. Until it was enough and the girl turned her face away, accepting him slowly from the grip of the painted woman's elderly hands.

Class. Harder with class. Needed to be. Class was narrow, wanted you out. Easy on yourself. Get there.

When he returned to the big room most of the guests had already left and the lights were dim. On the chintz sofa Dr Yakovlyeva and the little brunette huddled together like zoo birds on a swing, conversing brightly as though his absence had gone quite unremarked. He smiled and took the stool opposite, feeling tired and rather awkward. He did not interrupt.

"It's a question of pleats you see, darling," Marya, the dark one, was saying. "Mama simply has no idea how to fold them for ironing, and she *will* use starch . . ."

When Marya stood up to demonstrate, the white of her ankle-length skirt narrowed the flare of her hips against the scarlet silk wall-hangings. Slater knew she was sulking: had he no taste? Why not her in the room, alone, instead of the blonde? Or both together? Couldn't he see that her whole evening had been wasted? He had made her promises, too, not one of which, they both knew, he intended to keep. He had made them all promises except Dr Yakovlyeva who was too old. He was too old himself – at least, for sentiment. Tomorrow he would be home, thankful to have liquidated his obligations by expensive presents individually gift-wrapped which he had left with Vera for each of the girls. He made a mental note to leave his travelling iron as an extra for Marya.

By now the blonde would be asleep in the rumpled bed. It had been too rushed, already he was forgetting her, but Vera had crowded him for last-minute favours – messages, telephone numbers, a whole list. The woman was a fool. Back home no one was left who gave a damn about mad old Vera.

Glancing at his watch he rose to his feet, bowed to the women and took a last look round the room. He would miss nothing, and he knew that should he return after weeks, months, even years, everything, including the women, would still seem as cheap and second-hand as the plaster statuette of the Madonna on the corner shelf and the Pre-Raphaelite prints strung along the dado like so much coloured washing.

"So soon, Oliver?" said Dr Yakovlyeva from the sofa. The brunette looked away, reproving.

He dialled from the freezing hallway amidst the women's damp furs and galoshes. At one time he had been allotted a chauffeured car which was withdrawn after a fortnight. No one knew why. Since then he'd made use of Vera's black-market syndicate. He confirmed the booking, remembering to tell the driver to wait at the end of the street. Vera was neurotic about black cars drawing up outside the house. And she would not be seeing him off. Not after an evening of this kind. Her rule – never afterwards.

His gloves were at the back of the drawer in the hall stand. As he pulled them out a sheaf of brand new violet bikini briefs came with them. He remembered the girl. Where did Vera get such merchandise? He stepped out into the clammy air, suddenly glad he was going home. They didn't need him. They were doing very nicely without him, thank you.

After so many visits Slater could find his way in the dark. Beyond the main street, a steep rise, then the motorway three and a half kilometres west. At home there would have been allotments, garden sheds, a pub on the corner. Here, the country sprang up wild the moment you left the road.

Still, he'd been lucky spending so much time out of town. He hated cities. It must be the gipsy in him.

Long ago Vera should have done what he'd done most of his life: Vera ought to have taken a lover. Someone thirty years younger. He had told his wife that Vera was an old friend, a very old friend. He had to. He was with her so often. Of course, his wife might have suspected that Vera was more than a friend. But his wife's letters had been hard to interpret. She found writing difficult and her correspondence was merely dutiful. He had taught her that marriage was that kind of arrangement. Now he wondered if she had been childish enough to guess at the nature of the arrangement he had had in mind.

Towards the city the sky glowed brick-red. Soon the cab would come, soon he would be on the plane, soon he would sleep. Fifty yards ahead a flicker of movement parted the high grass by the roadside and two figures emerged to his left. With them came the smell of the river. Beyond, a waste of rubble from a derelict factory stretched down to the white strip of shore. Lengthening his step, Slater felt a sudden urge to reach the half-demolished wall before they came near enough to speak.

He'd left Vera's too early. The taxi might take another ten minutes. At least.

The men drifted towards him through the shallow mist. The taller wore a heavy close-buttoned coat. Police? Vera made jokes about the present-day police, so nobody took her seriously. But they still had jurisdiction. He must offer no resistance. He could still be charged.

The tall man hung back while the other closed up the distance. "Enough to do you a mischief, this damp," he said, falling into step with Slater. "Come a long way?" The accent was harsh, unfamiliar. Georgian?

"Oh, yes," Slater answered. "A long way."

"You'll catch your death," said the man. "Round here." He wheezed and his companion moved into touching range.

"That's a nice job," he said to Slater's cashmere overcoat.

They walked on either side of him, not too distant, not too close. Slater scrutinised the downslope towards the waste ground. He was a good runner.

"My eye," said the tall one. "I think we've met before. Don't you want to know me?"

"I don't think so," said Slater.

"Oh, yes, you do," said the big man.

His companion scowled. "Oh, no, he doesn't."

Oh, yes, I do, thought Slater. The type, I know the type. He began to jog, slowly.

"Sanya, your own mother doesn't want to know you. Why should he?"

Head to head with the Englishman the couple chuckled simultaneously without looking at one another. Slater lost rhythm. His legs were heavy, no spring to his heels. They knew he would stop. When he did, so did they.

"Look at the sweat on him," said the tall man, Sanya.

"He's a bag of nerves."

"Maybe he's been inside. Isn't that where I know you from, mate – from inside?"

"Never," said the small one. "But he's been places we haven't. He has, haven't you, old feller? You have all right."

"I can smell the drink on him," said Sanya. "And the woman. I can smell her, Vanka, smell her off his clothes, a woman."

"*Women.*"

"*Women.* And him a greybeard. Who'd credit it? One for the ladies are you, Pop?"

A sharp attack of cramp brought Slater almost to his knees between them. He gasped, "All right, all right. Who are you?"

Smilingly, in concert, Sanya and Vanka reintroduced themselves.

"No, no, no." Slater nearly screamed from the pain in his legs. "Who do you *represent*?"

"Represent?" said Sanya. "I told you, he's pissed. He's humped himself stupid on some tart, then got pissed. *Re-pres-ent*? Who do you think we represent, Jewbeard, the fucking Soviet Writers' Union?"

"He's a provocateur," grinned Vanka. "An unrepresentative provocateur."

From below Slater saw into the man's mouth. His upper set of teeth was false.

"He's an intellectual. He believes what he reads in the papers. He thinks things are different now, not like the old days. He thinks we're

7

properly going down the drain, nothing in the shops, no cars laid on, no nice accommodation any more, just a load of talk about how changed things are, he thinks it's changed, he thinks the communists have gone . . ."

Sanya kicked Slater's right calf. "Listen to him, Grandad, he's educated. Nothing's ever been got rid of in this country, even the Jews pretend to be communists. And the communists pretend not to notice because no one's supposed to think communism works any more . . ."

They were young, late twenties perhaps. Fit. He was fit, too. But over fifty nobody's that fit.

"We're official," said Vanka. "Plain clothes. See him – he's been in Vietnam. On business. Official."

Slater watched for a gap in the low brick wall along the waste ground. Vera had warned him about muggers. Even in central Moscow they would pretend to be official. Children were abducted at railway stations by bogus officials. It was kept out of the papers. Still. He began to jog again. They kept up.

"I don't believe you," he said.

Across the river was an unlit building as high as a grain silo. "That's our office," wheezed Vanka. The three were close now, bumping elbow to elbow.

"I don't believe you," repeated Slater.

His last girl, the blonde, she had been unusually reluctant. Were they somehow to do with the blonde? Boyfriends, brothers perhaps, out to roll him because of the blonde? He wanted to drop his briefcase and leap the wall but they kept him boxed in. Why the blonde? She had unhappy eyes. They all had unhappy eyes. Look at the country, look at the eyes.

"What's the hurry?" said Sanya. "You done something you shouldn't?" The words slushed out of his mouth as he breathed.

Vanka managed a giggle. "He knows, don't you, old feller, he knows what's what."

If they were related to the girl, their vengeance would be tribal. The humiliation was more appalling than the prospect of a beating. Would they drag him off, spreadeagle him, remove his clothes, break his teeth? In the light of the street lamp Slater caught the glitter of a spiked silver chain between the short man's gloved fingers. He purposely stumbled, breaking the rhythm of their run, twisted out of reach and raced back down the street in the direction of Vera's.

One kick at the door, a shout at the darkened windows before they had him again, jostling, cursing, kicking at his knees. He knew it was hopeless. She wouldn't open up once he'd gone, not for him, not for anyone. After dark, another inflexible rule. The house was full of women – who would protect them against night-walking strangers? Bitch.

At the far end of Vera's street one house showed light from a single first-floor window. Slater tore open his brief-case and tipped out the contents at Vanka's feet. His thick folder of work burst open, scattering over his two pipes, a half-litre of cheap vodka and 120 Deutschmarks in small denominations. The distraction was sufficient and he ran for the light and his life.

The wooden balcony was narrow but just low enough for a finger-tip hold. As he tried to swing himself up the window-blind between the shutters lifted, fell, then tilted sideways to reveal a small child in the triangle of brilliant yellow made by the line of the blind against the glass door leading out. When Slater lost grip the child did not drop the blind but stood motionless, one arm raised, pointing into the dark.

The men were walking slowly towards him, one spinning his chain, the other holding out the empty brief-case, as if about to hand it over.

"Why so drastic?" called out Vanka. "We've only just started and you've got all the time in the world."

They halted, still some way off, and looked above Slater's head to the silver-haired child who continued to watch from the window until, behind him, the lights were put out.

When they reached him Slater was holding out his wallet, his gold Omega wrist-watch and a pair of amber oak-leaf brooches which he had bought that morning for his wife's third wedding-anniversary gift.

At the touch of Sanya's mittened fingers on the exposed flesh between the top of his gloves and coat cuffs, Slater let out a high, animal scream and lashed out with his boots. The man backed away and stared down at the marks made by the ridged crepe sole on his immaculate jeans with an expression so piteous that for a moment Slater expected him to burst into tears. A second later, and the Englishman had side-stepped, fending off the second man's lunge at his coat-tails, and was on the run of his life to the waste ground.

Brilliant manoeuvre. No panic now. Just run straight, run with the ball. Beyond, the forest. You'll lose them in the forest. Losers. Bastards, swine. Have the trinkets, the trash. No one was having him. No one.

He forgot about the boots. He forgot until he had time to remember, a very short time, but long enough to condemn himself for believing that once more, for one miraculous burst, he could be as strong and astute as he had been with the girl, still young enough to have cleared the low wall with inches to spare. On his belly in the frosted rubble he cursed his age and his fate and the stacked rubber heel that had caught one of the ice-capped bricks of the wall, causing his right leg to fracture above and below the knee.

It was nearly over.

They came up from behind. He heard them stumbling, younger than him, so much younger, but more out of condition. He felt almost happy.

The silver-dollar weights at the end of Vanka's chain struck Slater between the rim of his Scottish tweed cap and the upturned collar of his overcoat. The force of it lifted his head very slightly so that he lolled into the next, presenting his face in three-quarter profile. The pain came then, with a pop in his ears which couldn't be swallowed away, ricochetting in pinball jinks from hemisphere to hemisphere.

"He's still breathing," whispered Sanya.

The shorter man squatted down and tweaked up Slater's left eyelid. In the light of his torch the pupil momentarily flinched. "Not for much longer," he said. "It's starting to sleet." Without anger he rose and stamped deliberately with the heel of his trainers on the grey satin lining of Slater's coat. "Here's one for the Tsar Liberator. And another for *demokratsiya*. And this," he shouted to the figure stretched in the snow. "This," he shouted louder, coming down with a crunch which splintered an underlying brick. "This is for *perefucking-stroika*."

Slater heard nothing, saw nothing, except voices in a light compressed within his head which hurtled upwards colourising the voices with fire.

"*You're a remarkable boy, Slater.*"

Flame picked at the closed line of his fontanelle cracking it free.

"*Unusual.*"

The whole of him surged inside the fire waiting for the break, doubled up, the soles of his feet tucked beneath his jaw, preventing speech, and his left forefinger was one with the eye of the flame burning out the dome of his skull.

"*Believe me, one day you will have a contribution to make.*"

The voice was spooning him out on to the finger and the finger blazed white. Now everything was in the beginning, and in the beginning everything was worth it. He had got away, away into the great timbered hall, into the foreign city, made addresses from the conference chair: *Doktor, Herr Professor, Sir.*

"*Everything is going to happen.*"

"*To me?*"

"*To you.*" said the voice. "*Now.*"

When the opening came he went through in the uprush, breathless with excitement.

From the zip pocket of his windcheater Sanya produced a little knife and began to unpick the exterior seams of the cashmere, humming under his breath. When nothing was revealed, Vanka helped him to turn Slater face-up.

The tune was catchy. While the man with the knife slit into the handstitched edges of the right-hand lapel, Vanka knelt in the snow, trying to recall the words. At length his companion, apparently satisfied that the coat contained nothing but Slater, straightened up and put away his knife. "Obsessed," he said to the body. "Couldn't leave it alone." And again he began to hum: "Dadada, dadada . . ."

They were almost at the riverline when the words came back to Vanka: "Mickey Mouse, In the house, Taking down his trousers . . ."

"You're a weird bastard, Vanka, you know that? Weird."

The smaller man stopped and whirled his chain at the silverwater moon. "I know," he said. "It takes practice. Times are bad for you and me. Where would we be these days without my sense of humour?"

II

LEFT TURN

Clacton-on-Sea and London, January–March

2

The yellow doubloon looked horribly fake against the royal-blue lining of the box. A cheap-looking trick, even in the shop when the assistant had handed it down from the shelf, NOW YOU SEE ME NOW YOU DON'T on the Day-Glo strip pasted down its side.

Kitty bit her lip and took a drag on the Sumatran panatella before trying again. The tray fitted smoothly enough. A little push, careful with the fingers, exactly the right pressure as the instructions said.

The tray slid past the magic point of no return and popped out to the right. Aha. In place of the coin a neat little cavity. Brill, as the paper boy used to say, *brillianteenissimo*.

In reverse no amount of effort would make the doubloon slot back into its bed. A dud. She picked up the conductor's baton and gave a smart whack to the box. Hey presto! The coin flipped out before she could catch it and dropped at her feet. Magic.

When Kitty Slater heard the front knocker, then the bell, she did not take her elbows off the card-table where the Tarot pack was strung out against the green nap like a run of chequered gaming counters.

The man outside under the cuckoo-clock roof of the porch bent down and peered through the letter-box.

In the glazed tiling of the hallway a choir of angels refracted the deadfall of afternoon light through the stained-glass conch shell above the transom. The mail had not been collected for some time.

"Hello! Anyone at home?"

Still as night. He straightened up in the salt wind and smoothed back his wispy reddish hair. There must be. In this job you developed a nose for habitees. He tugged on the bell-pull and waited for the mechanism to crank back to the kitchen. Huge, these old places, room enough for an army. The jingle of the clapper reached him as he was about to try again. In the remote interior nothing stirred.

In a precise, well-educated voice he shouted once more. "Don't give me that. You're not deaf. I know you're in there. I can wait."

Retracing his steps, he spotted the wrecked chassis of one of those expensive hand-crafted wheelbarrows that people stick plants in. It was half-buried in the hedgegrowth, grass looping through the wheel-staves. At the gate he paused to wipe the raindrops from his spectacle-lenses before carefully dropping the latch.

"Nice stonework," he said out loud. "And all that brass and marble inside. Cost someone a pretty packet, I'll bet."

Beyond the gate stood a '69 2.5 litre Daimler in metallic blue. He went round to the passenger side and adjusted the seat. Once inside he took an A5 ledger bound in scarlet rexine from the glove compartment and began to make notes: "Imposing residence villa-type (double-fronted). Good original features circa 1865. Some dilapidation."

Behind him there was a creak of leather as someone shifted on the bench-seat. The back window was wound down. "Just look at those turrets, Arch, Dracula's outhouse. Enough to give the peasants nightmares." The voice was husky from sleep.

Archie slid his ledger back into the door pocket. "Plenty of very normal people spend fortunes on places like that," he said, without turning round. "Holiday homes, Nazir, that's what we're talking about."

"So what are we waiting for?"

"We're waiting for them while they wait for us."

In front of the Gothic house the white of a Pompeian mosaic path silvered as the street lamps came on. Nazir gave a yawn and clambered over the back of the driver's seat. Side by side they watched for movement beyond the net-curtained bays of the windows. Nothing to see except the perpetual back-combing swish of the breeze along the evergreen hedge

"I grew up here, you know," Archie said. "Still got relations on the other side of town." He scanned the three-storeyed Windermeres and Hermitage Lodges. "Not this bit, though. Class, here."

Nazir settled back, closing his eyes against the bustle of the yew-hedge. "Give me the city lights any time. This is like camping on the steps of a tomb."

Suddenly it had become very cold. Kitty shivered through the thick coat. She felt tired, and her brief joy in the trick with the coin had passed off the moment the knocking came.

Now everything was quiet again she resisted her desire to cross to the dark front rooms. Instead she pictured the grey garden, its crackleglaze path plunged into shadow.

The callers had gone away. In the end they always did.

She wanted to urge herself out on to the street where the sound of the wind used to spin high from the breakers over the tip-tap of her heels, but the old despair came back and she rested for a while on the armless chair in the hall underneath the bentwood hat stand from which her dead husband's umbrella still hung.

The restaurant was too distant and so very awkward to reach. If she could manage tonight, then, after tonight nothing on earth would persuade her to fulfil another engagement.

I am becoming what I always dreaded to be, she thought. An amateur. And she shivered again.

When she rose Kitty almost stumbled. Anxious, anxious because the unkempt hem of her costume-skirt dragged at the chair legs, because the beaver-lamb coat was hideously matronly, and even her beloved 'cello in its plum-morocco case suddenly felt as tubby and unmanageable as a fish-kettle. Outside, as she turned to lock the front door top and bottom with the Chubb key which Slater had insisted she kept on a chain attached to her coat, the stone piers at the sides of the porch reminded her of the ruins of the fortress on the mountainside above her father's house.

"Mrs Slater?" said the man. He had come from behind the pillar so unobtrusively that she slipped past unalarmed, refusing to notice that he had made himself apparent – a trick which Slater had taught her in case of indecent exposers – but beyond the gate the outline of another man was shimmering under the street lamp.

They converged upon her by the carcase of the wheelbarrow.

"This won't take a moment," said the first man. "My name is Renshawe, Archibald Renshawe from Lambert R. Farncombe Associates, Authorised Bailiffs. Is your husband at home?"

Except for the word "husband" Kitty understood nothing. Instead she grasped at the tone, which did not sound unkind. She put down her 'cello. "Husband?" The aspirate was guttural, hard.

"Your husband, madam. Business. A private matter."

Husband. A pretty word, round, encircling, like the thick ring on her finger making her his.

"Not here," she said and picked up the 'cello case.

The first man kept up with her to the gate, the second passing through a couple of steps ahead. This one was dark. In his white suit darker, very dark. He did not smile.

The kind man began reading from a red book by the light of a pen-torch: "A filling station in Southgate. £422.11 pence. Barker and Rudd of Epping, wholesale stationers, £236.20. Shacklin's for men's toiletries, charge account, £136 exactly, now nine months outstanding and no response to numerous recorded deliveries. I could go on.

None of the sums or items disputed by one Professor Oliver James Slater residing at this address?"

"I don't know."

She did not look up but wondered, if she did, if the eyes behind the spectacles would be as kind as the voice and, if she looked into them, he would see that she was so very afraid he would touch the arm of the dark man and they would both withdraw, turning their backs to the light. Without warning her knees gave way. The pale man caught her fall and set her down on the domed end of her 'cello case in the middle of the pavement. His clothes had the smell of softwater-washed cotton touched by starch. Around his head was the blue-black of deep space above the disappeared rim of the sun.

"I really am very sorry but we all have our jobs to do," he said.

Nazir gave a chuckle. "It's only money, after all."

"*Money*," whispered Kitty. "In England always money. I do not speak English."

"You said money," mouthed Nazir. "I heard you. That's English. You said it in English."

"Always money," Kitty moaned. "A man dies, the woman weeps, the Jews come."

Both men flinched at the un-Englishness of the phrase in its application to them.

"She's a foreigner, Arch. A foreigner, dear, aren't you? What are you then – the *au pair*?"

She stared at the dark one uncomprehendingly, keeping him at bay. *Ach, miliy moy muzh, my sweet husband. I see you so clearly*.

"Swedish! They're usually Swedish. Listen, Frøken," said Nazir. "Where's the family tonight?"

Kitty turned up her throat to the sky. In the end it had come to nothing. "*Delo konchilos nichem!* Professor Slater *skonchalsya!* Passed away, dead, dead, dead!"

They sat in the back seat of the car with the woman between them. Because they spoke so softly and did not hurt her or forget her 'cello or her bag, Kitty let them continue to be kind. In England, she had learned, it was not the thing to confess that you were lonely or unhappy or even at death's door from fear and neglect. But this pale man's voice was so soft that she could not understand why she had at first feared him. "I must go," she said. "I have job."

In the phosphorescent green from the dashboard instruments Archie scrutinised her. Underneath the rusty house-clearance fur she had on a long starlight-silver robe embroidered with Oxford blue half-moons, stiffened at the high neckline with a goldworked pattern of bursting meteors and planetary signs. Out here, in the Clacton street, she made Archie feel like a kid who had thrown his line into the municipal pond and hooked a blue barracuda on his bent pin. He was sure of one thing: he was going to think twice about throwing her back in.

"Did he make a will, your husband?" said Nazir.

The widow gazed piteously from one to the other. "I have job," she repeated.

"This is crazy," said Nazir.

I have a job. Back home that was like saying, I have a mind, two legs, a heart. But here how splendid it sounded; and, for a lone woman, how brave. Kitty recalled the consternation of the other academic wives when her predicament was disclosed after the funeral: "You poor thing." "I suppose you'll have to . . ." "To make ends meet, of course." Her pride then had been fierce because in that sense Slater's death had been a boon: at one stroke she had regained her youthful independence. But the *job*, what a comedown that had been taken to be: "*Restaurant cabaret?* How exciting! But isn't it rather *seasonal*? Of course, one can't judge, never having experienced that side of life . . ."

If once in Moscow those same condescending ladies had ever performed an act, any act, in front of their husbands, as fine and outrageous and utterly feminine as she had performed before miners from the Kuzbass, soldiers, workers, nice, nice ordinary men who smiled and applauded, they would have known once in their lives what it was to be a woman at one with her talent.

"A job where?" said Archie.

He was nice, he really wanted to know.

"Seaside. Frinton. Boring."

He knew she meant the place. "Very boring," he agreed.

"Terminal," said Nazir.

There were some big houses in Frinton but her big house made them all look vulgar because it had the single original doorbell and there were no brass plates outside. Slater had taught her all those little snobberies but she had never told him how sad and out of place she felt in his house.

"What is your employer's name?" Archie asked, very slow. Maybe they could make a detour to Frinton on the way back and get some sense out of him.

Her eyes drifted. "I am magician. Hoopla!" she exclaimed sliding out a gold-tipped wand from the sleeves of her coat. "Tricks."

Nazir studied her fanciful clothing, the twist of her long fingers, above all, the hint of elegant mischief that gave her face such vivacity as she flourished the little stick.

"Go on, you're no Trix. That's a Page Three name. Alicia more like. Something with tone."

Archie tried again. "What is *your* name?"

"Slater."

"Yes," he said. "I know that. Your first name, your Christian name."

"Yes?"

Archie began to feel out of his depth. Her appearance and manner were so bizarre that he wondered how she could sit on a bus without molesting her fellow-passengers by her very proximity. Too close and they might start to feel like the sweaty toads which one glimpse of her moon-dusted eyes could perhaps turn them into.

"My Christian name, for example, is Archie . . ."

She shaped her lips imploringly in silent repetition. Suddenly it broke in upon her. "Yekaterina Aleksandrovna!"

Nazir snorted. "I told you, I told you in the first place. She's Swedish."

"Archie," said Mrs Slater. "Kitty, Kitty."

"Kitty, my dear," he said. "Tell me – about your country. Is it far away?"

The question paralysed her, not because she didn't understand it, but because of the immensity it conjured up in her mind. What could she say? That beneath the mountains the light turned blue among the trees and the air was so clear that you could see for miles? Even if she could have said such things in his own language this mild-mannered man would think she was an exaggerated person and lose interest in her.

She opened wide her green-cheese eyes which Slater had once so doted on, and smiled, trembling all the time because the worst thing about trying to come back to life when you felt dead inside was the necessity of taking risks.

"Very far," she said. Then she tried hard to recover the sentence, her party-piece Slater had called it, Katie's lifesaver, if she ever mislaid herself in Selfridges or took the wrong train at Liverpool Street Station. "Excuse me. I am Russian. I am lost. My English is not very good."

The face of the white man changed, and she took advantage of his evident surprise to construct more sentences: "I have job. I am late. I work for Mrs Sedgewick, Lyudmilla, she helps me. She gives me food and money. She will explain. You will take me?"

The men consulted together across the seat.

"Frinton? Why not?" said Nazir. "It's getting dark. God knows where she'll end up otherwise."

Archie looked back at the girl. "I don't think it's our kind of business. She could be a tart for all we know."

"What – with a bloody 'cello and a wand?"

Kitty felt in the pocket of her fur and brought out an antique silver-linked purse. "You need money? You take me and I give you money."

"You mean sod, Renshawe," said Nazir switching on the engine. "Put your money away, Trixie, I feel like a spin. He can come along for the ride."

They took the coast road to Frinton. It was warm in the car and the men were silent so she said nothing but turned to watch the sea which had roughened under the evening wind and was tumbling around the matchstick legs of the pier.

At the turning next to the courtyard of a high block of flats which faced out across the bay, Kitty remembered someone had told her that on a fine day you could see Holland from the roof garden, and she wondered what Holland would look like. But her pleasure at being quiet in the car with the two men began to waste away from the weariness she always felt at being a foreigner, having to hunt for the right words to say when the time came, as it had now, to give directions to Lyudy's restaurant: second left, first right, straight on. There, there, Lyudy's place, the Tsarina.

"You come with me," she said. "Tonight is grand opening. I invite you."

3

The Tsarina was on the corner between a side street and the main road. Nazir pulled in just before the lights.

"Hop out here," Archie said to the girl. "We'll bring the rest of your stuff."

Frosted on the glass of the double doors was a Janus-faced eagle that parted heads to let her through.

They had trouble getting the conjuring equipment out of the car boot and past the swing doors. Inside Kitty Slater was already grappling her 'cello up the steps of a high dais in a far corner of the empty restaurant. From behind an oriental screen a squat brunette in a scarlet caftan advanced upon them.

"One day," she said, "one day I shall take a boat from this place and never come back. The rain, the rain, gentlemen." Her breasts undulated from a deep, heart-rending sigh. "I do not want to die in the rain." Sidling away into the clump of little tables she began to make last-minute adjustments to the place-settings.

"I know the feeling," said Nazir, putting down Kitty's box. "It's the wind. Brings it off the sea, straight from the east. You'll get used to it, won't she, Archie? Look at me, I got used to it."

"My husband," said the woman darkly, "he deceived me, he promised everything, the earth. But the weather? Not a word about the weather. And now, at my age, I learn that England is a marsh bog." Beneath the caftan she seemed to puff up at each hoarsely articulated word. "You know what I would do to him, you know what I would do? I would . . ."

Before she could complete the sentence a pair of elderly ladies, one very gaunt and slightly lame, the other with a permanent wave the colour of stick cinnamon, presented themselves in the open doorway leading to the back kitchen. "This is so *exciting*, Lyudy dear . . ." said the gaunt one.

"Already I have guests." Lyudy Sedgewick indicated Archie and Nazir with a flurry of the rainbow serviettes which she was issuing to the tables. "These gentlemen are not being entertained. You play, I pay. Now you play."

The gaunt woman mounted the dais and sat down at the piano, and after dusting the keys with her plush velvet evening bag, crashed out a series of broken chords. Apparently satisfied, she got up and kissed Kitty Slater on the lips while Kitty went on calmly applying rosin to her 'cello bow, a slight smile perceptible at her profile.

Mrs Sedgewick motioned both men to a centre table. In the orange pan-stick bloom of her foundation her mouth was a moist terracotta bow. She planted herself down between them, eyes brilliant with tears. "I live in England seventeen years. Tonight is the climax of my existence, and I am nervous."

The woman with the cinnamon hair finished laying out the piano music before disappearing into the kitchen. On the dais Kitty arched her back and gave an audible sigh.

As if exasperated at this note of resignation Lyudy snatched at the low-slung chignon at the nape of her neck, extracted a long pinch-beck and amber pin and began to score the immaculate starch of the table-cloth.

"Frinton is hell. All Great Britain is hell. When I make a fortune from this place, I go on a cruise, I discover myself."

A consumptive-looking youth in a single-breasted dinner jacket and viridian cummerbund took his place on the platform. The next moment Lyudy's Tsarina was replete with the swirl of "Roses from the South", as arranged for string band by Arnold Schoenberg.

"Ah, how it gives me longing for my country, this music," murmured the restaurateuse. Archie felt his hand being gripped. "In Livadia orphan children play this music." The warm pressure of her fingers disconcerted him. She didn't even know his name.

He cleared his throat. "You have a great deal in common then, I imagine, with our friend over there at the 'cello."

Lyudy twitched away her hand. "That hunched-up girl-woman? She thinks she is Palm Court seductress on posters by Klimt but she loves her misery so much she drinks from morning to night. I am up to the ears in worry, but I take pity on others – who would employ her if they did not have my feelings?"

Without waiting for an answer, she turned away and called out something which Archie did not catch. A freckled lad in an ivory satin tunic shirt with mandarin collar, red velour breeches and ruched white boots came piling through the kitchen doors with a basket-weave tray on which stood three bottles of wine, one of them already uncorked.

"Vassya," said Mrs Sedgewick as the boy began pouring rosé wine into each of the four glasses on the table. "My youngest. Say hello, Vassya darling, to the gentleman who is Kitty's guest tonight."

"Hello," said Vassya gloomily. "They're all foreign here. You foreign, too?" He flicked the wine napkin at his crinkly boots. "I didn't choose this outfit, you know. My Mum did. It's foreign. I feel stupid in it." Stretching out his arms he stood like a scarecrow, inspecting himself.

"I think you look very nice," said Archie.

The boy shrugged and took away the tray. A little way off he spun round and fixed his mother with a malevolent leer. "That's what she says, too, but I know different. I'm English – Not *Vassya*. I'm *Basil*. That's English. Foreigners? I hate them."

Mrs Sedgewick let out a shriek. "Don't listen to him! At heart he is a good boy but he acts like a tragedy, the same as your 'cello lady, Kitty Slater. Her English husband dies and suddenly she doesn't know who she is anymore. One day she is sad – the next she is a perfect scream. Like me – today I am laughing."

And, for a little while she was, ringingly and open-mouthed, lip-gloss pearling in the glow of the mauve-shaded table lamp.

The music stopped then started again. A polka. "Donner und Blitzen".

"Do you ever go back?"

"To Russia? Of course – once a year, clockwork. In this English hole I am a joke, but in Leningrad, Moscow, I am a person. Anybody who is anybody there knows Lyudy . . ."

Archie could hear Kitty working her 'cello up to a bass rallen-tando and he felt a sudden impulse to turn round and watch. Mrs Sedgewick noticed. "You love her, that girl?" she said, filling her glass.

How could he? He could have said that he liked her. That for some reason he liked her very much. He didn't know why, but he might. "She's attractive. With the right clothes she could be striking."

"She has no money."

Ah, back to business. He had been forgetting. "Property, though, she has property?"

"The house? You see the house? After you see it, you think – who wants to live in such a place?"

"A matter of taste, Mrs S. I'm always surprised what people will put up with if they've sunk money in it."

"Lyudy." She snapped the name at him. "You call me Lyudy, short for Lyudmilla. You believe it is hers, that ghost-house? Well, I tell you, my dear, when I left home, my country of origin, I was a girl, thin as a stick, with oh, such hopes. How could I know that the public-school man who married me, my English Sedgewick, who opens doors and brings me flowers, all the time this person is betraying me with English ladies? One day I wake up and he is gone. He has debts. Tax. Loans. Banks. Pouf! My house goes, too, from under my feet." She shivered. "Bah, her Slater, I think he is the same. She has nothing, your quite striking girl – except her body and her stupid 'cello."

While she was staring at Archie unseeing, apparently entranced at this totality of betrayal, the boy in boots came through from the kitchen holding a long platter away from his chest.

It looked like rice-pudding and cucumbers. Reluctantly Archie put a spoonful to his lips. It tasted delicious. He took another. The boy watched him, amazed. Once more the music stopped.

From the dais Nazir, too, was watching. The fat lady was doing all the talking. Archie simply nodded now and again, and they both kept staring to where Nazir watched them, seated on the top step of the dais, fixing the spike of Kitty's 'cello into a crack between the boards. They weren't looking at him, they were looking at the girl, and the longer they looked, the graver Archie's expression became: tight-lipped, even grim. The pair of them were up to something.

Archie bent forward and touched the hand of his hostess who oozed herself closer. They were taking the girl to pieces, Nazir thought. She was foreign, hopeless, too pretty, a touch sluttish, and in love with her husband, who was dead.

"Maybe there is something – life insurance perhaps?" Archie was saying.

Lyudy shrugged. "But where is it, then, I ask you? She cannot afford stockings, and dresses like Oxfam. I think she is very sick."

"How did she find out he was dead?"

"God knows. Two months ago she walks in. I have the decorators, I am busy so I hadn't seen her for weeks. I say, hello, and, what do you want? And then she tells – My Oliver is no more. Just so. No details. Well, he was fifty-five years of age! A heart attack, maybe, a car runs over him, an accident? She looks vague and starts to laugh. All the time she is following me round my restaurant like a little dog and I am saying, start with a new slate, darling, wipe this out of your mind. She needs job, I give her job, all kinds of jobs but she is unhappy and cannot do the jobs properly because she still loves this husband who nobody sees any more. She loves him, she loves me, she loves everybody, even Vassya!" Lyudy tapped the side of her nose and leant nearer. "You know what I think? I don't believe in this love she dishes out. It means she has no principles."

On the bandstand Nazir was being introduced to the pianist. "Miss Kelch from Kaunus," said Kitty.

"Really?" he said. "I've never been to America."

"Lithuania," corrected Miss Kelch.

"I believe things are looking up, nowadays," said Nazir politely. "Aren't they, in Lithuania?"

As the trio struck up again he returned to the table. "We may get somewhere after all, Archie. A kind word, and the widow pulls herself together quite nicely."

Scowling, Mrs Sedgewick rose to her feet. "Soon she will be loving you also. Be sure not to let her love you to death. I waste my time, she wastes my time . . ."

"What was that in aid of?" murmured Nazir when their hostess had moved out of earshot.

Archie cocked an eyebrow at the girl on the dais.

"She thinks Mrs Slater knows where her husband is."

"Great! Where?"

"How should I know? Under the floorboards, in the deep freeze. Maybe he'll drop in later looking for a free meal."

At seven thirty the guests began to arrive and Lyudy Sedgewick flung herself into the role of hostess. A giant pot was carried to the centre table. When she began to dish out caviare *blinis* Nazir looked at his watch. "I don't know about you, Arch, but I haven't eaten since breakfast. So here goes."

Archie drank a glass of grapefruit juice and reviewed the position. The debts were substantial but there were assets. Despite Mrs Sedgewick's pessimism he felt that his questioning had been on the right track: there was money somewhere. The widow would have to be interviewed again. Meanwhile the restaurant became noisy and very hot. Archie dozed.

A roll of chords brought him to.

Lyudy S was by the piano, clapping her hands. At first no one listened. Then Kitty appeared on the dais with a very short skirt beneath the dark ankle-length cape. Without a word she began building something out of red play-blocks on the closed lid of the grand. Apart from an occasional creak of a chair as one of the diners leaned back, the restaurant had fallen silent.

In white make-up Kitty seemed less woman than child. At the back a man guffawed, and Archie said, "Shut up!" in a voice which sounded embarrassingly loud, but which caused no one to turn. Under the downlight a little house was taking shape. He admired the way she inserted furniture – stove, table, pictures, even a blanket-roll for the box bed – through the half-open roof.

All the lights had faded except for a halogen spot which shaded the well of Kitty's eyes. Suddenly a red-headed puppet in breeches and boots was dangling from her sleeve, and she had started to speak. This was Miki. The house was his.

An English person had evidently rehearsed her patter because she reeled it off without a stumble: Miki lived alone until one day Riki turned up. Riki came out from under her cape, three times Miki's size and wearing a peaked cap. She lurched him at Miki's door. Miki fell down the chimney. The house lit up and there he lay, downstairs, cowering underneath the stove.

It was quite skilful: you couldn't spot the puppet strings, and broken glass tinkled convincingly when Miki threw the furniture out. He sent the stove flying, and the chairs and the rest of the stuff. Riki cartwheeled round and round the house, laughing horribly until, in a thunder-flash roar, actual flames billowed out of the windows. Miki shot up through the roof, suddenly huge, huger than Riki, huger even than the house, and tore Riki apart.

The audience applauded. If she'd left it there, with a bang, they would have gone back to their desserts still loving her, but the Miki-Riki act was only the prelude to a succession of tricks so unaccountably feeble that long before the last, involving a wand, a red box and a disappearing coin, chatter broke out, jeers came her way, and finally she stepped down to a slow handclap from a party of men at the front who made way for her with exaggerated bows.

After her act Kitty stayed in the kitchen drinking from the schooner of wine which every so often Basil topped up for her when his mother wasn't looking.

Several glasses on she began to hum Riki's nonsense threats under her breath, "Oona moona buckettee, Ar bar beck". Each time she peered through the roundel of the service door the men at the table near the dais looked redder, more gross. She was convinced that they were making jokes at her expense, and that the evening would soon come to an end by the entire clientele following their example in a riot of contempt and loathing.

Relaxed by the wine she hated them back and returned to the dais. When a woman in an apricot ball-gown came up and requested a strict-tempo waltz, Kitty rushed off to be violently sick.

Ten minutes later the proprietress found her sobbing into the sink. "This is disgraceful, Yekaterina Aleksandrovna," shouted Lyudy in Russian. "Why do you think I work so hard? For you to turn my restaurant into a market beer-booth? I hire you out of charity, so you take advantage and do stupid things with children's toys. You are not at home, people in this country don't appreciate drunkenness, and I can't afford refugees who make trouble for me."

"I'm so sorry, Lyudy. For pity's sake . . . I practised so hard and I've felt awful for days. When those men started I simply went to pieces and kept thinking of Moscow and Slater . . ."

"You have no right, Yekaterina Aleksandrovna, no right at all, to reveal your feelings to strangers in a public place."

In Russian Lyudy sounded a very different person from the woman non-Russians thought they knew.

"This is immoral, unfeminine and quite indecent," she said. The perfume of her *Quelques Fleurs* mingled with the updraught of cooling *shashlik* as the extractor cowl sucked up the aromas from the hyperlit recesses of the designer kitchen. There was no time to run, and Kitty was sick again as she stood, face to face with her appalled employer.

At midnight, the cabaret over, Mrs Sedgewick came up and presented the bill. "You go now, Mister," she hissed at Archie. "And you take that damn drunk girlfriend with you."

Nazir flinched. "I thought it was on the house."

"On her house, not mine," said Mrs Sedgewick. "Your friend can collect from the fancy woman who abuses my hospitality."

On the dais, alone, Miss Kelch was playing the Russian national anthem.

Basil had followed his mother with the credit-card franking machine. "On expenses, I take it, for you gentlemen?"

"Not his share," said Archie, handing over his card. "Any drinks are down to him."

Nazir checked the items. "I only had a single carafe. Of the white."

"She had three in the kitchen," said Basil. "I thought they were your treat."

"Who?"

"Trixie," said Archie. "You can pay me her share in the morning. Where is she, by the way?"

Basil waved a bunch of credit-card vouchers in the direction of the kitchen. "There's been a dust-up. Mum's given her her cards. You can always rely on foreigners to bugger things up. God help you if she's your responsibility." He poked a carbon-smudged finger at the machine. "They've been interfering with this. Here," he confided to Nazir. "You look an Honest Injun, which way up is it supposed to go?"

"I thought you said getting involved with a client went against the business ethic?" Nazir complained on the way to the kitchen.

"I've got a living to earn," Archie shouted back, pushing through a crowd from the Chamber of Commerce who were mobbing the lone violinist for another Balkan *romanz*. "What are we on – twenty, thirty per cent of four thousand?"

Mrs Sedgewick swept through the kitchen doors radiant with false bonhomie. "You like to ruin my evening some more? The last time I tell you, take your beggarwoman and scram, hop it from my life."

Nazir held back. "You heard her, Arch. There's nothing down for us. La Slater's skint."

Lyudy dumped Kitty's 'cello at Archie's feet. "Hah! Listen to your black boy, Mr Kerbcrawler. She has not even bus fare. You must drive her." And with unmarred smile she made a bee-line for a reporter who had promised to drum up a feature on the restaurant's opening for next week's local free-sheet.

They found Kitty Slater on the floor of the staff washroom, fast asleep, the Miki-Riki house in pieces around her.

"You've got to laugh," said Basil, handing over a smeared card voucher in the vestibule. "Unless you're one of *them*," he nodded at the frail figure of Kitty supported between the two men. "And then I suppose you cry, like they always seem to."

"Swedes?"

"Yeah," said the boy. "Swedes, Poles, Czechs, Russkies, they're all the same underneath – miserable as sin."

4

"Where is this?"

"Home, Mrs Slater. Don't you recognise it?"

The house loomed black above its hedge. After the sparkle and hum of the restaurant the quiet of the street felt monolithic, vast.

The bottom sill of Kitty's door scraped the kerb, then stuck.

"I keep forgetting to have that fixed," said Archie, leaning over the back of the driver's seat to help. The touch of her hand was clammy. "Chilly, these winter nights, aren't they? Now, just give it a smart shove as I press down." Kitty did not move. In the candle-power glow of the courtesy light her eyes were huge from alarm.

Archie got out of the car and wrenched open the rear door. "There we are, no problem. Hop out like a good girl."

Suddenly obedient she put out a long leg and raised herself up. On the pavement she clung to his arm. "My instrument . . . ?"

Blast it, the 'cello. "Ah, nearly forgot. Where would you be without that? Hang on, I'll unlock the boot."

Glad to unclasp her hands he went round to the back, quickly heaved out the 'cello and her case of conjuring props and stacked them up by the hedge-gate. Already he was coming to dislike the black staring house in this queer soundless street, and the fact that he was affected by these things and that the girl had to live here, amongst them, alone. She was clearly in no state to be interviewed tonight. The debts would have to wait. Without looking he had already selected ignition from the bunch of keys in his hand. "Right, then. Good night, Mrs Slater."

"No, please. I am not well. You must come in home with me."

For a moment he gazed at the wide silhouette of her face quivering under the street lamp. She was a kid, a waif. He experienced a sudden surge of pleasure at the idea that she felt him dependable.

"I can't possibly, Mrs Slater, much as I'd like to, not at one o'clock in the morning. A matter of professional ethics, you understand . . ."

She didn't. "Ha! Your reputation. All right for me, I am foreign, I cannot have reputation."

A salt wind rustled in the winter jasmine along the York stone flags of the pathway to the house.

"Mr Renshawe, soon I will not be standing. Tonight I have drunk . . . I am still . . . *sloshed*."

"Steady on, dear." He took her by the sleeve. "Look, I'll come as far as the front door and wait outside until you find the switch."

She clutched his elbow and began to cry, and the more he tried to lead her in the direction of the gate the tighter she clung. This was going to be a facer. "Naz!" The loudness of his voice between the close-set houses made Archie feel naked. "Naz!" Any minute now a light was going to come on. He whispered, "Excuse me." But she held on and he had to hump them both in a three-legged jog to the offside door of the car. "Nazir!" he hissed through the open quarter light.

"Spot of bother, old chap?" yawned his colleague.

Archie sat in the kitchen. The Aga had gone out.

Her breath vaporising in the cold Kitty Slater perched on a high stool trying to light a cigarette. The matches were damp. Eventually Archie made a spill from the restaurant credit-card voucher and ignited it in the pilot light of an antiquated geyser over the sink.

In the flame she looked older than he remembered her that afternoon and he disliked the way her legs stuck out from each side of the stool. She didn't seem to care that her collapse might strike him not as vulnerable, but ugly. The way she dropped her spent matches to the floor irritated him; the red quarry tiles were dirty and, for some reason, that made it worse.

He looked round the kitchen trying not to notice her legs. Upstairs Nazir was nosing around to check for intruders. It was the bailiff in him: he loved sizing up other people's property. Not much in here, though, not even for house-clearers. A fridge that rattled, oil cloth on the rickety deal table, a few cookbooks slung on the window ledge any-old-how, a rotary can-opener coming unscrewed from the wall. Bird-nuts everywhere, unopened, in red-net bags, enough for an aviary; but no food, except for an egg-box in the onion rack and a shrivelling Polenta sausage left half-sliced on the back-ring cover of the Aga.

She had come to the cork-tip end of the cigarette, but carried on smoking. "I cannot go living like so. I kill myself. I am desperate woman."

Archie's breath frosted on the air. "Look, is there anyone I can contact? A neighbour perhaps? At least they could sit with you for a bit. Everyone has to have someone, people you can telephone. In an emergency."

"No one," said the girl. "No telephone."

In the dimly lit hallway Nazir tripped over the Riki-Miki house propped on the bottom stair. "It's a gold-mine up there," he confided after a perfunctory nod at the girl. "Late Victorian, big stuff. Why not make her an offer?"

Kitty's sea-flax eyes paled from tears.

"You're an animal," said Archie.

"What's the matter now?"

"She's frightened."

Nazir smoothed down the line of his Windsor-knotted tie. "Look here, Arch. How much English do you think she understands?"

"Enough."

"Well, then, put her on to the Samaritans."

"The phone's been disconnected."

Nazir took a step nearer the pathetic figure on the stool. "There must be someone, dear," he said firmly.

Kitty kicked the stool from under her and closed upon him almost toe-to-toe across the kitchen tiles. "You English!" she shrieked. "You bloody English! You listen. My man is dead and no one gives damn for me. But I am real, real!"

Out in the road beyond the garden a dog began to bark. The sound seemed to break into her poise, and Kitty slowly retracted. In the opening space between her body and his, Nazir threw up his arms and slid away into the hall where he brushed himself down before the hat-stand mirror.

"I'm sure it'll work out all right in the end, Mrs Slater," said Archie, gripping the towel rail of the Aga. The remark was banal and if he'd been her he would have screamed, but she simply got back on her stool and took out another cigarette.

"Now, I tell you something for nothing, Mister," she said in a calm, pleasing lilt. "You don't help me, I make trouble. By God, I tell you, no woman make bigger trouble than Russian woman."

Kitty had fully intended to create the scene in the kitchen. Earlier, in the back of his car when she had felt giddy from fear and so ill that she could not recognise her own street, this man had stared at her and in his nervousness almost blushed. It was then that she saw her chance. She needed someone and the moment he turned his open, bemused glance upon her display of craziness, she knew he was a man who would weaken. Englishmen, she had already decided, became tenderer when one succumbed.

32

Afterwards, hobbling through the dank garden, leaning against his shoulder, secure for a little while against the alien sea which crashed below her great grey house, she thought she could be friends with him; or someone like him.

He was that kind of innocent, easily moved, steady Englishman about whom, as a girl, she had read in books, and she would make him admire her; she knew how to do it. Her honesty would do it. He would admire her for showing her feelings, for allowing him to watch.

To have been entirely honest and told him the truth (which could only be partial since her isolation was such that she could no longer recognise what the whole truth might amount to) was beyond her linguistic skill. Renshawe obviously spoke no word of Russian and Slater had never troubled to help her learn his own language properly. Besides, she was idle; they were husband and wife; he ran the house, dealt with finances, correspondence and tradespeople, and Kitty was content, on social occasions, to let him speak for them both. When Slater read aloud to her in Russian and suggested that they converse in her language she was glad to comply because in their monoglot world they could be cosy together, away from the crowd.

Only after his death did she realise how much she had been deprived.

In the cold of the kitchen she started to tell Archie as much as her inadequate English would allow.

The day after Slater's funeral Kitty had found herself completely alone. No one came that day or any of the following days. But letters began to arrive. They looked official. They frightened her. At first she had put them with other things of Slater's which she disliked too much to have about her. Then she had cleared them away into the sunless front room where they accumulated into a deepening pile on the sill behind the window-seat.

At no time since her marriage had Kitty Slater been certain that she would not, one day, be deported. She had never felt sure that even marriage conferred on her any right which she could enforce upon her husband or anyone else, let alone the representatives of authority for whom she had preserved from her childhood a very reasonable fear. With Slater dead, the logic of her position seemed unassailable: as a wife she deserved refuge; as a widow she could be driven away. Ought to be, probably, for what did they owe her now, this foreign people which had taken her in?

She had told herself not to be silly, that there were laws, but she had no more belief in them than in herself. The monstrous letters had continued to arrive, and they still frightened her, but tonight, this man whose business was threatening by letters, he would explain them to her, wouldn't he?

In the front room Archie ran his thumb-nail along the PRIVATE & CONFIDENTIAL of the topmost envelope. "I shouldn't open these. That says I shouldn't." He flicked through the rest. "They're all personal."

Kitty thrust Slater's silver paper-knife into his hand, shouting, "Read me this personal thing!" furious with herself for the loss of those hours when, instead of refining the nuances of her late husband's Russian, she could have pleaded with him to explain how she could say: Please be so good, young man, my dear Mr Renshawe, Archie, yes, please read my letters and tell me the worst.

Archie felt the blunted turn of the blade. "Why don't you ask your employer, that restaurant woman, Mrs Sedgewick? Speaks quite decent English, doesn't she?"

"Once I was trying but Lyudy she can only speak. Not much reading. Also, I hate her already – she is one cat, one bloody big liar."

Again she wanted to say: Lyudy is no person to turn to, she would want reasons, want the whole story, and having discovered it, would use the information in some beastly devious way. Women were no good at secrets. I need a man, Mr Renshawe. I have always needed a man, a man who can help me to understand myself and enable me to deal with life. I am in mourning. The year is not yet out and I am still in mourning so I cannot bring myself to attend to anything beside the rituals of my grief. But if I could tell you this you would think me insane. Lyudy is a believer but even Lyudy told me I was insane.

"Help me – dear," she said tearfully.

Archie sat down at the bureau-bookcase. The flap of the writing compartment was shut and he whistled softly to himself while Kitty knelt by his feet to extract the key from the lock of the deep bottom drawer before releasing the catch, dropping the flap and sliding it out. "Hey presto!" she exclaimed. "Magic."

Archie had already made his decision but he lingered, inspecting the pleated green-silk blinds behind the pear-drop latticing of the bookcase until she had settled on the carpet by his knees.

"OK," he said at last. "Let's find out the answer."

"You go on with whistle," said Kitty. "I like that."

For the best part of an hour he read through the letters, occasionally forgetting to whistle as he came on something especially surprising. Then she would remind him that she was still there, by nudging his leg with her forehead. The rest of the time he could sense her watching out for his face, anticipating the expression it would have when he turned and bent down to tell her that he had finished.

Nazir came in from the hallway and did not look at her directly. "Aw, Christ, Arch, it's freezing, I'm dying out there."

Neither replied and he settled in front of the gas-fire. While Archie, too, remained seated, Kitty was no longer distressed. In this state of calm, not sad but not happy, she did not need to be able to speak this man's language but could think in her own, very clearly and plainly, her thoughts gathering round the picture of his sitting there, above her, gently whistling a tune which she had asked for but which she did not know.

He sorted the letters into three heaps: routine, urgent and lethal.

Gas and electricity would be the next to go and so would the water. Since he'd left for Russia Slater obviously hadn't paid a single bill. In fact he had failed to settle bills for nearly a year before that. The credit-card statements were worst. Credit limits – the lowest more than half Archie's yearly salary – spent up to the last penny or, in two cases, vastly overspent beyond the limit. No attempt had been made to reduce the balance, forward suggestions for payment, not to use the cards, or to return them cut in two.

At his feet Kitty stirred. "You don't whistle."

"I don't whistle."

Sheet after sheet, listing shops with unpronounceable names, cash withdrawals at airports, local currency conversions, every imaginable charge that the company could offer a client.

He tried to cash up the particulars but the subtotal made him light-headed.

"They do not send me back because poor Slater died?"

"Not a chance."

"I am safe?"

Instead of answering he shuffled through the heap of miscellaneous envelopes he had kept till last. Many had a divorce-court-registry feel to them, wastefully oversized. My God, Archie thought, this Slater fellow really took the biscuit for rampant irresponsibility. Probably these big letters came from some building society foreclosing on the mortgage. The widow could well be out on the street before Slater's headstone was cemented in.

An autopsy report. Subject, a well-nourished male aged fifty-five–sixty. It was like a butcher's bill – the man had been gutted. Heart, lungs, even the brain, removed and weighed.

Without going into detail he described the nature of the document to the girl. "You didn't attend the inquest?"

"I do not understand."

He felt her tremble at his knee. Over by the gas-fire Nazir drooped on the Aztec-weave armchair pointing the toes of his shoes inwards and outwards.

"Tell me," said Archie. "When exactly did he die?"

To this she had an answer, she would never forget. "Twenty-nine November."

With a sense of shock Archie suddenly realised that if Professor Slater had died on the twenty-ninth of last November then, despite his careless neglect of bills in general, he could not be blamed for exceeding the credit limit on two of his now-cancelled cards. Itemised bills from abroad had arrived almost two months late. Even allowing for distance and inefficiency, Archie knew at once that this last spending spree was not Slater's. No, someone else had used the cards after the professor died. Who?

"And what have you been doing since his death?"

"I am living," Kitty sobbed. "Here. What you think – I go on holiday or something?"

Nazir lay back experiencing the coffin-coloured wallpaper trying to imagine how it must have been for the girl alone, in this cold echoing room, while Archie, in his present hyperactive state, felt he might be driven to do something for Kitty Slater himself. Something Good Samaritanish, quixotic, the sort of thing in-service training sessions had tried to knock out of his head.

"Here," she repeated. "I die here. He dies in Moscow. Alone, like me. I die in his house, he dies in my home. Very funny."

This was almost the longest coherent sentence she had spoken so far, but when her voice broke under a fresh gush of tears, Archie got up and crossed to the fireside where Nazir sat, his heels propped on the black-leaded fender.

"Stir yourself, man. I've got my hands full with this woman and you're better at figures," he murmured. "I need you to take a look at some of this financial stuff."

When Nazir replaced his partner at the desk the girl edged away to the fireplace, still on her knees. Archie stood astride the hearth-rug, his back to the gas. He could see her scalp, white where the fringe parted, black from black.

"So you've not been back there recently?"

At first she seemed intent on the medallion of Britannia set in the burnished undermantel of the fireplace and did not reply. What age? Thirty? The B side of an old Rolling Stones record: "The Spider to the Fly. Thirty. Just about thirty". One day he might like to have a really hole-in-the-corner affair with a disastrously unsuitable woman who flaunted her emotions.

"My Slater has one sister," said the girl eventually. "Edith. A very old, good woman. She wants me to go back."

"For always?"

"No, no, she is not cruel. She says I must go there to see what he did in those last two months. See people he saw."

Her ignorance about the man was pitiful. What he did? Spent a small fortune, that's what he did. And so did someone else, with his cards, after he was dead.

"This is not woman's work," Kitty was saying. "Edith is old. I know!" she suddenly exclaimed. "*You*, you will take me. Yes? I find money . . ."

From the desk Nazir gave a deep chuckle. Mrs Slater shouted, "You! Pipe down!"

Archie took off his spectacles, examined the lenses and put them on again. Nazir was right. The invitation was grotesque, but with her now before him, rocking back and forth on her heels, her narrow back curved from the effort to find the right words to move him to go with her, he could be tempted, really tempted.

But his reply was professionally bland. "I'm afraid that's quite out of the question, Mrs Slater."

"You are not detective?"

He saw the glint of new tears. "Not detective. Besides, I can't speak a word of your language."

She pounced. "Easy! I speak English! I translate."

Nazir found voice again. "Attagirl, Mrs S. You stick out for what you want. Perhaps we'll all be going." He was smiling fatly, quite transformed. "We're home and dry, Archie boy, your number's come up at last. Our pretty little lady can hire a dozen interpreters, charter an aeroplane, whatever." He brandished a handful of the thick blue envelopes Archie had left unopened. "She doesn't need dictionaries now, do you dear? She's going to be rich, Archie, old chap. Very, very rich."

From the unlit dressing-room on the first floor Kitty watched them go out to the street where the red-haired one stopped to check the lock of his brief-case near the lamp post before motioning his colleague into the passenger seat of the long blue car. For the second or two that he fumbled in and out of the light he seemed to her so very anxious about nothing in particular that she recognised herself in the slight, rather awkward figure, uncertain which way to go, and she felt a desire to attach herself to him because there was something wise and safe in his nervousness, which was in her, too.

In a moment he was gone, and the street was as it had always been, and again everything new had gone from her life. Another drink? Soon, perhaps, another, and then she would come apart again and she would forget entirely what they had said.

The dark one had explained about the money. His eyes wheeled around her like brown moths, getting in the way. Already she had forgotten what he wanted her to want. The easiest thing to forget about a man, yet it was all she remembered about the man in Moscow. Quite a different sort of man waiting for her there, someone she feared and wanted to fear, but most passionately wanted to see.

Not Slater, but *the* man. The first.

In Moscow Klavdia, too, was waiting. Klavdia who thought that the only explanation of the terrible things in the world was that Jesus was not God but Lucifer.

Kitty Slater swept away the neat pile which the two men had made of her papers and found underneath the bundle of aerogramme blanks her husband had set aside for her correspondence with him while he was in Russia.

"*Svyet ty moy, Dymka*," she wrote. "Dmitry, light of my life, do not be angry when I come back to you in Moscow. I know you will want to hear this from me . . ."

As she wrote on in a quaint old-fashioned style all her own she thought of the other man, and how much she would have liked to be writing a letter to him: "Dear Mr Renshawe, Dear Archie, Something happened in Moscow three years ago, I married Oliver Slater instead of Dmitry Florinskii, and this is why I am here now, in this house, a lone woman who drinks in the day and weeps all the night . . ."

But that was Russian. She could only think and write Russian, and only Dmitry would understand that she could have such thoughts about another man while she was writing to Moscow, to him.

The way from Moscow to here had been long but the way back would be even longer and darker. Journeys from childhood, always journeys. She foresaw this one as obligatory, inescapable. The last. One she did not wish to undertake, but would, as an act of homage to the man she had married and to the man she had not.

To Klavdia she wrote: "*Nu, Klavshka, bud schastliva*. Be content. Pray to God. *Molis Bogu: on tebya nye ostavit*. He shall not abandon thee."

She sealed Klavdia's note inside Dymka's cover which she addressed very carefully without abating one word of his official title or the great Department of State in which he worked.

5

It had taken Kitty years to get used to the smell of Moscow.

Monday used to be her free day, and every Monday afternoon in summer she would cross the river by the Borodinskii Bridge to treat herself to a single fresh flower from the same woman hawker at the steps of the Kiev Station. Although the dahlias and gladioli were scentless she would bury her nose in their blooms and pretend they carried that brash tang of fern and grass which dispelled the fish-oil odour of the city. It took her back to that other place, more real than Moscow, where her girlhood seemed to locate itself unblemished within the tight fold of petals.

After two years on the outskirts she moved to a hostel in Silver Street and grew more accustomed to the city. But the other girls in the hostel, she never got used to them. They dressed poorly and wore too much make-up. At night the dingy corridors buzzed with their complaints, their silly, defiant gossip. Only outside, in the fresh air, could Kitty feel individual, although that was often more frightening than being one of a crowd.

In the narrow alley which unwound from the door of the artistes' dressing-rooms to the pavement of the six-lane boulevard a stall had been pitched for the sale of beer, sausage and chestnuts. When Kitty came out with the other girls after matinée performances the old man beneath the awning always served her first because she had an accent like his own; but unlike the others she did not try to hide it by affecting the high lady-like voice of a city-bred woman. Most of the girls in the troupe were emigrants from the provinces whose moderate abilities as acrobats, dancers, musicians and trapeze artists had gained them some status back home, but who, once in the capital, had quickly learned to defend their lack of talent and sophistication by aping city slang and manners, and being very blasé about men.

Throughout winter and summer the size of the audience hardly varied. Good attendances were guaranteed by the sale of seats *en bloc* to provincial delegations up from the country for conferences and meetings. Occasionally the cheaper end of the foreign tourist market might appear as a filler, if business were low at New Year, but parties like those were noisy and effusively critical (an all-female circus in a pokey part of town was a let-down after the splendours of *Gostsirk*), and then the girls, smarting from cat-calls and jeers, would become bad-tempered and take out the humiliation on one another, quarrelling on stage and in the dressing-room; afterwards even in the alley, in front of the old man in the booth, sometimes dropping their careful accents altogether and shouting country obscenities for the favour he showed Kitty by reserving her beer, and making a present of *zakuski* in a special cardboard box which he kept for her under the counter.

Kitty shared a couple of rooms on the third floor of the run-down hostel with Klavdia and two other girls. Klavdia who had brilliant yellow hair and a tip-tilted nose, worked as assistant to a huge Georgian conjuress and was Kitty's best friend. Klavdia wore a lot of lipstick and was self-conscious about her teeth, although the audience was too far away to notice their slight gappiness. The defect made her envious not of other girls' teeth but their legs and she was especially quick at picking quarrels with the dancers. As an orchestra girl, third 'cellist, Kitty was exempt from abuse. In the pit even the men in the front stalls could not see her properly so she was no competition.

After particularly well-attended performances Klavdia always rushed to the props-man who sat dozing in the wings. "Ilyusha, has anything come for me, dearest?"

And Ilya or his deaf son who stood in for him on Wednesdays and Saturdays would fumble in the plastic ice-cream tray where he kept his flask and thick sandwich, knowing in advance that no flowers or invitation had been delivered. But Klavdia was never dashed, and went on to ask next day and the next, just in case.

Sometimes the leggy girls got flowers from men. Notes, too, although this was strictly forbidden. The dressing-rooms had partition doors which no one ever bothered to close so that the women performers could see their neighbours. Once, when Ilya was drunk, a man strayed into Klavdia's dressing-room. Later, they saw him, three doors down, reflected in their long mirror, his head between the legs of a dwarf girl who had lifted the hem of her shift to get a better view of what he was doing.

Anyway, the letters didn't really count because they were mostly written by Russians pretending to be foreigners: Ukrainians who said they were from America, Sicilian Armenians – all crooks of one sort and another. Not that their propositions were necessarily dishonourable – a lot entailed marriage, but fall for a wrong one and you'd probably end up stuck out in the backwoods worse off than when you started.

Klavdia wanted a real foreign man, and she knew that every woman in the troupe was waiting for one, too. Where he came from didn't matter – even a dark one might do at a pinch – and looks were the last thing on a girl's mind. Yes, rich would be nice, but how could you tell? Unmarried, obviously – without family over there – how else could you get out? Or come back, just when you wanted. Two passports, see, when you're married. Travel on either. According to Klavdia, having that chance was the only thing that made a girl's life worth living.

"You dumb-cluck kid," she observed when Kitty said she was going out with a student agronomist at Moscow State. "Where's the percentage? Agronomy? That's farms. Before you know where you are you'll be pulling turnips while he does his Master's on agrarian administration. Find a nice American, a French Jew, anyone, so long as he appreciates you enough to take you with him." However, despite her shrewdness, Klavdia confided that the only non-Russian she had been out with was a fish wholesaler from Yokahama, married, with three children. "A girl can't be too choosy. Besides, they have divorce, too, don't they, in Japan?"

But, choosy or unchoosy, Klavdia had to admit that, like her, the other girls hadn't had much success. Out of her circle of cronies only Fat Carla managed to make it legal, in 1984, with a Tunisian. "Well, he had a kind face and how did she know it was really Africa?" But he had slipped out two days into the honeymoon and she never saw him again. "Letters? She can hardly read Russian, dear, never mind that sign language they write in those places. Still waiting, though, poor love, still hoping. Didn't have the education, you see, Carla. With that sort of man you've got to talk politics if you want to get anywhere. Invent a father who had beliefs and suffered for them. Or talk about what the Nazis did to your Gran in the war or how you were persecuted at school because you went to church. Believe me, sweetling, you'll never depart this vale of tears unless you make up a history to swank about."

One night Klavdia's conjuress demanded an extra hand for her act, and Kitty, for the first time, found herself in the ring.

"Perfect," said Klavdia afterwards. "With that dead straight hair you looked exotic – a Chinese doll in blue-black silks. Even the spotlight couldn't wash you out."

That was shortly before Kitty's student proposed. She accepted him largely because he had a room of his own and she was bored with being amongst women the whole time, so many in the hot auditorium, the little practice rooms, and nowhere to go after performances and rehearsals except back to the hostel where there was nothing but shop-talk night after night. Klavdia's scorn was tempered with philosophy. "You're a fool, of course. More self-discipline and you might have struck lucky, a girl with your advantages, but if you don't mind being poor all your life who am I to stop you? Oh, what the heck – let's celebrate anyway."

Dymka had proposed on the eve of his final examination, and, upon her acceptance, decided he must have an early night to be on top form the next day. That same evening, as it turned out, Klavdia had arranged her first rendezvous with an American. "Strictly platonic." But later, he had telephoned to ask if he could bring along his friend – a Russian.

"Take him on, dear," urged Klavdia. "You're not married yet, and you like them, don't you – Russians. And food."

Kitty agreed. In those days she was always hungry.

The men arrived early, while Klavdia was still in her slip. She swore and hustled them out with Kitty to wait in the alley. It was already evening and the pie vendor had gone home. They walked up and down past the dismantled snack-booth which was padlocked to the wall.

Kitty's Russian date was young, more boy than man. His name was Ben. "Tell me about yourself," he said. When she could not, he told her about his own life: he was working for a higher degree and the American was taking language lessons from him in order to qualify for a government post in his own country. The American was quite old with bad sinuses which crackled when he said "*Ochen rad*" and kissed the back of her hand. "Tell me . . ." he also began but she was even more tongue-tied than before and allowed him to tell her a long story about the city near which she had been born without revealing a trace of the terrible homesickness which still assailed her whenever she heard its name.

At the restaurant Ben introduced both women to an old friend, Professor Slater, the star turn of some cultural exchange programme; evidently quite a celebrity because heads turned when they sat down to eat. Later on, Klavdia said, at first she'd taken him for another fraud from the provinces because he looked so odd and his accent was too good for a foreigner. Certainly no metropolitan Russian would have been seen dead in those clothes: white trousers tucked into his socks, lumpy thick-soled shoes. Except for the fawn cardigan that buttoned down the front and a stiff-collared shirt, he could have been a hiker, a mountaineer.

After a brief initial exchange during which he brushed aside their preferences and ordered a different meal for each member of the party with a queer take-it-or-leave-it smile, he fell into deep conversation with Ben as though the rest of them did not exist.

Kitty was grateful to eat and be silent. Over *solyanka* and wedges of rye she covertly eyed the stranger, intrigued. Despite the white at his temples his hair still had the style of a young man's, long and smoothed back high from the forehead. The face was bearded, almost unlined even under his eyes which were grey, slightly too large, but very beautiful.

"God, you were rude," Klavdia said afterwards. "You stared at that professor like a cow at a meadow. And why do you eat hunched over your food – like the Government's going to snatch it away?"

Both remarks were true but Kitty could not tell her friend that when the American started to grope for Klavdia's hand under the table and suck his food through his teeth she would in any case have needed to turn her attention elsewhere.

Near the end, over tea and *piroshki*, Slater turned and spoke to her. How pleased he had been to make her acquaintance – had she enjoyed the evening? There was absolutely no sense of his being aware that she might have felt neglected. When he spoke to her directly his intonation faltered and he mis-stressed a word so comically that she giggled.

That, too, Klavdia had pounced on. "Well, what's so funny? How the hell was he to know what goes on in your disgusting little mind? You think you know foreign languages – you think they come out just because you open your mouth?"

Instantly Kitty was apologetic to the man.

A week later, a note. Not in Ilya's tub but left for her with the door-woman at the hostel: "Would you and your friend like to come to tea at my hotel?"

At first Klavdia had refused. Those awful trousers! Besides, she distrusted his hair. There was too much of it for a man of his age. And at that age men were normally married. If they weren't they either had no time for women, or you could simply never get rid of them. She might be his last chance but he wasn't going to be hers.

"How can you, Klavushka? Poor man – he must be very lonely, simply dying for company. Remember how courteous and open-handed he was."

The idea of pitying an attractive man was such a novel experience that Kitty almost believed herself. He was attractive, of course, distinguished even; and he clearly admired her – why else the note? But even though she decided not to tell Dymka about the invitation,

Kitty felt no qualms about accepting since she knew that in the end Klavdia would come, too, out of sheer envy.

Slater gave them tea and a bottle of sweet Martini and asked Kitty how old she was several times, the way a man might ask a child, until Klavdia said, "OK, you like young girls. What makes you think she's so much younger than me?" Klavdia's American had already told her why he thought she looked older than Kitty. He had even told complete strangers on the Metro on the way home.

"Why, obviously because of my frock, you great goose," exclaimed Kitty, slightly heady from vermouth. They had come straight from the matinée and she was still in a star-spangled dress with the flattening bodice. "These are my work clothes. Don't I look funny?" And she made a stage bow so deep that the fall of her hair brushed Slater's knee.

"Not at all. I wouldn't dream . . . And you, my dear," he said to Klavdia, "look younger than springtime." This was no sarcasm but a compliment. Ghastly, but well taken by Klavdia who perched on the radiator under the window and began riffling through the books on the sill.

"I believe you," she said. "Now, how about another drink?"

The way he truckles, Kitty thought, watching Slater swing open the refrigerator door and select something strong with which to placate her friend.

"Will this do?" Awkward, yet not inexperienced – his eyes had already envisaged Kitty's breasts crushed within the frock, worked her over, hip to hip – but over-eager, too ready to please.

It was an English drink, fiery, tasting of earth-worms. Klavdia sipped ungraciously. "How can you live here?" she said. "This place is a slum."

In fact the room was tidy, even his books ranged according to size like empty bottles. The drink made him cough. "One m-m-manages, my dear, one gets used to anything in time."

While Klavdia pursued him with tart advice, exacting revenge from one foreigner for her failure with another, Kitty began to feel sorry for Slater who responded so politely without realising that no one played the silly bitch better than Klavdia; then quickly, overwhelmingly, Kitty became sorrier for herself. How much she longed to depart from this city and set forth for the south: Alma-Ata, Pyatigorsk. Then Klavdia wanted to go home and only shrugged when Kitty said she would stay and talk to Slater about her past.

In fact she told him only a little. About her dead father who had been a music teacher in a provincial high school; her mother, of whom she had no recollection except the touch of a hand at the back of her neck and the glisten of patchouli in long-ribboned hair. She heard herself and thought: how this must appeal to him, how much he must want it to appear the way I make it sound — the only child, and talented, oh, so talented that her father had sent her away, while she still had other memories of her mother which faded with school after school, and had entirely gone by the time she reached Moscow. He was so proud! But at the Conservatoire she had no talent to withstand the noise of others: the incessant boulevard roar, the jingle-jangle from practice-rooms, above all the hard jabber-jabber of fellow students who wanted her to fail and knew they could talk her into it because she came from the back of beyond.

This was true, or not true, depending on how Kitty felt when she told the story. Sometimes it must have been true, sometimes not. Because Slater thought it true, now, she was pleased.

"I understand you," he said. "I understand because we both come from the outside."

"That is a very cheap thing to say." When she tried to get up the room slopped around her like bathwater. Slater stood up, embarrassed, without offering to help. She did not try again. "When there is a continent between us,' she said. "I hate this city and the rooms in this city. Your room and everything in it. *J'en ai marre de tout ça, j'en ai marre.*"

The French was to impress because he could say, "Look, it is in my power to take you, to take you to Paris, London, it is in my power . . ."

"Yes," Slater said. "This is not a nice place to be ill in. Wouldn't you feel better at home?"

Home was the hostel. At home they stole your soap and changed the sheets once every five weeks. His home was in a house. In his home would they have to change them every day? Do I remind him of his wife? Tears were gathering.

"You are ill. Shall I telephone the circus and say that you are ill?"

And Klavdia might come and take her back and put her between the dirty sheets of her own bed, tut-tutting, askance, "Did he take advantage? Did you take precautions?"

Take, be taken.

Telephone? No, no, really, not yet, defer pleasure, wait for it, for me. She turned towards him, powerful, secure, the first time she had been so secure for years. "I am not ill. I want to go downstairs to the Osborne Bar."

"Of course, I'm so sorry. I was simply waiting until . . . I didn't mean to keep you . . ."

His obedience was intoxicating. She took such pleasure in this man that joy in provoking him overcame all the guilt and contrition for playing fast and loose, and Kitty was seduced by a feeling of luxurious melancholy that went through her like pain. The scribble on the back of the bathroom door in the hostel – what did it say? "I simply adore men."

She allowed him to watch from a distance as she carefully repaired her make-up at the washbasin mirror. "Did you know I'm engaged to a brilliant young student who is going to be a diplomat?" There was nothing that jealousy might not achieve with this old man who stood behind her, motionless, watching. When he kissed her there, on the back of the neck, she would crumple tenderly and not resist the hand at her throat. He would be violent, even desperate, and need help with her clothes. She would fall into the embrace, bearing down against his broad, experienced fingers. Oh, she so wanted to do the right thing, to be buffeted, rocked against him, paralysed by the thoughts of what he would do to her. This is my chance. I can trust him. This is the man. I can feel him already inside me. Feel his feelings.

"You still look very pale. Are you well enough to go to work?" Slater said.

Work? She had just come from work – didn't he remember? He must have forgotten, he was tired, he had a lot on his mind.

Kitty dropped her rouge stick into the basin. "Get me out of here," she shouted, "before I kick down the door."

There was nowhere to sit in the Osborne Bar. She continued making up at a round buffet table. Slater bought Japanese whisky and sweet pastries. Under his pastry something moved. "I say," he said brightly. "Just fancy that."

Kitty looked down with half-powdered brow. "That is a disgusting but perfectly ordinary thing."

"Quite." He turned it on to its back with the rice-paper doily from his pastry. "My whole life has been Russian literature, but this is my first time, almost face to face with a true-born, live Russian cockroach. Let me tickle him."

Kitty snapped her compact closed. "Her," she said. "This one is female. Unfortunately I have experience of them."

If the cockroach had not happened the story might have ended there in the shabby Osborne Bar that rainy November night. If Kitty had been able to explain to Archie Renshawe what happened after the cockroach he might have understood why she treasured the memory as the best and purest of her life.

Then she only knew that Slater was lonely, would have taken her to bed, been nice enough afterwards to try to make a love story out of it, because she too was lonely and wanted him to, without any care for the consequences. Then she thought him vulnerable, in spite of his age and his being so clever. An innocent. She took pride in those perceptions because they led her to decide not to see him again. A really sensitive girl ought not to take advantage of an older man, especially one who might love her and have promises to keep.

She did not know then that Slater was far from being pathetic, quite undeserving of her showgirl mercy. The man was rich, unmarried, a widower without encumbrances. Not the Prince Charming of the circus troupe's collective dream but the man in his retinue who smiled in the shadow, knowing that he could pay for a hundred glass slippers.

So she told him she was shortly to be married and could not see him again. Slater simply laughed and asked if she would invite him to the wedding.

And that was how it all started.

Because Slater was clever and made light of convention, Kitty, who had never been clever with men, soon took her lead from him, and next time he invited her out she did not take Klavdia along. Eventually, one of the girls (she never discovered who) told Kitty's fiancé about Kitty's new friend, this Englishman, vaguely important, but old, really old, and there was a terrible row which ended with his storming out and her rushing to Slater for consolation. And in a muddle of tears and endearments, in his room, on his bed, he, as Klavdia would have put it, "took advantage". After that, no one at the hostel wanted to know her. Except Klavdia, of course, who was the only girlfriend to attend the wedding. Now Kitty could not understand why and how she had felt at that time, but once she had given herself to the man there was no going back. Even had she been able to recount the story in his own language to this Renshawe, it still would have sounded absurd, because it was absurd: Slater wore diamond-patterned socks to the wedding, and at the reception, which was held in the basement flat of one of his Russian colleagues, the lights fused halfway through the speeches and they sat in the dark for fully three-quarters of an hour. That day, she learned later, Dymka spent on his back from an attack of migrainous neuritis. Later still he sent back all her letters in a chocolate-box shaped like a coffin. She was terribly upset.

"It won't last," Klavdia told the circus girls after the wedding. "That old man of hers is on his last legs. She'll be back, you'll see, and then her dinky Dymka will take it out on her hide."

Klavdia believed you could never give destiny the slip.

6

"So, for two months this professor spends money, but all the time he's dead?"

"It happens," said Archie.

Lambert Farncombe squeezed the bridge of his nose before inserting an aerosol inhalant up his right nostril. "Today I feel seedy, young Renshawe, even my immune system is on the blink. Dispel my ignorance, lad, tell me my business."

"Electronic transmission of funds, Lambert, old boy. State of the art, software, the modern miracle."

While he waited for his employer to fumble the inhaler to his other nostril, Archie twirled his one-legged executive chair and surveyed Lambert's office.

It was certainly an unlikely venue for technology. Nestling among the hand-blocked gillyflowers and peonies of the cobalt-blue wallpaper was an ebony-framed Sunday School text: "If ye have not been faithful in that which is another man's who shall give you that which is your own?"

Lambert withdrew the tube of Vick and sniffed mucously. "Tchah – treacherous, treacherous. Don't trust machines, that's my belief. How else could your professor's money have been frittered away all over Eastern Europe at the blip of a touchscreen? Thank God, our writ doesn't run to foreign countries, either. We've got enough aggravation with our domesticated pillocks." As he leaned back anticipating the rush of vaporising menthol to his sinuses Lambert stroked his neatly brushed, very slightly oily blond hair which merged with the beaded corn ears of the wallpaper to give his long smooth forehead and full lips the overvarnished tinge of a Wildwood Man on a public-house sign. "I can't bear scandals that reek of unrighteous Mammon. Criminal capers, forgery, obtaining pecuniary advantage by fraud. Pass it to the uniformed branch, as they say on the telly. No, we're only chasing the HP arrears – that's where the honest profit ticks up."

"Yes, well, now the Slater business is being regulated on a proper footing," said Archie. "I've been helping the widow, you know, and

Professor Slater's professional colleagues seem to have rallied round."

On Lambert's seamless face – incredibly youthful for a sedentary man of over fifty – the smile came and went, a very slight smile, as if he were holding his breath against the sudden breakthrough of old age. "Ah, how I admire you, Archie boy, always ready with the helping hand. Be a good lad and pass over my drops. One of the drawers over there. Have to keep them out of the way – they bring on the cat's asthma."

Archie threaded his way through a suite of club armchairs to an octagonal library table, dark and heavily waxed. He tried the nearest drawer. "You've no soul any more, Lambert. Think of it, an affair like Slater's – big money, big fish, exotic locale."

Once the little bottle was on Lambert's desk Archie watched him unscrew the balled rubber cap with a flourish and sprinkle drops on to the back of his left hand. He knew Lambert of old. All this fiddling around was usually a prelude to bad news.

"I'll come straight to the point," Lambert said, relinquishing the dropper and reaching for the porcelain jar of crystallised tangerines which he kept beside the reading-lamp. "I've been contacted by a Sir Evelyn Tremayne. Mean anything to you?"

Archie nodded.

"Thought it would. A weird sort of herbert, but decent enough. Said he is definitely standing the racket for all Russian malfeasances and misdemeanours."

Archie sank down on to the spoon-backed nursing-chair which Lambert reserved for important clients. "But Lambert, you old twister, you knew that already. I put it in my report, remember?"

The older man began to lick the sugar frost off his tangerine with practised aplomb. "And now you've been deputed to make the financial arrangements, boyo, I've put you down to attend to Sir Tremayne tomorrow a.m., around at his place. That suit you?"

Archie felt distinctly uneasy. Normally nothing would have stood in the way of Lambert himself attending to this distinguished old friend of Professor Slater's whose intervention on Kitty Slater's behalf was one of the revelations Nazir had unearthed among the letters in Clacton over a month ago. "Why not you? You'd have jumped at it once, Lambert, moving in that kind of circle."

His employer raised another segment of baby orange to his lips. "I like to take it easy, nowadays, lad. It's less stressful living over the shop. Besides, I lack that essential something – can't help it – no breeding, see? Now to you and young Nazreddin Hus-sain" – Lambert was the one person in the office to have attempted to master

Nazir's other names – "to you it comes natural. Education. Refinement. You need that to predispose an exalted client."

Archie always winced when Lambert got to this point. Nazir had had the real education. At a real public school. And a real university.

"European Studies, wasn't it, young Renshawe? A BA degree?"

That was Nazir, too. "MA."

Lambert's Welsh lilt rode triumphantly high. "Who better to have on our books, then?"

"Well, you'd be better sending Nazir to interview this Tremayne." Lambert leaned out from his chair to pat Archie's knee.

"No, no, he particularly asked for you. Seems he's heard of your charitable deeds to the Slater widow woman. Can't deal with her direct – too emotional for him to handle, apparently. He needs a middleman to channel the generosity."

More than generosity. It was munificence: every item on Slater's accounts to be settled in full, if Archie's most recent enquiries were right. Then the hefty life insurance and pension plan, all of it paid up to date by this old chum and patron of Slater's whom Kitty scarcely knew.

"So out you go, Renshawe, my lad, and get the goods. I've no idea what else he wants, but keep him happy. We need the percentage. Agree to anything, within reason."

"Where's his money from, Lambert?"

"You never did keep abreast of your subject, Archie. Bugger the *Financial Times*, read the gossip columns. The man's rolling. Family fortune going back centuries, and he's the last of the line. Master of some Cambridge college once, but retired early to devote himself to his art collection. Lovely house. Robert Adam. I read about it in *The World of Interiors*."

Archie concentrated his gaze on the Victorian oleograph of Leonardo's *Last Supper* on the far wall of the office. Lambert was holding back. He and this Tremayne character were obviously cooking something up between them for a consideration. Something involving him. Exactly what he'd have to wait till tomorrow to find out. He'd never shift Lambert on a question of money.

When he got back to Endymion Road Helen was standing stark naked at the kitchen dresser, spooning dried oregano into a rose-bowl filled with cold ratatouille.

"Hello," she said without turning round. "A hard day? Take advantage of me if you want. I won't mind."

The voice strung out, running throaty. An assured, expensive forty-year-old sort of voice, a voice with open marriages behind it, thick with experience.

Archie squeezed past her to the end of the dining area and kicked off his shoes before flopping on to the day-bed in front of the television. "Don't mind what?"

"Being had."

"I thought we'd already sorted it out, Nell, your stuff and mine. Nobody's being had."

"I *know*," she sang out in cockney falsetto. "Ain't it a bloomin' shame. Look at all this – just going to waste."

Archie winced as she slapped herself with the copper ladle just where the curve declined into the straight of her right thigh. "Go on, dearie," she crowed, clashing the ladle along the deep-cut rim of the bowl. "Can't you see I'm dying for it? Do me now, right up – you know, how I like it, from behind."

"For God's sake, Helen, cut it out. I'm just not in the mood for your crotchless-tights act tonight."

She turned, hooked her feet into a pair of Dutch ceramic clogs which Archie had bought as kitchen ornaments, and clattered away over to the double drainer. "I meant well, *caro mio*. Only a *partenza*, after my positively last appearance. All I wanted were my catalogues and a final squelch."

Archie breathed in deeply. She was in one of those moods. For the last couple of months these unexpected visits had become rarer and rarer. How long since? Three weeks, perhaps less? He couldn't remember, but they always began with her cooking or ironing, and ended with her flaunting outrageously, nude as an egg. Next, the obscenities would come, precisely articulated so that he would get the full pleasure of hearing them from an educated woman who ought to know better.

"A quickie, sticky, fucking thrash, all the way up, Archie."

Devastatingly illuminated by the battery of strip lights over the work surfaces of the utility area, the white of her body reminded him of those dainty cream-whips in the confectioner's chill-tray, marine blue in the folds from the glare of the Insectocute. The whole neighbourhood could be looking in, too; she knew that, she did it on purpose.

He went over and pulled down the blind of the patio door. "Now you see me, now you don't. This has been going on for months, Nells." He settled down again on the day-bed, out of reach, and opened the local property free-sheet. "One protracted farewell I could cope with, dear, but this is a retirement concert, dear, the longest long goodbye in the world."

His weary unconciliatory tone distressed her, as he knew it would, and she began to weep, noisily, straddling the ladle across her long, flat stomach. "I've had enough, Archie. More than enough. I've been meaning to leave you for ages ... now at last I've made up my mind."

He shook out the paper. Every column-inch advertisements: "Executive mortgages for the financially aware." Relax, fabricate normality, she'll choke herself off eventually, always does. "Release the £££££s in your equity." Throughout Helen's affected sobs he concentrated on tomorrow's interview with Sir Evelyn Tremayne, touched by a sense of coming ordeal. She might be a help, though: she was older, fairly high up at her Museum, knew the academic score. "Helen, I'm sorry, love, when you've finished I'd be grateful for a little advice. It's this job tomorrow. Evelyn Tremayne. Ring any bells? Sounds a bit ivory-towerish to me."

"What do I care about your rotten job? I hope he bloody murders you," she said.

"A friend of yours?"

"Men like that don't make friends, Renshawe. They have acolytes."

He relinquished the tattered paper and looked up. Helen had put down the ladle and was coming towards him, her long narrow feet gliding the porcelain clogs over his most precious possession, the bitter scarlet Shiraz on which he had blown a month's salary the day after his wife had left him for good.

Inertly naked she was unaffecting; once in motion her slightly overweight body assumed the dignity that clothing always gave it and she appeared stately even now as she splayed her white legs right across his lap.

He waited. For her, their relationship could never be more exciting than when she was in the throes of putting an end to it. Any moment she might disengage herself in a wild fit of panic, reach for her clothes, storm out half-dressed on to the public road, leaving him mute and seething, determined never to let her near him again. Debating the next possible move was fruitless; whichever way he chose was bound to be wrong because she was cleverer than him, older, surer of herself, richer, and, most of all, still capable of inflicting that mixture of tedium, excitement and pain which he had spent two whole years of his life trying to shake off. And even now, although he could admit that he didn't love her and probably never had, he still couldn't fix on any other woman whom he more wanted and admired.

"Archie, darling, how can I bear to lose you?"

53

The image came to him of Kitty Slater's grey house and her face in vivid cut-out against the smear of a desolate sea.

"Don't start, Nells. I hear you but I can't listen any more."

She was undoing his shirt, wisps of her black straight hair catching round the button thread as she found the holes with her active, strong fingers. "It's that bloody job, isn't it? Who's a poor tired boy, then, slaving all day for that horrid, horrid little man?" A pricklish flush broke out below the line of her breastbone.

Once, in a rare moment of honesty, she told him that she had lost two husbands because they both eventually found her affectations intolerable. Archie had no objections on that score. No, as far as he was concerned, the problem was that she wasn't quite affected enough. With her genuinely exotic background – the Jewish-refugee father, a vaguely aristocratic mother who had died giving birth to the daughter – Helen's education, her easy fluency in a clutch of languages, her degrees, the classy job, even her unorthodox clothes – most men would have been pleased to be fascinated. But from him she mostly concealed these intriguing aspects of her present and previous lives under banal position-taking. If he betrayed any real interest she closed up and badgered him: why did he want to know? What difference could knowing such things about her possibly make?

He had long realised that the success and failure of their affair came from class attitudes. He knew he was a snob, and one of the worst kinds: eager to please someone only because they gave him glimpses into a world he had never entered. His exaggerated respect for the educated ought to have put Helen beyond his reach, alongside people like Slater and this unknown Tremayne whose palatial dwelling and academic eminence overhung the squalor of Archie's mean professional world. Helen had supplied him with a similar dream-like glamour, and he had given her exactly the opposite type of escape. She revelled in his careful economies, his few painfully acquired possessions that reflected his need for an abstract sense of good taste which she didn't even have to think about. Even his sordid cronies gave her a thrill. To top it all, he was shockable, and that made him extremely attractive. She liked shocking him. Sexually, she could be nerve-racking.

"Archie. I am happy. Let me make you happy."

It always started like this. They might be anywhere: a walkway on the South Bank after a concert, a pub car park, a deserted playground. She wouldn't even look round but keeping him at arm's length would back against the nearest fence or wall and pull up her skirts like a ballerina about to make a leap. He used to get frantic: there could be people walking dogs, hurrying for the tube, just being normal, but she'd stand there, luxuriating in the spread of herself (she never wore a stitch underneath when they were together in public), and squealing maliciously as if he'd been some lout assaulting her.

Afterwards she would press her lips to his neck and thrust her hands into his armpits. "You are so unextraordinary, Archie. How could you think anyone would have thought you were possibly involved in anything *flagrant*?"

And back home she would want it hard (her words, never his), lights blazing, curtains undrawn, on the high-glossed boards of the dinette floor. Anywhere, over a chair, doubled up in the bath, anywhere at all, except comfortably, in bed, like ordinary people who took all their clothes off.

"Don't let him do this, don't, don't . . ." It was working, it always did. She knew exactly what to do. After lifting slightly to allow room for his hand she settled back and wavered gently to and fro along the inner turn of his wrist. "That bloody Farncombe *patronises* you. It's pathetic."

In a minute she'd be unstoppable. "Helen . . ." If he didn't time it right she could turn vicious, give up, lose interest, simply because he'd started to, roll away saying it was no good, she wasn't in the mood after all, and then get half-dressed before telling him that having brought her so far he'd better make a real bloody effort and hold her down and force her, before it was too late.

"Helen . . ."

She found him and wriggled. "And the black boy, black all over, don't let them do it, let me, do let me, screw, screw, Archie, let *me* screw you . . ."

He had to shout. "For Christ's sake, Nells, stop thinking about yourself for a second."

"Oh, sweetheart . . ."

The trouser-pantomime was lengthier than Kitty Slater's Miki-Riki act. There was little he could do as she unzipped and unbuttoned, so he concentrated silently on Helen's brilliant fawny eyes while the full, squarish hands dealt with him beneath, practised and unhindered.

The morbidity of this laying out of his intimate body enchanted her to the point of climax. "Now, don't you move, don't say a word, let me try . . . What's this then, dear? Nice? Nice? But we're all hooked up, aren't we?" After two husbands she didn't need to see what she was doing. In a swift, undragging movement, she had him free and to herself without having ceased for one moment the circling of his eyes and ears with wet, clear-cut lips. Then and only then, was he permitted to take part.

Her habit was to sleep on him afterwards, unextricated, like a heavy pink cat with claws dug in. Although he had learned not to move, this time he didn't want to, and was reluctant when, as usual, she woke exactly ten minutes later and parted with him, brusquely, indifferent to the foolish spectacle he always felt he made, sprawled on his back among the cushions of the gingham day-bed.

Her clothes were in a rucksack next to the washing-machine. Unlike all the other women he had known, she dressed in front of him. Dreamily, slowly, as if she were making an act of will to recall what came next. And the more elaborate the garments, the more they seemed to try her memory. She went in for loose stuff with plenty of flow, and to look at her in the street you'd think she must be freezing. He had done, the first time they met, on that bleak December day by the Embankment with sleet flurrying up from the river. Then the flowers; vigils outside her office; theatre tickets; restaurants he couldn't afford.

He must have been insane.

"Nells."

The first brassière, a russet half-cup that he liked because it didn't quite cover her nipples, dangled unattached across her shoulder while she rummaged in her bag for the one that went over it.

"Archie?"

First she'd twist the red one round her neck, back to front, clip it to, stare down at her breasts as if they were in the wrong place, then undo it and start up from the waist.

"What's an acolyte, Nells?"

That way the underwiring always caused a faintly perceptible graze under the heavier right breast. A slight shudder and she was even and comfortable, prinking up the machine lace with the tips of her fingers.

"Didn't they teach you anything in that school of yours? It *was* a *public* school you went to, wasn't it?"

"In a way."

"That's you all over, Archie – devious. Everything's subjective, a manner of speaking."

The second bra was yanked downwards and she stooped herself into it. The material looked like wartime parachute silk, unboned.

"Leave my school out of it."

"Well, it'd make any woman furious, that sob-story. I mean, imagine allowing yourself to be thrown out of a place like that. *Unprecedented* – I bet it was. All because Daddy couldn't come up with the fees. And the rest – braving the world of work because you were too pigheaded to accept a loan and finish your education."

Above them boards creaked, there was a scuffle of feet, and a fine dust began to drift from the loose ceiling rose, spiralling down on to Archie's rug. Eight o'clock. The landlord's kids tuning up.

"You never got over it, did you, Archie? Well, did you? You told me that at the beginning."

He couldn't squabble now, before she told him what she knew about Tremayne. He changed the subject abruptly. "God, you look awful in that thing, Nells. What was it once – a mailbag?"

"I know," she said placidly, giving a slight twirl in order to catch the fullness of her own reflection on the burnished clockface of the automatic oven-timer. "Positively ss Bring 'n Buy, I quite agree, but extremely effective, nevertheless. Keeps them at a distance."

"Who?"

She smiled very wide. "Why, men, of course, dearie . . . Nipple watchers, rapists, public-school boys, that kind of chap."

When she flicked back her hair Archie noticed how grey she was becoming. He had never got used to the ritual of her post-orgasmic teasing. Six months ago he might have retaliated but now he did not even regret the lost opportunities. One day some really sadistic bastard would make her care.

The recorder band from upstairs struck up the first bars before tailing off unevenly to let in the treble screech of the landlord's smallest boy.

"Lavender's blue, dilly dilly, lavender's green . . ."

By now Helen was into her leading pair of knickers. Tight and semi-transparent they covered and revealed her at one and the same time, like a first layer of surgical gauze. Burgundy lisle tights went over the schoolgirl pull-ons. "Devoted followers, attendants, those who snuff the candles and mop the altar tiles. Acolytes, Archie, are skivvies who long to partake of the mystery. Now, how do I look?"

A black buttoned-down top with leg-of-mutton shoulders in deep pink came above a white skirt billowing to mid-calf. He gave her an absent-minded glance. "Swaddled?"

Helen pirouetted. "Perfect! Hardly an inch of visible flesh. Don't you just adore the thought of my body inside all this?"

He went over to the window while she put on her Reeboks. "Look, Nells, I know you like playing the silly bitch, but I'm not in the right frame of mind. I'm worried that Lambert's keeping me in the dark about this Tremayne character." Had he been honest he would have admitted to a more sinister intuition. There was something odd about the Slater business, odd in the way that too much money seemed to be flying around, dispensed with a weird prodigality that Archie did not understand. And, at the receiving end, was the bizarre, confused figure of Kitty, about whom he found it hard to think calmly.

As Helen did up her laces he told her about Slater without mentioning names. "Apparently your Tremayne had been paying enormous premiums on a life insurance for this professor, and not satisfied with that he's even topped up the lump sum with a further fifty thousand pounds *ex gratia*."

She put the last touches to her hair before the darkened window. "Well – that's his style. Grandiose to a fault. Where's your problem?"

"I suspect . . ." Did he? Well, surely no one would throw money around like Tremayne without expecting some *quid pro quo*? "I suspect he wants the firm to run a little errand for him. I don't know what for but I reckon I'm the one who'll be doing the running."

"Where to?" muttered Helen through a mouthful of hairpins.

Until that moment Archie had not asked himself the obvious question. Now she had, he knew the answer.

"Moscow. This professor died in Moscow."

Helen tested her French pleat with the last of the pins. "How bleak for the poor old thing. What did you say his name was?"

He hadn't. When he did, instantly she was facing him, lips distorted from an intense gasping cry. "Good God Almighty!"

"You know him?"

"Slater? I should say so. Everyone knew Slater." She came over, and for a little while she was silent until he took her arm and they stood side by side looking out over the dark garden. "We all knew him. He could be quite enticing in an old-school sort of way. I did a few jobs for him in the Manuscript Division, transcripts, photographs, simple routine. Earned me a lunch now and again. Always at nice places – typically well-researched, if you know what I mean."

"Did you fancy him?"

"He could make almost any woman feel she did. It was that type of charm." She seemed regretful. "They say he went mad, you know. Couldn't get any proper backing for his work. Tremayne was the only one to remain loyal, but he's always been a law unto himself."

This was news. Archie kept silent, waiting for the offer of more. But nothing came or would come and all she revealed to him was that apprehension, detectable behind an unaverted gaze, which he had come to recognise after years of experiences of doorstep encounters as the surest sign of holding back.

Ducking away to the rucksack she began to adjust the length of the back strap. He reached over to help her with the buckles. "Let me walk you down to the tube."

"I can handle myself, sweetkin, you ought to know that by now."

He followed her into the chill hallway, helped her on with the rucksack and handed her back the door-key which she had ostentatiously tossed into the fruit bowl. "You never can tell. So what more about Slater?" He ruffled back the fringe to brush a kiss on her forehead. "Why do you want to hold out on me, Nells?"

"The man's dead, Archie. *De mortuis . . .*"

"I know. I get that from his widow."

She gave a palpable shift to the weight of the rucksack. "Good God, of course! I forgot her, the shrinking Soviet flower! Your original immaculate refugee!"

"You know her, too?"

"Well, we've never actually kissed hands or whatever people of her sort do to ingratiate themselves, but I've heard about her all right. What a scream, Archie – aren't you the perfect gent? Oh, that reminds me, darling – your wife rang while you were at work."

He groaned. "Did she leave a number?"

Helen shook her head, the smoky glass drops of her earrings dancing beneath the globed light. "I'd put a stop to all that, Archie. You're much too nice to that cow. Why don't you tell her to fuck off?"

7

A continuous frieze of blue and white swags extended below the tall first-floor windows of the terrace. By the right column of porch No. 193 was a copper bellpush, beside it a tatty piece of paper with the message: RINGTHENPUSH. Archie did both before realising that PUSH meant the door which glided inwards with a kind of pug-dog snarl before his hand had time to flatten against the brass fingerplate.

In a recess at the far end of the marble-floored vestibule a young man with a crutch was seated at a card-table. Going up to him Archie gave his name. The young man said nothing but tugged on a cord attached to his crutch and the door slammed shut with an echoing crash.

There was nowhere to sit down. Archie looked round at the huge pictures on the walls, fiddled with the brass combination lock of his brief-case and thought of Slater. They wouldn't have dared to keep a professor waiting. He would have strode into this hall as if it belonged to him, tossed his attaché-case on to the table, flicked through the mail and barked at the cripple. Quite right. An ambiance such as this would give anyone ideas. No wonder Slater had wanted to live in a castle, even if it were only a Victorian Gothic pile in Clacton-on-Sea.

From within the cubby-hole a woman's voice sounded distinctly above the buzz and click of an ancient telephone switchboard. Archie heard his name being spelt out, the young man twisted round and pointed with his crutch to a cage lift. "Press 'four' and watch the gates."

The lift was lodged discreetly in an alcove between a white stair-case and a glinting mahogany door which curved away to accommodate the sweep of the rounded yellow-marble wall trimmed top and bottom with stucco motifs picked out in greens and greys.

All the way up Archie tried to remember what he would need to say, urging himself not to make a mess of it. This grandiose mansion with its art collection and library normally granted access only to academic researchers, restorers, historians, and those whose business lay in the world of connoisseurship. The whole atmosphere made him feel awkward and uncouth.

On the fourth floor he met Sir Evelyn Tremayne's personal assistant. She walked him along an astonishingly green carpet in a stiff, scatty way which he found disconcerting. "Sir Evelyn is expecting you," she said, and then laughed. And when she laughed her thin body contorted at the waist almost bending her in two, so the laugh came out harsh, like a cough.

At the end of the corridor they halted before a cream-coloured door under a shallow skylight. The assistant rapped twice with her keys on the brass circle of the Yale lock and pushed through ahead of Archie who paused, not knowing whether or not he was intended to follow. Through the gap he heard her laugh again, and then a quick whispered exchange between her and a man. Before Archie realised that their conversation was over, she was back on the threshold. On her way out she nodded him inward with a conspiratorial smile before slipping the catch and letting the door click to behind her.

Archie found himself in a small, very modern kitchen where a tall elderly man was holding out his hand across a round white table on which stood two full bottles of Gordon's Export Gin.

"My dear boy, how clever of you to find me. I've lived here twenty years, but I still get lost on all those stairs."

"There's a lift," said Archie, stupidly.

"Quite right, very sensible." The eyes were blue, soft, winning; the silver hair, a little too long in a man of his age, framed a sepia face which wrinkled into a crackle-glaze beam of whitish lines as he withdrew his hand from Archie's grasp. "I was just about to . . . A little early for you?"

The kitchen was very warm. Archie studied the foremost bottle of gin. Beside it stood a couple of tumblers like the ones that came free with petrol. There was nothing else, not even ice.

"I don't much, Sir Evelyn. A tonic, perhaps?"

"Of course, Mr Renshawe. I realise you must observe the niceties of your profession. But you don't mind if . . . ?" He filled one of the tumblers in brief, hesitant bursts: quarter, half, then half as much again. "An attitude I admire, greatly admire. Now, let me see . . ." Leaning back he flipped open the door of a mini-fridge behind his chair. "Doesn't seem to be much in the way of a soft . . ."

The refrigerator contained an empty bottle of Kia-Ora and an artichoke.

Sir Evelyn seemed genuinely puzzled. "I really can't imagine how that's happened. Living alone, you know. Very sad. Let's adjourn."

And, ignoring his guest, he sauntered off through a flush-panelled door by the sink. Before Archie had taken more than a step after him, the silvery head re-appeared. "Always forgetting. You know how it is, my dear fellow. Come along."

The room was long and low-ceilinged. At the far end an uninterrupted stretch of window took in the spread of tree-tops fringing a little square outside. The walls were covered with more gilt-framed pictures. Archie waited to be asked to sit down, relieving his awkwardness by concentrating very hard on a browny-green landscape dotted with trees in front of which a naked man was washing his feet in a fountain.

Tremayne followed the direction of his gaze. "Know it?"

Grouped around the fountain picture were others, with here and there a broken column protruding from undergrowth.

"Athens?"

"Rome, actually. But do forgive me. I'm forgetting the real point of our meeting." Before Archie could speak, the tall man was across the room with a sudden, energetic stride, ushering him to a high-backed, brocaded sofa.

"A wretched affair, this Slater imbroglio. Very good of you to come and see me about it, at such short notice." And having seated himself as far away as possible from Archie, in this museum of a sitting-room where every tick of the squat cupid clock on the chimney-piece seemed designed to make his guest feel loud and intrusive, Sir Evelyn broached the subject of Slater's death with surprising nonchalance. "Poor fellow, dying so sordidly," he said with a kind of simper. "Quite out of character for such a balanced individual. But thank heaven I managed to trace your firm and discover what was going on before more damage was done to his posthumous reputation."

"I gather you are willing to cover the entire amount, Sir Evelyn. A most extraordinarily generous offer."

A lengthy silence ensued during which Tremayne frowned, ejected an additional spasm of gin into the tumbler between his knees, then took a long hard swallow from his glass. "Oh, the debts, Mr Renshawe? Uppermost in your mind, of course. Quite understandable in your type of work. But the least I could do, the very least. Only too glad. Sure you won't . . . ?"

Archie could have kicked himself. It obviously wasn't, then, just a question of money. Now he felt squalid. A lout. Worse, because he knew that was how he was intended to feel. Once more he refused and waited in disquiet while Tremayne squirted himself yet another four-fingers-full.

"I'd known him for years, you see. Delightful man. A most extra-ordinary memory. An adherent of the truth, wherever it carried him, a disciplinarian who showed a certain honourable flair in pushing the purely scholarly side at a time when other academics were developing political and entrepreneurial skills in order to remain in business. That was Slater – no compromise. The work always came first. But you wouldn't be overly concerned, I imagine, about that side of life?"

Archie observed his own reflection between the embossed invitation cards tucked along the two sides of an ornate mirror-frame above the chimney-piece. Surely the man couldn't think he was that much of an oaf? "I've done my homework, Sir Evelyn. One has to in my business. Evidently a highly talented man. Mrs Slater was most informative."

The mention of the widow appeared to unsettle Tremayne, who began to revolve the glass between his long palms. "I doubt that, Mr Renshawe, I really do. Slater remarried late, you know. In earlier years he would never have been – what can one say? – so *insouciant* about his affairs. Take this silly business with the cards, for instance. You say you've done your homework, Mr Renshawe? Most unlike him, surely, once upon a time, to run up such enormous bills?"

Here Archie felt on safer ground. The old man apparently had no idea about the function of credit. He didn't have to. He was too rich. So Archie explained about the theft of Slater's cards and their misuse.

As he did so Sir Evelyn was drinking again, absently sipping from his glass in neat cat-like dabs, as if Archie's tale were so engrossing that a gulp might break its spell. "So his cards were simply a ghostly trace of this man, you mean?" he said at the end. "Fraud *post-mortem*. The plastic has a life of its own – non-biodegradable, I see, I see. Quite unlike our poor Slater, then."

For some reason the old man seemed to find this idea amusing and spluttered into the remnants of his gin.

Archie began to flounder. "Yes," was all he could say immediately.

His companion's voice trembled from silent laughter. "Russia, Russia, Mr Renshawe. *Such* a long way from home."

"Quite," Archie rambled on. "I'd always thought stolen credit cards would be useless in that sort of country."

"Too sophisticated for the natives?"

"I should imagine so."

Tremayne's sky-blue eyes narrowed. "One would need to be a foreigner to make use of such things?"

"Well, yes."

This exchange appeared to raise Sir Evelyn's spirits. "Out of my province entirely," he said briskly, tossing off the last of his drink.

"With this new-found openness over there, I am sure Moscow is as well-populated with criminal foreigners as London. Now, to business, young man. Why do you think I asked you here?"

The way this elegant, elderly academic could wrongfoot him was making Archie very jumpy and he said the first thing that came to mind. "Well, Sir Evelyn, given your outstanding generosity to her, it did cross my mind that you might want to hear news of the widow. As you probably know, she shut herself up, refusing to answer letters, but I've been able to make contact, and have done what I can."

"Splendid, Mr Renshawe! When I heard you had spoken to Mrs Slater I was immensely relieved that she had at last found someone to attend to her business affairs. Strictly between ourselves, though . . ." The voice became so small that Archie had to stoop to the words. "Slater's death has wreaked havoc on her. And female neuroses can be the devil when one is sorting through the aftermath. A delightful woman but needing just that little extra finesse. You appear to have managed her admirably."

How well Tremayne knew her Archie had no way of judging but Kitty had evidently led him a dance. "After the funeral I was naturally concerned about her future plans," the old man went on. "Did she intend to return to Russia, or remain in her late husband's house? I telephoned her on several occasions: the last time she actually screamed down the line – can you imagine?"

Archie could. He would never forget Kitty's first call to Endymion Road after her telephone was reconnected. "*I am going mad. Edith says I must return to Moscow. I will go mad there also. Help me.*" Then she hung up. "I can shed some light there, Sir Evelyn. It seems that Mrs Slater never revisited her country after her marriage. Seems to have conceived a slight antipathy to the place, but now thinks she should make the journey. Professor Slater's sister explained it to me. According to her the widow is understandably very confused, feels intimidated by some of her late husband's academic colleagues, but, at the same time, wants to understand a little more about what he was doing. I've no clear idea why. And I doubt if she has."

"Wifely duty, perhaps? Women have these fancies." Tremayne seemed eager to adopt his own explanation.

"I couldn't say. All I know is that she insists I go with her."

"Mmmm," uttered the old man. He seemed about to rise, but instead remained seated, staring at a point beyond Archie's left shoulder. "She is reluctant even so?"

I will go mad there.

Archie nodded.

"Then it is our duty to persuade her, Mr Renshawe. Imagine the therapeutic effect of such a pilgrimage. I would do all in my power to smooth the way – money, letters of introduction. Were I younger I should accompany her myself, but, alas, my days of adventuring in Eastern Europe are long gone." For a moment he was silent. "Doesn't this whole business excite you, dear boy? Would you refuse the chance to do someone a good turn, visit an exotic foreign country, perhaps even turn up new information about poor Slater's tragic accident?" Tremayne leaned forward, his lips pleating in a confidential grin. "You'll find this hard to believe, but as far back as I can remember I've always wanted to be a detective. It's a hard world that parts us from our dreams. But you are young. Now, what do you think?"

"I can't say. I've never really wanted to be a detective."

Slightly flushed, Tremayne shook his head. "No, no, of course not, not a detective – I should be very surprised if even a Russian detective could succeed in the matter I have in mind – but an aide to the unfortunate lady, an intermediary between her and her gruesome Russians . . ."

"But I can't even speak their language."

"Exactly. You have nothing to fear from her compatriots, so you can frame the questions. You ask, *she* will interpret. Think of it as a sort of memorial, a dossier of Slater's last acts." He scrutinised the rim of his empty tumbler, appeared dissatisfied, gave a loud "Hah!" as if the fault had suddenly revealed itself and strode off to the kitchen. From the sink his voice carried clear over the swirl of tap-water. "We can all benefit from others setting down their recollections of us. *Non omnes moriar.* Horace, you know."

Archie did. It had been his school motto and he didn't believe it now any more than he had then. "I need to know a little more. About Professor Slater. For example – when did he start to visit the USSR?"

Tremayne returned with the still-dripping glass and a fresh bottle of gin. "British Academy, sixties fellowship. A matter of public record. I suggest you look it up."

Testy. Archie was too old a hand not to seize the initiative offered by a client's reproof. "I have, Sir Evelyn. Rather frequent his visits, though, weren't they? I mean, for a philosopher – he was a philosopher, wasn't he?"

Tremayne seemed to wince at the continual mention of his title and batted the air with his left hand as if driving away a troublesome insect. "You may think so, young man, but to those who know about such things, he was more correctly spoken of as an historian of ideas."

"Ah, ideas, yes, of course. And, in your judgement, Sir Evelyn, would there be a lot of scope for the investigation of ideas in that sort of country? I've always been led to believe that they make do with one out there – a big one, but just one all the same."

In the kitchen someone opened and shut the refrigerator door. A frown collected above Tremayne's uncandid blue eyes. "You will forgive me when I say that the texture of intellectual discourse is made up of many threads, not all of which are palpable to the uninstructed touch."

An exasperated snort came from the kitchen followed by a clatter of plates.

"Besides, you never met him, young man. Slater felt as I did. We both delighted in the country, the literature, the history, all the broad richness. A love-affair, a love-affair. And then he was a gregarious man – friends of all types. A second home, you understand, a recourse for the spirit."

"Spoke the language, too?"

"Tolerably, I believe."

"Enough to court a Russian girl?"

Tremayne raised an eyebrow. "There was always that side to him. Quite capable of going native."

"Rather a catch, wouldn't you say, for the girl?"

The sound of humming floated through the half-open door. Archie twisted round. Standing in the doorway was a stout middle-aged woman in a navy lurex blouse.

"Dear me." Tremayne rose to his feet. "I quite forgot. Mrs Kavanagh. Mr Renshawe, this is Mrs Kavanagh. Today is one of her days."

"You'd think he was hard-up," said Mrs Kavanagh to Archie, flicking her duster at the door furniture. "Have you seen the state of his fridge?" She spoke like a mistress, totally without regard for time or place.

Although it was quite chill in the drawing-room, her blouse was sleeveless and dark at the armpits from sweat. Archie looked away to Tremayne who had stooped over the woman and was clasping and unclasping his hand on a level with her forehead.

"I left a glass for you on the draining-board, Mrs Kavanagh. Do make yourself at home out there, once the shopping's put away."

When Archie stood up Mrs Kavanagh glared at him as if he had committed an unpardonable solecism. "You just stay where you are, young man." And she bent down with difficulty to pick up a brightly lacquered wastepaper-bin by Tremayne's feet. "It's no good for either of us, you know." Her wheeze broke out into a *sforzando* hack as she straightened up. "All this ... this ... out-of-hours indulging. He'd starve if it wasn't for me."

Tremayne gave a subdued, acquiescent groan and felt for the inside pocket of his pin-striped jacket, enfolded the woman's shoulders with one arm and with the other was pressing a twenty-pound note into her duster hand.

"That's all very well, but you're not yourself today, I can tell. It's a shock to the system abusing your body at all hours. And as for you," shouted Mrs Kavanagh as Archie was about to resume his seat. "Mind your manners and don't go fingering the objects. I won't have you taking advantage just because he has a child's face on him."

Although his encounter with Mrs Kavanagh did not seem to have caused Tremayne the least embarrassment, the atmosphere had freshened, and beneath the languid mannerisms of his speech Archie began to discern a hard, unconvivial self-control.

"Come along, Renshawe, don't prevaricate, there's a good chap. Either you agree to accept my commission to act on behalf of the Slater family or I shall find someone else who will."

Kitty Slater had put the same point to Archie only two days earlier without receiving a satisfactory reply. Secretly Archie found the prospect of jaunting off with the widow immensely attractive, but he jibbed at coming clean with Tremayne.

"I'm not a free agent, Sir Evelyn."

Mrs Kavanagh chose this moment to burst into song.

Tremayne's smile was another grin. "For a fee your employer has agreed to dispense with your services for a short period. One week. And I shall pay *you* – and any assistant you might wish to accompany you – two thousand five hundred pounds."

"Each?"

"Each."

Two thousand five hundred. After stoppages, the best part of three months' salary. That did it. "I can't promise results, Sir Evelyn. This kind of job is rather outside my experience."

The old man shook him warmly by the hand. "Nothing to it, my dear chap. Just a few questions round and about the place. Begin with Madame Slutskaya, a friend of friends. Knows everyone there is to know in Moscow. Mrs Slater will supply her address. That should get you started. Then you might try the Soviet police. Papers, you see – Slater was robbed of his brief-case as well as his cards – something in this line could have turned up since his death."

The contralto rasp of "I'll Take You Home Again, Kathleen" passed through the door panelling as readily as a stream of neutrons.

For two thousand five hundred Archie was on, police or no police. One last hurdle – the conflict of interest. "I'd better be straight with you, Sir Evelyn. I was on the point of finalising a separate contract with Mrs Slater. Do I still go ahead and sign her up, too?"

Tremayne made light of the scruple. "Why not, Mr Renshawe? We all have a living to make. Besides, the position is clear. The welfare of Mrs Slater and my concerns for her late husband's work are one. One and the same." He paused as if giving Archie time to grasp the concept.

"There's nothing – sensitive – about his work, is there? I shouldn't want . . ."

Tremayne gazed at him almost fondly. "Not the merest whiff, young man. Slater's was one of the most remarkable talents in this country. But, well . . ." Here the voice declined to a whisper. "At the end of his life, something of a broken man. He came to see me last year in desperate straits, unable to obtain the necessary funding. He applied to me. What could I do?" He sighed and spread out his hands. "I felt it my duty to help him."

And now his widow. Was that duty also? Archie didn't ask Tremayne. He asked himself. Was generosity on that scale believable? The man must either be mad or a saint.

The sound of heavy objects colliding with a hard surface came through the wall. Tremayne suddenly leapt to his feet with such force that Archie started back as the old man's six-foot-six angled through the gap of the partly closed door. On the kitchen side a conversation ensued in which only Mrs K's contribution was audible. Archie seized the opportunity to assess his position.

He had never met Professor Slater. He knew nothing about the stress of an academic career (except that judging by Tremayne's intake of gin it could be acute), so he was prepared to believe that Kitty's man had gone off his head in Moscow just as Helen had said he had in London. And that Tremayne, not altogether happy about this, needed reassurance that his protégé had done nothing disgraceful after he flipped.

Very well. What could be odd about Tremayne? He was a distinguished man, slightly eccentric but clearly beyond reproach. Only the day before Archie had checked his credentials in the local library.

"That's totally unacceptable! I'm already out of pocket from the last time." The voice was Mrs Kavanagh's, vicious, slanging. "No cheques. And that reminds me, Evie . . ."

Evie? Evelyn. Evie.

"Evie. There's a crate to bring up, that's man's work . . ."

Eccentric, yes, absent-minded, bullied by his daily. Unorthodox, unconventional – wasn't that it? The kind of insider/outsider with a leaning for the tackier side of life?

His comments about the widow, though, had been disturbing. Had Archie been all along looking in the wrong direction by suspecting that Kitty was the injured party in her marriage? Overhearing the one-sided row between employer and employee now taking place in the kitchen, Archie suddenly grasped the nature of Kitty's relationship with Slater, the dry-sherry man, the aloof, apparently dominant partner. It must have worked because she instinctively played up to what he expected of her: tears, rages, prostration – the full-blown, glass-smashing sensibility that the literature had led him to expect of true-born Russian blood. Mrs Kavanagh likewise had her role off to a T: the washerwoman biddy, as Irish as stage-green whiskers. To Tremayne she was evidently straight off the boards, a stunning queer fish, just as Kitty must have been with her Slater. And Kitty, like Mrs Kavanagh, had fully intended to keep it that way. How else to explain three years holed up in Clacton with a man who, she claimed, wouldn't even teach her his own language?

Tremayne slid back through the doorway, fingering the disarray of his sideburns. "Now, where were we?" He moved away from Archie to an upright chair with a striped satin seat.

"The Slater case," said Archie. "I accept."

Tipping back his chair the old man explored his empty tumbler as Mrs Kavanagh swept in with a plate of sandwiches rolled up in a savagely ironed table napkin. Tremayne unfastened his lunch as if it might disintegrate at his touch. On top lay a long envelope, the same shade of blue as those Nazir had opened that night in Slater's Clacton house.

"What's this?"

"Your *billet doux*, Mr Renshawe." Balancing his sandwich plate across his knee, Tremayne seemed more relaxed. "An agreement which empowers you to act for me with a minimum of fuss, and send out any of Slater's work through official channels. Instructions enclosed, plus a letter to the Cultural Section. And, of course, your cheque."

Slightly dazed at the speed of this transaction, and the realisation that the agreement must have been drawn up even before his arrival, Archie accepted the envelope from Mrs Kavanagh's hands which were warm and red from washing-up water. Tremayne was still talking money as he nibbled his Italian ham with an air of distaste. "A small contingency fund. If there is anything you need please don't hesitate. And should this venture succeed I may wish to retain you on a consultancy basis. Privately, of course. No word to your employer."

At last Archie was being offered job security.

A probationary acolyte.

Outside the sun had gone, and a fug from the early-afternoon traffic along Gower Street was starting to undercut the keen midwinter scent of the little square. Archie had not felt such triumphant justification since he passed his driving test. But this was better, this was best: he had stuck by the girl and now he was vindicated. The song was a portent. "Kathleen, Katherine, Kitty come home again."

Twice he made the circuit of the square, head up, hands deep in his trouser pockets, cocky as a street kid who'd turned up a tenner in the gutter-trash, relishing the prospect of the here and now: from the seal-back grey of the naked trees against the pasty afternoon sky to the liveried awnings of the smart shops, the stiff porticoes, the numbered parking bays reserved for the highly distinguished, set about him now in unforbidding glamour. After all those years of side-lining he had come central, a fixer, an object of discernment. A consultant. By appointment. It was as if all his life he had been his own picture on someone else's wall waiting for the light of recognition to dawn in the eye of an equal. And that could have been for ever if dotty old Slater hadn't taken a queer turn at the end of his life and delivered himself into the arms of the unpredictable Kitty.

It was miraculous how well things had fallen out for him. But at times like these, Lambert always maintained, when you're stilt-high to the world, thinking nothing can trip you, that's when you've got to hang on to your brains.

God, how I hate him, his slop-shop office, his assignments to hustle single mums who've got behind with the tally. But I'm climbing out of it now, Lambert. *Adios.*

III

SEVEN MOSCOW NIGHTS

Moscow, March

8

After having booked Mrs Slater, Nazir and himself on to the only package-tour which could find room for them so late in the season, Archie spent the next fortnight accommodating his new client's fears: should she really go back to Moscow? Would she be allowed in? If she were, did he think the English would permit her return?

He was able to reassure her on all these points but she soon disclosed fresh anxieties: was she stable enough to deal with the trauma of return? How would she feel, confronted with her dead husband's friends? Would he keep with her every step of the way?

Why he was never rude to her Archie did not know, except that she was so disconcertingly exotic normal rules did not seem to apply. It was strictly none of his business yet her physical condition, for example, touched him. She looked undernourished. Too professional to cloud the issue by suggesting she ate more, he found himself dwelling on her skinny girlish figure and the faintly bluish pallor of her lips. If, like him, she converted to wholemeal and vegetables, would this look survive?

Then there was the atrocious Mrs Sedgewick who had evidently patched up the quarrel with her protégé because, on one of his visits to Clacton, Archie came on them, cheek to cheek over a Dulux paint catalogue, planning a new colour scheme for Slater's Gothic kitchen. Kitty's diet? Her pasty complexion? Lyudy had the answers. Marriage to Slater had been one long dormitory binge: *chorizos*, hamburgers, ice-cream, *babas au rhum*, blended whisky, *blanquettes de veau* and Mars Bars. It was simple reaction. At home in her village they ate nothing but fruit and freshwater fish.

But why did she smoke so much?

"If you had seen one part of what she has seen, young man, you would be smoking worse than Sherlock Holmes."

Kitty Slater, Archie had concluded, was hardly his type of woman but they might have jogged along quite comfortably if she had not invited Mrs Sedgewick to come with them to Moscow. That, and her subsequent behaviour, was downright unethical.

* * *

To make sure they arrived at the airport on time he had arranged to drive down to Clacton to collect her, but the night before she cancelled, instructing him to wait for her at Gatwick. When they finally met outside passport control the flight was being called for the third time. Even then she had vacillated and he guessed from the shadows under her eyes that she had probably spent a sleepless night.

They touched down just after six. Beneath the livid snow-cloud rolling over the tarmac Nazir's complexion looked olive green. He grumbled all the way to the Customs Hall. "Mrs Sedgewick hardly let me get a word in for the whole three hours, and now the widow goes emotional the moment she catches her first glimpse of the old homestead. I'm shattered."

While they filled in declaration forms Archie tried not to notice Kitty who was slumped in a corner, glaring from him, the furniture, the omnipresent figures in shabby uniforms loafing at exits and entrances, to the huge spread of the runway where the familiar aeroplane stood alone, suddenly inaccessible.

He took his turn in front of the glass box through which a spotty youngster in an open-necked khaki shirt scrutinised him with blank concentration after glancing down at the passport photograph. On the verge of incontrollable giggles Archie was about to turn his head away when, with calculated tetchiness, the boy soldier rapped sharply on his desk and Archie snapped to attention, continuing the mute, inimical stand-off until his rebellious English hatred of authority welled up, freckling his throat and cheeks with salmon-pink hot spots. He had lost. He felt the blush like a nerve-tingle and saw its effect in the slight pucker of amusement on the lips of the lad as he handed back the visa, and operated the foot-pedal which slid back the gate, enabling Archie to escape into the vast chairless Arrivals Hall.

Kitty came through with the face of a sleepwalker. That earned her a smile to which she made absolutely no response but they didn't even open her hold-all.

"Well?" she said afterwards, handing over her bag for Nazir to carry. "This is beginning. You like it so far?"

Archie smiled. "Not much of a welcome they give you, is it?"

"Welcome? You wait seven days and see what their goodbyes will be like."

The pavement seemed wider, the traffic sparser. The only scale memory had kept intact was the spread of the night above her, huge and engulfing. Across the street a neon sign ticker-taped along the top storey of the opposite block: DO NOT CROSS UNTIL THE LIGHT IS GREEN.

Kitty wept. It was like being in a foreign country.

"For pity's sake, darling, do stop." Mrs Sedgewick bustled past into the spacious vestibule of the hotel. "Just thank your lucky stars you don't have to call it *home* any longer." She was unimpressed. "So repulsively bourgeois, these international places, I always think, but my relatives simply adore them." The next day her sister would be flying from Siberia with her children, her in-laws and their children, each loaded down with ethnic items from the steppes. "All for Frinton, of course, expressly selected. That's the joy of family – so reliable! Come to Vnukovo with me tomorrow, darling. We could always do with an extra pair of hands. I'll be off out of this place just as soon as the family's had a quick tour of the amenities."

Kitty wondered if she would ever be able to set foot outside her room, let alone on the public street. In Clacton it was bad enough. Here, the sense of space crippled her.

"It's only the first step that hurts," exclaimed Lyudy, checking the contents of her duty-free carrier. "So you'd better make it soon before emotion lays you out completely. Look at me – who'd have thought I was once in love too, buried alive in Frinton with a rotter?"

Had the worst moment been when Dymka was not at the airport, and Kitty realised that he had never really intended to meet her, or when Lyudy, who had only heard about him from Kitty, was so certain that he would turn up?'

"So what's new about men, sweetie? Forget him. This is a holiday. Let's freshen ourselves up and see some life."

The first whisky in the all-night bar made Kitty feel better. She decided to get very drunk. After her third Archie found their table. He was unusually elated. "It's really only ten past nine," he said, raising his glass of *citron pressé* to the sunflower dial of the clock above the bar. "Nazir's gone to bed but I'm as perky as an owl. It's thawing outside. Anyone fancy a stroll before turning in?"

Kitty visibly trembled. "I am not here," she murmured in Russian. "I cannot believe I am here."

Lyudy interpreted. "She is let down. Her boyfriend. He does not come to the airport."

"It is finished," moaned Kitty in English. "I do not care."

Over her glass of *crème de cacao* Mrs Sedgewick squinted round the bar. "Things go to the dogs wherever you look."

Archie felt for Kitty's fingertips. "How about a breath of air?"

* * *

In the street Kitty said, "Take my arm – please."

They walked along a subway flanked on one side by little kiosks shuttered for the night. Although it was late, the subway was quite crowded and Archie took the right lane presuming that the flow of people, like the road traffic, kept to the continental side, but after several side steps to avoid oncomers, he did not resist when Kitty steered him gently to the left. Once above ground again, it took him some time to re-adjust, and crossing the road he looked in the wrong direction.

When he apologised Kitty only said, "I, too, forget."

They sat on a snow-covered bench in the gardens below the Kremlin wall watching the trolley buses.

"*Shto dyelat* – what can I do? I want to see him. Also I do not want to see him. He was not there."

"Him?"

"Florinskii. Dymka, of course."

Oh, that him, of course.

"If I were you I'd get him right out of your mind." Archie was sick of the men in her life. Faced with her now, wittering anxiety to the skies, he could see how dispensable any man might find her.

"He lies," she muttered. "It is his business."

The wind was blustering sleet in their faces. In this mood she might fancy sitting out the whole night but the cold raked Archie to the backbone. He suggested a move. They left the snow garden and trudged up against the river breeze into the unsquare Square. In the starlight the fairy-tale walls looked flimsy, the outworks of a child's toy fort. Here and there flashbulbs popped among the knots of late-nighters sauntering under the lee of the battlements.

"I hate him," said Kitty loudly in front of the Tomb. The air had stung violet prickles on to her cheeks.

"Steady on," said Archie, turning her away from the guard of honour.

"Not him, *him*."

Ah, of course, still that him. Her him. Dymka-him. Sooner or later he was going to have to ask what edge Dymka had over all men, living or dead. But for the moment Archie wanted home. "We don't want you getting into a state, Mrs Slater, and if I may say so, you're looking rather windswept. Shall we make our way back?"

She pinched him hard underneath the elbow and set her mouth defiantly. "The river. We go by the river."

There is was colder, raw as fish. A litter of ice-floes clogged the free water. Archie shivered. He thought of Captain Scott adrift on the polar sea. It was dismal.

"Watch," said Kitty. There was nothing to see except the jiggle of slab against slab between the warm smudge of the embankment lights.

"You must really feel at home here," he said.

"I have no home. I do not belong."

He saw her point. This broad, flat city was soundless, choked dumb like the river beneath its covering of snow. Since their arrival Kitty herself had grown icier, less humane.

"I am thrown in the gutter," she murmured. "I am dead, killed by that man."

It was too cold for melodrama. Archie shrank into his coat and grimaced against the bitter air. "Do you always have to bloody exaggerate?"

She whirled at him, open-mouthed, her chin thrust out beyond the red-fox edgings of her hood. "What do you mean, swearing at me, Mr Detective? Don't say anything you will regret, this is not play, this talking. In England you say, 'Tell me everything so I can understand.'"

In the wind strands of her hair strayed across her face. Catlicking them away from her lips she continued to scrutinise him through the murk. Had she made a mistake? Was he reliable? Would he help?

"I'm sorry," he said, "but I don't quite know what you want me to do about *him*." How was he to know that some man who'd allegedly done some terrible thing to her in the past was supposed to be welcoming her at the airport yesterday? "You never mentioned him before tonight. Why so secretive?"

She caught at his sleeve. "I am guilty, forgive me, I am silly. This man was my fiancé. We do not marry. Instead I marry Slater and Dmitry, Dymka, he is very . . . insulted because . . ."

". . . Because he is your fiancé and you do not marry, instead you marry Slater. You throw him in the gutter. Right? So he doesn't come to the airport with flowers. So that makes him – what – a man with a price on his head?"

He had to explain what the expression meant.

"Archie." She rarely called him that. Now his name tipped from her mouth like a pearl into the black river-night. One day he would tell her exactly that. "I am not his, Archie, but he does not accept my intentions. I think he searches for my love."

To Archie this didn't seem so much of a problem, let alone a crime, but she was obviously enjoying her fairy-tale situation, letting down her hair for Dymka but, unlike Repunzel, complaining when he began to climb. Hide-and-seek, Catch-me-if-you-can. She loved it, that side of love, the precipitous aspect. "I am bad, always bad for him. A bad girl."

And if I lay down in the snow and begged, Mrs Slater, would you be bad, be bad for me?

When they arrived back the hotel foyer was deserted except for a man in a parka reading the *Kabul Times*. "Hey," he called out as they made for the elevator. "Somone's been enquiring after you."

Archie recognised him from the plane. English. One of the tour group. He'd tried to chat Kitty up on the journey.

"Oh God," she whimpered. "Not this Gavin. I think he is mad."

Gavin loafed across to them. "Slater. A message for Slater. That's you, isn't it?" He smiled at Kitty.

She flicked back her hood and looked away. "What message?"

"I'm not sure what message. Just who to. Some foreign bloke. Rang reception, and then the bar, then me, too, in my room. Been ringing all evening for Katerina. *Blaya, blaya, Katerina, oy oy oy.* I had to ask him to slow down and speak English. Even then I only got one word in two."

Kitty went white. "Sweet man, my dear, I beg you, my message."

Visibly startled Gavin made a powerful effort to recollect. "I wouldn't hang for it, Miss, but I think this was the gist . . ." He took a deep breath.

"*Radi Bogu . . .*" whimpered Kitty.

"Florence says she's sorry she didn't meet the plane yesterday but tomorrow she'll take you to the circus."

There was a brief silence. Archie tried not to look at Kitty's face. "Did he leave a number?"

"Who?"

"Florence. She's a man."

"My God," said Gavin. "You can't rely on anyone these days."

9

Next day lunch was served at eleven thirty a.m. Archie showed up late and very tired. The dining-room was empty except for Kitty and Nazir. There was no sign of Lyudy Sedgewick, Gavin or even the tour guide, Maroussia.

Over *kotlety* and rice he began to explain their programme for the week. Back in Clacton he had realised from conversations with Kitty and Lyudy that it might be unwise to attempt to clear Soviet customs with a notebook filled with names, telephone numbers and appointments. Consequently he had been unable to draw up a proper schedule.

"Kitty can supply all that," said Nazir. "She's going to do a list of addresses for you to show the taxi-drivers."

The girl looked from one to the other. "Today, please, Archie, you visit Mrs Slutskaya, Verochka, and I take Nazir to the circus."

Archie nodded irritably. At the moment it looked as if Nazir had taken charge of the arrangements. Kitty was going to look up her old circus contacts, many of whom had met Slater during his final stay. He watched her take several sheets of thick paper out of her bag, clear a space amidst the half-eaten salads, and begin to write, occasionally asking a question, but soon lapsing into a withdrawn silence.

On second thoughts, perhaps she had made the right choice. Nazir could be crass. It might be risky delegating the Verochka visit to him, and Archie himself could easily snarl up the circus business if, as he now suspected, the aberrant Florinskii, her Dymka, were to turn up there too. Quite possibly Kitty was now regretting last night's river-side *tête-à-tête*.

She sat apart, as intent as a child on her imposition, pausing to sweep back her hair and look beyond her companions to the long veiled windows where the waiters stood in a group to one side, watching the street wind dither snowflakes above the massed passers-by.

"Try not to let her out of your sight this evening, there's a good chap," said Archie quietly.

79

Nazir smirked. "Keep your hair on. I won't let her vanish into thin air. Which reminds me – what's happened to Prof. S's writer chum? Kitty tried phoning this morning, but there was no reply."

Archie glanced at Kitty's scribbled list. "Dr Yakovlyeva you mean? Maybe she'll turn up at the circus, too. Anyway, make sure you keep an eye out. Observation's never been your strong point."

"The big top!" exclaimed Nazir to the girl. "Fire-eaters, the Indian rope trick. It'll be like being a kid again. I'm going to enjoy myself."

Kitty came out of her dream. "Not that circus. My circus. My circus is different. All women. Young."

Nazir rubbed his hands. "Better and better. All right, Archie? We can leave the old ladies to you."

For Kitty the mere fact of compiling a list stirred up unwelcome memories.

That last time Slater was away in Moscow she would wake before dawn, switch on the flasher of the digital clock and watch the seconds mount into minutes, the minutes into hours while she lay rigid with jealousy of the people he might be with at each successive interval. Three hours ahead, 08.30: a stand-up breakfast, perhaps with Ben Karpinskii, in the long bar on the ground floor where the queue never seemed to shorten and people had helped themselves and finished eating long before they reached the cash-desk. He liked all that, the hustle, eating on foot, on the way somewhere, already hatted and gloved for the first snow which crackled underfoot with the noise of ground glass. Today, after his spell among the boxes and folders of his obscure little archive tucked between a cobbler's and the Institute of Military Science, he might go skating, and shop on the way, joining the crush at the bakery for those white sweet buns which, at six, came out warm to the touch in their tray.

Morning after morning she had perpetuated this vigil. Cloaked against the deepening light by those horrible red curtains he liked so much, now grown purplish in the sea-blown air of this strange country, Kitty had tried to stare down the recurrence of such images against the tireless jitter of the clock. Sometimes, later, when the dark was not dark enough for the red whirr of the clock to mask the white walls, she would get out of bed and open the doors of the huge press in which his clothes were kept, and hold them to her face along the stitching of the folds where the smell of him lay deep and full.

In Russia, he never grew tired of people. In England, they scarcely had a visitor. Just before he left he had said, "Edith, there's always Edith. Edith won't mind."

Setting out the addresses crosswise on the broad areas of writing paper, Kitty could not prevent her hands from shaking, so that the letters began to reformulate themselves into others, like the figures on her clock.

Edith, Slater's sister, older by ten years, perhaps more. Quite an old lady. Or woman – that was how he always spoke of her: a good woman, a good face, a pink, soft, good face. Archie Renshawe's face was somewhere behind it. Very English, but old, very old.

Edith used to tremble, quite without reason. A nervous complaint, her brother said: inherited. Kitty wished that Edith were here. The thought of Edith's secret, incorrigible taint made her feel unblemished and, while she remembered it, calm and purposeful.

He didn't have a lot of friends, my poor Slater, she told herself, not nearly enough for such a vulnerable man. But the people he *knew*: important people, people with influence who respected him, and stood up when he came into a room. The little people too: Slater's protégé, the brilliant young Karpinskii, retired Academician Savlyevich; the Borisovs; Dr Yakovlyeva, the children's writer. Everyone.

Having managed to overcome the tremor in her writing hand, Kitty set out the names and addresses on separate sheets, first in Cyrillic, then in Roman. Afterwards, she numbered each one.

"Take taxi tonight," she said to Archie.

For a moment he was slightly taken aback at the length of Verochka's address. "He'll know?"

"He will know," she said.

"Fine." Archie folded the paper into four and tucked it behind the handkerchief in his breast pocket. Perhaps miracles happened here. In London he'd never known a cabbie to take him from Liverpool Street to St John's Wood without asking directions. "How do I get back?"

"Verochka will telephone taxis. Don't worry this much." And, for the first time that day, she smiled at him, relieved that the funereal list was completed, but glad that he had at last started the investigation.

"All done," she said, capping the nib of Slater's expensive fountain pen. "Except my man's friend, Academician Savlyevich. His letter came back: NOT KNOWN. Perhaps Klavdia tells me at our circus. Maybe. She knows everything."

"OK," said Archie. "But one thing at a time, eh? This Verochka – she's expecting me?"

"I telephoned and she awaits you at six o'clock."

"Friendly?"

"Yes, yes, yes," she exclaimed. "Believe me. It was very bad line."

Archie pondered this ambivalence before turning to Nazir. "That's settled, then. Tonight I trust myself to Moscow Red Cabs and you accompany Mrs Slater to her circus."

She wondered why sometimes he called her Kitty, and sometimes Mrs Slater, as though he had suddenly remembered who she was and recognised a need for restraint. Her own sense of herself seemed to shift according to context. A moment ago an employer; before that, making her list, a widow. Now, dwelling excitedly on the prospect of seeing Klavdia and the girls once again, who was she? The old Kitty, the Kitty from before? That Kitty had a home, her home had been here. Could she come back? Yekaterina Slater, a Mrs Russian-English relict of the late Slater man: *Kate, Katya, Katkin, you've got to think of something, Katyushka, you've got to make a plan.*

Before Archie came Nazir had made her laugh with his list of English words he said she ought to practise: spoony, slithering, smarmy. Dymka might come to the circus to meet her. Yesterday her tears were for him, but Kitty had always known that if she once showed her real feelings he would go away for ever.

Never weep on the street, Mrs Slater. Only with this Englishman, Archie, who shyly does your bidding, you might, in private, you might. Because although he is almost as timorous as you, he is more afraid for other people than he is for himself.

Unlike Dymka. Spoony, smarmy. Dymka, the slithery man.

After a nap, shower and shave, Archie felt human enough again by late afternoon to be in a state of pleasant anticipation. Kitty had occupied her time on the telephone, arranging appointments with various of Slater's acquaintances whom Archie and Nazir were to interview.

"What's this – a census?" Nazir had expostulated after a dozen or so calls. "We've only got six days left. Where's my snooze-time going to be fitted in?"

"You stick to that girl. I'm worried about her."

And myself, thought Archie after an hour or more's tossing about naked in the stoker-hold heat of his room. But under the shower, he could relax at the thought of picturing the evening ahead as a cool interlude amid the frenetic comings and goings which had so far marked his experience of hotel life: a colloquy with a quiet elderly soul: Verochka, the gracefully-aging academic who had been Slater's dear friend for over twenty years. Even Tremayne had vouched for her charming hospitality and the excellence of her English. Kitty, it seemed, had never actually met her.

Verochka sounded too good to be true.

Once in the forecourt he breathed in so deeply that his eyes watered. After the clogged, re-circulated air inside, the atmosphere was intoxicatingly keen, cold enough to make him cough. A blue-cheeked lad in commissionaire's rig had followed him out.

"*Taksi?*"

"*Takskii*, yes," said Archie, looking down at the row of chequer-doored cabs on the cambered ramp of the hotel entrance.

The boy squinted briefly at the paper which Archie passed over and handed it to the first driver in line. Glaring at Archie, the man muttered something, spat and wound up his window.

"Village," said the commissionaire in barely recognisable English. "Too far. Not allowed."

Archie's white breath snaggled upwards into the green neon fuzz of the hotel logo.

"Nobody go there," said the boy.

"I go there," said Archie. "Me. I go."

The commissionaire grinned and thumped on the nearside door of the next taxi. The woman driver released the catch on her quarter light. "*Dollary?*" she said through the gap.

Archie caught on quickly. "*Dollary*," he repeated.

Before getting in he showed her a twenty-dollar bill, just to make sure, and then gave the commissionaire two one-rouble pieces which he had intended to take home as souvenirs.

"OK. *Gut*," said the woman, shifting the gear. "*Sprechen Sie Deutsch oder Französisch?*"

"*Englisch*," said Archie.

But for the whole of the journey the woman addressed him in German, asking no questions but apparently content to shout out the name of every public building which they passed in the course of their drive from one end of Moscow to the other.

10

The road had dwindled to a track between snow-furred pines.
"*Scheisse!*" said the woman, braking.

There was no street, nothing except forest above and around. She put the taxi into reverse, then swung hard on the wheel, spinning the tyre-walls against the rutted snow. "*Hier!*"

Archie wound down his window. The only sound was the twig-crack of frost among overladen boughs.

"*Nicht hier*," he said.

"*Doch, hier. Das Dorf liegt geradeaus.*" The meter blipped white in the darkness. "*Fünfundzwanzig.*"

Archie paid her off in one-dollar bills.

No sooner had the cab pulled away than the moon disappeared behind a tatter of cloud wrack. He stumbled a few yards before reaching for his pen torch and Kitty's sketch map. The path should end in a rise which gave a view of the river. In the glow of the returning moon he traversed the incline. At the top he was again plunged into darkness, but from here he could see light. A glimmer from a faulty street lamp which turned off and on every few seconds, giving him just enough time to pinpoint the features outlined by the girl: a fat curl of river, waxy under the moon, catwalk jetty poking into the ice, the jib of a crane pointing skywards.

A ninety-degree turn, then straight on to intersect the main street almost under the lamp.

From way off he recognised Verochka's house from Kitty's three-dimensional picture. Two-storeyed, beset by a ramble of sheds, one big window near to the ground. By the time he came up the window was a rich beetroot-red from the blind within and the light behind. He thought of scalding hot tea with honey, and the presence of women. Uncleared snow lay fresh on the steps of a little porch alongside the window. There was no knocker.

He thumped on the unpainted door with his forearm. Would that have been what Slater used to do? Nobody came. It was very cold. Archie hammered. Still no one. So he did what he would have done at home, and found his way by torchlight round to the back, through a sagging gate into a covered alley-way stacked on one side with empty cardboard boxes stencilled in English "Toshiba, Hitachi, Handle with Care". Here the door was makeshift, simply wooden slats shuttered across a frame. Before he had time to knock there was a henhouse scuffle inside, followed by the slip of bolts above and below, and his eyes flooded from light round the shadow in the doorway.

A blodge of a woman against the flare of the kerosene lamp. Wide, droopy. Hair in a longish bob swept back from one temple by a white butterfly slide.

Archie enunciated very precisely. "My name is Renshawe. I am calling on behalf of Yekaterina Aleksandrovna Slater. I believe she made an appointment . . ." Shifting from foot to foot on the ice-scraped earth he had time to listen to himself trotting out his door-step formulae rehearsed in the taxi. "Her husband, Professor Oliver Slater, was one of your . . ."

Flat to the light the woman was all the while rocking between the door-posts like a flabby black kite. "No more appointments," she said. "Slater is dead." The English was faultless.

"I do beg your pardon, the *late* professor, of course . . ."

"Of course." Within the voice was a simper of malice. "Consequently, *molodoy chelovek*, I am no longer at home to persons of your sex." In her mouth the English sounded older than the Russian: stilted, regal, pre-war.

Groggy from cold, lack of sleep, and the increasingly creepy sensation of having strayed into a replay of his old life on the doorsteps of Seven Sisters Road, Archie mentally fumbled with his tally book and pencil, playing for time. "An appointment, you see. An appointment was arranged this afternoon. You are Mrs Slutskaya? Verochka?"

"Don't you understand your own language? She is not at home! Be off with you before I call the militia!" A younger voice, strident, tart.

The old woman began to shuffle backwards, receding into the passage, the end of which Archie could not now see because a smaller figure had darted in front blazing the storm-lantern up to his face. "Be off with you," she repeated against the hiss of the gas. "Have you no shame?" Black-butter eyes kindled in the shining; the hair darker, glossy from warmth.

"Bugger *orf*!" shrieked the old woman, one arm tight to the breast of her quilted wraparound, the other clawing the wall. "Push *orf* out of it, you bloody little snooper, go to hell, to hell, to hell!"

Down the passage a door crashed shut and Archie suddenly felt the heat of the lamp at his chin as the brunette raised it high to inspect him. Her fingernails were false, sea-green, as long as mussel-backs. Kitty was a witch. She'd sent him to the witches to be blinded alive. Witches in a burrow, all going mad.

"Forgive me," he murmured. "I must have taken a wrong turning. Could you direct me to the high road?"

Aaaaah! The answer was a sound of pain threading into the desolation of ramshackle barns and sheds which Archie sensed at his back like some vast agronomic sore running from here to the forests of Poland. "I've rather lost my bearings, you see. Do you think I could possibly telephone for a taxi?"

The brunette stared into his eyes, lost in an unquellable dream.

No proper map, torch or boots. Panic rising within him, Archie dared to turn his face to the night. It wasn't a village, it wasn't even a street, it was a thing that had petered out over aeons into a job lot of ruins.

"The last man," began the dark woman in her stiff, foreign English, "the last man who took a taxi into that, he never came back. Tonight I thought he was you. But you are not, you are his friend." She doused the light. "So God forgive me, I shall do to you what I would do to him."

They were late for the circus because Kitty had insisted on stopping at a hard-currency shop to buy presents. She took a long time. "I'm only tired," she told Nazir. "You think I look sad? So maybe I am happy when I look sad."

They took the shortest route from Prospekt Marksa, changing to the Circle Line at Byelorusskaya. Slater never went anywhere by Metro. He said it was riding on convict-bones. Beneath the platform Kitty imagined an array of rib-cages twisting away from the stab of her heels.

When they arrived the performance was more than half-over.

Nazir followed her backstage where they waited among buckets of whitewash scattered with sequins, and he watched the trapeze girls massaging their thighs while Kitty smoked her long, half-hollow cigarettes.

At the close Klavdia came in, sweat pearling between her breasts. She threw her arms round Kitty. "Believe you me," she announced to her dressing-room mates, "three years ago this kid was just one of us."

Nazir opened the wine which Kitty had brought and a frail-looking girl still wriggling out of her tights kissed him with open lips and gave a "Hurra!"

When the wine had been round twice, Klavdia drew back the curtains so that the entire row of windowless alcoves became suddenly visible.

At first Kitty drank sufficiently little for everything to seem amusing, even comic. Fat Carla who was heftier than the men who raised the big top, sat on a stool half-stripped, bellowing an old German love-song: "*Es war noch Sommer . . . als wir . . . in Portofino . . .*"

"Nostalgia!" shouted Klavdia above the gasping accordion. "For somewhere she's never been. Isn't that sad? Don't you feel sorry?" She looked thinner with her yellow plaits gathered from her face. Moodier, too, the tears edging quicker along the sweep of false eyelashes gummed to her lids.

"It's not so awful here, though," giggled Kitty. "Not as bad as it looks . . ." But when the wine took effect, she saw that it was worse. Stairs narrower, passages darker; under the greasepaint the skin of the girls was unblooming.

Nazir, full of the nearness of these excitable, semi-nude women, could not know how their costumes were skimped, how, since Kitty's day, they had had to make do, unpicking and patching, waiting, waiting for some imported ensemble which was all of one glorious unseamed piece. A girl called Zoyka sat with him, knee-to-knee, passing out snapshots of her brothers and sisters, and he tried not to stare at the tight swell of the leotard between her partly-opened legs.

Klavdia was tossing through Kitty's parcels. "Tea? Did you bring tea? Tea we can't get . . ." There was laughter. "And coffee . . . And sugar . . . And butter."

Kitty knew then that she no longer had a place here. It was not enough. It would never be enough. She had become a foreigner proffering tokens of goodwill. As the paper wrappings were trampled underfoot her expression was savage.

"Cheer up, duckling," said Klavdia. "We're not proud. Remember the sausage?"

Kitty shuddered. "Dead baby" they called it. Flesh embryonic, the colour of wallpaper, size, texture – unaglutinated gelatine. Grit-grey in twenty-four hours.

"We can still get that. A good thing I've got black-pudding blood in my veins," Klavdia went on, stroking her 140-rouble floral shawl. "Otherwise I'd never stand up to matinée days."

When the supervisors came in, having heard the racket from the front office, the girls' festive mood shrivelled and they attended to themselves individually with an air of desperation, suddenly as isolated, crankish and ill-turned out as the circus orchestra striking up the intermezzo at the penultimate interval. Kitty went stiff from the old, ingrained fear that they had come to look her over, silently, as they used to, with unblinking, glassy-eyed scorn, before recording her inadequacies in their assessment. But they, too, had changed, and not changed. Old Mikhaila, still dressed like a man in collar and tie, positively bustled up to Kitty, followed by the silent, hook-nosed Masha whose gold-rinsed hair had become quite grey.

"Katyushka, darling," breathed Mikhaila. "Tell us about England, tell us everything."

Nazir had taken Zoyka on his knee. "You carry on," he whispered to Kitty.

Klavdia was laughing. "Nobody's really afraid of them nowadays, except that you never can be quite sure who's up and who's down. Isn't your black friend a hoot?"

Despite her invitation, Mikhaila did not allow Kitty to speak. She knew it all before, from the rest of the troupe. That had always been her way. "D'you know what I think?" she murmured, bushing Kitty's hair back from her face and fastening it at the nape of her neck with a high gilded comb. "You ought to turn round now and go straight back to England. Now, right now. Go back to your lovely life and never try to remember this nightmare." Almost languorously she dabbed a kiss behind the girl's ear. "Poor dear love. Hubby's dead, child. Don't you be sentimental about him – or us. No one knows what is just round the corner. It could be dangerous for you here. Go home, darling, go home soon."

Later on Kitty said, "I must see Ben." And Klavdia took Nazir's pocket-book from inside his jacket, and was writing down Karpinskii's telephone number. Ben ... Ben ... Another Slater protégé. Did he have others whom Kitty did not know? The pocket-book matched Archie's. American Express. How good Archie was. How spineless she had been to send him off alone to Vera's.

Oh, why do I deceive him so? Because of Dymka, of course. And I deceive him also. Why did I telephone Dymka and agree to meet him here, tonight?

Because I must be mad.

A wind sprang up from the dark, bringing snow. And on the wind the snow smoked white and enveloping. Archie stooped into the curtain of flakes and made headway for the place where the woman taxi-driver had dropped him. It was uphill. After twenty minutes he felt like a child left to cry in the night.

He cursed Kitty who had brought him to this, cursed Evelyn Tremayne. But above all, he damned Lambert, safe back in England, damned him to hell.

Before Archie had left on this fool's errand the widow had offered him a hat, a silly squirrel hat, Slater's, never worn, and when he refused she had forced it into his pocket where he felt for it now, suddenly grateful. Inside the hat Archie's skull felt shrunken. Slater was high-domed, a man of superior parts whose head evidently stopped his hat falling over his eyes. Slater needed his head. All that intellect. The brain on him fascinating women by degrees, juggling with witches. How many in the blood-red house?

Archie blundered on. Upwards the going was heavier. An old one, a young one. Red and black shimmering on the lamp-glass. *Push orf! I want to lie down. Why don't you? Bloody little snooper – push orf!*

He reckoned he was almost at the foot of the rise when the blizzard lifted on a freshening wind. Around him the snow-flurry died and he could see again. Below, Verochka's street lamp was still winking, the light still shone at the window, but the pine trees on the summit were no nearer. Damnation. Instead of uphill he had been working sideways.

A voice lilted from the valley calling out strange words. Archie moved towards it stiffly, without question, knowing by instinct that the voice was directing itself to him. As if in a dream he saw a car made of snow, and beside it a wide-bellied snowman, beckoning him on.

The voice curled away, dwarfed on the wind, high and distant. A troll's voice.

Archie stumbled forward to the snowman hump near the car and fell to his knees, almost delirious from cold and relief. The snowman came up black through the top-spinning drift, black and heated, woolly as a ram. Archie had to be dragged. Round the car air steamed amber in the headlights. He felt himself being heaved into the passenger seat.

"My friend," said the man in the sheepskin sitting beside him, dusting off his high astrakhan hat, "you are a very lucky man."

The heater was full on, blasting warm gusts of oil-tainted air into Archie's face. His body shuddered uncontrollably. "So cold, so cold."

"Too cold, too jolly cold," said Sheepskin, jabbing at his chest with a pudgy forefinger. "I speak English. I am your very own policeman, Boris Kirillovich. You call me Borka." Even the name sounded cold. He leant over to wipe away the snowflake melt from Archie's eyes and cheeks on the sleeve of his peasant-tanned coat. "I bet never have you been so glad to see a policeman?"

"Never," said Archie. "Ever."

The fat man gave a sharp chuckle and started up his car. "That is good for my reputation and our public relations. How goes the Kipling? 'Yours not to question why, ours but to do and die . . . ?'"

Archie turned Slater's squirrel hat inside out and gave his hair a vigorous towelling with the warm lining. "Lord Tennyson. And the word is 'reason', not 'question'."

Borka changed down viciously as they bumped along a track fringed with huge snow-laced beeches. "I do not like lords. I can say this because your are not an English lord, I presume?"

Archie said not and introduced himself.

"So, Mr Renshawe, tonight I find you running round in one little village, way out of town. You doing marathons at night for Soviet charity? No, no, I take your lord's advice – reason. I reason, and reason tells me you are up to something."

Archie would have liked to tell the truth, but he felt the truth would be less plausible than any lie. A Russian female cabaret artist, widow of an English professor some thirty years her senior, was hiring him and an Indian to visit circuses and a crazed old lady in order to find out how her husband met his death in the Moscow back of beyond.

"There's been some kind of mistake," he said at last. "My taxi-driver lost the way. She only speaks German."

"No mistake, Mr Renshawe. I followed you from the hotel. You and I need chinwag. OK? You talk, I understand. England! I love England. By God, how I love England."

11

Kitty immediately disliked the room. She disliked the plain white walls, the smooth unpanelled doors leading off to bedroom and kitchen, the subdued lighting.

Florinskii's taste had obviously progressed in step with his career. He was secure, and that instinct for solid opulence about which she had often teased him when, almost penniless, they had made forays to the second-hand shops in the Arbat, had at last been indulged and the force of it was now set about him, materialised into heavy, reliable furniture.

While he was busy at the switch panel mediating the fall of light, she broke the silence, feeling oddly afraid of this Dymka whom she had thought she knew so well. "You must be extremely well off." The release of spite braced her. "Not that a man in your position would have had to pay, I suppose. No doubt this has been provided for you." Selecting the least comfortable-looking chair, she sat down, uninvited. "Strange," she said when he took no advantage of her pause. "I can't help remembering that dingy three-roomer on Yaroslovskoye chaussée that you shared with Freddie and Zhenya. How fortunate you thought yourself then, in spite of the leaky refrigerator and the beds on the floor."

He turned to her with an unreminiscent smile. "Ah, but Kat, that was only a refuge. This is a home."

Outwardly, he had not changed; not even swollen to his role by putting on fat. A touch of stoutness might have matched the consequence of that alien world into which he had so easily passed. Still trim, still too much the boy, awkward and alert, he stalked the room at a distance, pausing to admire a picture as if he were his own guest, but gradually advancing to where she sat inactive in the darkest recess.

He came upon her out of the light, placed two short-stemmed glasses on a circular table at the left of her chair, poured for her from a blackish squat bottle, hesitated over the amount, reflected, poured again before straightening up. "Cognac?" he said, instantly moving away to fetch an ash-tray and the cigarettes which he kept in the top drawer of his bureau.

"For God's sake, man, can't you ever keep still?"

Florinskii sat down at her feet. "Like this, you mean?" he said, assuming the pose of a Buddha. The next moment he was on his knees. "Or this? Or this?" Each time he froze, transfixed in a different attitude which brought him nearer. When at last they touched, Kitty slanted aside. He grabbed her hands and began to cry.

"You are perfectly all right, Dmitry Pavlovich, do stop it."

"I'm a fool," he murmured. The tears on his cheeks were real enough. "I don't know which way to turn, sometimes. I'm such an appalling fool."

Anything but. With her, she decided, he had always known what he was doing. The job must have reinforced his second nature, deployed it as part of the training. At first she tried to push his hands away and slither back against the hard frame of the chair but when she moved he gripped her more closely, and as he continued to kneel, head bowed, she felt her embarrassment cool to a revulsion at herself for not being able to control her delight at his shameless performance.

"There, there." She allowed her hands to go limp in his grasp. "You were good to me. You mustn't blame yourself. We were both at fault."

"You always bucked me up – you know that, Kat, always, even when we thought my career was finished. How could I have lost you so utterly?"

He knew perfectly well how: in Dymka's circle there was less scope for bohemianism than outright treachery. They had called her "the witch". He had taken the hint.

"Not utterly, my dear, or why would I be here?" The remark was only well-meant, but he acted upon it as if it were a prologue concluded, and scrambled to his feet.

Kitty felt cheated. She reached out for the Cognac and drank off half a glassful.

"It was wonderful of you to come back, but Katyushka, I shall be no use to you. Drunk too much, you see. Before. It's always the same story with me, nowadays, I'm afraid." While he stated his position, Kitty admired his striped silk tie, his beautiful straight-edged nails, the sweep of hand to mouth as he brought up his cigarette. Now he was in movement again, jerky, smoking, pacing in and out of the shadow, accompanying each phrase with the febrile inconsistency of gesture and speech of a character in an unsynchronised film. "I'm a ruined man, in spite of what you see, a total failure. I failed you, too, didn't I? But there you sit, untarnished, no older, looking no older"

– she smiled at the typical qualification – "the same woman, radiant, the neat heroine of romance without a blot on her conscience. Oh God, Katya, I feel so *ashamed*."

He must have something to tell her; something important. Meanwhile Kitty might have to suffer these preliminaries indefinitely unless she distracted him – and herself. "Three years is a long time, Dymka," she said. "I know you have been abroad. Tell me about that."

"Unexotic jaunts, mostly." He looked away. "But I learned a great deal. I developed a taste for people. You know, à la Tchekoff. Street-hawkers, three-star generals, actresses, pilgrims, the high and low of the world. It shakes one up, being forced into contact, you know, makes one . . . mmm . . . flexible. Yes, that's it." Evidently pleased with the word he repeated it several times.

Beside her on the rug was one of Dymka's inputs from abroad: a melamine globe of the world in a stainless-steel cradle. At the touch of her shoe the globe lit up from inside and began to spin. "You must come to England one day. It would suit you. Most bizarre, full of oddities, a very strange country."

He frowned. "So I am told, Katya, my dear, but why should I go to England when you have come back here? Do you feel less welcome there than back with us?"

"I can't tell. Last night I wept until dawn. You are the traveller – one can be homesick for a place which was never your own?"

"Of course not." He flicked ash on to the electric green of east Kent. "Yesterday you were simply upset because there was no one to greet you. I let you down. I should have been at the airport with flowers."

Of course. That was all there was to it. What more could any woman want? This man was always so damnably careful.

"I was confused about the time difference. Everything to do with you mixes me up. Believe me, Kat, I'm agonisingly sorry."

"Do have a sense of proportion, Dymka, it was hardly a tragedy."

But he had slipped too far down his penitential well to accept rescue quite so soon. "Some of the chaps in the department took it out on me after you left, you know. Still do, as a matter of fact."

"That was three years ago. They can't still hold it against you."

"Oh, of course, they don't put it like that exactly. No, it's a joke. 'Remember old Florinskii's thrash with his magic-woman? Well, she's got the nerve to be coming back after three years without a word or a sign. Some girl, eh, Dmitry Pavlovich? We don't blame you, but then, you're not married, are you, *golubchik*? Isn't it time to settle down?' Kitty darling, you can guess the kind of thing. The worst of it is, I feel guilty twice over – to them and you."

"Rubbish," she said. "What a portrait you must have painted for your colleagues. Wild-heart Dymka languishing after – what was I for their benefit? – A tightrope dancer? Bear-leading gipsy-child? You were ashamed of me, I was a nobody, I came from the back of beyond. Even then you were ashamed of wanting me. But I was silly, lonely and loved you . . ."

"How could you?" wailed Florinskii as if the promise had been made and broken the day before yesterday. "And then run away with that – that, I can't *bear* him . . ."

"That middle-aged foreigner?"

"Precisely," said Florinskii. "I hate him."

"He's dead."

"I know, I know, don't pester me with details. Anyway, it makes no difference. I trusted you and you eloped with a person old enough to be your father, my father, the head of my department's father for that matter. It was base, Yekaterina, vile."

"I treated you abominably?"

"Unspeakably."

She burst out laughing. "Oh, Dymka, my sweet, you have become so pompous!"

"Have I?" He shifted closer, edging round the globe to take up the matches. "It's the milieu, I daresay – niceties, always niceties. Admit it, though, Katya, I was pretty decent, wasn't I, giving you plenty of time to ponder? In any case, that was in the bad old days when an exit visa could take months, years even, so what was the hurry?"

"You never rang, you never wrote, you might have been dead for all I knew."

His image fined down in the stroboscopic jitter, the line of his jaw becoming tenser, the press of his lips around the cigarette sculpturally fine. It was no good. She didn't care what he had failed to do once, so long as he did now, taking her hands and twisting them upwards to kiss the palms.

"They said it was a ruse, that a woman could sell herself for a foreign passport, but I never believed them, not when the woman was my Kat, my Katyushka, my own . . ."

Kitty was unresistant. Let him have his justification, only let him go on, like this, the touch of him everywhere, invasive, making her slide, slide back to where, with him, she had uniquely once been.

"Katya, darling, it was pique, wasn't it pique? Tell me now, you can tell me, what does it matter now? You never loved him, how could you? Pride, pride, my bloody-minded little angel, all because of pride?"

Pride? Was the man quite so obtuse or was he simply in need of a woman? Shame had bound her to Slater. Desire for him used to sweep over her so suddenly that were he in Dymka's place now, she would have fallen on her back there and then on his tasteful granite-grey rug and begged to be taken.

"I loved him, Dymka, I'm not ashamed to admit it." Oh, she was, how she was. Then and now. "Can't you understand that his death has smashed me up, broken me? Can you imagine what it must have been like to have survived such a thing?"

"There, there," he said. "I'm an oaf, darling, an absolute oaf. How you must have suffered." His breath smelt of dentifrice. Behind the louvred doors of his kitchen he must have been cleaning his teeth in readiness. He didn't believe a single word she said. Nothing had changed.

He must think she had behaved like a tart three years ago and that tonight she ought to behave like one still. That is how he is going to treat me and I won't mind because he is right, it's how I want to be treated, because I deserve it. God forgive me, it's what I came here for.

With his hands on her breasts he could go on thinking whatever he liked, so long as he remembered that whatever she might say would be bogus and that she was ready to do what he wanted entirely.

On their way to the city snow came again, this time windless and unflustered. Borka had to stop to clear the windscreen. By the kerbside Archie watched the underbelly scud of cloud.

"Marvellous," he said, warm from the car. "A real storm."

"Only occasional shower," said his companion pulling out into the express-way. "In real *metyel* I could not have found you and soon you would be dead. But if it was gales, then *buran* and in *buran* I, too, would be dead."

The dashboard intercom crackled every time they passed under motorway signs, and snatches of pop music broke over the official radio traffic. Borka turned it off. "Pirates," he said. "Once we had anti-social elements. Now they are called pirates. I ask you, my friend, what has happened to the dignity of my profession?"

"Nothing. Same work, new job-description, that's all."

Borka slid into the slow lane where the car's poorly sprung suspension made the lights appear to swing like pendulums. "You talk through your hat!" he exclaimed. "There are more bad people now.

Out in all weathers, lacking respect. Excuse me – I know this, it is my business."

"Is that why you followed me?"

Borka turned to him with a gesture of such violence that for a split second both his hands were free of the wheel. "You say the taxi-driver lost you. Imagine! For this the poor woman could lose her licence. But at the hotel you show her an address, written in a fine Russian hand. I think you know exactly where you are going. I follow. And your life is saved. Now, Mr Renshawe, does not one good turn deserve another?"

Across the carriageway the uplit façade of the hotel loomed yellow in the snow-mist. When Borka drew up outside the portico Archie made to get out. "Yes," he said.

Borka grabbed his elbow. "Then not so fast, as they say in the English movies. I have a favour to ask. Business. I scratch you, you scratch me. OK? Allow me."

He did not let go of the Englishman's arm until they had gone down the fire stairs, through a windowless passage below the hotel foyer where a dozen or more uniformed men sat behind grey metal desks, and stopped in front of a cast-iron door stippled bright apple green.

For the first time since his rescue Archie experienced real fear.

The bedroom was hot and white. Even the roses on the white table were white. But apart from the room everything was as it had always been. As usual, before, she shuddered in spite of the heat, and he, as usual, shut the door behind them with his foot and pulled down the blind. In a moment he would roll back the sheet and place the white pillows one on top of the other.

Watching Dymka strip the narrow divan of its quilt, Kitty unexpectedly panicked, backing away, feeling behind her for the handle of the door, but he caught her round the knees and slid up from the bed against her, very close, so that the front of her body felt the impress of every button and zip-tab on his dark suit.

"That's rather silly, my sweet," he murmured. "Why would you be here if you didn't know what you wanted?"

She had forgotten how firm his grasp could be, how incisive his movements as her scalloped black jacket fell away to her waist before she quite realised what was happening, and she was outstretched on the divan, her bare heels ticklish against the weave of the carpet. And she expected herself not to say: the last person who spanned my breast with his hand was not my husband but you, and I remember you now because my husband is dead and will never do that, and I am glad that you can be so entirely different from him.

Florinskii did not kiss her, caress her or waste time in leading up. "I want you now. Every day for three years I have wanted you."

Always banalities, expressly because he knew Kitty's boundless appetite for cliché at the most intimate moments. Slater had baulked. He had tried to be original. It was no good and she had to teach him what to say. But Florinskii was a natural. His novelettish tributes rushing in her ears, Kitty floated her white body in the white-carpeted room, avidly comparing. It had not often worked with Slater because Slater could not pretend. But with Dymka she knew now it could never work because Dymka could always pretend.

"I used to dream of you," he said. "Once I dreamed that you were dead and I had killed you, and when I woke I was glad I could remember my dream."

An old game. No threat but a provocation, once as inviting to her as to him.

"How killed me?"

Florinskii placed the straightened edge of his hand under the fall of her right breast and chopped inward.

"There?" She hooked her thumbs in the material of her teddy, hassling down past her ribs. "Feel," she said, pressing at him. "Feel how it would be."

Could she tell him? Before it had been – imagine how white and still I should lie beneath you. Now it was: fulfil us, let you and me experience the outcome. Kill me now and we shall know what once we both pretended to want, and the ghost-print of Slater, Slater the skull with eyes, still live in the bone, will fade out with my breath. "Be strange with me, Dymka. Treat me like something in your way. Can't you see? You must do that or I shall never forget."

Next moment she was away from him across the white carpet, face set in a glazed smile, slowly pushing out her hips from the black trousers, and allowing the silk to rustle down her legs until it was flat around her, and she could step out, not entirely naked, but sure now that he would blind her to those images which the memory of Slater had evoked. I shall destroy every trace of my husband's letters, all thoughts of Slater, when I go home. Strip away every mark of him from me with acid and flame in that cold house by the sea.

He took her, riding her forward and back like a doll on the rack, whispering that he loved her, how he still wanted, needed, how long the wait, he must, she must, he must. This time.

He must think it's simply a matter of technique, she told herself, jostling like a wet fish under his weight. "I can't," she broke out. "I can't, don't you understand – I *can't*!"

*   *   *

97

The room was stuffy. There was no furniture except for a couple of tubular metal chairs placed side by side behind a desk.

"Take a pew," said Borka, unbuttoning his sheepskin. Archie sat down, still in coat and gloves. The policeman took his seat on a corner of the desk and wiped the uppers of his wet ski boots against the foam rubber cushions of the other chair. "Life is a bitch," he muttered. "A bitch. How often in this life did you know a man who is immediately a pleasure for you to know, Mr Renshawe?"

Archie leaned away from the oniony blurt of raw spirit on the policeman's breath. "I don't know. Once in a blue moon."

"You know how many times I have this experience with a colleague from my own country? Never! With you, straightaway. The first once in the bloody blue moon. Let us drink!"

Archie pressed himself against the canvas back of the chair. "Look, if it's all the same to you, time's getting on . . ."

Borka glowered down at him, a snappish twinkle in his black eyes. "Scotch, Irish, USA Bourbon, Tennessee Snakebite, take the pick. Here all international tipples are at our disposal." He suddenly slammed the ball of his fist on the desk top. "*Ivan Ivanovich!*" Behind him a panel slid open in the wall revealing a dazzling white rectangle.

Out of the brilliance came the rattle of glasses.

Borka dropped to his feet, turned and thrust his huge head through the slot in the wall. After a few whispers he emerged with a bottle and a pair of heavy tumblers.

Archie took off his coat and folded it across the back of his chair.

"A good suit, Mr Renshawe. English." Borka held out a glass full of clear liquid. "*Nu davai*. Let us drink to your suit."

The vodka was tepid and undiluted.

The policeman drank swiftly, uningratiatingly, downing two glasses in succession. Before Archie could take a second gulp his tumbler was snatched away and topped up to the brim. "Before, I watch you. Tonight, I meet you. I like you. I think you could be my foreign friend. I could take you under my wing." The drink was heady. When Borka smiled, Archie smiled back. "But you tell me lies, you bastard!" bellowed the policeman. "So who in hell are you, Renshawe-bastard, eh, eh?"

The switch was so unnerving that Archie experienced it like the vodka as a wild rush to the head. He could have burst into tears. "I thought I was your friend."

Borka took a long Havana cigar out of the desk drawer and waved it at the blue-shirted men visible through the ribbed safety glass of the partition window to Archie's left. "Appearances! You see that?

You see *them*? Where do you think you are, my friend?" Now the dark eyes were alert, inimical, unteasing.

"A police station?"

"Bloody spot on," exclaimed his companion. "*Militsiipunkt*. In jug, old chap. My jug."

"Christ," breathed Archie.

"Precisely."

"In a hotel?"

"Under a hotel. In England you do not yet have policemen under hotels?"

Archie thought of Torquay. "Not yet."

"It will come. Now, let us proceed." Rootling deeper into the desk drawer Borka produced a thick manilla envelope and jostled out a clutch of passports. "Renshawe. How are you spelling Renshawe?"

Archie spelled it as it was spelled, the way that Borka could see it was spelled in the white rectangle on the front of Archie's passport. So that's where they went after being taken from you at registration.

The fat man flicked through the leaves several times before flattening them down at the photograph page and carefully tracing along the entry under "profession".

"'Consultant'," he read aloud, "'Executive Legal Consultant'. Explain."

Archie did his best but the sight of his passport in alien hands was provoking. "Look, if you don't mind, I've had about enough for one day," he said, finishing the strong drink in one gulp.

He was almost on his feet when the other man swung a foot forward forcing him back into his chair. "Times have changed. I know English detectives. These days I can speak to them in England by telephone. What you take me for — some stupid *muzhik* cop who thinks you are Scotland Yard? You do private work, old man, dirty work. Shifty, shifty, shifty. A secret man," whispered the Russian, revolving the cigar between his teeth until the band came away, bringing with it a tiny curl of the wrapper. "A cloaksman. One who pretends to be here on his holidays but only goes out at night." He leant forward, shredding the cigar between his baby-gherkin fingers. "I, too, have kept watch in this same little village. And the English private detective knows the street. He speaks no Russian, this is his first visit, but he even knows the house I am watching. Tell me, why did you assault that old lady this evening?"

He brushed past to sit beside her on the edge of the bed. The wardrobe door, disturbed by the draught from his movement, swung open revealing an inner side covered with mirror-glass tiles.

"Look at yourself, Katya. See how beautiful you are. How could you – with that old man?"

In the flat, uncomplicated light of the room Kitty's cigarette smoke fazed her reflection. "I made a mistake no English *lady* would have made. I thought I had married an old man for love, and did not think that because of it everyone would laugh behind my back. You would get on very well with the English, Dymka. They also cannot forgive passion – or mistakes."

"And to think I once almost came over to London to track you down."

"What prevented you?"

His fingers explored the nape of her neck. "Well, to be frank, it wouldn't have been very sensible, I suppose, career-wise, to have taken that kind of snap decision. Anyhow, my superiors out-English the English in the personal sphere." He laughed. "How could I have got clearance – on compassionate grounds?"

"You might have tried."

"You forget, my love – you were married."

She could never forget. He would never understand why she could not. There lay the impasse. How could she explain about Slater, even to herself? That she had not married him out of calculation but innocence which when she was with him had made her feel perfect? Slater never held anything against her. Even when she was outrageously drunk, cruel and insulting, invented affairs with other men at his squash club, refused to launder his shirts, wouldn't cook, spat at strangers who came to the door, Slater would sit in their bed, scrawny as an owl-chick, nibbling toast and tut-tutting, not at her but at the crossword. In his eyes she could do no wrong, and in time Kitty came herself to believe that for him the whole duty of marriage consisted in her being true to a nature which no other husband would have tolerated for twenty-four hours. "After he died," she said, trailing her reminiscence aloud, "I think I went mad."

A nerve flickered under one cheekbone and Florinskii drew his mouth in very straight. "Never mind that for the moment – you wrote that you were coming to see *me*. And I find you messing about with the scum of the earth – policemen and blacks, God knows who."

"Oh, is that all? I thought you truly loved me, Dymka dear, but you simply act out of pique. I could explain but you wouldn't want to know, would you? How much nicer to believe I'm still the slut you took me for when you brought me here tonight."

"God-Christ above, Katya, do you still think the world is some kind of circus? You can't get away with these weird liaisons. There'll be trouble in the end, terrible trouble."

She slithered off the bed and began to cast around the floor for her belongings. "You always put me in the wrong. Oh, God, where are my clothes?"

The weave of the teddy ripped against the points of her fingernails and one nipple poked through like a brown eye on a ladder. "Hell, hell!" He offered to help. "Don't even breathe on me, you swine. I knew I oughtn't to have come." Having buttoned down her blouse in front of the door-mirror she turned to him, hands on hips, apparently oblivious of the unclothed half of her body. "Listen, Dmitry Pavlovich, my husband died unexpectedly. That was a shock. After the funeral everyone went away and that was another. But the worst was not knowing the first thing about how he died, or what he had done those last few weeks of his life." Suddenly she became aware of her half-stage nudity.

Her tights and the rest were under the quilt. Without a glance she stuffed them into her bag, then bent away before flicking up the black Mussulman trousers from the floor with her toes.

"So when his business affairs were settled and I discovered I had money, I employed English professionals to find out. Private investigators. They are discreet, sympathetic, and personally rather kind. They're here to help me on a quest, if you like, a harmless, harmless quest."

"In your book it may be," he said. "In mine it's police work. Call it off while there's still time."

The palms of her hands were cold as she gathered her blouse into the waistband and the odd thing was that now she was dressed she couldn't understand why a moment ago she had stood intimately naked under his gaze, and before, had wanted to lie in his arms and be touched. Now she was clothed he was vicious. His tone was vicious. "There'll be trouble if you don't, I promise you. Get rid of those sharks, pay them off. I'll do their job for them – for you, and for free."

What old lady? Slutskaya. That old lady. The sheer absurdity of the accusation made Archie blench. "*Her?* She's mad. I made a civil professional enquiry and nearly got blinded. The woman's insane. And so are you if you believe her. But you're all lunatics together in this country, aren't you, all of you flailing at the mad-house walls?"

Borka gave a satisfied intake of breath. For a while there was silence broken only by the clink of glass as he tried to balance his tumbler on the neck of the vodka bottle. "Quite so, old chap. Mad as the hatter. Proverbial. Maybe after all you can do me a service, young fellow."

Old chap, young fellow, do a service. It was nightmarish to have to listen to this Soviet State employee dredging his word-bag for the idiom of Piccadilly Jim. "In return I offer you help, co-operation. But only when you are fully honest. I ask again, what are you doing in my country?"

"Doing what you're doing, *old chap*, if you must know – trying to earn a living, that's all."

"Your career. Tell me about this."

"It's not a career, it's a job. I trace people's whereabouts and try to turn up when they least expect me."

"Confront them with their past?"

"Their present usually. But the two have to fit together."

Borka licked his lips. "Miscreants to misdeeds. A fine exercise, healthy for the soul."

"It keeps the wolf from the door, put it like that."

"Ah, money, Mr Renshawe. You have come to the wrong country. Who has real money here?"

"I've already been paid. There's nothing to collect."

Borka left off the game with the glass and lit his Havana, dropping the matchstick into the splatter of vodka on the desk where it flared blue in the spirit. "Tell me more. About your accomplices, for instance."

"My *what*?"

"Your *acc – om – plices*, Mr Renshawe." Borka felt round to the back pocket of his stone-washed American jeans and pulled out a wedge of documents fastened round with a blue elastic band. On each Bible-thin wafer of paper was a portrait photograph, over-stamped in violet indelible ink. Tipping one out he presented it upside down to the Englishman. "This negro, for instance, what is his relation to you?"

"He's not a negro. He's an Indian. The picture's over-exposed."

Borka re-inspected the photograph, then passed over a faded snap of Kitty Slater. "And this woman?" Under the dazzle of the ceiling spot she looked an old lady.

"She's Russian," said Archie.

Shuffling up the photographs Borka replaced them in his pocket. "Now, I tell you the bad news – Archie. I may call you Archie? You are not very clever Englishman, Indian and Russian. In fact, you are stupid, very stupid. You are in danger and put yourselves at risk by not coming to me first."

The man seemed genuinely concerned, a touch sorrowful even.

Risk? Danger? For the first time in his life, Archie realised how it must have been for the tearful housewives at the receiving end of his tallyman's guff. Only one thing to do, as he'd counselled so often: give in. "I've just been trying to cope on my own. You're right, but I don't understand this country."

"Never mind," said the policeman. "Better late than never. Perhaps we can help each other. Let us meet. Tomorrow. I help you."

Anxious to bring this unexpected interview to a close Archie agreed. Tomorrow. Borka's office. Four p.m. But the policeman had not finished with him. "At last we are in touch, Archie. Now you tell me the whole story. Take your time. Another?"

This time Archie accepted the drink gratefully. "Well, about seven months ago an Englishman . . ."

Borka began to take notes.

". . . a professor, came out here on a research visit . . ." He held nothing back but went on, listening to his own words as though they might yield some interpretation in the telling which he hadn't yet grasped. "There was a farewell party at Mrs Slutskaya's house the night before he left. The toasts must have got a little too frequent because they found him next day lying dead in the snow near the place you rescued me from tonight."

"Slutskaya was the last to see him alive?"

"Yes."

"And the family of this man asked you to revisit the scene?"

Archie nodded.

"So this Russian lady, Mrs Slater, who is in your tour group, is the professor's widow – why should this lady employ executive legal consultants like you and the Indian gentleman to pay last respects to the memory of her husband? Did you not suspect that your client was making use of you? Pulling the wool, old boy?" Borka got to his feet with a lurch. A broad yellow ring gleamed on the hand which clamped Archie's shoulder. "As a man you could be a companion, but as an investigator you are already an atrocity, my dear. You see, I, too, know of this professor. He was accidentally dead. The case is closed."

12

The room was hot and dark. Archie blundered against the hard-edged divan under the window and put out an arm. The sleeping figure heaved and rolled over. "Mmm, that's nice. Give me some more."

Archie found the switch. In the skin-pink light of the bedside lamp Nazir's sleek face crumpled but he slept on, crooning baby calls to his bolster. "Lovely, just as it comes, nice, oooh, nice . . ."

It was disgusting. The man's appetite for sleep was gluttonous.

"Leave off, you indecent little ape; wake up, why can't you? You're supposed to have news for me. And where's Kitty?"

Balling his fists into Nazir's chocolate throat he repeated the question until at last the faint voice issued. "Went off, didn't she, with that diplomat? Big noise, big car." The memory of the car seemed to give him a jolt and he turned on to his back, eyes still closed.

"You mean you let her go?"

"What d'you think I could do about it – tie her to my leg? She's big, too, Archie. Know what I think?" murmured Nazir, still unawake. "I think she'll marry a big shot and have a big family."

Twenty to midnight. Archie counted back: six hours, each of them feeling like a week; and the people filling them up – the hotel doorman; that Verochka; the bloated policeman with his sinister old pals' act. On top of it all, he had to sleep with an Indian who'd probably talk to himself all night. "God, you're repulsive," he said, glaring at the foetal hump under the heavy blanket. "Bloody abject." He sat down hard against Nazir's ankles. "Wake up, blast you. I'm losing track of what's going on. Somebody says the Slater woman's setting us up. Got an opinion, have you?"

Nazir gave a violent gulping snore and jerked sideways across the bed.

"I'm not putting up with this, you know," Archie shouted. "We're here on business. I'll make out a report on you, that's a promise. And Lambert can sort you out when we get back. It's a conspiracy, this, a conspiracy. You're probably in with them, trying to discredit me, you're after my job, you want to ruin me . . ."

Nazir suddenly opened his eyes and bared his uneven teeth in a long sleepy grin. "It's late, Archie. I'm always telling you, you're too conscientious. A little nap, a little shower, and you'll be right as rain. Who needs reports? Count yourself lucky – that Tremayne's already paid us, and old Lambert's pleased. So the lady knows a thing or two? Relax, at least we're not robbed and she'll pop up again."

Archie took a moment of silence to congratulate himself on having held back about Tremayne in his talk with Borka. That had taken nerve. Nazir was right. No point in getting jumpy over incidentals. Damn that vodka, but his head was clearing. "Next time don't lose her so easily." He prodded his companion's dense black hair. "She's our only official customer and we need to hang on to her. I know it's not straightforward, I've already messed up the Verochka business, but at least one of us will need to keep his wits about him."

Nazir fell to nuzzling his pillow again, his smile warm and glassy at the prospect of more sleep. "No more prangs, eh, Archie? That lady is perfectly fine, believe me. I only caught a glimpse of the boyfriend but they looked made for each other, real cream and sugar. Well in, he must be. That car." His voice began to trail away but the smile remained fixedly broad. "A dealer in something naughty, bet your socks. La Slater's friends hinted as much at the circus tonight. Apparently the place is full of them nowadays. Shallow end, though, I should think, no high finance. Still count in beads, don't they, out here?"

The girl on the landing desk was a peach, heavy-breasted and made up to the eyes. She watched him bang on Kitty's door, then try the handle. No luck. When he sauntered back she smiled over her spectacles and wished him good night in German.

At the end of the corridor he found a deserted tea-bar which stayed open all night. Knowing that he would not be able to sleep until Kitty's return, he took his seat at a little round table furthest away from the counter and ordered tea by pointing at the electric urn and miming at the beautiful statuesque blonde who towered over it from her high stool in front of a row of cordial bottles. The tea was the colour of beer and came in a glass. Archie wanted to ask for milk but the girl had already placed the glass before him with such evident, inexplicable contempt that he smiled up at her white apron without meeting her eyes and began to unwrap the little packet of cube sugar in his saucer. She returned to her stool, crossed her legs, and stared away from him at the curtained window.

The tea-bar was really only one end of the second-floor landing, partitioned off. Behind him was a glass wall through which the long sweep of the corridor extended past the row of room doors to the left; turning to his right he could overlook the lift exits. Just after one o'clock Kitty emerged from the most distant. Archie caught up with her as she stood on the rose-flowered carpet waiting for the German-speaking desk-girl to hand over her key. The blonde from the tea-bar came after him.

"Thank God for that." He took the key and pressed it into Kitty's hand. "I thought you were lost."

She swung the key by its oval room-tag. "I am perfectly able to take care of myself, thank you."

"I know it's very late, but could you spare me a moment – in private?"

He had intended to lead her back to the tea-bar but Kitty had already unlocked her door. After switching on the hall light she turned on the threshold and gave a brusque signal of invitation. When he hesitated she flung off her jacket. "My, my, look at him," she said, her naked throat and arms startlingly white against the black satin trousered two-piece. "He is afraid. This is night, this is some crazy girl, this is bedroom."

At his back the desk-girl and the blonde began a high-pitched conversation which broke off in loud giggles. Archie shut the door behind him. "What was all that about?"

"Oh, them." Kitty kicked off her shoes. "They think we are lovers but the fair one says you are too young for me. Is that true?"

Archie stepped back. "Look, I'm awfully sorry, Mrs Slater, but now's obviously the wrong time. I'll drop by in the morning."

"You shut up. I pay, I am the client. You will do this for me. You will stay." Her eyes were slits. In a minute she was going to cry. Archie made his way through the litter of discarded clothing and paper bags blocking the narrow gap between the twin beds, gently took the tortoiseshell holder from her trembling fingers and inserted an untipped cigarette from the packet of Senior Service on her lap.

"Tonight Kitty raped herself. Hey presto, no trousers. On the floor. How do you like that?" He lit her cigarette with her own lozenge-spangled *briquet*. "I am not a nice girl," she said, sobbing out smoke. "With men I do dreadful things." Wet mascara clogged her eyelashes.

"You're just overtired," he heard himself saying. The sentence completed itself like a line from a radio play. "Or you wouldn't be telling me this."

She responded out of character, with a heavy sniffle. "Yes, I would. Who can I tell? My dead Slater? Ha! Who else do you think – my mother? Is she in the room? No, no. No husband, no mother. I am alone in the world. Except for you. You I pay. I am the client so you listen. Any case, you want to. You are a man, and men, I know them, they would pay *me* money to hear dirty stories."

Already intrigued Archie sat down on the opposite bed, hoping that Lyudy wouldn't get back from visiting her relatives before the end.

"Today a man comes back into my life – yes?"

Archie was following. Yes. That man.

"Ages ago, this man takes a deep fancy to Mrs Slater, before she is Mrs Slater, you understand, this Florinskii, Dmitry Pavlovich. To us – Dymka. Once, ages ago . . ."

Oh, Lord, she wasn't going to have the vocabulary.

"Your client, your Kitty, she could play Dymka like an instrument."

"Like on an instrument."

"The same thing, I'm telling you," exclaimed Kitty wildly flicking ash at the headboard. "But not tonight."

Given her tears and general disarray, that much had been evident from the beginning, but Archie allowed the following silence to brood darkly between them.

"Tonight I become an instrument and Dymka the playman. What do you think of that?"

"To be honest, at present, I haven't got much to go on . . ."

Kitty squealed triumphantly. "I am right all along, you are a man, you want pictures!"

"Not really, but I'm a bit in the dark still. I mean, did this –" *Dymka?* "Did this person, did he . . . I mean, what did he do, actually?"

"Oh, *him*," shouted Kitty. "What not? He was so good, a holy man, the virgin, so modest, disturbing, sad. What he has done to your client is make her feel a bitch, a bitch, a bitch!"

For a long while she wept, luxuriatingly, clasping her own slight body in her arms as if it were a child's toy cast aside in a fit of anger only to be caught up moments later in a smother of kisses.

Archie was mildly disappointed at this feeble dénouement to a promising story, and also very embarrassed. Obviously he couldn't simply walk out on the woman. God only knew the extremity of distress that a girl of this sort might drive herself to. "Perhaps you misunderstood," he said, trying not to stare at the bleary wreck she was making of her face. "Diplomacy. That's a busy life. Perhaps he was tired."

Kitty checked a sob and drove in upon him, hollow-eyed. "What you're saying?" She drubbed the heel of one hand across the taut planes of her forehead. "A time like this and you give advice?"

"Try and see it his way," said Archie in his mad-quiet voice of the professional counsellor. "I know what it's like – a long day and you come home tired, need a drink, time to unwind."

Across the gap her mascara-blodged face loomed at him like a Rorschach ink-blot. "Serious, you mean this, serious?"

Archie gave a polite cough and stiffened slightly. "Worth thinking about, I'd say, before jumping to conclusions. People are funny . . ."

Kitty shot out an arm and grabbed at his lapel. Involuntarily he bent closer.

"You know something, Mr-bloody-Archie? You, you are funny." The whisper was beckoning, intense. "You like jokes?" With the other hand she freed her shoulders from the halter-neck of the two-piece and wriggled at him, the smell of her thick and warm on his cheek. "Look at me, tell me, you are the man, is this a joke?" Even if she'd given him time to answer, he might still have been dumbstruck. Instead, she screamed, and as she screamed, hellishly, implacably, without a thought for him, herself, the innocent guests stacked around and above and below in this great pea-pod of an international hotel, for no one except this Dymka out of whose arms she had fallen, the right lapel of his jacket parted at the hand-stitchings, and came away entire in her hand.

At two o'clock he stood in his shirtsleeves drinking tepid mineral water from her tooth-glass while Kitty, slavish from remorse, sat cross-legged on a pillow searching her workbox for matching thread. The colossal outburst unpent, she was garrulous. "Not always deep, that man," she said, finding the right shade of twist. "Not deep. There is a word for him?"

Archie knew one or two. "Superficial."

"Superficial. Superficial." The repetition seemed to gratify her. "He was not the lover of deep feeling. At the end he gave me only cuddles. Listen, Archie."

Archie felt no doubt that he had to. "That sounds all right. Quite nice, I'd say, thoughtful . . ."

Under the shade of the bedside lamp she squinted for the eye of the needle. "At the end, Archie. Afterwards the woman likes cuddles. Not-at-the-end." She caught at the wisp of protruding thread, and yanked it through.

"I see. Then you'd have been better staying at home for the evening, tidying up this place. I don't know how you can stand it." He started on the English Sunday newspapers cluttered beneath the wash-basin. "Need this stuff?" he asked, rolling up the colour sections.

"Dymka likes it for motor-car pictures but I forgot." She did not protest when Archie went on to stuff the rolls neatly into the wastebin, empty the ash-tray and arrange her shoes into pairs. After the empty bottles had been stacked on the bottom shelf of the wardrobe, only her clothes were left.

"Do you mind?"

She smiled at his hesitancy. "Please . . . I am grateful."

He folded the star-spangled black cape over the back of the chair. "Nice things. But they'll spoil, you know, get creased . . ." The floor clear, he sat again on Lyudy's bed, clutching a carrier bag full of Kitty's minimalist underwear. All the while she had worked silently, deftly, and his jacket was almost ready. "Now, as soon as you've made me respectable once more, I'm off. If you want a word of advice to sleep on – don't go throwing yourself at foreign men, even though you think you know them. Nazir has already told me about your diplomat friend."

She turned back the cloth and contemplated her stitching. "That Naz, you know, he is sweetie-pie man. My circus friends they take him in their hearts, speak English with him. On this dreadful, dreadful day I am lucky because Naz is so sensitive."

Mention of her night with Nazir suddenly reminded Archie why he had come to see her in the first place. "Listen. Last evening while you were both at the circus . . ." It was no hour for lengthy explanations so he gave a rough-and-ready outline of the Verochka fiasco, concluding with his miraculous rescue by Borka.

By the end she had already snipped the final thread from his jacket. "All Katya's fault," she gaily announced, tossing it back at his chest. "You are alone. You are a man. She is frightened. And you cannot speak Russian. This is the explanation of tonight. Next time we go together."

Archie slowly pulled on his jacket. Not half as frightened as he'd been of Verochka and her accent. You could butter loaves with that accent, it was so rich. No more visits, if he could help it, to her, or the lady with the lamp whose fingernails were the colour of rubber surgical aprons. "To hell with Russian – she speaks English better than me. I'm not going back there without an escort."

Instantly Kitty was on her feet, taunting. "I know! Only with him, your horrible policeman!"

Lord, not again, not another scene. It was unnatural. Didn't these people ever think of sleep?

"Come off it, the man saved my life. I'd have died in that snow."

He fumbled with his jacket buttons. The woman was becoming twistier than a mongoose and he suddenly wanted to damage the intimacy of their last half-hour. "And I feel bound to say, Mrs Slater, that my colleague and I seem to have achieved so little that you may be well-advised to drop the whole matter in your own interests."

Dymka's thoughts, Dymka's words: *call it off, drop it, before it's too late.*

Her mouth creased in anguish.

Oh, Lord, now he'd gone too far in the other direction. After all that work at her English lessons in Clacton she understood more than he had bargained for. Archie backtracked. "Listen, Kitty, my dear, didn't you say that your husband had a lot of friends in this city?" Silence. This was murder. If she now went pathetic on him he'd never get to bed at all. "Well, it's very odd because as far as I can see, no one wants to know about him, or you, and least of all, me. You were on the telephone most of yesterday afternoon but few of his friends seemed exactly available."

"Oof!" cried Kitty, bunching one of her supple musician's hands into an arthritic claw. "This is old people. They forget. Tomorrow we see young people."

"Oh, God, don't you realise what time it is? It's tomorrow now."

Her face lit up in triumph. "OK, is today already. Today we all go to Karpinskii. Ben. Ben is a boy to Slater. Yes, Ben is *synok* — Slater's little Russian son."

Next morning Archie came down late. The table was set for six but Nazir sat alone breakfasting indiscriminately off his own and other people's tea and rolls. "You look ghastly, old chum," he said, making room for his companion on the red plush bench seat at the head of the table. "Have a dose of Vitamin C."

Archie pushed away the glass of unnaturally vivid fruit juice and cracked a white-shelled egg on the ash-tray. The yolk had a green tinge.

"Feeling squalid this morning, are we?" Nazir appropriated the egg and dried it on the table napkin of an absent guest's place-setting. A broad-shouldered waiter glared at him from the tea-kettle trolley but Nazir was on top of the world. "Marvellous . . . this kiddies' tuck." He gulped down the egg in two successive bites. "And it will be lunchtime in a couple of hours. What's the matter with our lot?"

Archie yawned and beckoned the waiter. "Sleeping it off, I should think. Tea, please." The tea was the same colour as last night's. Nazir unwrapped the sugar for him.

"They keep on disappearing," he said, with a glance at the waiter's retreating back. "I can't make it out."

"Having a drag in the kitchen, aren't they?"

"No, not the tea-boys, Arch, the people that came with us, I mean. The *group*."

The night before they had sat down five at dinner: Kitty, Nazir, Archie, Lyudy and Gavin. Archie looked round the dining-room.

Nazir laughed. "Gavin got stinko. Where does he get the stuff?"

"Bars. They have more bars here than lavatories, or haven't you noticed?"

"Not what he's debottling, his supply isn't labelled. No, he's on to the home-produced product. There's a fortune to be made in this country, you know, just out of raw materials – a few sacks of sugar, brewer's yeast . . ."

Still brooding on his small-hours suspicions of Kitty Slater's good faith, Archie drank three cups of tea and waited for Nazir to run out of entrepreneurial steam before retelling the Verochka story over his black bread and cheese.

Long before he had finished his companion was in fits of laughter.

"You? Help a detective? Come off it, Archie, someone's having you on."

That, after last night, Archie felt bound to admit, was probably true. "But it's perfect, don't you see? Tremayne gave me instructions to contact the Soviet authorities and this is the opening we need – informal, semi-official, no red tape . . ."

"But we're booked up today. Kitty said we were supposed to be meeting an old pal of hubby's. What shall we tell her?"

"Karpinskii?"

"That's the boy," said Nazir. "Ben."

Benjamin. Slater's little Russian son. Kitty must have made the appointment last night, before her meeting with Dymka. What was she playing at? "I know," said Archie slowly. "He speaks English, so we can interview him on his own. The woman's too emotional, she'll only get in the way. She can take us to his place, make the introductions, then you can bring her back here and wait for me." He tore a page from his pocket diary. "That's Borka's full name, rank and extension number. He speaks English, too. If I'm not back by four this afternoon, give him a ring. If Kitty turns funny, tell her it's a new line of enquiry. And, by the way, congratulations. I heard you went down well backstage at the circus last night."

A brimming smile spread over Nazir's khaki-moon features. "Is that right? Well, great. You should have been there. My eye, what a stunning bunch of girls." Elbows wide on the tea-spotted table-cloth

Nazir embraced the entire dining-room with his smile. "You know, I really like it here, Archie," he murmured across the punctured egg-shells. "Give me a native dancing-girl and I'm sure I could settle down very nicely."

13

It was past noon when they turned off a deserted side-street into a courtyard surrounded on three sides by nineteenth-century low-rise tenements. The two men loitered by the drifted snow at the entry-way, feeling redundant and a little apprehensive while Kitty checked the name-boards at the bottom of each staircase. At the far end of the nearest block, a pair of tailless cats rubbed themselves against a grating through which clouds of steam were escaping from the boiler-house plant. Despite the thick covering of uncleared snow on window-ledges, roofs and the stumpy birch-copse in the centre of the court, the noise here was worse than on the street; an alien, anachronistic noise of too many families in too little space.

In this, the most inner of cities, Archie could hardly have waited for the decay to begin; to escape and plunge away into the shadows of the encircling forest. About that, as so much else, Nazir obviously didn't give a hoot but struck out, under Archie's gaze, from drift to drift, tilting his autofocused Minolta at the dusty yellow buildings. He was the one who ought to have looked out of place, reflected Archie, but then, wherever he was, Nazir made it home.

When Kitty came back scowling, the ridge of each lower lash-line stiff against the waxy green of her eyes, Archie saw that she, too, was made for the snow-light. "Ben is gone," she said. "And his girl. Both gone."

Aloud Archie said, "Thank God for that. Time we were gone as well." But in the end he had to let Kitty go on ahead because Nazir was reluctant to abandon the snowman he had made on top of a bicycle ramp. As he hopped back to where Archie stood at the farthest side of the yard, a dwarf-like old woman in felt ankle boots came out of one of the entries with a bright green tin dustpan which she banged against the gutter downpipe. In an instant the cats came racing towards her.

Archie swore. "Let's bugger off out of this before the neighbours join in."

On the way out Nazir waved to the woman who gave a bow.

"Don't be so self-conscious. This is Europe. People understand child-hood reversion. Anyway, what's the hurry?"

"Kitty made a mistake, they're not at home."

"I don't know why you rely on that girl. She'd forget her own address if it wasn't on her passport. Never listens to directions, either – that's what the circus people told me yesterday – nobody here seems to know where anyone lives. Look at her now."

Three hundred yards in front of them Kitty stood on a patch of cleared pavement by the traffic lights studying the German street-plan which Archie had bought at the airport. "Here," she said when they came up. "Along the boulevard and right at the *kinoteatr Rossiya*."

Nazir took the map, folding it with difficulty in the rush of air from the heavy lorries speeding along the multi-lane ringroad. Archie groaned. He'd studied that map on the plane and worked out the scale. Another mile at least, another traipse past more iced-sugar frontages devoid of life or colour.

"I thought we were going home." Odd how cosy their anonymous hotel had come to seem after an hour in this blank townscape.

Nazir took Kitty's mittened hand in his. "Clear off if you're going to be so lacklustre, Renshawe. Nobody'll miss you. I'm still game and she reckons she knows where this Benskii character's stall is."

"His what?"

"Stall, stall, you know, barrow, pitch, retail outlet. He trades – on the street."

Once on the broad pavement which had been scraped clean of the under-snow ice, Archie could stride out fairly comfortably and followed the couple, keeping several yards behind, nevertheless, feel-ing sore at being inexplicably excluded from their private party. It was all the Slater girl's fault: if she'd only got out of bed at a reason-able time, the Karpinskii street-hawker would still be back at the tenement and might have offered them a cup of tea. He was dying for one now, even the milkless stuff served up in the hotel tea-bar. No cafés round here. Nothing. Just old folks with bags and kids lashed up like wobbly parcels against the cutting wind.

Kitty and Nazir suddenly pulled away to the left, off the broad sweeping road into a less imposing neighbourhood of crooked alleys and basement flats with grilles at the windows. It was quieter here, the howl of the traffic cropped to a buzz by the happen-chance lie of the streets which mazed deeper and deeper into the heart of the old city. Even the crowd on the sidewalks changed. Here every second person appeared to be foreign. Thronging amidst the *Glasnost* T-shirts and Texas Ranger boots Archie experienced a sense of solidarity with Kitty and her kin. If this was the new politics it felt like being on Leicester Square tube on Cup Final night.

The destination they were making for was a triangular patch of frost-bloomed grass, hard in the shadow of a rustic-hewn statue of a man in a cap. A mob of hawkers jostled round the plinth, swearing, wheedling, bargaining with the onrush of tourists who flocked round the monument fingering haphazardly at the goods on display. Ahead of him Archie saw Kitty drop Nazir's hand and plunge in where the crowd was thickest. In the blink of an eye she had emerged with a deathly thin girl whose apricot hair was pared down to within an inch of its roots. This was Karpinskii's girlfriend, Stassya.

"First you buy something," said Kitty. "And then Ben will speak with you."

Archie inspected the merchandise. "You want one?" he asked her, holding up a necklace of red and white beads.

"Buy," said Kitty impatiently. "It is expected."

The beads were rubbish, the cane tea-glass holders were rubbish: and the crudely painted brooches. And, like all street-vendors' rubbish, outrageously dear. He wanted to tell Kitty this but she had sidled away to stand at a distance watching and pretending not to watch. He bought a soapstone frog for the equivalent of thirteen pounds.

The transaction seemed to jerk Karpinskii's girl to life. "He is saving up," she announced in English.

"Is that right?"

"Yes," said the girl. "Quite correct. You don't believe me?"

Another female, much older, with frizzy bobbed hair, moved alongside and began to finger Archie's coat. The touch was fierce, almost possessive. She winked at the Karpinskii girl and muttered something.

"You don't believe me," repeated Stassya, this time not as a question.

The frizzy woman gave a sort of snarl and lunged at Archie's lapel with her teeth, then dabbed a kiss behind his ear.

"All right, all right," he said, backing away. "I believe you. He's saving up."

"To to go USA."

"OK, to America, so he needs it. So I bought his frog. OK?"

"You come from America?"

Kitty was over the road, out of reach, in the midst of a crowd of student-looking kids.

"No, I don't come from America, I've never been to America . . ."

He had one foot on the pavement, the other in the gutter when both women barred his way with their match-girl trays. "Kitty!" he called across them. But before he could finish a powerful hand had yanked him round by the collar of his Simpson overcoat, and Archie found himself staring up at a lanky young man in a black sheepskin jacket, whose eyes were a remarkable periwinkle blue.

If this Heathcliff-looking boy were really Ben Karpinskii he obviously wasn't pleased to see Mrs Slater. Deep in his stomach Archie experienced the familiar swallow-dive of apprehension: not another mad one, for God's sake, not another Verochka. Obedient to previous orders Nazir was at his elbow instructing Kitty to leave Archie alone for his talk with Ben, while Ben stood apart, looking insulted already, glaring down the side-slope of his long nose at Archie and muttering things to his punky-waif girl without creasing his lips.

Kitty tried to smile. "He speaks English," she said, under the smile. "Better than me, Archie. But only at bus-stops while he waits for the bus. He says it is only that way. Now I take Nazir. It is time for hotel lunch."

Archie complied cheerlessly and took off for a secure bus-stop with Ben and the girl. Two streets away was a glazed-in shelter awash with brown snow. This, he told himself was what he had come for. And, despite exhaustion, hunger and desperate queasiness at being abandoned to the care of these unpredictable strangers, he felt relief to be on the trail at last.

"I am here to represent Mrs Slater on a personal matter. You're not obliged to talk to me, but . . ."

"OK, OK. What you want? You some kind of policeman?"

"Her friends told you who I was yesterday, didn't they?" *If they'd got out of bed yesterday and could remember who they were when they had.*

"Yeah," drawled Karpinskii with uncannily hip American intonation. "I said already. They told me you were some kind of policeman." He suddenly danced round Archie splaying his bandy-ish jockey legs.

To a man the bus-stop crowd looked at their watches, their newspapers, the buses that weren't there; anywhere except at what might, at any moment, be transformed into what they spent their street-lives evading – an incident. Only Stassya watched, accustomed, and clearly fascinated by the mannered gestures with which Karpinskii reinforced his quaint American.

Archie stiffened against the unvandalised glass of the shelter. He'd been told that Slater had some odd contacts but this one was a public liability. Already the crowd was edging out of one corner.

Instinctively he made to join them, relying on their number to shield him before he made a run for it along the high exposed kerb.

The girl caught his arm. "No, no, you stay. He is serious boy. Professor Slater loved him very much." Her speech was measured, unaccented, BBC World Service. "He will tell you." Then she kicked rapidly and very hard below the washed-out right knee-fold of Karpinskii's right jean.

The young man laughed, scissored his legs one last time before the sheepish crowd, then lounged up to Archie brandishing his rabbit-skin hat in an exaggerated bow.

The humour of this transformation was lost on Archie who almost cringed but the crowd was so deeply gratified at the turn of events that a tall man in a navy-leather coat looked up from his book and winked at the back of Karpinskii's bare head.

"Some woman, eh, my woman? You wanna see her in bed."

"I beg your pardon," Archie began.

"Yeah," said the boy. "You wanna see her."

The girl slipped a gloved hand into the pocket of his padded jacket and smiled at Karpinskii, unoffended. "Don't mind," she said to Archie. "He doesn't mean this. He learns English from Slater."

"Videos," said Ben. "American. Jeez, I love that language."

A bus drew alongside and there was a scrum for the doors. When it pulled away they were three of a dozen still waiting.

"I'm cold," said the girl. Archie let her lead him back inside the shelter which was now empty except for an elderly couple with a child and the tall man who stood back to let them through.

The conversation about Slater continued. Yes, old man Slater had been Karpinskii's friend – Ben, please, yes, Ben, OK? – More than a friend, more – charitable, patronising. Right?

"Wrong," said Stassya. "Ben always says the wrong thing. This is his problem."

"I know," said Archie. But Professor Slater, he wasn't a problem? *No, no, no*, a good man, in Russian, *dobrozhelatyel*.

"His well-wisher," explained the girl. Who brought Ben things from abroad, nice things, expensive things; helped his career, used influence for him. Someone you could look up to, admire. Out of love.

"Benefactor?" said Archie at last, remembering Kitty's lopsided marriage in which Slater had maintained the imbalance out of sheer suffocating love.

Right. Slater was a great man, one helluva guy, sometimes a pain in the ass, but *so* distinguished. Ben had treasured the acquaintance (her version). Yeah – well, right – when he wasn't being a jerk (his).

"You see, he liked to fuck," said the girl rather wistfully, quite unaware of the impropriety of the verb.

"Her problem," explained Karpinskii. "He wanted to fuck *her*."

The next bus was boarding. Everyone got on except the old couple with the little girl, and the tall man.

Ben couldn't recall exactly when they met but it must have been sometime in his first year at university when Slater delivered a lecture series on the ethics of the Victorian novel. The lectures didn't interest him but Slater had kept open house in his flat; there was always decent food and a lot of drink. People came and went as they pleased. He showed films, too. Those nights you could hardly get through the door.

Archie glanced at his watch and suddenly felt immensely tired. Back at Lambert's he would just have been returning from lunch. Here, beneath the seamless bank of cloud he felt victimised by the queer muted light in which neither he nor his companions cast any perceptible shadow. Already the broad tracks of the boulevard were coalescing into a single thick smudge which ribboned down to the skyline.

Like a son, Kitty had said, this Karpinskii, not the tatty free-loader he was fast making himself out to be. The girl was different. He could understand what Slater might have made of the girl. An oldish man, his time running out, might have been very tempted to break into that. Had he? You couldn't ask.

"I'm sorry," Archie said to the boy. "I seem to have been mis-informed. I thought your relationship with Professor Slater was closer, somehow, rather special."

Stassya was quick. She noticed the shift to formality. "We must not part." She touched Archie's cheek with her loose hand. "Not like this." She must have read it somewhere, expropriated it from some romantic story, but because she used it now, imperfectly, the phrase assumed the force of poetry. Archie shuddered.

"Hey, man," exclaimed Karpinskii. "You gotta insult me? How you think it was – that I should let him fuck *me* instead?" He pulled away from the girl, stepped in and out of the shelter, pointing at his chest and repeating the same question indignantly, in English, to the blue-coated man, the old couple and, much to Archie's distaste, the little girl, who stared up at the young man impassively, twirling the tassels of her headscarf.

"Like a son," murmured Stassya using Kitty's exact words. "A beloved son." For a second time Archie shuddered. Through the glazed rear of the shelter they could see Karpinskii, arms out-stretched, violently shaking the iron railings which ran along the far side of the pavement. Ben was rude, she excused him, but then, he was sensitive, understandably so, because with Slater Ben had made the running. The man fascinated him.

A natural diffidence – yes, yes, it was true, in spite of appearances – prevented the boy from shining in the kind of distinguished company which Slater kept, so he took to following his professor round the streets until he became a nuisance. Late one night Slater, who had some experience of being followed in Moscow, cornered him in the Metro. When the truth came out, the professor was flattered. Ben was young, Ben was fun – that was obvious, wasn't it? For a while they went everywhere together – bars, restaurants (Ben knew all the dives) and the younger man was enchanted with his privileged new friend. Then Slater took up with some showgirl and dropped Ben, just like that. No explanation was necessary – everyone knew about Slater's girls – but Ben thought there was, and when none was forthcoming, he was devastated. The next thing they heard was that the professor was actually marrying his floozie – Ben always called her that. He had met her once, and an invitation arrived for the wedding reception. He didn't go, of course, but Slater must have had a fit of conscience because after the couple had returned to England Slater began to send out books for Ben's linguistics course, then letters. Somehow the friendship was renewed and when Slater came out last year it had become closer than ever.

Was Ben at the farewell party, the night before Slater was due to fly back? Not Ben. Much too shy of all those greybeard academics. The morning after he had gone to the hotel to say his private good-byes, but they told him that there had been some administrative mix-up and that the professor had already left.

How did he find out the truth?

"Oh, quite casually – from a girl on the desk." By that time the militia had come for Slater's baggage. They saw no reason to keep quiet about an old man's death. A heart-attack. It happened all the time.

Snow began to fall, a sprinkly dust at first, then fast, thick, cluttering the narrow space between earth and sky. The girl hammered on the shelter with her fists. "*Ben, Ben. Poshli! Avtobus prishol!*"

The boy came over, dragging his feet through the slush of melting flakes. But, again, it was not their bus, nor the blue-coated man's. The elderly couple waited until enough passengers had disembarked for them to board without the little girl's being jostled. "Bye, bye," she said in English turning back on the mounting step to take a last look at the strange young man who had rejoined his friends.

Ben gave a broad grin. "Byee, byeee," he called as the bus slithered away into the mainstream traffic, and he waved until the child's face was indiscernible amidst the fuzz of brake lights and fog lamps.

"You still here, man?" He turned to Archie. "You got no place to go? I got some place, she got some place, so why don't you just fuck off?" This came out accompanied by an expression of such total amiability that Archie began to see what Slater might once have seen in Karpinskii. He didn't talk to you, he used you for practice; to him, apparently, English was less a language than a repertoire of shocking things to say, the effect of which you couldn't judge except by saying them and watching the other person's face. Karpinskii was a child; an old man's child; a last child. Archie was beginning to understand.

"I'll stick around," he said.

"Whaddya know? He's gonna stick around," said Ben to the girl. "You encourage him, you dumb kid. She encourages you, mister police-dick, she's crazy. What she tell you, this crazy girl? About Slater? That stuff? You know something?" he went on, taking a sudden interest in Archie's fur hat. "You're a cop, right? Undercover, right?" Archie submitted. "OK," exclaimed Karpinskii. "First rule – never be conspicuous. See this hat?" Archie couldn't but he felt it being whirled back to front on his head. "A dick who wants to be private in my country, he learns which way round his hat goes."

This done, Ben Karpinskii sat down on the floor of the shelter and crossed his long legs, apparently satisfied.

"Thanks for the tip," said Archie.

"Aw, nix," said the boy. "What's it to me? Tips I give to Slater – d'you think he gave a damn either? He was the bastard who prided himself on never owing anyone. To think you'd done a favour made him mad, real mad. Then he'd spout horseshit about pride at being his own man. A mad bastard." For some minutes he was silent, pulling up the legs of his jeans to reveal the lacings of a pair of knee-high paratrooper's boots.

The boy's contempt for Slater seemed so genuine that Archie kept silent, anticipating a continuation of the outburst. When none came and the boy proceeded with great care to undo one boot after the other, Archie looked to the girl who had slipped back her headscarf and was absorbedly brushing her spiky orange hair.

Slater was devious, that was clear. Doing Moscow's night-life with a sullen adolescent lad can't have been much fun for a sociable intelligent man longing for female company. He was using Karpinskii. Poor little devil, stretched on the concrete, fiddling with his leggings like a destabilised Pinocchio, you had to feel sorry.

"Here." Archie dropped to one knee to help by threading the right boot while Karpinskii finished off the left. "Allow me." When the boy responded with a generous smile Archie thought, Slater, you knew what you were doing, Slater, you sod.

"He gave you money, your professor?"

"He gave nothing, *your* professor," said the boy without bitterness. "He made promises. And things – he made things, he made them up." The obsolescent Yankee flip had gone and Karpinskii began to speak like the girl, who, having tucked back her hair into the scarf, now stood with her back to them, cowled in the snood of her fur, watching the road.

"Like?"

"Like his life. Like a past. Like he was once very poor, a poor boy whose teacher encouraged him. Oxford. He talked about Oxford. Say – you know Oxford? I know Oxford from Slater. I bet I know Oxford better than you." Ben chafed his numbing fingers against the metal eyelets of the boots. "A hard life, Mr Slater said, a hard life teaches you conduct." He laughed and pointed to his chest. "He tells me this over and over, so I get bored and tell him back – what's new? All my life I've known this – chin up, chest out, look the world in the eye. Boy scouts. I know this already, I told him. Then he gets mad, like I said, and tells me stuff I don't want to hear."

Archie's boot was nearly done but he slowed, taking time over the final double knot. "What stuff?"

Embarrassed, Karpinskii reconstituted his accent. "Aw, the kinda stuff people say when they want you to think they're so *tough*. A load of rules: Never thank him, never admire him, he wasn't worth it. People weren't worth it. Once he'd admired someone a lot, some guy, even loved the freak, but they'd turned bad on him. Months I believed this crap, a year, more. See her?" He nodded at the girl's broad back. "It broke her up, me not trusting her either. She cried, gee, how she cried. And for why? For nothing. Only because old man Slater had found out he'd married a tramp – the little *russkaya* was fooling around, having a ball."

Kitty? Not Kitty. Archie couldn't believe it.

"Suit yourself," said Karpinskii, hauling himself up. "I copped out of Slater's mess a long time ago, like I'm copping out of yours, and that's my goddamn transport."

This bus was twice the normal length, newer-looking than the previous type, and split into two sections like an articulated track. The stop must have been a transfer point because twenty or more people clambered off, twisting back in the wheel slush to lift down suitcases, parcels, cardboard boxes, even skis. As the driver revved, fumes of unburned oil gassed from the double exhausts, rippling through the crowd and heightening the irritation. They struggled to clear their possessions from the roadway. At the front, a solitary unencumbered passenger sprang down the steps of the exit by the driver's cab; a cocky young fellow done up in a feathered pork-pie hat, nonchalantly chewing a toothpick.

At the kerbside, standing a little behind with Karpinskii and his girl, Archie suddenly spotted the blue-coated man who had been hanging round the shelter. This wouldn't have been his bus because the doors had already clattered to, and the driver was engaging gear ready to swing out of the bay, but Blue-coat jumped on the bottom step just as the gritted wheels began to hiss on the ice, and grabbed the chap in the hat, swinging him off his feet on to the sidewalk where they embraced, once, twice, slipping and kissing like lovers well met.

Evidently thinking he had made a mistake by stationing himself at the wrong end and not realising that this bus went off-service at this stop, Karpinskii dashed into the road and banged his little case along the nearside windows. In the crowd a woman gave a hoot of laughter. As the blow-back of fumes dissipated behind the retreating bus a ripple of contentment passed along the bystanders. Archie shivered and pressed closer to the girl.

Karpinskii was trudging back, head down, pressing the spring catches of his case. Caught in the spread of the lamplight, he hesitated and looked up. And with this look it seemed to Archie that the traffic noise instantly died and the attention of everyone present cut away to the hiss of the arc in the high lamp above the figure of the boy.

The girl stepped awkwardly off the kerb, stumbled and fell to her knees. Karpinskii saw and began to run towards her, away from the light. Nobody else moved except the blue-coated man who sprang from the embrace of his friend and leapt at Karpinskii over the kneeling form in the gutter. For a moment it occurred to Archie that man and boy must be friends; that they were rushing to greet one another; and he had time to admire the grace of the tall man's swing as he reached the boy in a hurdling stride which threw the whole weight of his body aslant the impetus of Karpinskii's run.

The girl gave a stuttering, hideous scream, tried to rise, but fell back against the snow. Why the boy went down Archie did not understand. There was only a hustle, a commotion of limbs swarming between the two at chest height to which the boy inexplicably succumbed. He did not get up. Perhaps he knew better than to try to get up. Perhaps it was better to allow what happened then to happen there, on the ground, the road running protectively under his back as he rolled over and over, under the lofting kicks of the blue-coated man.

Twenty seconds from beginning to end? Less, possibly, even than that. But enough for the boy to lose any sense of where he was, and who he was, and what would happen next. Archie did not know but the girl knew and had screamed because she knew. And the crowd was silent because the crowd also knew, and was waiting.

Blue-coat gave half a turn away, sought for his friend amongst the onlookers and having found him, smiled as he had smiled when they met on the bus. The boy rocked gently in his own embrace, making no noise.

An old yellow bus rattled round the curve of the slip-road sounding its horn at the obstruction. From the back of the shelter came a high-pitched elderly voice. Afterwards, when the girl had explained, she had remembered this the most clearly: "What d'you want to do? This is a human being. D'you want to kill this human being?"

Archie had pushed forward, dragging the girl to her feet. The bus lumbered on, flooding the afternoon twilight with its headlamps. The man smiled again, at the voice and them all and, with an act of supremely casual effrontery, sailed a final kick into the boy's half-open mouth.

Archie knelt in the gutter with Stassya. Around them, passengers were milling for the bus. No one paused. Blue-coat was last. He bowed low from the mounting step before the doors closed.

Karpinskii lay chest-up to the sky respiring his own lung-blood with the air and breathing out a froth of lavenderish bubbles which bletted pink on the snow.

"Don't try to move him," Archie said to the girl. "Wait for help."

"There is no help." Her tone was quite without rancour.

Archie took her scarf and bunched it beneath her boy's neck. The pupils of Karpinskii's eyes had diminished to the size of pinhead screws. "An ambulance. A doctor. Do you want him to die?"

"You have brought him to this," she said. And she did nothing for the boy except mop at his mouth with the silk-tasselled fringe of her bag.

Archie sprinted across the empty bus-lane into the main road where a long stream of traffic had halted for the lights. Banging on the nearside of cars and trucks he ran down the line until the driver of a minibus taxi leaned over and slid back his door. "*Shto ty suma soshol shto li?*"

Had Archie known what it meant he would have shouted back "Yes", at the moment he felt he was going out of his mind. Instead he began very loudly in English, "Someone's been hurt. ACCIDENT. Doctor. Hospital. Doctor, hospital . . ."

In the back of the van they sat opposite one another, Karpinskii laid between them on the metal floor. He looked bad.

"Just then I did not say the right thing," said the girl as the driver wove in and out of the trolley-buses jamming the route to the clinic.

"That doesn't matter. It was hardly the time to pick words."

Near the Old University building she tapped the driver on the shoulder and he pulled in opposite a tobacco kiosk. "This is very central." She opened the door for Archie to get out. "You will not have far to go."

From the kerbside Archie took a last look at her and Karpinskii. "What did you mean – you said the wrong thing?"

Stassya spoke through the gap of the closing door. "I meant you brought *him* to *us*, Mr Englishman. How can you bear to be one of that kind?"

14

Kitty slid closer to Nazir on the stacking chair and fingered the top fastening of his open Antartex. "We should not come to this place, Naz dearest."

They sat in the airless waiting-room of the subterranean police station and confronted a veined marble plaque extending from floor to ceiling.

"That Ben is hooligan, Naz. He does not tell Archie the buses."

The entire length of the wall was covered with similar plaques incised with shallow lettering. At intervals lists of names were broken up into groups, headed by various conventional symbols: crossed swords, little speedboats. Over the briefest list was the computer-disk radiation sign.

"You listen, Naz – at this time now Archie is not finding the bus."

"You're right," breathed Nazir. "He'll never find us here. They've brought us to a fall-out shelter."

Borka came in without introducing himself and demanded to know why Archie was not with them. Before they could explain Archie arrived, looking washed-out.

Kitty gave a cry. "Archie, you are so white. I think you are not well."

"I got waylaid." In the stale bunkerish air of the waiting-room he felt the colour draining from his cheeks. He turned to Nazir. "I've just had the worst experience of my life, out on the street."

Borka intervened briskly. "Wonderful, Mr Renshawe. You are late, but you are English, so I wait for you. Today, you have a moral experience on the street. Tonight, you will stop being stuffed shirt and understand even more about our country. Now, we go."

Kitty felt cold. Being afraid always made her feel cold and when she felt cold she felt hatred. She hated this oblong slab of a room with its surgical light and dead men's names on the wall.

Her access to Archie was suddenly barred by the fat policeman.

"You shan't stop me," she said in her quaint, southern-accented Russian.

Borka whistled through his teeth. "You are a good girl and understand that there are reasons why you must let him come with me. And I claim the authority to keep such reasons from you, and from him, and you know that I possess that authority."

Over by the door Archie and Nazir were muttering together.

"If you really care for this man," said the policeman, "it would be better if you left the explanations to me."

Archie had no idea of their destination. One part of this darkened city looked so like another, that it was almost bound to be indistinguishable from the rundown blocks of assembly-built flats which stretched ahead of the car, mile after mile, to a greeny moonswept horizon.

"All in good time," the fat man had said. And he said it so comfortably, transferring a pat from his own cheek to the Englishman's like a blown kiss between very good friends, that Archie fell in with his companion's lack of urgency and made himself as comfortable as he could in the cramped front of the little pug-nosed Lada.

At any event, Archie persuaded himself, Borka's invitation was a godsend after the disastrous encounter with Karpinskii. The policeman had whisked him away so quickly that he avoided talking to Kitty. She would have harassed him for an account of his meeting with Slater's Little Boy Ben. How did it happen, and why? As they overtook a bus slithering to a stop by a clump of young girls at the kerbside, he rehearsed the questions but came up with no reply, except that it had happened as it did and he was helpless to prevent it.

"Home sweet home," announced Borka out of the blue. Archie shook off his reverie and peered ahead.

The car was threading between the pillars of a narrow entrance to a tiny parking lot set about with what might once have been a lawn. Borka leant across to open Archie's door. "Not bad, not good," he said, indicating the entrance to a modernish brick-built apartment tower. "Rome was not built in the day."

"Or the night," murmured Archie, taking a closer look from the outside at the slapdash pointing of the porch.

"You are the guest," said Borka sharply. "Be polite. See here." He pointed to a row of balconies three storeys up. "All day she is cooking for the guest."

"I didn't realise you were . . ."

Borka jiggled his topboots on the lamed grass, centred his chest to the moon and breathed out expansively. "This is real Russian home. Leave everything to Mamochka!"

"And do you have any children, you and Mamochka?" Archie asked on the way up.

"Mamochka – yes. Only one!" exclaimed Borka, inserting his key in the lock. "Male, Caucasian, 220 pounds. You love your Ma, too, Archie Renshawe?"

With Archie gone, Nazir said, "What was the name of that girl again – the one with the plaits?"

"Klavdia."

"Klavdia. Is she on tonight?"

When Kitty turned in surprise the look in his eyes was narrow, dissatisfied, insolent.

"Again?" she objected.

"Yes," he said, taking her hand while they crossed the twisty side-street between chocolate-coloured buildings on their way to the Metro. "I like the way she can laugh about living in this place."

On the train Kitty stared at the old people, and prayed that God would spare her from living long. So many lies left to endure. That disgusting policeman whom Archie liked so much, he would make these people angry and afraid. Men of his kind never changed. He was making a fool of Archie by pretending to make a fool of himself. And now all Nazir wanted to talk about was Klavdia, the girl who did tricks.

". . . I love the skittery dance she does after the first interval, you know, the funny way she uses her hips . . ."

I should never have come down from the white mountains to this staid city where the red-legged scissor men murder children's dreams. I should not have come back because no one listens to me.

A bearskin rug hung above the wide feather-bed in the smaller room of the flat, nailed to the unpapered wall with blue-headed tacks.

"I shoot him for Mama," said Borka, proudly flexing the stiff fur at the neck to show where the bullet had gone in. "He makes her feel warm. One day she wants to be buried in him, would you believe?"

The other room was a little more spacious. Here, where Borka slept on an old Army truckle bed that packed away under the mahogany sideboard, Archie was introduced to his mother who rose to greet him from across an ancient pedal sewing-machine. They touched hands shyly. Archie called her madame, and she smiled. He was invited to look through a photograph album containing nothing but pictures of her son. In baby frock, shorts or his first long trousers Borka was recognisably the child of the man. In one picture, naked except for a towel and thick socks, he was skinning a bear.

When Archie lingered they formed a trio with him on the settee. "My God, once I was twenty years of age," sighed the detective. "Now the bear he is older than me on that day." He began a long reminiscence about the hunting syndicate he had once belonged to. His mother went away. Presently the smell of basting fat drifted in from the kitchen.

"What did you do with the rest of him?" said Archie, still eyeing the haunches of the upside-down bear in the photograph.

"Eat! What you think? Elks, too, boar-pigs. You want us to waste them?" From the window Borka pointed out quartered carcases hung in string nets from the balcony coping. "You look ill, my friend," he laughed. "In England you never eat from the deep-freeze?"

Before he took his seat at the kitchen table, Archie decided it was too late to plead vegetarianism. In front of him Mama Borka was already unmoulding an intensely dark-looking terrine.

"Wild ducks," said her son. "Very à la française. Wine French also, especially for you. Bottoms up."

The wine was Moroccan, tasting of cassis. A glass and a half fortified Archie against the pâté which contained tiny specks of pulverised bone. "Awfully good of your mother, all this . . ."

Between mouthfuls Borka relayed the compliment to Mamochka who shuffled up from the stove in her slippers to stroke Archie's hair with one hand, while with the other setting down a long wrinkly crusted pie that smelled of mushrooms. Archie did it justice. "That was superb," he said afterwards. "Tell your mother I really feel at home."

The fat man's eyes gleamed from the wine. "Now you learn to put up with us, eh?" He began talking about his labrador bitch that had died the Christmas before. Because he hadn't the heart to replace her hunting had temporarily lapsed. "Your country is the home of dogs. Perhaps one day I visit and buy retrievers?"

The old lady returned with a bowl of apple compôte and sour cream.

"I'd like to express my gratitude," said Archie. "Does she understand English?"

Borka got up, took the dish, whispered volubly in his mother's ear and sat down again. She leant over Archie and kissed him on the brow. "I – love – you," she said in laborious English. Then she smiled, more broadly than ever, displaying bluish-white false teeth. Embarrassed, but oddly pleased, Archie stood up and bowed, before getting down to the apples which his companion had already divided between them.

His mother out of the room, Borka slurped through his portion of fruit. "Mamochka is typical Russian," he said, pushing away his plate. "Extremist. For example, she will not permit smoking in the flat."

"That's all right. I don't."

"Me. I do. We go outside."

On the landing they stood at the top of the stairs by the lift. "Here it is different." Borka sighed. "Here we may talk unofficial."

It was very cold. Archie waited for the fat man to light up. The entire evening had probably been devised round this interlude.

"I would like to talk about a present problem." Borka replaced the cigar unlit in his top pocket. Although the approach was not unexpected Archie declined to co-operate.

"*Re-lax*. Perhaps you worry too much, you know that? You are perfect guest. Perhaps you worry about Mama too? Relax. Mother washes dishes every day, she washes now so that we can be alone. Man to man. *Re-lax!*"

With the chill off the shuttered concrete walls misting through his lightweight suit, Archie was finding it difficult even to keep still. "How many more times?" he said, jogging up and down on the brown linoleum tiles of the hallway. "I don't go poking my nose into other people's affairs just for the hell of it. I like to mind my own business."

"But, Archie, business is business all the world over."

"Don't you believe it, old chap. Not here it isn't. Not here."

This response obviously touched some chord in the fat man who suddenly grinned broadly and closed his fist round Archie's four-buttoned cuff. "Now for brass tacks, Renshawe my dear, how about this as they say – you scratch my back I scratch yours? Now I help you. Now I tell you something."

"And I thought your mother really liked me." Archie tried to duck the oncoming confidence with a Nazir-type disclaimer. "I should have realised you people are never off-duty. All that . . ." He waved towards the padded rexine door of Borka's apartment. "All that was just kitchen-Russian for tourists, wasn't it? If you want to talk shop then talk to your mother. I'm freezing to death out here."

"The wine has gone to your head, Archie, shush, shush . . ."

And Archie, in spite of himself, did quieten, conscious that beneath his companion's close, easy familiarity, there was now, as before, more than a hint of distance which imparted a weird severity to the fat policeman's toddler-talk.

"Shush. A man is known to me, this man is a dealer, dealer in all objects – drugs, women, stolen things – what shall I call such a man?"

At this Archie relaxed: Borka was educating himself. He wanted the slang. "Definitely rather shady, I'd say."

The fat policeman clapped his hands. In the corridor a woman peeped out from the last door but one, and quickly shut herself in again. "Wonderful, wonderful! 'Rather' – a tiny bit, given that way. Wonderful! There is more?"

"Pimp, pusher, fence."

"The Georgian fence, my Mr Zhikadze. Before I cannot touch him. But now," said Borka coming so close that he had Archie knee to knee against the entry wall. "Now, with you, I am hoping to catch this man."

"Me?"

"Each other, together. Us."

Beyond Borka's head Archie watched the outer door of his apartment swing open. The old lady stood on the threshold, her wide, blunt hands shiny wet from the dish-water, flapping at her son.

"Boris Kirillovich! Telefon!"

For a moment Borka seemed not to have heard and his mother stared, not at him but at Archie who was struck by the fixity of glance in the slanty clay-brown eyes which narrowed the stare to a studied expression of sympathy, as though he were a child who had strayed beyond call across a dangerous street.

The telephone conversation was brief. Afterwards Borka called out from the hallway, "Archie. Hurry. We make tracks *now*," before rushing into the bathroom and locking the door behind him.

The old lady helped Archie into his overcoat. "It's a pity we can't talk to one another," he said. "I never knew my own mother. Your Borka is a lucky man."

From behind she adjusted the hang of the coat, smoothing round the run of the collar into the high lapels. When he thanked her, using up almost all the Russian he knew, she turned him towards her gently, stood back a little to smile in acknowledgment, then squeezed his left wrist with both her hands in a final gesture, which, besides goodwill, communicated a sense of almost raffish matiness.

As he skipped down the steps of the emergency stairs – Borka was too impatient to wait for the lift – Archie could still feel the impress of her strong fingers. Once she must have been someone; someone really to know. He would rather have stayed.

By the time he reached the first floor Borka was at ground level, and a sudden rush of frost through the opening double doors whirled up the last bank of stairs making Archie catch his breath. He stopped on the turn and looked out from the half-flight window. Ahead of him, just in sight, Borka's bulky mass was ploughing a line through the new-fallen snow straight to a car in the forecourt. Not his car, but a Polish Fiat, parked askew the exit to the main road. In the glow of the headlights was a cluster of men in felt boots stamping down the snow and shouting at the oncoming figure.

The ring-mistress in stove-pipe hat and rusty frock-coat had the same horsehair moustachios she'd worn in Kitty's day, but now her own hair had gone completely grey. Kitty wanted to cry. The show, too, had come apart. Even Nazir sensed it, which was why, in Kitty's mind, whenever Klavdia rode no hands on her aged monocycle or the juggler managed not to drop her sequinned swizzle-sticks more than once, he clapped so very long and loudly.

Backstage, after the show, Nazir clasped Klavdia's hand and kissed it on the wristbone.

"Good Lord," she exclaimed to Kitty. "That's hasn't happened to me with a sober man since colour television. Are they all that nice where he comes from?" And the withholding, rather haughty expression that she had assumed at their dressing-room meeting quite disappeared and she became, in her violet slashed skirt and glass-beaded top, almost her old flashy self. "But listen, chick, are you sure it's safe to be seen around with you or your foreign pals? That crazy girlfriend of Karpinskii was here today full of woe. Apparently the pair of them were set upon in the street after rendezvous-ing this morning with some English detective."

Kitty put her hand to her throat but did not speak.

Nazir watched Klavdia's mouth as she talked, enchanted by the glisten of her heavily rouged lips. "Tell her it's on me. Champagne. Anything she fancies, so long as she laughs."

Kitty did so.

"Isn't he peachy?" said the girl. "But tell him a square meal will do, in case he thinks I cultivate this famished look for the good of my soul."

In the taxi she started to cry. "It's so awful to be alone when things are bad. We fight for scraps. Russian men are such predatory swine, I don't give a damn about loyalty now. If you want to get on or get out, pick an outsider, even the dusky variety." As they neared the hotel she repaired her make-up from a little vanity case. "Kat, promise you won't repeat what I said. He's really nice. I can't talk his language but I've only got four days to make him sit up and beg. I'm desperate. It's purgatory here. I can't stand it any longer and that's gospel. For the love of God, don't tell him, though, *pleee-eease*."

Before they reached the hotel she wept once again, more

controllably, affording Nazir the opportunity to put his arm round her waist and press his silk Dior handkerchief into her hand.

"I know it's none of my business," he whispered to Kitty as they bustled Klavdia through the lobby, "but what exactly is the matter with her? I'd like to help."

The doorman followed, demanding their passes. When Kitty swore at him in English very loudly, he touched his cap and withdrew. She would have liked to swear at Nazir also: yes, you can help, you silly devil of a man. Marry her. Tomorrow. That would bloody help. The girl is at the end of her tether. But he was an idiot, like all men.

In the lounge bar she tried to tell him what had happened to Ben but with Klavdia nearly in his grasp he was impervious to reason. "Muggers. Nothing sinister. The same the world over. If you think it's bad here, try Brixton on a Saturday night."

There was no sign of Archie. If she rang Dymka, would he spirit her away from this ghastly couple who were starting to do things to each other's knees under the table?

About the fate of Ben Karpinskii she dared not even think.

15

It was Vera's place. Surely. This is where he'd come the night before. Down the wide lane — you couldn't call it a street — to her tumbledown house at the end of the row, there, under a lamp, still shorting on and off in a burst of white sparks.

Archie strained into the dark for a glimpse of the familiar: the low broken wall down one side of the waste ground, a boarded-up gateway, a jagged fence. "Borka," he shouted above the howl of the disengaged clutch as the policeman fought the Lada across the loose pebbles of the unmade road. "Where the hell are you taking us?" But Borka's answer was only to skim his near wheels on to the concrete sidewalk and race the car at a sickening angle to the uprights of the fencing.

Finally they stopped and Borka sat tight, mumbling to himself in his own language. Without asking again, Archie shouldered open the door and squeezed himself out into a narrow gap between passenger-side and the timbered wall of a two-storeyed building. After the hot interior of the car the biting cold was refreshing. Above him projected a narrow balcony, also of wood. Leading on to it were three bay windows blanked by louvred shutters one of which had lost its restraining bar. Over time the slats had eased loose so that now, in the wind, they gave an unpredictable clatter which spoiled Archie's pleasure at the stillness of the night. Neither Borka nor the crew of the following car showed any sign of wanting to join him, and besides the snap-snap of the defective shutter the only sound that came to him across the snow was the ping of contracting metal as the bonnet hoods of both vehicles cooled in the frost.

Although Archie could hardly distinguish what sort of buildings these structures were, he knew instinctively that within their listing façades no light would come on and no one would emerge to investigate. The silence was too dense for habitation. And, for the first time since his arrival in Moscow, he felt secure. Professionals had taken him along for the ride; and the sensation of being quite without status in some important event in their lives was exhilarating. Because he knew nothing they had a duty to protect him.

He clumped down from the unlit vehicles, through well-stacked drifts to a tall stand-pipe situated at the crossing of his street with another which bent crookedly away on one side, and quite straight on the other. He was on a rise. To the right between more shed-houses, an uninterrupted view ran down to a wharf or embankment: against the creamy moon reared the black-iced struts of a crane. Not a whisper of life. The other way was the way they must have come. Vera's way. And, sure enough, there it was again, the crazy lamp, its pole hidden by the twist of the street, still blue-dazzling the panoply of white roofs.

Behind him something gave a sweet throbbing chirrup. The shock of sound sent him sprawling for cover before he remembered that, after all, he was not alone. He lumbered to his feet, feeling stupid and redundant in the faces of his escort, one of whom, a broad-cheeked lad in mufti, was leaning out of the driver's seat, a dog-handler's whistle in his mouth.

Borka stood astride, hands on hips, watching Archie return. "Who you think you are – Father Christmas?"

"Sorry. I got carried away."

"Before they don't like you, old boy – you know that? Now they will kill you, my skinhead Ivans, when you act silly arses again. Not nice people, eh? Like this one." He jabbed at the gabled posts of the balconied house with a dinky-looking automatic pistol.

The youngster in plain-clothes came up first, the skirts of his unbuttoned greatcoat swashing at the hard-topped snow. Ignoring Archie, he conferred with his superior for a moment, then whistled up the uniformed troops from the second car. At Borka's command they each unbuckled the belt strap of their own pistols, canted them high to pull back the sliders before replacing them, cocked but safety catch on.

Archie tried the door of the Lada.

"I lock it," grinned Borka. "Even round here. You never know. Now, Mr Renshawe, the man in the house, he owes us, so how you like to do some real business?"

Before Archie could reply the fat detective had thrust a heavy torch into his hand and was leading the way to the front porch. The tallest *militsioner* shouldered open the door and stood astride the threshold while Archie played the torchbeam up and down a narrow wooden staircase which ascended almost vertically from the dry-earth floor of the entry-way.

He took a step forward but the man barred his access and looked beyond him to Borka. A staccato exchange took place between the two Russians at the end of which Borka gripped Archie's elbow and gave a deep growl. "He suspects you. Anyone suspects everyone nowadays. I tell him you come as the observer. He tells me that is why he suspects you. Promise not to do any stupid things."

In the oblique torchlight the *militsioner*'s nose cast a pirate-patch shadow on his left eye socket. Archie promised.

They mounted the staircase in procession, Archie last, angling the torch to light the risers for Borka, the morose pirate and a couple more uniformed officers, barely out of their teens. A fifth remained on guard in the porch. When Archie looked down from the head of the staircase he saw the flare of a lighter as he lit a cigarette.

At the end of a long passage stacked with primed canvases and what must have amounted to thousands of books, the pirate tossed over a heavy bunch of keys to Borka and they waited in silence while he rattled about feeling for the right one. The door was iron with an insert of glass no bigger than a matchbox. Through it Archie saw light. Pistol held across his chest, Borka turned the key and gently pushed. The door swung open as if a watchful servant had anticipated their arrival.

It was the balcony room. Quite deserted but almost welcoming in the mustardy glow of an oil lamp set on a shelf beside the street window. Beyond it was a long-tubed astronomical telescope bolted to a table the legs of which were elaborately carved in the form of plumed female caryatids. Borka reholstered his pistol, went straight to the table, knelt for a moment, then rose to beckon the Englishman over. At the same sign the pirate and one of the youngsters retreated to the corridor, closing the door behind them.

Archie crouched into the shadow below the great table. The wings of the caryatids swept downwards to form a central pillar which supported the entire mass. There, where the feather-tips merged into a single swirl of intricate carving, he saw the head.

He had no knowledge of death. Everyone he loved had died in his absence, a long way away. He knew the reasons, of course: his father's long illness; the absurd accident which had killed his mother, but that was only like knowing how to turn the key in a lock, the mechanism of which should remain inaccessible to a person of normal curiosity.

Since Archie could not know what to expect, everything he saw was compelling, fresh and quite unalarming. The man's eyes, for instance, were long-lidded dark eyes, still open, finely set below the strong flat brow, staring back without looking, into the torchlight, dead and un-dead, like glistening snail-pods in their shells. He had evidently slithered to the floor from a battered chaise-longue where, in order to keep warm in the barely heated room, he had begun to wrap himself in the fringed batik coverlet, one corner of which had caught on the nose of a cherub ornamenting the back-rest. The tautening fabric had broken the man's fall and he lay not quite touching the boards, his body stretched lengthwise to the triangulated cloth like the sprit of a dhow sail.

He had been small, this man whose feet poked out rigid from his winding-sheet on the litter of tissue paper and shavings strewn across the floor.

Borka called the plain-clothes lad by name, and for a while all three knelt in silence around the body. Archie was nearest.

"Feel under," said Borka in soft-toned English.

"Under what?"

"Under *him*. He does not mind."

"But he's dead."

"Exactly so, Mr Renshawe. Tonight is his funeral, not yours."

Archie did as he was told. There was nothing to it except a sensation of weight quite out of proportion to the slight build of the man. At the small of the back his fingers closed on something hard and rectangular. Afterwards they passed it round in the torch beam.

"You know what that is?" said Borka.

Archie knew. Everybody knew. It was a toy bus, an old-fashioned horse-bus, die-cast, expensive. There were even little figures climbing the spiral steps to the open top deck.

Borka knocked the torch out of Archie's hand. "I wanted blood. Instead I find playthings. Kornei Ivanovich," he went on in Russian. "Perhaps we are not too late. Search the house."

They were almost at the door when the Englishman realised what was happening. "Hey! You can't leave me with him." But they could, bloody Borka could. The man was a sadist. "Hey! What if he's not dead? It can happen. I don't even know his name." The torch kept rolling nearer the body at every touch.

Borka gave a roar which sounded off the ceiling of the room. "*Zhikadze*, Yosip Stepanovich. But if he rises again – *Mister* to you, old fellow, remember."

His torch eventually recovered, Archie checked again, just in case. No sign apparent on the shrouded parts. As for the rest – no ligature, contusion, bruise. No trace of blood except a razor-nick below one earlobe. That had been powdered. A meticulous man, attentive to himself. Even the grip on the shawl thing looked dainty until you tried to separate finger and thumb. Archie had wanted to do it because he felt that the man would have wanted his eyes to be covered because the stranger under whose scrutiny he lay found them impossible to close, and the man would have done it himself had he realised the stranger's helplessness. Like Slater on the waste ground, junked, simply in occupation of space; once he, too, must have looked as pitiable an encumbrance, asking to be bagged and chuted. In the face of this, the knowledge that Zhikadze was a fraudster, a thief – everything that Borka had said – and more, brute, assassin, was as useless as standing over Slater's body sprawled among the half-bricks of that derelict croft and invoking his professorial dignities.

The lights came on, all at once, all around, in a row along the picture-hung wall and above from a pear-drop chandelier; and the first unmellowed objects which Archie had seen since entering the house was a stand of artificial purple tulips in a blue stoneware jar. Their hideousness made him feel human again. Despite his taste for antiques and collectables Zhikadze must have enjoyed a joke because the bad taste of the flowers seemed a careful affront to the elegance of the surrounding furniture.

Archie got to his feet, slowly brushing the dust from his knees. In this vaulted attic where book-cases and heavy elaborate dressers had been arranged, giving form to a space far too broad and high for comfort, he might have been in a church. From an apse-like recess at the far end a clock struck twice. A thin, homely sound, quite out of keeping. And somewhere above he heard the hiss of a faulty cistern. The noises lifted his spirits. Only a house after all. A squat in a basilica. How that would have tickled old Lambert! The furniture, too, was right up his street: pew-dark strapping pieces, fit for chapel. Some were damaged and marred by clumsy attempts at repair. The smashed column down one side of the mirror-fronted press had been replaced by softwood. And as he roamed amongst the pieces, Archie realised that as well as being a queer kind of home, this whole place had functioned as a depository and workshop. One archway led on to an elliptical alcove snicked away from the rest of the room by piles of rush mats twice, three times taller than Archie himself. In here the bulb of a hanging lamp had burned a hole through the shade and the lines of the floorboards looked skewed under yellow and scarlet stripes. The things in this part were pure kitsch: a bamboo cakestand with a tin-plate handle in the shape of a dolphin; nude onyx girls astride an ash-tray. Trashy, flimsy stuff that people turned out of cupboards when he used to serve distress warrants.

Borka came on him silently while he was riffling through the open drawers of a repro Second-Empire secretaire which was stuffed with sheet-music of some Russian's *Fantasiestück*.

"Browsing. A man of peace. Normally I like to see this, but be careful where you are putting your feet, my friend. A man's grave is here."

"Borka, how long has he been dead?"

The Russian gestured about him at the strange contents of the room. "Who knows? Maybe he came with the furniture. Never mind this detail. My men now search the building. My eyes are not so good. You search here."

"What for?"

"For me. For the clues."

With no idea of what he was looking for Archie fumbled around, opening cabinets and pulling out drawers. He found a box of chocolates, an air-pistol and a box of .177 pellets on top of a massive video. When he switched the set on two naked girls appeared, silent screen, doing things to one another with floor brushes.

"Good God above," he said very loud.

His noise caused another, also human but small and indistinct. Behind the video was a blond-haired lad of about six dressed in a powder-blue sailor suit. He was clean, rather plump and secured to one paw of an ebony sphinx by a silver-chain anklet.

"*Zdrastvui*," said the child sleepily. "*Gdye dyedushka?*"

At the sound of his voice Borka came over very quietly and pushed Archie aside.

"*Shokolade.*"

In response Archie wanted to touch the boy but the detective laid a hand on his arm.

"What's he saying?"

"He wants Grandaddy, then he wants chocolate."

"Who's Grandaddy?"

Borka turned to where the corpse lay under the table and spat on the floorboards. "Grandaddy is not. Grandaddy was. *Ponyatna?*"

Archie understood.

"Do not grieve for our Mr Zhikadze, a trader in many types of merchandise."

They fed the child chocolates one by one from the box on the video and watched in silence as he slid from the brocaded nursery chair and began to range a set of his soldiers along the ramparts of an antique toy fort, the interior of which was stuffed with imported chocolate-bar wrappers – Ritter Sport, Lindt, bitter Suchard. Archie knelt before the little boy and began gently clearing away the rubbish from the fort's tiny parade ground. At the back was a recess evidently intended for stabling the horses of the toy artillery train. Inside lay more paper, some sheets torn into longish fragments, others whole, neatly stacked above a tin of *Caran d'Ache* crayons which he only managed to pull out by dislodging the papers.

His eye was caught by snippets of English handwriting. " . . *Initially I thought her somewhat freakish* . . ." he read. "*Bitch! We never . . . God, such exquisite . . .*" Before his brain registered hand and tone he saw the name, and then more bursts of exultation. "*!!! Again and . . . !!!*"

"Fool!" Borka hissed in his ear. "Now cannot you see?"

The wind suddenly gained in strength flapping the pales of the broken shutter against the verandah window at the far end of the room and the golden-haired child reached out for the end of Archie's striped tie and put it in his mouth.

Slater. Papers, notes, a diary perhaps. There had been more. It was here. He scrabbled at the ripped-up sheets. "*Verochka's for 9 . . . She knows nothing, knew nothing . . . Nothing . . .*" Archie collected them all, even down to the smallest triangular flag which the child had cut out and pinned to the castellated towers of the fort where it now tremored in the draught like a minuscule pennant of war.

An hour later they stood in the snow watching a pair of female paramedics slide the black-bagged corpse into the rear of their ambulance.

The little boy sat astride Borka's neck unstringing the earmuffs of the detective's fur hat. Round his neck was Archie's tie.

"Will he be all right?" He stroked the child's uncovered head.

"He is lucky. He is fine. He will be taken in by good people. Other children stolen from deep in the country before him, they will not. Tonight he is lucky because you are lucky, too. All thanks to me, wouldn't you say?"

Feeling inside the pocket of his overcoat where he had crammed the remnants of Slater's papers and credit cards, Archie was nevertheless too wary of his companion to agree. "This was arranged beforehand. You knew I'd find them here." And, he added silently, you knew in advance that someone would be coming out from England to track Slater's last moves. Who tipped you off? Why were you so anxious to make my acquaintance?

"A put-up job? Yes, I am clever. I did not want this petty business of your professor interfering with my case." Far from triumphant, Borka sounded dashed. "But, no, I did not put those things in Zhikadze's room. It was not meant badly, but, I beg you, Archie, do not yet show those writings to Mrs Slater. She may be very angry."

Archie did not need to be reminded and his suspicions of both Borka and Kitty deepened. After all, only she had known where to find Ben Karpinskii that morning, and she had left well before the attack. Borka had surely known where to find Slater's cards and papers. Now Karpinskii was out of contention, Renshawe the only one still at large, nursing pocketfuls of Slater's lost manuscripts – the ones Borka and Evie Tremayne, too, did not want Kitty to see.

Deep play, Mrs Slater. But what is your game?

16

Klavdia spoke only Russian, but gazed at Nazir as if he understood her. "You know what gets me down most? Where I live. I have to live in this place twelve stops out by Metro. In summer it's the colour of cardboard. And the dust! Thank God for winter when I get back in the dark and can't see it. You ought to come in the day and take a look. It'd cheer anyone up, knowing they weren't stuck out there like I am."

Kitty looked at her watch. She was sick of translating. Later there was to be a cabaret, but at the moment it was too early, even for drinkers, and they were a party alone in the bar of the Starlight Lounge overlooking the city.

How Klavdia went on! Would Archie ever come? Each time she heard the elevator gates slide apart in the glazed assembly area behind her, Kitty did not dare look. She knew that if she turned round he would not be there. But turn or no turn an hour passed and still he remained absent. The heat! It was even worse up here than in her superwarm room downstairs. Her palms were humid from sweat. Perhaps she would fall in a faint? Better not. Eventually he would come as long as she sat with her back to the lift.

"Can I fetch you anything?" said Nazir, puzzled by her growing reluctance to translate anything Klavdia said except for the occasional "Yes", "No", or "Soon".

People were drifting in from dinner, unrowdy but elated, set on making a night of it. Soon the bar would be crowded.

"Cognac," said Kitty.

The amplified roxy-pop which had made conversation difficult died away and a saturnine young man in a white linen suit appeared on the round stage mid-way between bar and exit. He had a balalaika. The newcomers applauded. Kitty felt like getting drunk.

"Large!"

The man on the stage gave a peremptory strum on his balalaika and began to sing.

"Oh, God, it's him," said Klavdia looking as though the audience ought to be informed. "The one who fancies himself – I got on a tram with him once – you'd never believe what he tried . . ."

"There you are," said Nazir, placing a brimming glass before Kitty. "*Odin bolshoi!* I'm learning," he smiled, resuming his place at Klavdia's elbow and watching for Kitty's reaction. "The barman told me."

At least a treble. It was good brandy, and enough to get her started. Away from this silly couple who touched knees under the table, and the horrible moon-spangled ceiling, and the men-tourists in linen slacks downing Pilsner and cracking jokes about their ridiculous wives. The dark man in white was singing about a hill where he used to meet a girl on summer mornings. One day he told her that he was leaving her for ever.

"Typical," whispered Klavdia. "Smooth as they come."

But Kitty would have given anything to be the girl because the girl had stayed where she belonged. The earth under her feet was as much home as the wobbly newel at the top of the stairs outside the bedroom in Slater's weird old Clacton house had been Kitty's. She knew then that she was nearly drunk and, because she was, Archie would absolutely let her down, never arrive *ever*, and that by the time he did, she would be so drunk that if he didn't stop her she would do something so outrageous that he'd wish he'd never been born.

"Another!" she called out, waving her empty glass at Nazir. "*Yesh-cho odin bolshoi!*"

Nazir half rose. A tall man holding a wide bouquet of silk orchids close to his chest, came up to their table, bowed to the women and passed a remark in English which caused Nazir to sit down again, Kitty's glass still in his hand.

Klavdia touched Kitty's wrist. "Won't you just look at those flowers?"

There was no response.

"Sourpuss," whispered Klavdia. "If looks could kill! Aren't you going to invite him to join us?"

But Florinskii did not wait to be invited. He took the seat directly opposite Kitty murmuring, "*Katyushka, Katyushinka, Katya prily-est.*" Klavdia was thrilled.

"Another," said Kitty to Nazir. "Bigger."

Florinskii snapped his fingers. "*Champanskoye!*" The waiter came scurrying from behind the bar.

"Oo – ee!" squealed Klavdia. "Treats! Come on, Kat, why can't you be nice to the man – he was your man, wasn't he? – I mean, *before*?"

*　　*　　*

Kitty refused the champagne. She huddled back in her chair gulping down more of the Cognac which Nazir felt obliged to provide. He had sensed her mood, and had already learned early. One cross word and she could cause a riot. Besides he was making progress with Klavdia, and since this Dymka guy seemed only too happy to act as interpreter, he should make more before the night was out. So he left Katya-Katyushka to sulk while the conversation burbled on merrily, in English, in Russian, sometimes in both.

Kitty hated them. She was pleased that she hated them. She was pleased with the brandy that allowed her to hate them. Brandy never consoled, Slater used to say. But who except fools desire consolation? But their talk! It flew with the wine, freer and freer. So commonplace, so vulgar, the ghastliest chit-chat. Dymka asked for Nazir's impressions of Moscow, and Nazir enquired if Dymka had ever been abroad, and Klavdia expressed a life-long desire to see the Taj Mahal. Everyone agreed with her that India must be very hot, especially in the summer.

The subject of heat gave rise to indecent jokes between Klavdia and Dymka who interpreted them to Nazir, embarrassing him so much that Kitty almost intervened. Noticing her fury, Dymka shifted ground to the general question of pitfalls in translating from one language to another.

They were making a lot of noise. People turned to look. And Kitty found it almost unbearable.

Dymka was a perfect swine. She had expressly invited him tonight in order to tell him, once and for all, that she did not love him. But there he was, laughing, showing his fine white teeth, allowing her no chance to be serious.

Now she hated the others less than him. "I am feeling rather unwell from the noise," she said to Dymka in Russian. "We must find a quiet place to talk."

Klavdia stopped giggling and looked at Nazir as if afraid that he too would go with them. But Nazir did not want to break up the party.

"Are you all right?" he said to Kitty. "Take it easy, I'm sure Archie will be here soon."

At her side Dymka stiffened, but said nothing. He would not run away, not before she said what she wanted to say. She put her hand on his shoulder and murmured in English, "Nazir, M. Florinskii and I must talk a little, more private. We have business. Unfinished."

"Katya," whispered Dymka, also in English. "Remember. I have come here tonight because I trust you."

Kitty got up slowly, and Nazir too rose, also speaking of trust.

"Archie said I shouldn't let you out of my sight. Can I trust this friend of yours?"

Dymka smiled. "You may trust me with her life."

The balalaika man had left the stage and, for a moment, the crowd at the bar was almost silent, waiting for the next thing to happen. Nazir was not a fool. He was not unhappy to be left alone with Klavdia, but had she been only a little less inviting he would have had second thoughts about the diplomat, who led Kitty into the night with the air of a man who had already settled something of great importance.

Outside, on the pavement, Kitty recovered her good nature. In the car Florinskii came straight to the point. "The old man's taken me under his wing. He'll see I get what I want. One grade up and I'm at principal level."

Had he not noticed how drunk she was or was he drunk too?

He did not seem to care that she was scarcely able to take in a word. Watching his lovely forehead in the driving mirror she wished he were uglier, and that she were more sober and therefore less easily swayed.

"He's simply waiting," said Dymka.

"Where?"

"It doesn't matter *where*. The point is – he's waiting."

Kitty caressed the velour head-rest with her cheek. In the refracted street lights his silhouette seemed to crease and shimmer. "Who is waiting?"

"Oh, don't be so stupid, Katya – my departmental chief, of course. You must remember Abramskii."

She remembered Abramskii. He was fat. His hobby was cooking. He had written a book on milk puddings. She giggled. "Then let him wait."

"You're not listening, Katya. I want you to listen." How patient Dymka could sound. But that wouldn't last long. "It's entirely in his gift, you see, but first he must know how I measure up to things." Oh, how beautiful his hands were. "This is my big chance – a posting. Abroad."

"Come and see me," she murmured. "Abroad."

He pulled out suddenly to overtake a cement lorry and cursed when the automatic kickdown failed to respond, leaving him nose to tail with the truck for a long stretch of boulevard.

"For pity's sake, Katya, pull yourself together, talk sense. This is no joke. The old man is waiting for me to settle down with the right woman before making up his mind. It's marriage I'm talking about."

"Is she nice, this right woman?"

They stopped at the lights on Kropotkinskaya, still behind the truck.

"You shouldn't drink, you really shouldn't," said Dymka sounding his horn the moment the lights changed to green. "Last night you were sober, you believed what I said. I need you, Katya, I need you . . . I must have you back . . ."

"Something would be bound to go wrong." For her it always had. Why not for him? Just because it never had, so far? Dymka thought so. His life got better and better. Take the car, for instance. She had never been in such a luxurious vehicle before, not even in England.

She heard herself sounding incoherent. "Dmitry Pavlovich, is this a proposal?"

Red came up, then green again. Dymka kept his hand on the horn. The truck remained stationary. At the next red a workman in a sleeveless body-warmer got down from the truck and began to kick the rear-axle stub.

"Of course it is, you stupid little bitch," Dymka shouted.

The workman rapped on the car window. Dymka opened his door. The workman saluted. "Got a tyre lever, mate?"

"Dymka, my love," whispered Kitty. "All my life I've tried to belong and I've always failed. I'm no good for you. Wouldn't it be better now that we were simply friends?"

By this time the truck driver had also clambered down from the cab.

"You do not need me. You will get your chance," went on Kitty. "Someone better than me will come along and you'll have your post in America."

"What's up?" the driver asked his mate. They were both staring at Dymka.

"He's going to America, but he won't take her with him."

"Bastard smart-suit," said the driver, bending over the man to take a long look at the woman. "I know the type. You're better off without him, love."

"He hasn't got a tyre lever, either," said his mate.

"Dymka, we cannot talk here – take me back to the hotel . . ."

"Hasn't got much else either from the look of him," said the truck driver standing back to size Dymka up. "Bound to be a disappointment. I'd give him a wide berth, dear, hotel or no hotel."

Both men glared as if the diplomat had insulted them. Behind, the line of stationary traffic steamed in the bitter night air.

"I'm not talking about an affair, woman. I'm talking about love, marriage," exclaimed Florinskii, his door still partly open; and, selecting "Drive", he wrenched the wheel round, and thrust hard on the accelerator. With the snarl from its faulty gearbox the automatic leapt diagonally into the off-side lane, and collided with a tow-bar bolted to the rear of the truck.

The driver strolled up to where Dymka and Kitty stood examining the damage to the car.

"Don't say I didn't warn you, dear," he said to the woman. "Your American's just vandalised state property. I'll have to report him."

They returned, not to the hotel, but to the flat, Dymka's flat. After abandoning the car in the middle of the road, doors open, its engine still running, he had dragged her across the central reservation and flagged down a taxi going in the opposite direction. When he gave the address, Kitty had protested until Dymka took her hand and crushed her fingers together so hard that the diamond cluster of her engagement ring cut into the skin. After that she knew further resistance was useless, and sat back, transferring the bouquet of flowers to her unhurt hand, resigned to the inevitability of yet another confrontation with this man who had never learned to take no for an answer.

Despite her fears of what Dymka might do after she had rejected his proposal, Kitty had rather enjoyed his embarrassment. The truck-men had been fearfully rude, even obscene, when they discovered he held an official position; and it was pleasant to see Dymka nervous for once, quite unable to trade insult for insult with the two burly men who found her so evidently vulnerable that, if she'd asked for protection, they would have knocked him to the ground for her, on the spot.

Nevertheless, as they drove to the flat in dead silence she prayed that he was brooding more about the accident than about her, but with such a man how could you know what he was thinking?

The moment they came through the door he went on the attack. "I made you an offer. An honest, respectable offer. Why don't you believe me?"

"I believe you," Kitty said, caressing the waxed silk flowers at her breast. "I am so tired. Will you make me some tea?"

"Why don't you believe me?"

Over and over.

Still holding the bouquet she sat down in the same uncomfortable chair she had chosen on that last disastrous occasion. She should never have allowed herself to be persuaded again. It was madness. "For pity's sake, don't be unkind, Dymka dear. Leave me be."

For once he did as she asked, and left her. From his swish bachelor's kitchen came the clash of spoons and saucers. "*Avec de la confiture?*"

"*Pas de confiture, Dym.*" Practising his examination French had once been a pet-game between them, and with the words came the inevitable onrush of sentiment. Because he was different and she was not herself, Kitty wanted to remember him *then*, as he had been, pitiable, endearing and unchallengeable. Not the man who had to trick her back to his expensive flat in order to "discuss matters". Things which all along Kitty had been clear-headed enough to perceive were things concerning Dymka alone; a plan born of some desperate calculation which, from the start of the evening, he had before his mind and which the collision with the truck seemed to have intensified.

"Isn't serious – the damage?" she said when he came in.

"Bad enough but less than meets the eye. We can patch it up."

On the tray was one cup of tea already poured. Kitty relinquished her flowers. "Are you sure?" she said. "It looked quite extensive." Her hand wavered as she picked up the cup and put it down again almost immediately.

"Drink your tea, Katya. I made it because you told me to and you know how I hate to be ordered about." He banged the tray with the flat of his hand. Splashes of tea flecked her bodice. Miraculously the cup remained upright. " 'Free-and-easy Katyushka, the slut with soul' – very available nowadays. Isn't that how they see you, for instance, your precious circus pals – *for instance!* For instance!"

"Who? Who could say that? Dymka, why are you frightening me by telling me these lies?" She watched his hands, the slow, heavy way he had with them, straightening the fingers away from the lie of his palm, and, for the only time in her life with him, she was truly afraid.

"*For instance* – that Detective Superintendent English creature."

Kitty breathed out in relief. "Oh, Dy-mka, is that all? You don't understand. He's nothing but an employee, a man who runs errands for me."

"You employ policemen? You expect me to believe this – in my country, our country – you pay wages to a foreign policeman?"

"It isn't what you think."

"He isn't your lover?"

"He isn't a policeman."

"He isn't a policeman but he is your lover?"

It had been stupid to feel afraid. How could she fear him, this man who had been little more than a youth when she had almost married him. "I have no lover, Dymka."

"He was in your room last night, after you left me?" Dymka smiled at her surprise.

"How can you possibly know? You weren't there . . ."

"Ah, my dear, don't be so naïve – in the hotel business there are many devoted employees who do not even have to be paid."

He stared at her obsessively, his face too close; by turns savage, mocking and mad. She looked back because without leaping sideways there was nowhere else to look, but she tried to appear helpless in his gaze as though he were making love to her. And she could not remember ever having been young, or free of the anticipation of death or the pang of dereliction which came over her at the memory of Slater. Death was like opening a door into another room, someone had said at Slater's funeral. What fool would walk into a room where the door became part of the wall the moment you turned your back?

The door behind Slater was shut fast on him and her. There was no astral regression through chinks in the brickwork. She was out of bounds to Dymka; and he knew it, poor love; but before the sense was full he was going to pour himself out slowly before her, like honey from a bottle.

17

B y the time Archie got back to the hotel it was two a.m.
The lift stopped two floors up without opening, returned to
street level, then began to climb again. He found the floor number
on the console and kept his thumb over the button until it stopped
again at floor twenty-five. He walked down ten flights.

His door opened at his touch and Nazir stood in the hall-light,
naked as a baby.

"We thought you were hitting the night-spots, Renshawe. You
could have bloody warned me."

A scuffling noise came from the double room before resolving into
a feminine squawk.

Archie suddenly felt very frail. "For Christ's sake, I've paid money
to sleep here. Get her out."

Nazir slammed the bedroom door with a backward kick of his
heel. "Have a heart, old man. What did you expect me to do – watch
TV till you got back from the job? You know how it is – a few
drinks, a bit of this and that, and before you can say . . ."

"Get her out! I'm dead on my feet. Get her out now!"

"OK, OK. We'll buzz, we'll buzz, but do me a favour, Arch, give
us a chance to get dressed. This one's serious." Nazir's voice became
lower. "Modest, you know, not in the habit of . . ." Archie took a
step towards him. "OK, enough said. What the hell – I'll fill you in
tomorrow, but be a white man and slip into the bathroom while I
take her through. A shade retarded about nudity, your average Russian, or so I'm told." He grinned down at his own slim, dark form.
Bare feet pattered on the tiles of the bedroom floor.

"Two minutes, you horny black goat, otherwise she'll find herself
three in a bed." Archie shut the bathroom door and sat down on the
WC.

Nazir hadn't said who she was. It could be the guide, Maroussia,
Lyudy, Kitty. Ah, Kitty. It might well be Kitty. Archie wouldn't put
it past him, or her. Did he care at this precise moment? Did he hell.

Exhaustion, and the feeling of continuous unease which had begun
on Day One, rendered him almost exalted: Kitty's gone to bed with

Naz. OK. He addressed his profile in the mirror-tiles above the bath-tub. You couldn't blame her. Look at you – stubble-chin, haggard eyes, crumpled shirt, no tie. That suit would never be the same again, either.

Through the flimsy partition he could hear Nazir soothing his woman with loud purry hoots. The answering rustle of bedsheets and clothes made Archie feel suddenly very sexy, but after a final glance at his reflection he turned to his shirt cuffs and began to extract the gold links. Bloody stuffed shirt. That's what Borka called him. That's what Kitty probably called him.

He banged on the wall with the base of Nazir's tooth-glass.

When his colleague put his head round the door, Archie was already under the shower. "I hoped I'd seen the last of your black behind," he said, fumbling for the soap.

Nazir handed it to him, then began to arrange the discarded clothing along the chrome towel-rail. "Well, we're off, then. You look a mess," he said to Archie's reflection in the washbasin splash-back. "What happened when you went away with that copper this afternoon? I was left with a lot of explaining to do . . ."

"Never mind that. Clear up the beds before you go. I'm not sleeping in your polluted sheets."

"Thought you were all-in, old lad – and what's a bit of crumpled linen between friends? Anyway, you're not exactly a novice at that kind of game. Just because I fancy the sensitive types too, you reckon you can barge in on me willy-nilly."

Was it really Kitty? Archie felt too glum to ask outright.

Crouched beneath the tepid shower, hosing off the sweat of a Moscow day and night, he experienced guilt. Karpinskii had been deluded about Slater. Slater had slept his way round Moscow, deluding Kitty who was probably doing it to him as well as having it done to her.

In bed he tried to sleep but behind his closed lids the day came up, fragments of colour: Kitty's eyes jade against the snow, the jaunty line of Karpinskii's cheek dappled red from Blue-coat's lunges, the dead antiquarian shawled in his Rajput blazon, the silver-white child.

Twice he shifted, switched the bedside lamp off, then on. The day had gone too far to be overcome. For a while he lay motionless trying to cajole away thought but the image persisted, and he decided to make himself physically busy by punching up the bolster and re-laying the sheets. Soothed by the new order around him, Archie looked for occupation.

Then he remembered Slater's papers.

* * *

After an hour Archie had mastered the handwriting. At first it was daunting – very small, cramped, running out of space all the time as if the man had hated to waste the paper he was determined to fill. Hard to find the thread.

The stuff at the beginning was routine: notes for a lecture – Pushkin on Tacitus, the Russian angle. Quite interesting once you got the drift. The prospective audience obviously needed spoonfeeding because Slater kept writing questions to himself between the lines: "*(too abstruse?)*", "*(use simpler approach?)*". The notes stopped abruptly at the foot of sheet two, and were succeeded by thirteen immensely detailed pages of conversation between Slater and a VS.

The style here was quite the reverse of the previous: very unbuckled. A feisty old boy – Karpinskii's girl had been right – not one of your sub-fusc prose artists like Sir Evelyn. This professor evidently wrote as he'd lived, heart and soul in every sentence. Even the punctuation looked throbby. There were dates, sometimes only the month – October and November mostly: occasionally seventeenth, eighteenth, twenty-first. But never the year.

"*I wouldn't have dared ask for more but could I stop her? No! Wonderful! Yes, yes, yes!!!*"

This preceded a string of similarly excited remarks extending lengthwise to the diary entries down one margin of each sheet: left for odd numbers, right for even. Because the writing was larger and clearer Archie read these first.

"*Blondish. 20s. Again and again and again.*" Three downstrokes. "*20.x – again! cf. 27.x.*" Sure enough in the margin four pages on: "*Tired. Less resilient. Jaded?*" A single downstroke. "*Cf.29 x. Red-head, over-waved hair. Persuadable eventually. Came like wolf-bitch. Felt at height of powers.*" Four downstrokes, very deliberate.

Archie examined the diary entry opposite. This was quite different in character: "*VS rather reluctant, but I explained the position. Nowadays her recall less forthcoming than in the old days. Rusty, out of practice. It has been a long time, that was the problem. Eventually agreed on whole day, 25.x. Arshino, free of distraction. 9.38 p.m. Down platform.*"

Archie went through all the other entries for the fortnight from mid to late October. Each was extensive. Slater had spent day after day in conversation with VS who seemed to be some kind of naturopath because there was learned talk about wild plants, herbs, hidden fruits of the forest. While Slater made lists of their Russian names and English equivalents, VS reminisced about expeditions deep in the country, thirty, forty years before – at which Slater and people known to them both had gathered cuttings and specimens. He was clearly trying to draw her out. "*Why was X always so reserved? Was Y never indiscreet?*"

As Slater, according to the marginalia, plainly still was. "*At – all afternoon. Relaxed with Marya, the brunette. Wildly drunk. Can't remember except that she wouldn't give way. A beautiful savage caught in a trap, claws out, tormented and tormenting. Next day – only dyspepsia!!! Can't behave decently when drunk. But can't find the nerve without it.*"

Drink evidently affected performance. Two strokes only. Meanwhile VS was becoming a trial. "*Harps on. Obsessed today with horoscopes. The exact time and place of my conception. As though one could have asked! But 'nothing is accidental. Therefore no regrets'. Has deteriorated into egocentric fatalism without realising what a ghastly laughing-stock she has become. Boring, so boring, my God!*"

So VS was a woman. But well past her prime. "*The years have taken toll. Recall the time when poor old V wasn't like this!*" No strokes for V then. What can he have seen in her?

The writing bit blacker as Slater resumed conversations with his elderly lady. VS had come down in the world. Once she had been a woman of consequence, courted, lionised, even. Now, after some kind of breakdown, she existed chiefly on memories but had the knack of retaining names and a feel for the long-past situations in which Slater had some inexplicable interest.

Other initials began to crop up: "*Dr Y quietly informative: A remains as usual. B smoked incessantly and complained of being ignored.*" Towards the end B appeared almost as often as V. An erratic, demanding type, given to moods. "*Hoping to obtain his invitation to Paris colloquium.*" A man at last. *B.* B for Ben. Archie remembered Karpinskii.

Kitty might have known these people. For a moment he dwelt upon their brief closeness when she had written out the names of Muscovite friends with that same fat black and gold pen which Slater must have used for this diary.

Back in the margin things were hotting up. Early in November Slater appeared to be losing his touch. "*Sick to death of her flirting. Decide to keep my distance, then she'll come running.*" The scrawl was wide and topped off by exclamation marks stabbed clean through the paper. The teacher in him.

It evidently worked. A few days and he was back on form. "*Rendezvous at V's. Total surrender. Bliss.*" This time Archie did not count the strokes. Whoever she was she wasn't unique. He isolated at least a dozen encounters, each with a different woman. On one occasion, two on the same day, double-marked, morning and afternoon. Always at V's place. What did *she* do during these high-jinks? Participate? In the heat of his bed Archie shuddered.

Towards the end of the month a new initial appeared, T. "*Mustn't get carried away. A job is a job. T thrives only on fact. Every craze, every enthusiasm, however apparently innocent. Keep her talking, talking. Something is bound to crop up. So far nothing except the girls. Enjoy yourself! she insists. 'Take the fun while it lasts!' Uneasy, but co-operate.*"

You bet, thought Archie. T had scruples, though. "*T doesn't appreciate that aspect of life.*" Slater had no such misgivings. "*12.xi. Marvellous. Felt 21 again. Five times!!!!! B buys flowers. Owe thirty roubles.*"

Sick of initials Archie decided to christen T Tutu and VS Viki. By the middle of November the professor's private life was clearly out of this world, but Viki had wilted. Another breakdown, it seemed. Tutu became very pressing. "*Two messages uncharacteristically insistent. T wants the lot. Not a care that V's mind is at risk.*"

Archie got up and went to the bathroom for a glass of water. Between them Slater and Tutu must have been driving the old dear mad. Tutu wanted something very badly from her. Mistake, inadvertence, confidence? The pursuit of information formed the bulk of Slater's diary, but Archie couldn't tell what Tutu was after. Neither, evidently, could Slater. Tutu was looking for something, the significance of which he alone would be able to discern. Slater, consequently, could not afford to miss anything out. Hence the boredom and complaints. Like Archie himself he was working in the dark to a commission. "*Several calls to and from London. Discreet reassurances offered but everything put down to special pleading as if I were in a deep game of my own. No excuses accepted for an overwrought VS. Mystified and exasperated. Beginning to feel v. afraid.*"

The remaining pages were taken up with the professor's accelerating tension. Pressured by Tutu's threats and blocked by Viki's neuroses he had evidently become desperate. "*Can't sleep. Think I'm being watched. Search revealed nothing. T says imperative I find material but won't specify what. Yesterday even suggested I contact police!! Not a word of this before I came here. Now, life or death. A nightmare!*"

Was VS easing the strain by providing him with women? Was it her means of a livelihood? Or had she thought he could be diverted from the task which he was under such pressure to complete? If so, she had reckoned without Tutu whom Slater feared with utter conscientiousness. "*No result, no future. His words. Death, or ruin, or both. Got away with similar for forty years. Ruthless.*"

Although the nature of Tutu's quest remained as elusive to him as it had been to Slater, Archie read through to the end of November when the diary suddenly stopped. He had expected mention of Kitty. There was none. The final lines. "*For other eyes recast diary in acceptable style and write report before destroying originals. One last meeting. Official arrangements to send this out. Defy T!!!*"

Two hours after dawn Archie awoke very hungry. He lifted the telephone receiver, dialled room service and spoke the only Russian which Kitty had ever taught him. "May I order breakfast?"

"No," said the voice.

In the little refrigerator were the left-overs from Nazir's previous night's entertainment: a jar of pickled herrings and a packet of airline biscuits. He opened the jar with a five-kopek piece and ate with his fingers. His sleep had been short but undreaming. After that and the scratch meal he felt recovered, almost brisk.

Nazir had failed to return. For all Archie knew he and Kitty could be married by now. Then let Nazir stand the racket and pocket her fee. Archie had already made his own decision. One official call to the Cultural Relations Section would rid him of the chronicle of Slater's indiscretions. They could decide on its suitability to be forwarded to Tremayne. Then, the airport, where Russian or no Russian, Archie intended to book himself out on the first available flight.

The telephone sounded several times while he was dressing but he ignored the buzz. His last job was to re-assemble Slater's papers before sealing the entire sheaf in a portly manilla envelope, the defunct credit cards clipped behind the lecture notes. Address? What was the point? They all knew one another, these people. Sir Evelyn's name would be enough. Lambert would reimburse Mrs S for monies advanced. Duty discharged, Archie was free.

Having packed his bag, he stretched for a moment along the hessian cushions of the single easy-chair, watched the snow clouds bloom above palace cupolas and thought fondly of the sleek paving-stones of Endymion Road.

The telephone started up again. Outside, someone began hammering on the keyplate of the door. Archie quickly stuffed Sir Evelyn's envelope into his travel bag and secured the zip by its padlock. Then he slipped the catch of the door and peered out.

"*Do svidanye,*" said a tall dark man moving closer. "Florinskii, Dmitry Pavlovich. Pleased to make your acquaintance, Detective

Superintendent. I am Katya Slater's lover. Would you please tell me what you have done with her?"

They went to the park.

"In a place like that you do not know who you are mixing with," Florinskii said, waving an Orkney-tweeded arm at the high curve of the hotel esplanaded before them across the busy road.

At the entrance to the underpass Archie had refused to go down the steps until his companion had once more insisted, this time with a gun. Archie thought he was dreaming but it felt real, poked in his side through the lining of his companion's raglan.

Which was why they were walking here together, along the broad walk, past busts of deceased rocket designers and astronauts, with Florinskii clacking away like some pensioner on the municipal bowling green.

"Katya ran with me from the company in this hotel. Then she ran away from me, also, into the dark. She was beyond reason, intoxicated. All night I have searched for her, for you, the whole night. In that place, all other places she might be – with friends, the circus, then back here again. I adore, adore her. Where is she?"

Although he spoke almost without accent and was dressed in expensive English clothes, his manner and speech were so brigandish that Archie felt obliged to consider him one of those foreigners whose passions might cause blood to be spilled. Instead of answer, therefore, he gave a grunt.

The noise seemed to exasperate Florinskii even more. "Although Yekaterina Aleksandrovna is a fastidious woman, Superintendent Renshawe, there are times when even the most fastidious woman is obliged to make use of men in your position, mere operatives. But the fact is quite without social significance. Do I make myself clear?"

Sir Evelyn could have put it no better. "Perfectly."

"So what have you done with your mistress?"

"Client."

Florinskii showed his teeth, literally. "Client, customer, dupe – you think I care for your jargon? Where is she?"

Archie exhaled very deliberately. "Calm down," he said as much to himself as the diplomat.

Florinskii hurled aside the cheroot he had been smoking. It fell at the feet of an old woman in a shawl delving for empty bottles in a snow-topped litter-bin.

"Calm! Calm! What can you know of deep feeling? A man of your sort would butcher children for money! I repeat: where is my *affianced bride*?" His shout startled the old woman who looked from him to the still-smoking cheroot.

Affianced bride? That was news, Archie thought. And very quick work. If this man were speaking the truth then Renshawe, the hireling, had indeed neglected his duty by sleuthing around with officer Borka last night, thinking how clever he was to have secured Slater's diary. In his absence Kitty had been driven by God knows what impulse to become re-involved with this badger-toothed creature.

The thought recurred that last night had been planned in advance. Why else should Borka have let him hold on to Slater's papers? "Kitty paid me to know where she was at every moment of the day. It isn't entirely my fault ... but someone's been ..." *Pulling the wool, Archie, pulling the wool?*

"Hah! So you admit it?" But Florinskii sounded untriumphant, in effect, slightly dashed. Largely because at that moment the old woman chose to shamble up and offer back the cheroot with her blessing. While the diplomat fumbled for small change, Archie had time to contemplate the whole duplicitous mess of the last three days. "It was that bloody policeman all along," he muttered. "If any harm comes to Kitty ..."

"Hypocrite!" bawled the diplomat, distraught again. "Don't you dare claim that you minded about her when all the time you were busy looking after number one. You were flattered because that idiotic detective pretended you were important. You think the real police can learn anything from you? You are an incompetent, dangerous fool, Mr Renshawe!"

Florinskii went on remorselessly until Archie was weak-kneed from conscience and shame. How could he blame Nazir for deserting Kitty when he himself had been fooled into deserting them both? Florinskii was right. Archie thought he was being clever, trying to do two jobs at the same time. To make matters worse, he now saw through the huff and puff of the diplomat's tale about Kitty running away. With his gun, his threats and his talk about hirelings and butchers the man must be pathologically disturbed. If there'd been any estranging of an affianced bride he'd already done it himself. Now he wanted her back. Archie wanted her back. Two birds with one stone?

First, the real story. Last night – how exactly did it happen?

"Let's take it step by step ... Dimka ..."

"Ach, call me Paul."

"OK, Paul." Mustering a deep breath Archie pronounced it to rhyme with Raoul. Florinskii winced. "Last night you and she had a little squabble. A lovers' tiff?"

Paul/Dymka gave a sulky nod.

"So she flings out into the snow?"

"Mmmm."

"There's no reason to suppose her in any danger." Remembering the body he had seen last night Archie suppressed a shudder. If Dymka were pressed too hard about Kitty's whereabouts he might panic and Archie would get nothing more out of him.

The Russian took another cheroot from the shagreen case in his pocket. "Very well. But as you say, this is, nevertheless, your fault, Mr Renshawe. You neglected this poor orphan girl-widow who has not a soul in the world." Lighting the cheroot with a cheap French *briquet* he began speaking faster as though suddenly determined to express something which before he was trying to conceal. "You were her paid guardian but took no care of her. I was her first lover but treated her ignobly. She married Slater and he abandoned her. Slater, Slater, always the dead man coming between us."

They had reached a dip where the end of the path suddenly broadened to embrace the portico of a tiny cinema, the doors of which were barred by a chain threaded through gunmetal hasps. Together they took a turn behind the classical mini-columns, examining the stills of the forthcoming feature. There were a lot of fish-eye shots of people in Bacofoil space-suits manning banks of computers.

Florinskii breathed hard and long at the picture glass, puddling the thaw with the sleeve of his coat. "My poor Katya, she had come to the end. She wanted to make a last pilgrimage to the place where her husband met his death." A pause before the COMING ATTRACTION board. "I did not want to tell you this, but Yekaterina Aleksandrovna wished to confess."

Archie had had enough. "Oh, for Christ's sake, cut out the kit-kat Pimkerina stuff. Confess? What to?"

"Why, naturally, Mr Renshawe." Florinskii smiled with his many teeth. "To the murder of her husband."

No. Not Kitty. No.

"Russians have no feelings. They are barbarians. So here he finds Russian playmates, toy-girls, dupes. Even my Katya."

Archie recalled how the night before he had dropped off to sleep, his counterpane strewn with sheet upon sheet of Slater's lickerish marginalia. He knew the whole story then, this dressy fellow. Knew what Archie knew about Slater's underground life. Had that caused the row between Florinskii and Kitty? Had the bastard told her?

The diplomat shook his head impatiently. "The widow was informed when she was not yet a widow, long ago, in England."

"The house, the girls? Everything?"

"Everything."

Archie's mind raced back: Kitty at the house, the restaurant, in the kitchen. If she'd known then, surely she'd have been different? But she was different in the first place, of course. Inscrutable. A magic actress.

"She was the real victim – not Slater. My beautiful innocent child." Florinskii began to weep. At first gently, then with increasing vigour. "You must forgive me," he sobbed. "I am overcome, distraught. My Katya was a gipsy child, suckled by wolves, pagan. Civilised scruples about murder have no hold on such a mind. Her instinct was to take revenge."

"Do you know Clacton, Paoul?"

He did not.

"Clacton-on-Sea, a resort about seventy miles from London. They don't have gipsies much in Clacton. A fortune-teller on the pier, perhaps, at bank holidays. They're not exactly overrun by wolves, either. No, the worst you get in Clacton are droves of hairdressers from Ongar lined up on the sea-wall eating ice-cream and catcalling beachguards dodging their Kawasaki power boats in and out of the pier legs. That's where your Ka-Katya lives." Archie carefully anglicised the initial vowel. "And has lived quietly and respectably for the last three years."

Florinskii attitudinised against the backdrop of the melancholy picture-house, hinting darkly with hand and eye. "Others do her bidding. Last night she told me everything. Six months ago it was arranged for her husband to die the night he went one final time to sleep with his mistresses." He suddenly flung an arm round the Englishman's neck and kissed him on the cheek.

Archie broke free. "You're crazy. I saw the pathologist's report in England. Slater wasn't murdered. He had an accident after drinking too much."

"So you *are* a detective." Archie did not contradict.

Apparently gratified at his own shrewdness the diplomat came up with yet another switch of mood. "Take no notice of me, Inspector Renshawe. Last night in the hotel I drank too much and became enraged by jealousy. I wanted to shoot you, then, myself, outside Katya's room. The woman has driven me mad."

By now the Englishman himself was so weary of Kitty Slater and her turned-over stone of a country that he almost sympathised. "So you shot her instead?"

Florinskii gesticulated hopelessly at the evergreen shrubs adorning the walkway. "No, no, no, of course not." The pistol wasn't even loaded. But he had done something far worse. Would an Englishman understand?

He could listen.

Well, what happened was this: After Kitty married he fell ill. When he recovered Mrs Slater had left for the West with her new husband. He never expected to see her again, but, quite by chance, he learned from an old university friend that the husband still made the occasional research visit to Moscow, but was never accompanied by his wife. Driven by morbid curiosity Florinskii caused enquiries to be made. Eventually Slater's whorehouse secret was discovered.

At first Florinskii thought it incredible, then disgusting, then wondered how much the wife knew. Last evening he finally realised the extent of her ignorance when, in a burst of jealous spite, he had hinted that Slater was not all he seemed. Kitty had become hysterical.

She would, Archie thought. Yes, for far less than that she would, too. "Rather ungentlemanly, Paoul."

"I am not a gentleman. I am a real man. Passionate. She too is passionate. She even scratched me, see?" It could have been a razor-nick, anything. "Then she ran into the night."

"Yes, you told me before." Archie looked at his watch. "Almost twelve hours." She could be back in Clacton. Or a couple of miles off, buried in the snow. Inside he felt an unfamiliar twinge as though peasant fingers were poking his liver.

The diplomat was convinced that she had gone to the village. To Verochka's. "To find out the truth about her husband."

"And you let her go? To *that* place? Alone?"

Florinskii fell to his knees before the severed stone heads in the alley-way. "What could I have done? Oh, God, forgive me, but what could I have done?"

Archie remembered the brunette with the fruit-green nails. And the lipsticked hag: *No more appointments. Slater is dead.* Had they let Kitty Slater into that house? If they had, what would they have done to her by now?

"I have a car," Florinskii was whimpering. "I could drive you. She might come to her senses if she sees you and me together."

Florinskii apologised for the car. The exhaust baffle was defective and the CV joints ground alarmingly when he swung off the highway into silent suburban by-ways.

They passed a tiny church, a chink in its dome covered by sacking. Even the snow on the brief expanse of tree-dotted park between the acres of high-rise blocks seemed pitted and shallow. Archie at last succumbed to the townscape but came to when Florinskii lost the city and began to jerk in second gear along a slithery lane between masses of ice-frosted brush.

"Welcome to Rimovka," sang out the diplomat. "One store –

burned out last month and not yet rebuilt – one church, used to store timber – and one eye. In the Great Patriotic War Rimovka was at the extremist range of German artillery and no one cleaned up the mess. Approach from the east, one kilometre." He drove on until the lane became a path before closing up altogether in an overhanging crush of topgrowth. They both got out of the car and waded into the snow. The sun was high behind the cloud.

Segmented by the trunks of sand-pines was an opalescent glow.

"The river," said Florinskii. "Eight hundred metres south-east. At the near bank turn right and you are at the western end of the village street. There you will see one damaged street light."

There was no need for more detail. Archie remembered. Vera's. Where else would Kitty have fled to? "I know," he said, turning. "I've been here before." But Florinskii was back in the car. "Hey, you said we were in this together."

Archie tried to run. The engine cut in and the diplomat reversed along his own tracks. "I have business to attend to," he shouted over the whirr of the car's chainless tyres. "And you said you knew the way. Don't worry, Inspector, we will meet again on the other side."

Before Archie reached the spot where the stationary motor had melted the ice, Florinskii's car was deep in the sinuous lane, invisible except for the jet of brake lamps as the driver twisted round the bends. Quickly, even that was extinguished and Archie stood alone in the sere air, his back to the river, kicking at the ruts and damning himself for his own gullibility.

18

In the bedroom with moss-green walls Kitty felt safe.

On the other side of the window clouds were bundling along the line of the bank. When she had crossed ice shifted beneath her feet. Soon there would be a *buran* galing steppe-snow on the river wind.

The distant cry of a child came to her, its brilliance rifting the solitude. A child with a dog racing down one of the finger-quays which hedged the frozen waterway. And Kitty felt suddenly replenished by the presence of the child; her fear ousted by a sense she thought she had lost – the sense of complicity with a landscape which unfolds itself before you, cajoling you in.

"*Papa. Make me a boat.*"

Like Dymka, her father had spun a globe: the Baltic *sund*. Midway, the Kattegat, Ascension, the Molucca Straits . . . "*All the seas, Papa, and everything in them.*" The Black, the Red, the Yellow . . .

"*Too far, too much, Kitaiyoza. Miss Chinese eyes . . .*"

Her breasts ached from Dymka.

Even at night the place had looked squalid. By day it was worse. The heavy fall of snow lay uneven, deep in the hollows corkscrewing down to the bank of the frozen river, merely a fine sheeting along the apron of the abandoned wharf. In the distance, a child in yellow gum-boots and bobble cap played alone among the trucks on a narrow-gauge rail track, hop-scotching from sleeper to sleeper.

Exhilarated by this one patch of colour in the monochrome waste, Archie plunged downwards into the mist coming off the ice, and followed the line of the river. Though the snow here was hard-grained and dryish, after about half a mile his legs began to stiffen. He rested on one knee by the ruined shell of a rowing-boat half-lodged in the ice. Around him, the mist was thinning and he could make out Vera's house, its window silvered by the rising light. He was about to get to his feet when two figures in silhouette crossed left to right a hundred yards ahead. Turning on to the higher track they came towards him in parallel, a few feet apart, a taller man leading, the other holding back, watching to the river side.

Had they not trodden so carefully, heads bowed as though hunting for something in the snow, or had not been so well-dressed, the Englishman might almost have been glad of their company. As he passed above Archie, the first man gave a genial wave, then halted and smiled back at his companion before strolling on. The pause was enough for Archie to place that smile. The grin of the lout who had savaged Karpinskii. Blue-coat. No need to peer at his follower. Head down. Pass by.

Already it was too late. The second man stopped, let out a barbarous yowl and leapt down from the slope straight into Archie's path. A moment later there was a butterscotch crunch of breaking top snow as Blue-coat came down behind, cutting off retreat.

"*Zdravstvuy, señor*," said the smaller one, brushing ice-crystals from his feathered hat.

Archie said nothing but stood motionless, his back to the slope, looking from one to the other while Blue-coat threw a cigarette to his companion over the Englishman's head, and they both lit up leisurely, without venturing nearer to each other or to Archie.

Did they remember yesterday? Had they come for him? Had Dymka sent them? Could he make a run for it, should he yell? For God's sake, hang on to your brains, don't make a fuss. Propitiate.

"American cigarettes?" he grinned at Feather-hat, scooping non-existence goods from the air like a child playing shops. "*Playboy?* Whisky?" He started to back up the slope. What was the word, Kitty-word, the word that obtained everything, everywhere, that was worth obtaining? Sterling, yen, dollars. "*Valyuti?*" he said.

With outstretched arms encircling an imaginary bundle, Blue-coat staggered forward under the weight and let it fall at Archie's feet. His breath was heavy with the glycerine-sweet fume of grain spirit. The cigarette still between his teeth, Feather-hat slid to Archie's uncovered side and with a tight-lipped guffaw, dashed the dying stub at the Englishman's mouth. Involuntarily Archie jerked away and Blue-coat had him from behind, dragging him further up the slope in a lock that crushed the breath from his windpipe while the other man thrust two-handed into the buttoned-down pocket inside the overcoat where Archie kept his passport, wallet and credit cards.

He let them do it. Would have helped them if they'd let him. But they didn't want his co-operation. That seemed to be their point. In the process they didn't want to damage him much, either. Not yet, anyway, because Blue-coat quickly relaxed his grip and pushed

Archie into a drift while both men sat on their heels in the snow sorting the spoils. They took their time, even when Archie began to yell for help in every language he could think of.

Florinskii parked the car at the end of the narrow snow-blocked lane between two yellow pinewood *dachas*. Both were empty. The owners were colleagues. No one came out in wintertime. It was safe. From under the driving seat he took out a sports bag. Inside were a thick-knit Norwegian jumper patterned across the chest with blue musk oxen, two pairs of jogging pants, a violet wool hat, soldiers' woollen gloves, a pair of paratroop ski-boots and a Soviet officer issue 7.65 mm pistol with two spare magazines.

He changed outside the car in the bitter cold. The pistol came last, strung from a length of khaki tape looped round his neck. He was fitting on the skis when he heard Archie's cry, and the sound of it so infuriated him with a desire to act violently, unthinkingly, that he wanted to swoop down on the man who had broken his silence and punch him until he fell, face down against the earth that lay rock-hard beneath the snow.

"*Au secours.*"

Once a plea to him from Katya. Now a call to her. To Kitty with love, from the Englishman. He groaned aloud. The fools had not done their job. He would do it himself. He would pound the earth with the Englishman, rock to rock.

Kitty wanted to mount to a high place and allow herself to fall. The house within the village within the city within the forest would come drifting up to her in a blur of green ice. After all, she no longer had a plan to fulfil.

"I am tired," she had said to Dymka. "I shall go home."

"England?" He spoke the word in English, un-Englishly. "England is not your home. England was not your husband's home. How could you be such a child? Don't you know why he came?"

"He was a close man. And vague, so very vague . . ."

Then Dymka had begun to tell her. About Vera, about Ben's girl. And the other girls.

"Stop it! Stop it! You want me to die?" He went on and on. "Madman! I thought I knew you but I am the only one who is known. Why must you tell me this now, about Slater?"

"*Slater, Slater!* All he gave was his name and the name was all that was desired of him — even by you."

When she had reached for the door he had spread his hand to cover the latch. "I love you."

She laughed and he came at her, scratching her wrist and she fought back at the look in his eyes – rigid, crazed, piteous – and she was afraid because she could back away no further and had to release herself to him, allow him to strike her face with the straight edge of his hand so that she swung loose from side to side until she fell, catching her temple on the library steps at the foot of the bookshelves. While he stood over her, she had sobbed, watching the trickles of blood from her nails mar that white forehead she had once thought unblemishable. "You know nothing of him as I know nothing of you, except that you lie, you lie . . ."

"On the contrary," he had shouted. "I knew about him. And you. Both. Why do you think he had to die?" Then Dymka had told her. Then she knew everything: that he had never wanted to marry her because he had never desired her. Never. His only desire was that Slater should possess her, and after he had possessed her that Slater should go on to possess others like her. Why? It was simple. Because, once betrayed by her, Dymka would have her betrayed, again, and again, and again.

The man in the hat had come upon Archie's pocket-knife lodged in the folds of the spare handkerchief which he always carried between his diary and the NatWest deposit-account passbook. Intrigued by the nail-clipper attachment the man rose, knees askew, and bent towards the Englishman, snipping at the white puffs of his own breath condensing on the air.

Blue-coat caught his mate by the flare of his gaberdine trousers, felt for the ankle, and with one quick twist sent him sprawling into the snow. For a split second Archie thought he was saved. His thieves were about to fall out. But they laughed. They laughed until their faces were wet with tears. The one in the hat had fallen like a boxer taking a drop, restful, entirely relaxed, his hat wheeling towards Archie along the ice-crust of snow. His hair was full blond, cared for, parted neatly down the middle. From where Archie lay he could smell shampoo.

Blue-coat kicked up the hat on his heel and handed it back, still laughing in a breathless falsetto that sounded like the stutter of some gigantic bird, *Miki-mao-miki-mao*. Then, centring on his mate's forehead, he kicked him just above the bridge of the nose.

The room was close but Kitty did not remove her coat. Expensive fashionable clothes hung from the picture-rails – fringed dresses, well-cut coats and skirts, bodices made of satin, underclothes, an entire collection. Vera kept dashing in with warm water and towels, tea, Cognac, even *kvas*. At last Kitty took off her coat and sat down on the sofa, removing her shoes then her stockings. All the time Vera was watching her through round spectacles.

"Your stockings are laddered, that frock is torn. You must have others. Choose. I have everything. You should change everything. You must change . . ."

At the urging of Vera, who, Kitty now knew, had performed exactly similar services on behalf of Slater, the girl allowed herself to be undressed completely, before resuming her fur while the woman flicked through the hangers for a suitable outfit, each item of which she subsequently helped Kitty put on, standing back every so often to admire shade, cut, and finish as, step by step, the girl reconciled the pallor of her nakedness to the berry-green of the walls, by accepting garment after garment.

Against the drag of the wind Florinskii came down slowly, in and out of the trees.

Fighting his way on hands and knees in the snow up the slope between the parallel paths, Archie saw him first. "Keep away from the bastards," he shouted. "They're raving mad!"

The Russian slalomed round him and came to a halt, the prow end of his skis pointing downwards to the spot where Sanya and Vanka lay tumbled together on the bottom path.

"Swine!" Archie gasped, still climbing. "They tried to kill me!"

Behind the half-mask of his ski-goggles Florinskii smiled. This must be as it had been with Slater. He, too, would have misunderstood, even at the end.

Twenty feet below, Blue-coat responded to the commotion with a flick of his head that seemed instantly to sober him up. For a moment their eyes met. Florinskii could have been looking at himself.

With him you couldn't afford to take any risks. Not with him. "*Zdrastvui, San, zdrast Vsye khorosho?*"

Before Blue-coat could reply Vanka had scrambled to his feet and smoothed back his hair. "Flor?" It was a nickname no longer but a challenge. "Flor, what the hell are you doing here?"

Crouched forward, his weight swung to the ski-sticks, Florinskii studied the smaller man. Once, there was nothing Vanka wouldn't have done for his Flor. Tip Vanka the wink and all's said and done. A bribe, a beating, timber for the new *dacha* floor, silver to eat with, silver to eat off, clean women to lie with between clean linen sheets. The diplomat shifted, angling the tape loose under his sweater. "Hoy, Vanichka! Up here! Quick – we'll finish the job together."

At the foot of the slope Vanka hung back. In the man's face

Florinskii could almost read off the images flickering behind the eyes: Vanka hatless at the door of the flat in Bolshaya molchannaya holding a parcel. Couturier clothes for Dymka's woman, his Kitty, stolen from Frenchies at the Rossiya, whose suite was festooned with Parisian lingerie. Vanka did things unflinchingly. Vanka killed Slater. Vanka had nerve. Was utterly loyal. Who could betray him?

"You ought to have done him this morning," he called out, signifying Archie who had broken off his scramble and was looking back, blowing on his purple-nailed fingers. "Saved our arses from the frost."

Sanya, drunker, still on his back, kicked up his heels in the air and let out a disconcerting scream of laughter. "Thought it was a game, fucking nancy-boy, thought it was a game, thought we was fucking a cir-cus . . ."

By way of salute to his mate Vanka blew his nose between finger and thumb before carefully testing the grip of his boots on the loose-drifted snow of the rise. Apparently satisfied, he began to ascend, wide-legged and head down. As he approached Archie slithered crab-wise across his path, still anxious to protect Florinskii whose exchanges with the couple he had not understood. The first shot came as he was fumbling off his spectacles with frost-raw hands. It took him completely unawares.

Vanka's friend, the man who had attacked Karpinskii, gave a sudden belch, leapt to his feet, took a stride forward, then stopped and looked round him to the river and trees.

Vanka came up at a run. "*San – ya, San – ichka!*"

Another fire-cracker pop blurred the still air. The syllables of the name ribboned out into a long, whining keen. "*Sa – ni – ch – ka-a.*"

"Florinskii, watch out," the Englishman yelled, flattening his hands into the snow. "They've got a gun."

Blue-coat leapt at him, lofting for the upper slope where his friend twirled on the spot clutching a hole in his throat the size of a five-kopek piece.

"*Sa-a-a-a-n!*"

A burst of rapid fire cut short the cry. Then a moment of silence. Then the punch, punch of hard-shod feet getting nearer, louder.

Archie raised his head. "Paul, Paul, I can't see you, are you hurt, Paul?"

Florinskii had his story. Out ski-ing he'd come on them by chance – a pair of thugs attacking a foreigner. Scum. Why shoot them? Was he expected to wait until they tried to kill him? Besides, what did it matter? He had friends in the right places who would turn the trick for him. And the victims were scum, unrelenting scum. They'd killed Slater, then robbed him because they were drunk. Zhikadze, too, after selling him the credit cards. That was not drink, but sheer panic. They thought he was about to turn them in for murder.

Renshawe would be their innocent victim, uniquely so, shot by accident in the *mêlée* by the man who had come to save him. It was a pity. One dead foreigner would mean live ones coming out to investigate. Florinskii would manage. He had managed after Slater.

It had been a personal matter, too personal, but how could he have borne to let that old man get away with everything: the girls here, the girl there, his girl, his Kitty? A beating, only a beating, he should have done it himself. Vanka always went too far. He drank, they all drank. What could you do? The Englishman, the Englishman, just frighten him off. Trust Sanya to think any man speaking English was the right one. At the bus-stop he'd nearly killed Karpinskii, but Renshawe was still here, sprawled on his belly, blind as a snow-worm.

Well, so was he, and this time he would take care of Renshawe himself. Then, afterwards, the woman.

"Paul, Paul, is that you?"

He should have answered. His silence was the thing, his silence and the crash of his boots on the drifts. Archie felt him at his side like a shadow, and rolled. It was then that a word would have been enough because Archie saw neither body nor gun, only a disfiguration of the light at which he flung himself sideways, chopping up at the blur with outstretched arms.

The blow was Archie's supreme effort. He did not know or care whom he had dropped, only that someone was finished. A long way off dogs were baying and men shouted under the wip-wop flail of helicopter rotors, but he was in another world, in a white warm burrow where he could huddle in and glory in his best hit – ever.

He woke up very cold. It was nearly dark. Someone called his name. In the distance a squat figure had broken away from an unfocusable group and was plodding upwards.

Even without spectacles Archie knew him. "Borka?"

"If you are weeping," came the familiar growl, "do not expect me to join you."

Wondering how long the fat detective had been out here, watching over him, Archie tried to rise but his legs were too shaky and he fell back into a sitting position. "Kitty – is she safe?"

"She will never be safe until she is dead. But she is not dead."

Eventually, with Borka's help, Archie got to his feet. Down below a single arc-light played across the river from bank to bank. By some fluke Archie's spectacles had survived intact. He put them on. Dotted round the light were several uniformed men. Further off, caught intermittently by the beam, lay three stretchers. On one crouched a dim figure in crimson.

"Florinskii. Is he hurt?"

"Not much."

"They tried to kill me."

Borka paused to re-light his Havana. "They did not try very hard, Detective Renshawe. If they had tried hard you would not now be feeling your backside grow cold in the wind."

"Swine."

"You are harsh," said Borka. "They were ignorant boys, up from the country, proud to wear good boots. They were bad at their work. So who is perfect?"

"But they attacked people."

"They were bad at that also. They killed your professor by mistake. Florinskii told them to hurt him a little, but they hit him too hard."

"Killed? Florinskii had him killed?"

"Indeed. He was unlucky to have such an enemy."

Poor terrified Slater, thinking he was going mad from distant Tutu pursuers and forgetting to look over his shoulder.

"They kill the monster Zhikadze because he used Slater's credit cards foolishly and they attacked the boy Karpinskii because he speaks English and they think he is you . . ."

"You knew about that?"

"Of course. I also now know that the man they should have killed is the man who killed them, and would have killed you."

Nodding in the direction of the stretchers, Borka spat. Archie saw the red figure kneeling on the ground. Some way off stood two women, one round shouldered, almost stooping. The witch. The mad one. *Push orf.* The other he would have known anywhere, despite the queerly outmoded clothes.

His throat had begun to ache from the struggle. "Kitty. She might have been dead, too. That man must be insane."

Borka withdrew his supporting arm. "And then she would have been pitiable and beautiful and men would weep over her body. Such romance! But what does she do instead? I will tell you — undressing herself and changing her clothes. For one whole day she dresses and undresses. Now is that something for a man to weep over?"

* * *

The door of the house stood ajar. Through the hinges Archie saw Kitty moving in and out of the lemony kerosene light attending upon the red-haired woman whose staccato whisperings – "Here. Just so. Be still for a moment" – came down to the men on the threshold. Borka blocked the doorway, making heavy work of unlacing his boots but preventing the Englishman from doing likewise until he was sure they had been overheard and the whispering had died away.

Kitty came out of the lighted room and stood at one end of the passage, pale and unsmiling. She had on a high-necked lace blouse with long sleeves. The lace was the colour of copper. Through the bodice Archie saw the white of her breasts. The skirt was belted, black, and came over her shoes.

"*Zdrastvuitye, gospazha Slater*," said Borka. "We are calling at an inconvenient time?"

Kitty turned without answer. They followed into the room. The floor was littered with women's clothing. The old woman lay full-length on a battered ottoman, her vivid hair spread out over the scroll end. "I told you before, little snooper," she said to Archie. "Why didn't you bloody push orf?"

In his stockinged feet Borka shuffled up to her through a heap of underclothes, framed her brow with his wide palms and kissed her twice. "Verochka. Be nice. He is only a policeman. Like me, not good, not bad, only a policeman."

Kitty held erect from both men, hazy-eyed, always within reach of the old woman's touch.

"Snooper!" Vera hissed. "Look at this. And this, and this!" Her hands were too small to span the finger bruises bunched on Kitty's face and on the underside of her breasts. Beneath the skirt were more, high above the fawn webbing of the stockings. "Sadist! Wife-beater!"

Archie did not look away until Kitty, still cold, still inexplicably distant, let fall the hem of her skirt and bent down to the old woman, speaking Russian into her ear.

Vera whimpered. "How am I to know? Too much to remember, far too much."

Borka padded over to the window-seat and sat down. By now feeling dazed, Archie was glad to follow suit. "She likes to confuse herself," confided the Russian policeman. "It is the privilege of age. For her one man is like all other men – with women a pig in his heart. You like tea now? Hoy, Katyushka," he suddenly called out very loudly to the stock-still girl by the ottoman. "*Chay budyet?*"

"*Seychas budyet, gospoda.*" Kitty went out of the room. Vera shifted on the ottoman, twanging a spring. "If it wasn't him it was the other thug. There was another." She was restless, forlorn, piecing together fragments of memory. "A name like a café. *Le rendez-vous le plus intellectuel de Paris*. Flor, *le café*. Flor. Flor . . ."

"Florinskii," supplied Borka.

"Nearly there. Thank God for what's left," said Vera. "Dead is he?"

"Not yet."

When Florinskii was brought in Vera drew the curtains across the square little window. Like every other pair of curtains Archie had seen in this country, they did not meet in the middle. Outside the night was clear black.

"How companionable are the stars," muttered the old woman, setting a kettle next to him beside the tea-things on a heavy elm table. "You should have kept to the open, young man, and left yourself to the mercies of the sky. I tried to warn you, but you are English and the English are stubborn." Chuckling, she served him first.

"So are you." Archie watched the tea accumulate until it reached the stephanotis painted round the rim of his cup. "*Vera*. Not *Vyera*."

She glanced sideways at him, eyes a fish-grey behind the thick spectacle glass. "Vyera, Verochka, not Vera. Vera was a long time ago. Nothing lasts."

He did not drink but placed the cup at his feet. While Vera busied herself amongst them, offering, carrying, attending to their requests before serving herself or Kitty, the men had begun to raise their voices.

Florinskii, his elegant clothes spattered with slush, had a split lip and blood on his chin. Once he shouted and shook a fist at Archie who was on the other side of the room, but Borka stepped between them, speaking rapidly in a soft, menacing stammer which caused Kitty to look up and Florinskii's colour to subside. In the doorway Borka's two aides grinned at one another and shifted their feet.

The broken skin round Archie's knuckles had begun to prickle in the hot unventilated room. "What's going on?" he whispered to the old woman when she came back to the kettle.

"Official. None of our business. Have you learned nothing? Don't ask questions." She pushed the tea-tray to the far end of the table, wiped the unpolished top with a dish-clout and sat down close to him, sucking on a piece of loaf-sugar. "Listen. Watch."

He did both, but could derive no sense from either. Eventually, the argument, not a word of which he understood, was concluded at a signal from the fat detective, one of whose men came forward and tapped Florinskii on the shoulder. The diplomat drew himself up, glared at Kitty who was about to say something when Borka waved in the second man, blocked off her view as Florinskii was hustled past and out of the room.

Vera crunched the last of the sugar before dusting down her skirt. "A – a – ah," she crooned over the tea-cups.

"Are you all right?" Archie said.

"A – aa-aaah." It was a sigh and a growl. Archie shivered. His hand throbbed. The heat was penetrating. God, they're all like her, eaten up with themselves and living in their own worlds.

"Are you all right, Mr Renshawe?"

"No. I'm not all right. And what's it to you?"

Borka was leaning over, examining Archie's damaged hands. "Mrs Slater, too, is not all right."

Vera's keening sounded in Archie's ears like a lullaby. "Mrs Slater is never all right," he said. "If you want to know, Mrs Slater is a long-term mess . . ."

To his own indignation Archie suddenly found that he could speak no further because either the room was too hot or he was too cold or the old woman was poisoning him through his right ear and Kitty was inserting fish barbs between his finger joints and ribs. He tried to get up to shake them out but a wall came towards him full of faces and the last thing he heard was, "Shock. Catch him . . . A – aa-aaah."

19

Nazir sat on the floor between the twin beds, his back to the wall. "Boy, am I glad to see you! I even asked the guide if she knew where you were but she only burst into tears. The last straw, apparently. Everyone except that Gavin bore has been out of sight for the last forty-eight hours."

At his right Kitty shifted under the bedspread. "Poor Maroussia. Maybe she loses her job."

"Poor Maroussia nothing. You know what she said, Archie? She was going to report us. You know, like we were cars parked on a yellow line. She got that out all right, between sobs."

Archie lay on his left side wedged around by pillows. When he tried to move the pain in his ribs was intense. Nazir looked from him to her and back again. "I mean, I thought this was supposed to be a country, not a boarding-school."

"Don't expect sympathy from me, you little shyster. Where were you when I needed you? I'd have to put you on trial the way you skipped off last night."

Nazir hung his head unremorsefully. "You know where I was. You threw us out, remember? Anyway, it's your fault for being so late back. By the time you turned up that Floritsky character had got Klavdia and me on to the same wavelength and then decamped with Kitty. What was I expected to do afterwards? Tell her no girls are allowed after lights out?"

"Florinskii," moaned Kitty.

". . . inskii, itskii, who gives a damn, the fellow was mad as a hatter."

Archie lurched at him from the pillows. "Can't you see the woman's at the end of her tether?"

Kitty drew the counterpane fringe up to her eyes. For a while they discussed her as if she were a situation, not a person. Archie was anxious to distinguish truth from fiction in Florinskii's elaborate tales, Nazir to demonstrate his competence once more by professional co-operation.

"Queer," he said, after hearing the whole story of what had passed.

"I always imagined a diplomat as the soul of discretion. Lebanon, Kabul. You hear them on the radio, measured, laid-back, bags of tact, even when the mob's howling round the compound. But yours sounds like he was on the wrong side of the gates."

"Playing up to the national stereotypes. I should have realised at the time. It'd be part of the training, wouldn't it? Under pressure, feeling Slav reverts to soul in order to outwit unrufflable Anglo-Saxon. That sort of ploy."

"Anything to stem the tears, old boy. I know you. So did he, apparently, because if what you told me is true, Itsy-Bitsy really took you for a ride."

Kitty groaned again. The two men had tried to put her into her own bed, in her own room, but she refused to leave them until they had heard her side of things. And now she raised her head and insisted on talking, just as she insisted on smoking, and once started on either there was no stopping her.

The trouble with Dymka, she told them, was that whatever he said always sounded so preposterous that when you discovered it was true in some particular, you felt unsure about doubting the rest and were swept along by the lie. Archie had been fooled in exactly this way. Now Vera, on the contrary, Vera acted up to her name: with details she could be hazy or devious; on big things she was absolutely reliable. She knew men, Slater was a man; therefore she knew weakness. He had gone to the village sometimes. Often? How often was often? Every night. Very well, often but not quite so often as that. Many times, certainly. Alone? Eventually alone. The routine was to spend late afternoon, early evening with the Karpinskii boy, or some other harmless innocent he'd picked up in the course of his work. Always male. That was the cover. Slater was another type of liar, the adolescent type, with a taste for glaring half-truths. He made out in letters home that he and Ben were constant companions. Which was true, most days and most hours of those days. But night-times he kept to himself, coming out in the twilight by taxi or in a borrowed car, Soviet registered to lessen the chance of being checked en route. Because it was risky, of course – the village was out of bounds to foreigners, although nowadays no taxi driver paid much attention to strict interpretation of that rule.

He used to joke with Vera about the room hung with fancy clothes. The dressing-room, the green room, the green girls undressing and re-dressing in the make-up, make-believe room. Always nice girls, nearly always one at a time, occasionally at weekends when he had more time, two, two at once. Nice, clean, young; good daughters, educated, ambitious for themselves, who were flattered, who needed money – the real kind that crossed frontiers; who required introductions to younger, unattached men from abroad who might make the offer, take them out properly, as no Russian could – right out, out of the country, as wives. He acquired quite a circle. He liked to think he could help. Perhaps he did, who can tell? He was in the academic swim and knew most of the Western students in Moscow. None of this, though, was openly stated, part of the pleasure being to imagine that the girls did what they did for him and for him alone, because he was so sexually attractive. He would have to have believed it; Slater was that sort of ungrown-up clever man. But Vera never did. She instructed the girls. She knew what they wanted and what they could be brought to perform in order to obtain it.

The two men let Kitty run on for nearly an hour, having to prompt her, search for the right words, in effect construct a narrative from Kitty's broken-up speech.

"Well? What the hell did they want, Slater's women? Did they know? And if they did, did they get it?"

She gave Archie a bleak stare. In the artificial light her bruises looked worse. "How many times, I am telling you? These girls are Russian, they want to be married."

"Want or not want," exclaimed Nazir. "But that's the indispensable *sine qua non*, my dear Renshawe. Without it they're left behind still doing queue duty from morning till night. Marriage opens up vistas. Marks and Spencer, Sainsbury's, even popping into your corner Patel's on a Sunday night for sliced white and tea-bags. It's an image of plenty, old chap, an absolute dream. I've heard nothing else from Klavka over the last twenty-four hours. And she didn't need a grammar book to put me in the picture. There's a universal language of signs about that kind of thing. She wants out for good and next time she wants me back here officially, with a ring."

"Good God, man," Archie said. "Don't tell me it's serious."

"Why not? At least she knows I won't be taking off to Poona, and the way I see it, it's quite a good deal all round. She'll be so dependent on me for the first couple of years – culture shock, language barrier, you know, etcetera – that by the time she's acclimatised I'll have a neat little family: one kid, another on the way, devoted wife and no in-laws. You don't imagine any English-bred Moslem girl would be as helpless and docile as that, do you? Besides, she's a blonde. I really fancy her. I've always fancied a blonde."

"Where's the romance in all that?"

"Search me. I'm just a family man. You'd have to ask Klavvy. Or her." Nazir nodded at the pathetic figure of Kitty huddled up in a blanket.

She swallowed Nazir's cynicism with a despairing laugh. Of course, he was right. Slater said he believed in romance. And when he said so Kitty had believed in it, too; believed that he had loved her as she believed she had loved him. The trouble was, he believed he loved them all: Ben's scatty girlfriend, Academician Savlyevich's daughter, Marya, the dark one, all of the women in the house – red, blonde or brunette – even Verochka perhaps. In England he had been as good as gold, the perfect husband, but out here, well, no wonder none of his Moscow friends could look her in the face. They all used to go with him to that infamous house. Joined in. Women, too. Klavdia? Oh, not circus girls. They weren't the type for Vera's circuit. No education, no connections. In any case, they might have told Kitty, and Slater didn't want his Kitty ever to find out.

With a shudder Archie recalled the crowded downstrokes in the diary margins. Yet there was much more to the diary than the simple "bang-bang-look-what-a-big-boy-am-I" kind of record. Never mind what might or might not have been discovered about Slater. What had he unwittingly found out about Vera which Tutu was so desperately anxious to know? "But your Dymka," he said slowly to her. "Your Dymka, Kitty, was your friend and he found out. How did he do that, Kitty? Do you know?"

The question was unexpectedly brutal but for the moment she declined to weep. How could she know? "Perhaps through his Department. Maybe he followed Slater one day? With Dymka everything is possible. Always –" Her tears, now. Profuse. "Always, that wicked person, he told me that I am no better than Vera's girls – always after passports, money, the free life. That is why I make eyes at a disgusting old man, and I am more disgusting because I am successful and get the wedding ring. But I loved him, my Slater, once I loved him so much . . ."

Passing a hand over the bruises on her forehead Kitty fell into a loud hawking sob.

"Did you?" said Archie. "Did you really, despite the wrinkly old body?"

"Yes!"

After Kitty had left the room Nazir said, "Was that absolutely necessary?"

Archie shut his eyes. "Slater was murdered. You didn't know that, did you? And she might just have known about it. I don't think so, but she might, she might."

*   *   *

175

Kitty opened her door to the blast of Frank Zappa and the Brothers of Invention coming from Lyudy's cassette portable. The room was ablaze with light.

"Won't be a moment, dear," called out the restaurateuse, luscious in cerise bra and panties. "I'm having problems with the swan. Been on a real spending spree these last three days."

Kitty peered into the fat cardboard box jammed between the beds, full to the top with red and gold beakers, napkin rings, bread boards, painted jugs and very many horribly primitive-looking wooden spoons. "What's all this, Lyudy?"

"Can't hear a word. Be a love and shut that man off." Mrs Sedgewick caressed the neck of a glass vase blown into the shape of three cygnets nestling among lime-green weeds. Kitty did as she was asked and repeated the question.

"For the restaurant, of course. I know I've gone overboard and bought too much. Those swine at customs will break my heart. Buy, buy what you want; oh, yes, we want your money, real money, but see how they'll enjoy themselves taking an axe to your property." In despair she plumped the cygnets, beaks down, on a platter expressionistically decorated with nectarines and withdrew bust-first from the box. "Sweet God," she gasped, catching sight of Kitty's bruised cheek bones. "Don't tell me – you've been mugged! *Sovyetskiye huligany!* I knew it – one breath of freedom and it's terror on the streets. Call the militia. Ice, we need ice!" Dashing a heap of *Melodiya* tapes from her bed she smoothed the cover and made Kitty lie down.

"Don't fuss so, Lyudy. I slipped in the snow; it was my new boots."

"You live in Russia twenty-six years and now you slip in the snow? What do you think I am – some old *babulya* out of her mind? This was a man, Katyinka. A true Russian man. I know the signs."

And when Kitty persisted with her story Lyudy knew that indeed it had been a man but that she herself must not persist. "*Nu,*" she sighed, patting her newly-set hair. "A woman knows her own business best."

Dressing in the bathroom she came back wearing a root-ginger brown shirt-waisted frock which she asked Kitty to button at the back. Everything in order she sat at the girl's feet.

"I want to stock the Tsarina with genuine articles. This is enterprise, originality. So I ask our fellow-travellers, Tories to a man, 'Help me share the burden.' But what do they care, these yuppies? What is in it for them? Is this a philosophy or an excuse? And as for my family, all they want is to sleep in the hay. You know, Katyinka, sometimes I think I like England. I love this democracy, but is there something wrong with the Conservative Party?"

Kitty iced her temples with Lyudy's Boots' Cologne stick. "I'm sorry you've had a bad time, Lyudy, dear, but we all seem to have, one way and another."

Mrs Sedgewick choked back a sniff. "Nobody like me. Nobody suffers like me. I am lonely, Katyinka. You disappear, everyone disappears."

"Think of your family, darling. All the way from Khabarovsk."

"Them? Who cares about them? Russians used to have pride but now they read the newspapers like everybody else and learn to dream about being rich. Something has died. It was a long time dying, but now it is dead. Stone dead. Now they are worse than anyone, worse than the English. Faith has died, love with it, and trust . . ."

"Ach, Lyudy, don't go on so. I'm hurting all over," murmured Kitty. "I must sleep."

Mrs Sedgewick crossed Kitty on the brow with her thumb. "That reminds me," she said, after the blessing. "*Dyevochka*, what shall I do with my carpet?"

Kitty felt hysterical laughter welling up in her throat.

"Maybe I could cut it into squares with my Ladycare razor and everyone in the party could carry a piece. I worry myself sick in this place. Years ago when life was hard here everyone looked forward. Now my Vassya will never see the land of his ancestors."

Kitty lay on her back shutting first one eye, then the other, and observing with pleasure the resultant shift in position of the fat yellow globe at the centre of the ceiling. Soon it would be morning. Soon the light would merge into the colour of day.

From her own bed in the big comfortable room Lyudy continued to talk but Kitty heard her without understanding. Yes, Lyudy was right, nothing was as it seemed. If they slept, when they woke the light would not have gone out but would simply be glowing unperceived. Her faith in people had died, Lyudy said. Yet the light had not died, but only appeared to have extinguished itself. It was almost a cosy feeling, this sense of betrayal, as if instead of the four Evangelists, Nazir, Archie, Dymka and Slater were standing at each corner of Kitty's bed.

Everyone had deceived her but that was in the night, and in the Soviet night anything could happen. Yet here she dreamt, damaged but unhurt, waiting for dawn and the reflorescence of trust.

Archie had prayed for a featureless day spent wholly in bed. At ten o'clock Maroussia was at the door. When he opened up she almost fell into the hallway.

"Steady on." The touch of his arm prompted an outburst of tears.

He sat on the luggage table next to Nazir's *Matryoshka* doll.

"This is the most horrible group I have ever conducted. I shall report every person except for you."

"Ah," said Archie. "I agree there's been a certain laxity in the matter of excursions."

Maroussia raised a tear-stained face. "You sound just like Gavin."

"Where is Gavin, anyway?"

"Last night he conspired to interfere with one of our waitresses. A married lady with children. Fortunately she saw through his evil designs. Tell me, Inspector Renshawe, would such a thing have happened in England?"

Archie thought of Slater, Slater's diary, Verochka's place. "Probably not. The English wolf needs abroad to come into his own."

After Maroussia had departed still threatening to report the group *en bloc* he went back to bed but sleep would not come. His last remark to the guide was depressingly accurate. Abroad the English hunted in packs: Nazir had his teeth into Klavdia, Gavin was stalking his Russian girl and Slater had them at leisure, like lambs in a pen, one after the other.

He managed to sleep for the whole afternoon and by evening felt almost human again. When he went to visit Kitty it was with an invitation, which she refused.

"Just as you please. But Klavdia will be there with Nazir, so Borka's mother will have at least one Russian to talk to."

Kitty sat between the beds on a pile of ragged-edged carpet squares blow-drying her hair. Draped over the window radiator was a set of unmistakably large underclothes but no other sign of Lyudy.

"Archie, I have something to say." Her hair hung glossily back from the dryer, folding and unfolding like a sheet of plasticised ink. In the grey jersey frock she looked youthful, almost demure as she tilted her head to the blow of warm air. "I do not understand all that happens to me. One day I think I am dreaming, then I dream that I awake. Sometimes I am not even afraid – what more can be done to me? And you, you are the only one to understand how it is to feel as I do. So I don't want to ruin your life. I am a terrible person. A great fool. If you tell me to go, I will go."

He reassured himself that he didn't know what she was talking about. Go where? To Borka's? Dymka? Back to Clacton? Or did she simply need a man, any man when she was in this kind of state, to tell her to go to hell?

"Fine. We'll go to Borka's."

She switched off the dryer. "Then I go back to Clacton. There is nothing left. I was mad to come back here."

20

It was all right for Nazir. He was stroking Klavdia. And Klavdia felt fine because she had on her very best blouse, a frilled turquoise wraparound whose seersucker sleeve warmed beneath his hand. In return she would wait until Borka's mother was busy at the stove before running her fingers along the seam of Nazir's trouserleg.

Borka took no notice. "You have not realised, Mr Renshawe, how I am so very clever?"

It was even better for the old lady. She was devoted to her son, besides not understanding a word of his English. A quick scuffle in the store-room and out had come her elk pâté, lumpfish roe, a little red cabbage salad, bread, all for him and his guests to nibble over their tiny glasses of Hunter's vodka. To Archie, who was drinking only mineral water, the past hour seemed to have gone on for a fortnight.

Could this fat man be as boring in Russian as he was in English? In English he simply asked questions. "You tell me, dearest friend Archie – what is the cleverest trick in the whole world?"

In England people asked this kind of question on phone-ins. Late at night after the pubs shut. Archie said what the man on the radio said. "You tell me, Borka of Moscow, what's the cleverest trick in the whole world?"

The old lady sipped dark beer from her tankard, eyes soft with regard for her son who conversed so readily in foreign tongues.

"Never, never to show your hand, darling," crowed Borka, draining his glass in one spasmodic move. His mother faced back to the stove and crooned at the gas-rings.

"Your Mrs Slater, she is magician!" exclaimed the fat detective. The heat from the oven was overpowering.

Archie undid the lowest button of his waistcoat. "She's not my Mrs Slater and anyway women can't be magicians. The word you want is witch."

Borka was dashed. "Then your Mrs S, she is a witch?"

"A conjuror, Boris, a person who plays tricks and those tricks are eventually pretty feeble."

"They always are, my dear," said Borka flashing his little black eyes. "I told you this is all a question of style."

Archie had an image of Kitty wedged between her 'cello and prop box at the garden gate in Clacton two months before. She had style all right, but it was wholly personal. Doing a job professionally never came into it. The only spectacle she could make was of herself. Take tonight. In the end he was obliged to leave her behind, hunched on her hotel bed, trying to mask the bruises on her face with greeny foundation cream, whimpering to everyone who came to offer sympathy, as Nazir, fat Lyudy, even the fourth-floor key-girl – had done, that now her face was ruined; that was perfect because so was her life; for the thousandth time they could all go to hell; and no, she would not put on silly frivolous clothes to attend that horrible policeman's surprise party, where he would never stop boasting about what he knew – why Slater had been killed, why Archie had *nearly* been killed, why Dymka . . . Yes, Dymka too, that swine.

Otherwise she had been oddly reticent about Dymka. Slater was the one. She said things about Slater in Russian that drove the key-girl back to her landing, clutching her brow.

"Houdini," mused Borka. "There was style. Jesus, now, he comes back from the grave but I am asking you, who saw this? Our Houdini had the audience."

"*Our* Houdini?"

"Sure, he was Russian before American."

Archie sniffed his hazel-coloured tea. It was weird. Spiritually exercised for passion by Dostoevsky *et al.*, you came thousands of miles for a taste of the exotic only to end up knee to knee in a cramped Russian kitchen being conscientiously bored by the kind of man who, in any saloon bar back home, would be left enough space around him to accommodate a coach-load of day-trippers.

"Resurrection!" Borka shouted, making digging motions with his broad hand. "Bah! Resurrection, the sawn-in-half lady. Bah! This I got to *see*. Hey," he went on, as if remarking Nazir's existence for the first time. "You Christian? You believe that stuff about angels?"

"Excuse me, old chap. We're just popping out for a smoke." Nazir smiled his charming apologetic smile and, taking Klavdia's hand, rose from the table.

As they passed the old lady, her face creamy and inscrutable beneath her pewter-grey hair, whispered something to the girl who nodded and waited in the hallway while Borka's mother helped Nazir into her son's black sheepskin coat.

"Very cold in the corridor. You know what I like about Houdini?" asked Borka when the couple had disappeared.

Archie said he didn't.

"He was after my own heart. It is a well-known fact that this man really appreciated his mother."

Nazir gone, Borka came very close and reaching out a fat arm, encircled Archie's shoulders, hugging him fiercely. The kitchen seemed to grow hotter and smaller.

"Dear friend, don't worry, I will try not to allow anyone to kill you . . ."

As Archie jerked from the embrace the old lady looked up benignly from the pistachios she was chopping on the dresser slab.

The Russian matched the scrape of his companion's chair across the linoleum until Archie was backed against the gas range.

"You mean someone's already nearly got permission?"

Though there was no one left to overhear except his uncomprehending mother, Borka dropped his voice to a growl. "I mean, don't you want to help me help you? Or don't you?" he added, after a pause.

Archie wriggled off his jacket into the gap between his chair and the oven.

"How would you say if I tell you that maybe this Slater, *akademik*, who could not keep his hands to himself, was also the undercover man, foreign specialist in criminal investigation?"

"I'd say you spent too much time talking to policemen."

"Ah, you are educated man, not a policeman. Imagine how such men think. You read Slater's diary – how often did he travel to Verochka's house?"

"I'm not sure. Several times a week, perhaps."

"For two months he travels away from his research in Moscow, three, four days, every week. You remember the place? For tourists there is nothing in the village."

There was nothing for villagers in the village, as far as Archie remembered.

"Exactly. So facts are noted by men with know-how, men of discernment – my type. They keep watch."

"You're saying he was followed?"

"No, no, Archie, I have only you followed. The professor was unlucky. They sit there already watching another man, Zhikadze. They are bored so they write in their notebooks and talk on the radio. He is amusing, this gentleman who comes in the night, a specimen of human nature. Other guests of Verochka come in moderation, but Slater, he is always there."

"They knew about the house and what went on there and no one tried to stop it?"

Borka shrugged. "It is a joke, not important. Life is short, they hate paperwork. The girls are nice to them."

"Nice?"

Borka's glance quickly took in his mother who was bent over a bowl decorated with gilt and orange flowers, doing something to the contents with a long wooden spoon. "How can I say to you, a pure vegetarian, above the flesh — but nice, nicer than nice?"

"Good God."

Borka ran a finger round the sticky rim of his empty glass and, without rising, stretched across the little table to the sink-top where an open half-litre bottle stood next to a neatly rinsed row of tumblers. "Now I am carried away." He helped himself to a fresh bottle and glass. "Such bawdy-house detail is not for you. I apologise."

"You misunderstand me, Borka. I'm a very average Englishman — no prude in that department, like Slater, not innocent, but quite harmless. I can understand one of the girls wanting to kill him, though."

Borka touched Archie's forehead with his full glass as though in benediction. "Girls, our girls, the most beautiful in Europe, *ach*, with natures so submissive, no girl would kill your precious Slater. Verochka's place was famous, a haven for this distinguished gentleman. Nothing under the beds. Verochka's dead husband was a man of position. It was allowed."

"And Slater was allowed, and now he's dead too."

"Alas, poor Slater, I knew him well."

"Never mind that, why should they have wanted to kill me?"

"I told you before, I am very good detective, but there are some things which are still puzzling me."

At first the job had been routine, round-the-clock surveillance on Zhikadze, observe the callers, cars, that kind of thing. Among Borka's HQ staff were a few disaffected souls who detested his methods. "The new broom, Archie, sweeps clean." Borka openly admitted his faults. Devotion to duty, overwork, and perhaps a little conceit had not been conducive to good relations, but his orders were to clear out backsliders. This he had embarked on, mercilessly, and in spite of some resistance the campaign had been going well until Kitty Slater's arrival in Moscow. Then, a new line of enquiry had opened up.

Archie could not see the connection between her and Zhikadze.

"There was none, dear man. The investigation was about you, the Renshawe interloper, and set on foot by senior diplomat Florinskii. I am clever but that man was more clever, and greatly more powerful. He ran many things, including policemen, for his own gains. When Mrs Slater brings you and your colleague to Russia you do not understand that this is not a sentimental journey to nourish tender memories of a dead husband but a ruse to seek out her old lover. You were only the . . . what does one say? . . . the trimmings on the cake – the disguise to impress Florinskii. And he becomes again mad with jealousy."

Had it all been such a humiliating farce? For a moment Archie almost believed the man, but sensed too that Borka was probably incapable of playing on the square.

"You were betrayed by your client, my friend, as I said you would be."

No, no, the compassion was too sanctimonious. The Russian was playing with him.

"I don't believe you. She's not that clever. Anyway, I was paid. Cash. So why should I care?"

Twice over, he thought, remembering Tremayne and the job which lay ahead. If anything convinced him that Kitty was an innocent dupe it was the knowledge that all three men – Florinskii, Borka and Tremayne – had, in their different ways, distorted her nature for their own ends. But the doubt remained. Who was she really? What was she? Would he ever know?

Head down, Archie tried to concentrate on his pudding. The Russian appeared to be so deep in the thick of his own woods that he had lost all relish for food. Yet the pudding was still good and Archie hungry. He ate on wolfishly. "I'd say you were the one to be let down, Borka," he said at last. "By your own men. That Wanka and Tanka who killed Slater and then took a crack at me, they were really working for you, weren't they?"

An apparently casual remark between mouthfuls. Borka was stung. Archie let him expostulate. Working for him? For him? He was the new broom, specially ordered to scour out the filth of the old regime. With Renshawe's help he had succeeded beyond dreams: Vanka, Sanya, the big fish, Florinskii, even the Georgian. "Zhikadze had already made the big mistake by using Slater's credit cards. He might make more, bigger mistakes. After you and I were seen together they could not permit him to live. The rumour was you were some foreign consultant, imported on behalf of Western credit-card companies."

Archie skimmed the inside of his bowl with the broad wooden

spoon. He could well guess how anxious Borka must have been to start that rumour so that the cat would jump. "How come there was no proper investigation of Slater's death?"

"He was too much at Verochka's. Many people here, important people, natives, drop in at this superior whorehouse. They will be embarrassed at the investigation. In this country we prefer to keep such facts of life to ourselves." The policeman plumped a nicotine-stained thumb over a smidgin of cream Archie had dropped on the tablecloth. "I tell you this though, old boy, in confidence – a very important person hated Slater. That same person hates you. He dropped a rumour, I believe, that our professor was not what he seemed."

Archie pushed away the dish, suddenly sated. He didn't know who but he could guess. Even if he guessed right, however, would there be any response from the water-rat eyes of this man who claimed to be his protector and friend?

"Florinskii? No love lost there, I suppose, on account of my involvement with Kitty Slater. He even tried to persuade me she'd planned her own husband's murder ages ago, back in England."

Not a flicker.

"Vera? She wasn't too keen on me, either."

Borka simply shrugged. "That hag-witch? What could she do?" He rose and dragged Archie up in a full-hearted embrace. "You do not understand this country, my dear. Now, why not stay and learn to love our ways?"

Next day Archie walked the streets alone. A light rain was falling. On a wet playground children in dungarees and reefer jackets clustered at the end of an ice-slide which had shrunk overnight to the width of a shoe. Tomorrow was the last day. Tomorrow, in the evening, he would inhale the scented air of the cabin of his 727 and be anaesthe-tised against the pathos of this city. But today he needed to be alone, with time to evaluate this nightmarish trip and fortify himself against the looming Night Six when there was to be a banquet for the tour group which, Archie knew beforehand, was going to be a ghastly fiasco. Only the freeloaders would turn up. The food would be uneaten, all the drink, drunk. Maroussia would weep.

He'd go, though, just as self-centredly, simply to divert his mind from what he had to do next day, the last day, the day before he flew back to the nest. North London. From there he might make sense of the whole twisty game Kitty had forced into play that night in the salt-sea garden two months before.

IV

RIGHT TURN

London, Clacton-on-Sea and Oxford,
March–August

21

At Endymion Road the storage heaters had been off for a week and the flat was bitterly cold. Archie switched on both bars of the electric fire in the lounge part of the thru-lounge-diner.

"Sorry about this," he said. Kitty hunched towards the fake coals from her seat on Helen's Spanish leather donkey. The tip of her nose was bloodless, her entire face white as bone. Even her English seemed to have drained away. "Home," she murmured. "I must go home."

Archie crossed to the freezing kitchenette and filled the kettle. "I thought we'd just been there," he called out. "*Rodina mat*, as they say in Moscow — Mummy Russia's. Wasn't that home? Remember?"

Silence.

Remember? He'd never forget: every cross-purpose, hitch, balls-up and moment of terror was graven on the inside of his skull. Home? Like hell it was. This was home, spooning Brooke Bond into your own teapot, the Marley tiles plastic under your feet, the gas burning a nice Tory, un-Siberian blue.

Searching for cups he noted with dispassion that Helen had evidently been in and removed the last of the decent china. Eventually he found a pair of Royal-Wedding mugs at the back of the cutlery drawer. "Come on, try to pull yourself together. You found what you were looking for over there, didn't you? That's some consolation."

She almost choked on the hot tea, fetching a tinge of colour to her cheeks. "So I know the truth — men are pigs. What are you saying to me now — be happy because I know it? Truth is like your tea — disgusting. I need cigarettes."

Archie went out into the hall and returned with two long packages. On the plane the thought of Mrs Slater's return to that mausoleum of a house in Clacton without essential supplies, had been too affecting for him not to splash out on her behalf. The girl had the grace to blush for her previous sullenness as he undid the container of Marlboro and threw over a pack before slitting the cellophane round the brandy.

"So, so kind, a darling, dear, my best man. I am sorry to be trouble."

"The least I can do in the circumstances. After all, Nazir and I weren't much use to you in Russia, were we? Total wash-outs in fact. So take it as a little treat."

"What is treat?"

Archie elucidated the concept neutrally, convinced that judging by his recent experiences, few Russians would ever fully comprehend it. "Shaking a tiny fist against the bloodiness of life. Like making up for the fact that your employees discovered nothing in Moscow that wasn't useless, unpleasant or unwelcome."

She looked imploringly from him to the bottle of Cognac before reaching out and helping herself. "Forgive me, Archie. I am very stupid, but there is something you have not told me?"

That made two of them. Beforehand, in Clacton, what hadn't she kept from him? His scalp prickled at the memory of the unexpectedness of it all. They'd been barking mad the Dymkas, Veras, Borkas. It was on his own conscience, too, that he'd never come clean with her about Tremayne. He felt shifty. He must have looked it. "OK," he said.

"Archie, this means you are saying something?" The set of her shoulders loosened suddenly. For a second he thought she might drop her mug but she tightened up again and held it towards him like a chalice.

"Yes," he said. "There is something I haven't told you."

Immediately Kitty was on her feet. "I know it!" she shrieked, pointing the mug-handle at the leather donkey's behind. "These things are not your things!"

He looked furtively round the room. "What things?"

Kitty cast an anguished, inimical glance at the donkey. "This is the animal of . . . of *your wife*. Yes?"

"Well, no, not exactly." Damn bloody Helen, not clearing out her junk. "It's more complicated . . ."

"Your mistress?"

"Well, not really that, either. Not now."

With one impassioned lunge she had grabbed the donkey by the tail and waggled the mug above its ears. "But you are not married?"

"Yes and no. Well, more no than yes, if you understand me. But that's not her donkey."

The resultant scream must have percolated through every partition wall from Archie's lounge-diner to the Kebab House on the far corner of the road. "*Svuki!* Filthy dirty little bitches, this and this, take from me this other stupid deceiving man!"

Afterwards her penitence was characteristically abject and he was reminded of that first evening in Clacton when she had knelt before her own gas fire, hands clasped in supplication, imploring, "*Come with me, come with me, to Moscow, only one week*."

"Look, it's all right," he said, still embarrassed by his initial response to her outburst which had been to stuff a handful of Kleenex down the donkey's ears to mop up the brandy. "My wife is an ex-wife. She's gone, like the girl. They've both gone."

Apparently heartened she got to her feet and picked up her coat. "In my country all the women do not behave this way. I am a little drunk. Archie – please to forgive me."

He put on a show of reluctance but she looked so woebegone that he had to relent. "All right, Kitty, but just remember, in this country women don't ask questions about other women unless ... Well, unless they've the right."

"Archie, dear man, if I am your wife, you can have mistresses, too."

He gave an exasperated swipe at the donkey which toppled over, its dun morocco heels in the air. "And in this country, women don't make proposals to men, so for God's sake, if you want that lift down to Clacton, stop making fools of us both."

From the side pocket of her coat she took out a slim carton lettered in gold: *Ivoire de Balmain. Eau de toilette. Vaporisateur*. At one end was a red sticker saying, *Gratuit. Bienvenu à Londres*. "I am *koshmar*," she said. "The Russian nightmare. Now you show me washroom where I make myself look English."

Outside a red tricycle with its front wheel missing had been propped against the dustbins. Kitty regarded it dolefully. "You like them?" she said, on the way down the path.

Archie was feeling for his car keys. "Like what?"

She pedalled her hands. "Children. Them. Their toys. The things about children."

To Archie they were simply a fact of existence, like the weather.

"*Gospodi*," she exclaimed to the sky as he swung open the gate for her. "How I adore them! Me, I shall make five, six, seven. Before, I have none. Slater did not want."

The gate wouldn't shut. Archie inspected it. Someone had stuffed chewing-gum under the thumb-latch. "No. I don't imagine he did."

Her eyes glistened. "I am nearly old, Archie. Seven is very many. Soon I must start."

In the car she fell asleep after drinking more of the brandy. On the outskirts he stopped for petrol and covered her with the plaid travelling rug hoping that she wouldn't be sick because it had just come back from the cleaners.

Along the A12 a fine rain came from the east mizzling the wind-screen. In order not to waken the girl by overtaking he drove in the slow lane amongst the straggle of container lorries and pantechnicons on their way to Harwich. Behind the old-fashioned instrument display along the walnut dashboard he felt comfortable, orderly, almost happy.

Children? Marriage? His marriage to Harriet had been nothing to write home about. An outsider might have said it was because he'd married above himself. Beyond himself would have been a more accurate tag.

Her people were nice people, yes, charitable, even good, but Archie knew they must have thought he was some kind of comedown, even for them, let alone the girl who was the only child and one day would come into Daddy's money. But Harriet wanted him and Archie was flattered.

So he had let himself in for her with total candour, her accent, her clothes, her poise (she told everyone her fiancé was a debt-collector – wasn't it a perfect scream?), but principally, Archie remembered, her childhood. As if, by marrying her, part of the sheen of it would rub off on him.

He didn't love her. Most of the time he didn't even like her. In the end he could have killed her.

That was all there'd been to it: he had married himself off in order to obtain a foothold in someone else's past. It had been the one bizarre, inconsequential act of his life. Had Kitty Slater made the same kind of mistake?

After Harriet left him the parents offered Archie the house. He couldn't accept. After all, he had a job, and Harriet might have come back. When she didn't it was already too late to salvage anything from the wreck. And now Kitty had bobbed up on the swell. Would it be unsporting to fish her out? She, too, was well set up and perhaps rather taken with him, but you couldn't be safe with a woman as scatty and berserk as that. Ever since that first evening at Lyudy's restaurant he'd indulged himself with her. He'd liked her a lot, had led her on, in fact, bent the rules. But after this last exhibition, better leave her alone, write correctly reserved letters, if she persisted. Illness. Pressure of work. That kind of thing.

The old car tracked on sedately, heavy as pudding. The only piece of solid quality he had ever owned. Compared to it Endymion Road was a squat. Soon he would have to find somewhere else. There'd been too many rows. Helen had smashed things. There would be other Endymion Roads. Tally ho. Work hard, get nowhere, pass through, never settle — the feel of the car talking, rakish, devil-may-care, opulent.

The reddish-brown composite of the road leading to the pier was flecked with sheets of tabloid newspaper which lifted in the wind from the sea, bowling round lamp-posts and the dwarf conifers planted in between the front lawns of the ranks of Bed and Breakfasts that extended from the station to the promenade. Archie guided himself by the signs "To the Front" along the high street, now and again catching sight of the slate and cream breakers which seemed irreverently primæval in face of the big-windowed building societies, offices and knick-knack shops lining the route.

"Another couple of minutes," he murmured to the girl who did not respond except to whimper in her sleep and give a cat-like quiver.

"What a place to come home to," he said, loud enough to wake her. When he switched off the engine outside the house the only sound was of the constant wind rattling the catch of Slater's garden gate.

He woke her gently and helped her out with her carrier bags and hold-alls that bulged with mementoes from her circus girls. At the front door he was suddenly afraid that she might have mislaid her keys but she yanked them up from the front of her coat on the same forget-me-not cord to which Slater had once attached them as a sign of his care.

Once in the dark hall Archie became aware of a smell: a dank, tangy aroma as if the deep stomach of the sea had evacuated its contents over the ground-floor rooms and volatilised puddled dead sprats, trawler-bottom rust and tide-creeping animals into one communalised stench.

Kitty took a deep breath apparently invigorated by familiarity and slid past him into the spacious front room where Nazir had opened her bills and Archie had found his way into her life two months before.

Reminiscent and dreamy he did not at first interpret her cry but saw it somehow as part of the house, a feature that went with every other feature, broken and foreboding like a bird flapping in the fire-basket beneath the tombstone chimney-piece.

"*Kosli*, the bastards, swine . . . Archie!"

She laid her hands to Slater's bureau as if to the lips of a dead child. The whole magnificent front had been levered off and inside lay a ruin of smashed drawers. Every paper that Slater had ever kept here had been ripped to shreds and drenched with the carmine-coloured ink that he had used for proof corrections. Underneath, the double-fronted cupboard had been kicked in.

Nothing else in the room was touched.

Without word or movement he watched her reach for her bag, unzip it, feel for the packet of Marlboro. The fish-crap stench was worse here than it had been in the hall. Now she had the cigarettes. Next the lighter. Her thumb was on the striker.

A fossilised sewage-stink of myriads of antedeluvian mites rose from the North Sea. That was it. Christ. Death reeking of death.

He leapt at her, clawing for the lighter, the gleam of the flint hard before his eyes, and in the clash of arms, the lighter flew upwards, then fell from them both on to the little blackstone tiles of the hearth. Before he picked it up he knelt for a moment and listened to the hiss from the unlit fire. That was it. The outstream aroma of the grave.

Kosli. Bastards, bastards. The swine.

22

"They look for only one thing, I think," Kitty whispered.

She and Archie were standing in the red-curtained bedroom. Against the far wall was a squarish marital bed canopied in rat-brown silk muslin; at its foot an ornate wardrobe – three drawers below a hanging press – which might have had its heyday in a *fin-de-siècle* Parisian hotel, but where here, in the side-chapel gloom of Clacton twilight, seemed as inappropriate as Art Nouveau fittings on a mortuary cabinet.

Kitty had been trooping him over the house, apparently searching for someone or something that she couldn't identify; in the frowsty cubicular dining-room, empty except for two chairs, a clock and a pot cat grinning from the fire-grate, other similarly sparse chambers on the ground floor, then upstairs, room after room strewn with piles of newspapers, potted plants long dead from neglect, and furniture of most styles from Second Empire to G-Plan, all reeking of salt-spray and damp. Archie had conceived such a loathing for the place and its contents that he could empathise with the intruder who had so nearly blown it away.

And if it hadn't been for the kiss he might have known how to proceed. He had kissed her outside in the garden, where it was cold, where they had first run from the gas; kissed her with no thought except that the warmth of her body was comforting through the heavy coat and her lips were dry under his mouth.

Now he wanted to touch her but she wanted to talk. "If they cannot find what they want maybe they return soon."

He crossed to the right, bent over and raised the valance of the Miss Havisham bed.

"Not there!" exclaimed the girl. "You think I am old maid, imagining men? Now you look in right place, in his cupboard."

"I feel like a burglar who doesn't know how to steal. What do you want me to find?"

The look she turned on him had an elderly, scornful gleam. "It is a wardrobe. Are you frightened of wardrobes?"

Her man's wardrobe contained only her man's clothes. Nothing

193

seemed to match or belong together, or even rest easy within the cupboard which looked and felt at odds with the room, as the room still seemed disjointed from the woman urging him on to unparcel every last bit of her husband's bits and pieces.

When he reached the bare shelving Archie felt he'd hit bone. This stuff should have gone after her man, into the grave.

From the bed Kitty watched him shut the press doors. "They did not come in here."

"You can tell?"

"I can tell."

He sat down beside her. "How can you tell?"

"They have not come in here because they want to come back. They are telling me there will be a next time. Next time they will come back to the last place that is mine."

"A warning?"

"A joke. They are funny people. They like a joke."

She sat trim on the bed, bolt upright, her hands pressed down in the lap of the tight flounced skirt. He had no idea what she was talking about so he touched her, and when he touched her her forearm quivered and she stared at him with such clear-eyed blankness that he felt ashamed, not because of what he had done, but because he did not know what else he could have done.

And if he didn't know that he knew nothing about her. He never had. How could he be expected to know? She'd lived so long in the dark she was blind to the light. Either that or, like her other funny people, she simply liked a joke.

"You've lost me," he said. "I don't understand. What are these people who frighten you so much?"

She shifted away. "Like you," she murmured. "Men of this world."

Archie clasped his head with both hands. A man's world, the world of this room. Slaterman's cupboard for her. Fusty, mismatched. On the ashwood bedside table a *netsuke* figurine of a Japanese peasant carrying a pig under his arm stood next to Roby's *School Latin Grammar 1899*. Even the tall brass taps of the thirties handbasin in the corner seemed dislocated from their bowl of male contraceptive pink. "Men of *the* world," he corrected wearily. "With a talent for winning people over, gaining their trust in order to manipulate them. Not that I wouldn't have liked to be one but I've always lacked judgement. I wouldn't be here now if I hadn't."

She did not contradict him. Quite the opposite. "Like my Slater. He did not see far into things, and all the time his mind was changing. I remember when I asked questions – why do you go there, why do you trust them? – he said this sentence: 'I am,' he said, 'an *ineffective* man.'"

Exactly, exactly, thought Archie. It was the reason Sir Evelyn had chosen Slater to do his dirty work in Moscow. Then Archie himself to tidy up afterwards. Lambert recommended him. Helen had known why. "*Because you're dense, Archie, my love. Everything's so simple to you. You just swallow things whole. You can't see the trees for the wood. That's why Lambert employs you.*"

"Haven't you left it rather late, telling me this now?"

Kitty separated her hands and smoothed down the material between her knees. "How could I know this until I watch you in Moscow doing strange things? In Moscow I was afraid. What is he doing next? Is he mad? Here it is different. In England it is safe to be a fool. You tell me – 'In England you are safe, Mrs Slater.' So now I know you are a fool, like Mr Slater."

It was too much. "You sly little bitch," he cried out in genuine distress. "I'm bored to death with your states of mind. You can't distrust the whole human race. It isn't logical because you leave out yourself and what's so bloody marvellous about you, eh?" In a wild burst of hatred and frustration he picked up the Latin Grammar and threw it at the portrait of Slater in doctor's scarlet hanging above the washstand. "I was educated to put faith in people. Men like him. Decent people, unworldly – there's your word – the educated, decent sort, educated better than me, the right sort. I couldn't get enough of them. People better than me in every way. And I still can't, despite finding out that your husband was a lying, posing, lecherous little bastard . . ."

Swift as a cat she had him round the waist with one arm, nuzzling up, forcing herself on him, along the curve of his neck, tonguing him like cream. "Not *svina*, you not swine, not bastard, not you . . ." The breast of her blouse split apart under the jerk of her shoulders. "*Nye ty*, not you, *sokrovishchye moye*, my treasure, not you, you, you . . ."

And before he could look down at where she lay on him, blatant and exposed, she had knocked away his spectacles and passed into a flow of Russian that moved from her mouth as fluently as the clothes from her back.

They lay on the bed gazing up at the strapwork of the elaborate ceiling. He was still in his overcoat, she naked to the waist.

"Archie, is this nice for you?"

At the beginning his anguish at her mistrust of him had been superseded by a desire so violent that he had fought free of her. It would have been only too easy to throw ethics and caution to the winds, but the house was wide open. Anyone might wander in.

She turned on her side. Her figure was fuller than he had expected, whiter, too, very white. He had to say something, so he said "Yes." It was enough.

"And this, Archie?" This was her head bowed, cupping herself, the fine white nail of one little finger traversing the horizontal slit at the peak of each wide areola. The contrast was intense. She was dark, shockingly dark. "Archie." That rift in her voice again.

He tensed. Oh, God. Not now, not more speculation about fate and Slater and Moscow and policemen and the meaning of life, not with her stripped to the skin, musing on the astonishing fact of her being, and offering it up to him with that slack, heavy mouth.

"Archie?"

"Yes?"

"Do something for me, Archie." She did not leave off touching. For all she seemed to care the house could have been full of murderers. "Say *grudy*."

He said it once, then again and each time she heard it, Kitty tightened her naked forearms across her breast and uttered a deep, lascivious groan.

Trying surreptitiously to unbutton his overcoat Archie carried on with the word. Whatever it meant it was working on her as effectively as her noises worked on him. It made him want to do what already he ought to have done — to tear off every stitch of this woman's clothing, in this stuffy old man's room, and without regard for the consequences turn the groans into screams again and again and again.

He was down to his shirt but still in shoes and trousers when deep in the house something whirred. There was an answering clank, then a brief moment of silence. On his knees above the girl who was still making noises that sounded like speech but were not, and who was crying without actually crying, and every so often attempting to thrash off the tight unslit skirt, Archie froze. At first she went on unaided, as though he weren't there.

"Shshshsh," he whispered.

After one last burst of kicking and gabble the girl fell quiet, too.

Another clank, then a series, one touching off the other until the boards of the floor began to shake and Archie dropped four-footed to the bed in order to keep his balance. "What the hell . . . ?"

Kitty stretched up an arm and pulled his hair so savagely that he swore, slipped out of her grasp and rushed from the room.

*　　*　　*

Today she had meant to say, Please do not misunderstand me because I love you. One day you may even get used to the idea.

Her wrist-watch clicked in the quiet, a pernickety old-fashioned sound, like the nagging of a spinsterish bird. When he came back there might still be time to tell him. But it would be a while before he tracked the noise to its source, above the box-room under the roof. Their peeping-tom lodger, Slater used to call it, the rackety old cistern which always seemed to start thumping on the ceiling moments after they had begun to make love.

She rolled over and with an athletic tilt of her long legs sprang from the bed and took the opportunity of his absence to order her thoughts while cooling her wrists in the flow of ice-cold water from the washbasin tap.

Her chances of winning over this man were not great, she had to admit. And the greater her need for him (which lately had become almost an obsession) the less she could control herself in his presence, and she would be bound to flare out in that old extravagance of feeling which she now detested in herself and fought to suppress. With Slater and Dymka she had been secure in their response to her rages and wildness, confident that she could take any man she wanted, but this one was dug deep into himself, wary, guarded, a distant man. To reach him she would have to outfox her old self, be clever, self-controlled, nurse him, smile when he smiled, obtain her desires without appearing to have them.

Turning off the tap, she crossed herself breast to breast with the chill tips of her fingers before drying off her palms on the front of the skirt. Where was he? What was taking him so long? He should be here, behind her, lifting the skirt over the back of her thighs, finding her out. Instead she had to lean forward, unclothing herself for him beneath the dark skirt, imagining his hands between her.

This bedroom is awful. It smells of wet linen. I must possess myself, I must be good. Under the skirt I shall be naked and because of the skirt he will know that I am and therefore desire me.

She just had time to fold away the discarded clothing, strip the cover from the bed and compose herself. His step was on the stairs, weighty, making no haste. A dreamer. He looks for ghosts and encounters machinery. After this perhaps we shall never be naked together again.

When Archie came in the curtains had been drawn, the brown coverlet was gone from the bed and she lay on her back, the candy-striped top sheet drawn up to her chin. In the aura cast by the strip lights above the handbasin mirror he saw her shoes on the armless chair at the foot of the bed, the grey stockings coiled within them. Underneath, neatly folded was something that looked like a man's purple handkerchief. Without looking at her face he pulled back the sheet. Her skin was tinged bluish pink from the lamplight but Kitty was not yet quite naked. The skirt was still on, rucked back along the knee.

At first he had no thought of pleasing her. He had tried too hard before and she had frustrated him. This time he wanted to be selfish in a way that he had never been with a woman, not to care for her, but make her care for him because he wasn't going to bother himself about her. Not a bit, especially with preliminaries. Let her take the consequences; after all, she'd got him up here.

The odd thing was that when he forced back the skirt to the thickness of a belt around her waist she didn't seem to mind and he felt that this time whatever he did she wouldn't mind. So he tried her, and she didn't, not even when he surprised himself by brusque demanding inquisitiveness that up till now he had never experienced about the body of a woman. More simply than a desire to see, it was an urge to gloat over his power to make her let him look. He dealt with her roughly. He thought he did. For him, at any rate, it was — quite startlingly so — but she shut her eyes on what he was doing, and smiled sideways into the Slater family bolster, talking out one continuous battle of unworded sound through the edges of her teeth. And that was while he handled her hard, mounting her up on the second of two Indian cotton pillows, and pressing wide and down. She could never have seen what he saw, and while he sated himself he marvelled that to her it was nothing, and had no meaning outside this present time, when it signified to him the whole of her being. Dark, swarthy, roe-red. A queenfish. A prize.

"*Kak ya khochu tebya rodnoi, kak ya khochu.*" came the voice.

"English, woman, English! Say it in English!"

Her eyes snapped open and in them he saw himself as one bodiless head, sweat peardropping from the distorted bulge of his brow, trying to pass back into her like a genie through the neck of his lamp.

"Dear ... Sweet ... you ... I want you ..."

It was quick, much too quick, and something to do with the words because however hard he tried to stifle them in her by an onrush that cramped her legs wide against his chest, she kept ahead. "*Khochu Khochu.*" Faster and faster. Until to his bewilderment and chagrin she took him in with a convulsion so narrow that he had to force himself to think away from her to anything, think of anything in the world that wasn't her or this, or what she had done, like this, before, the furl of her lips gapping, showing her teeth, expelling those same words in harsh asthmatic bursts, "*Tebya khochu tebya khochu tebya khochu.*" Too quick. Then in her throat a scream building, and he could dismiss the world because he knew where he was and what she was about to do.

The scream was freedom. Down went the corpse-yellow figurine of the Japanese ornament, down to the pine of the stripped Slater boards. Gone under the hard soles of her feet that lashed out in marionette jerks as he held fast under her thighs, watching and waiting for the last shudder to come and the noise to die to a whistle in this hermit-crab, old-man's cell.

When it was over he had hardly begun and he kept her under still gulping, still flickering, quite undistressed.

"You let me go now, Archie?" Peremptory, almost a command.

He wouldn't, though. "You selfish little cat – what about me?"

Her reply was to needle the gathered flesh of his armpit with the points of her eyeteeth.

"You like this?"

"Not much. Not as much as –" And as he said *that* he responded within her as far as she went. When he had made his first move at the beginning she was so ready he thought nothing could be easier but now it was unbelievably easy and becoming easier and easier.

"You like to stop now?" She licked his ear. Softer phrase but still contradictory.

"No," he said to her. "No, I would not."

Her fingernails were at the hair on the base of his skull, exploring, digging in, she drew his head towards her crooning in her barbarous language.

"Slater was nice man, nicer than you. Slater, he stopped."

Not that Slater had been an inadequate lover. He had liked women too much to be that, but from the moment Archie first touched her she knew it would be altogether different with him. Something undreamt of by Slater. Although this new man was clumsy, almost puppy-like in his enthusiasm, that quickly gave way to a ferocity which set her free to drift passively into any role she might choose – weakling, martyr, criminal – knowing that afterwards she would not despise herself for the fantasy. Slater had known that side of her nature, too, had incited it by artificial restraints both mental and physical, been heavy upon her, made her ache in mind and body. This man was gentle, then hard, then gentle, but all the time without any thought for her, as if, from the first, he had realised intuitively that what he did must be for himself alone since only then could she respond without inhibition. This man was in charge in a way that Slater could never have been because he had not divined her needs.

There were secrets between this man and her. There lay the novelty of difference. There is a coarseness in me, she used to tell herself, a flagrancy that any man must dislike. But she did not feel that this man could even sense it, let alone be repelled, because, holding her down, inflicting himself, he was not acting out his nature consciously, but was submitting to it as beneath him she was compelled to submit to hers. His desire was the positive of her own villainous cravings. He could choose or not choose to hurt her, she would never have objected because not knowing if or when made Kitty offer herself up as one continuous wound.

Be sparing, she told herself. Do not let him know you all at once now that he finds himself out in your body. He could be your life come back, and through him the life of childhood that never comes back except through a man. So be respectful and unscrupulous and quite unfair because the other women he has loved still flitter behind his eyes. I shall be underhand and ruthless, liquidate them, and he will be astonished at the extent of his power over me.

"You can forget Slater," Archie yelled. "This is me." And before the girl could resume her outlandish jabbering he had set her at the correct angle, then, turning her on to her front, weaved himself down. "Here. This is me. And here, and here." She urged him on by whispers the language of which made sense only to her but which closed around him in tiny palpable spasms.

"Dead, dead, dead." She wheeled corpse-like below while above her the man performed his ritual slaughter.

"Ach, *prilyest*," gurgled Kitty when he had collapsed on her, gripping the hair of her neck. "I say terrible things because I want to make you happy."

From the start he had been surprised by her zest. Now he began to feel jealous. Not of other men – her previous history was nothing to do with him – but he was jealous of the way she took such unashamed pleasure in her own body. No man could have taught her this because the pleasure was too inward, too self-regarding to be appreciated by men, most of whom, as he guessed, did not enjoy or even tolerate her kind of self-display.

With Kitty, apparently, all a man could achieve was to make her at one with herself, not with him. Slater must have known this, encouraged it, perhaps. If so, there was a lot to be argued in favour of age: an old man learns he is not required to win every point in the game. The idea gained on Archie as he drowsed with the girl in his arms. Insurance, comfort for the future. There would be consolations.

"Very good, very nice," she said, giving a brisk smack to her navel that brought him to with a start. "Now I make baby."

His heart bounded so strenuously that he hiccuped, and before he could get out a word Kitty had slid out of the bed to the washstand where she pattered about amongst the pill-tubes and bottles of patent medicine littering the floor beneath the basin. Eventually, finding a toothglass she filled it from the tap. "Drink it wrong side, dear," she said, coming back to the bed. "You must be well now you are papa."

It had been planned for weeks. After the Tremayne windfall she had taken advice. First Lyudy, then her GP, then a consultant. Privately? Of course. Kitty was rich. Nazir had said so. Rich! No worries. In the bedside drawer was a reticulated sheet from a Soviet child's arithmetic book with rows of boxed numbers inked neatly in pink and blue.

"This is pink time, Archie. Pink time we do it often." The pink days seemed few and far between. She'd worked it all out, there was the cross. Today, her best day, her pink-flag day.

"Hey, just a minute, you've kept very quiet about this. I mean, you've been married, you didn't get ... Look, this isn't on ... Anyway, I can't, I'm still married myself. It wouldn't be right ..."

Ignoring him Kitty propped the chart against her knees, the broad flush of crinkly black high on her belly fringing the lower edge of the paper, and ticked off the blue boxes with an eyebrow pencil.

"You mean you don't care?"

"Married man – phoo! Husbands, weddings – phoo! Yes, I don't care. For Slater I took pills. Ugh! Slater is dead. Now I am free. I choose. Here is my house, money, rooms to spare, so I choose. There is something wrong with you, maybe? You don't like making a baby?"

He said he might have done if he'd known that he was.

"OK, we try like this again. Then you know."

While she was arranging herself somewhere at the end of the bed Archie retrieved his spectacles from the crack between the headboard and the mattress and put them on. My God, she meant it. "Did they recommend that, too, at the clinic?"

Kitty was draped right over the back of the chair, her head out of sight. "I read in the book, Archie. Very deep ..."

He shouted, "Get up, I've had enough of this, you stupid big kid, get off your knees, I'm a human being, not some farmyard bull."

His tone was enough to bring her upright but she answered back, in spite of the threat of tears in her eyes. "Lyudy says men are pigs so your husband will like this. In clinic they say, too, this is exciting for him, let the husband make use of the wife. You are not excited?"

The word "clinic" acted on him again like a misapplied antiseptic douche and Archie leapt to his feet in the middle of the bed, stark naked except for his spectacles. "I'm not your husband," he yelled.

"No, you are not. You are cruel, cruel, pig-man. I hate you. This morning I tell you lovey-dovey Archie, I want seven children. You kiss me then. Now you scream like beasts . . ."

Hunching forward to mask her breasts from him she sat tailor-style in the three-legged chair and began to weep. Suddenly embarrassed by his own nudity, Archie snatched the counterpane from behind her back and tried to swathe it round his middle but she had folded it so small that he had to spend time flapping it loose.

Meanwhile Kitty found voice again. "You are the greatest wicked, wicked man. How can you do this when you have your wife?"

"I haven't got a wife. Well, not really. I suppose I have legally but that's neither here nor there, and certainly nothing to do with this."

The sobbing became more restrained but she continued to beat herself feebly, rocking to and fro, taking an occasional peep at the absurd spectacle he presented. "Look at you, you are not human being, you are ape man."

Archie bestrode the yielding mattress in a desperate attempt at dignity. "You knew I was married." The counterpane stank of mildew and was sticking to his skin.

"I choose you, stupid man. First time I see you I say, that is the man. I want this man for my baby."

There was no point in being too indignant, but he watched her in the salty-aired room where she must have lain on this bed, night after night, ill-starred by nightmares of loss and betrayal. Eventually he moved and caressed the nape of her neck under the shoe-black hair. Did she think she had succeeded in making him love her? What was more, did she love him?

"I will tell you a story." She might have been making a speech. Each word had been well-rehearsed. "When we go to Lyudy's restaurant that first night, I think *maybe* I can make you stay with me. So I behave badly, get drunk, throw myself at your mercy, but I do not speak about love because my husband is dead only two months and because I sound stupid and because you will leave me if I say it. Like now, Archie. Will you leave me?"

When he failed to reply she did something he had only read about. She gnashed her teeth. "I come back to England for you . . . I am giving you this house, Slater-money, anything if you stay. Say you stay. For a little bit – stay." Eyes suddenly dreamy she cradled an imaginary infant to her breast.

"I've got nothing to offer you, Kitty, nothing. Especially not now. I was no good as a husband, and I'd make a worse father."

"I do not want husbands," she murmured. "I need bodyguard. Is that not your calling, Archie dear?"

After dark she slipped from the bed and opened the window. A wind lofted in from the foreshore, smelling of sage, circling in the folds of the curtains.

Under the covers Archie stirred. Instantly she was on the alert. "Tell me what you want. I will get it for you. Only, you must stay. You promised me to stay."

"I just thought we ought to get up but when I felt for you you'd already gone."

"I watch you." She clambered back to his side. "I love to watch." She would invigilate every passing minute of his life so that he could never escape. "Let me watch."

He scraped back the boot-black hair from her temples, framing her brow where the skull lifted high and warm under his fingers. Even the bone of her imparted pleasure. "The rubbish you talk, Kitty. My God, the rubbish you talk."

Arching her spine like a hackling cat's she burrowed beneath him with thrusts of her hips. "*Yshcho*, Archie, another, *odin bolshoi*." Her bar-talk, set it up, a big one this time.

He did what he could without quite laughing aloud, but the idea that he could find her amusing in this situation bewildered Kitty. "I never know what you really think," she whispered. "Say to me, Archie, it will not always be so?"

But he wouldn't and she felt her eyes prickling against the sombre gaze of the man, weighted down under him, absorbed in the mass of her body.

"You're tired, Kitty love. Go back to sleep."

Instead she drew his hands downwards twisting them round until his knuckles divulged the clear line opening at the rim of her belly.

Child or no child she would make him stay for a while.

This time it was better and worse because he eventually gave out with more than the well-bred shudder she had grown accustomed to from her men, but when he had shouted she was afraid because she did not know, after that, how she could bear the thought of living without him.

"I need Cognac," she said. Then she kissed his hand saying, "No, I do not need." At the inner side of his wrist, her lips touched his pulse.

It had begun to rain. A long way off church bells sounded, the peal of the tenor chiding like a voice, the voice of practical reason. Klavdia. "*Leave him before he leaves you, darling. He's bound to get used to you and then where will you be? You know how it is — men always get used to you. Slater did, Dymka did. Why should it be different with this one? All men are the devil in torment delving for the crack in our souls.*"

Kitty sensed the flood of shadows moving under the trees in the aquamarine garden.

"Don't ask me to do things that you know I can't do," Slater had said, that last time. "Have I made myself perfectly clear?" Then he had coughed because he was starting a cold, and because if he coughed she would pity his weakness. "I cannot take you with me, and I cannot explain why until I return." And he reminded her never to answer the door in the night-time and to keep the appointment book in the car. As Kitty watched him pass through the departure gate she had thought, he doesn't know me. He doesn't know me at all. If I went on my knees he would still never understand that he ought to be incapable of leaving me like this.

But he went, and she hadn't got her own way. Not with Dymka, either. Perhaps with this man she would not even try. What was the point when they only hardened upon you like skin that flakes away the moment it is disturbed?

23

Kitty would neither leave the house nor allow him to do so, even for the ten minutes it would have taken to pop out to the Indian take-away on the corner, so, as they waited for the central heating to take the chill off the surfaces of the dank kitchen, Archie helped them both to the contents of the walk-in larder – sardines in soya oil and a tin of coleslaw. In the meat-safe he found half-a-dozen bottles of Slater's home-brewed stout, one of which Kitty sampled before emptying all six down the sink and topping up her brandy glass with water from the tap.

While he ate she watched his every movement, continually getting up from her stool to touch his face, hands, even lips – as if at any moment she expected him to evaporate. And talked. Lord, how she talked! Here, at home, Kitty was unloosing herself in a barrage of self-recrimination. She was responsible. It was her fault. Everything. Ah, and how she loved him. This she had known from the very first, and stupidly, thoughtlessly, she had brought him great danger.

Slater? Not Slater, that was gone, had never existed, no, no, no – *him, him*.

This sort of thing Archie wished to postpone. Later on he might be able to get to grips with his new rôle in her life, but, for the time being, Slater's ghost stood between them, unstilled, and Archie forced her to concentrate on specifics.

Had there ever been a diary? Had he begun one before leaving for Moscow?

She seemed to remember he had, about a week before "to get himself in the mood", he had said. Out there he certainly intended to keep a record of some kind. He'd discussed it with her openly: if she was not to accompany him, he ought to keep an account of his doings which they could enjoy reading together when he came back. But, yes, he must have started it well ahead because she'd been struck by the way he was writing that week. Of course, he was always writing, but his academic papers were usually worked over slowly in her company, while this other writing was in solitude, and very, very fast. She had shown interest only once and he had opened the book:

lists, page after page, very neat and small, and quite unreadable to her. Things to do, he had said, business matters, all v. boring.

His papers? His papers were eventually returned to her, sealed by the Embassy people after his death, but she'd left the package untouched for weeks, and when she finally opened it, there seemed nothing unexpected: just lots of English notebooks she couldn't read, and transcriptions of rather dull Russian manuscripts that she didn't even want to read. So they were bundled up and stuck in his bureau with the rest of his belongings.

"Like dead men's shoes – who wants them?"

It was time-consuming, making sense of what she tried so hard to express in her inadequate English, calming her down in the meantime so that she could think herself back to those desolate months, yet Archie emerged from the ordeal not only with a fairly reliable picture of what Slater had been about, but a powerful sense of his own guilt in the affair, because, whatever Kitty thought she had done or not done, Archie knew that the real charge lay against him.

Why hadn't he told her about finding the diary in Zhikadze's room? Because of what it proved? That Slater was no grand romantic, undercovering round and about an enemy capital, but a sexual underachiever who tripped to Moscow rather than Bangkok, because there, with the connivance of Vera, who thought he had influence, the old man could bed as many girls as he could manage without it costing him a kopeck. But since Dymka had told her, what would have been the use of the Renshawe firm chipping in with even more revelations in her dead husband's actual handwriting? Kitty was already unbalanced and he didn't want to be the person who actually tipped her over the edge.

So, that last day at the Embassy, he had parcelled up the diary with Slater's miscellaneous papers for onward transmission to Sir Evelyn, purposely omitting a covering letter. What could one add? Here's your reputable scholar, look how he spent his free time: going native on institutional grants and buying in the local talent for hard currency cash.

As night drew on Kitty relaxed. Once she even laughed in a relieved sort of way, after he had assured her that the break-in was probably the work of kids, and nothing to do with her late husband. After all, he was almost a detective, wasn't he?

He couldn't tell whether or not she believed him, but he was glad that, for a moment, she looked happy. When he pushed away his plate and took her hand she smiled and made to get up, evidently misinterpreting his intentions.

Archie shook his head. "Plenty of time for that later."

Her face puckered like a slapped child's and he kissed the tips of her fingers. "I'm taking you away. But first you must trust me and wait until I sort this business out. I won't be long, and I don't think I'll find anything terrible, but from now on we both have to be careful."

She refused. She didn't understand. She thought it was all over.

"Listen," he said, trying to sound both stern and comforting. "You expect a lot from me – protection, loyalty, commitment, even a family, for heaven's sake – so from now on you do exactly what I say. I shall need time. And a great deal of money. Meanwhile, you are not to argue but stay quietly wherever I leave you. Not ask questions. Understand?"

"You promise to come for me?"

"I promise, but I may be some time."

He could have moved her further inland to his aunt's villa but round there they were all OAPs with little on their minds except bowls, their gardens and the price of cat-food. Kitty was too striking not to attract gossip by her very appearance. In the end the solution came from the girl herself: Sussex. Chelwood Gate, near Forest Row. Edith. Slater's sister. Her house.

Archie watched her long fingers compose the number on Slater's fifties-style handset, musing on the fogeyish affectations of a man who, at home, lived so old, but abroad was as spry as a jack-rabbit. The contrast exhilarated Archie, and after Kitty had made her arrangements – yes, Edith was only too happy, no, she had not been asleep, tomorrow then, early – they went arm-in-arm upstairs to the dark brown bed where, eventually, they slept.

Edith's house was weird, too, like her brother's, but unthreateningly, childishly so: a barley-sugar twist and sweet plum of a house. The roof ran down and around, mob-cap shape, curling over deep wooden casements which kept back the light from Edith's vast collection of water-colours – whose fondant pinks and yellows toned up the browny shade of her brick-and-beam sitting-room.

Kitty slipped as easily into the sister's life as she had into Slater's. After breakfast she set up her music and gave a spritely rendering of Bach's first *Praeludium* for unaccompanied 'cello. At the conclusion of the piece, Archie kissed both women, wishing desperately that he could have stayed.

※　　※　　※

Next day he telephoned the office. Nazir answered. "Where the hell have you been? Lambert's going barmy."

"I need help. Take the 11.05 to Clacton. I'll meet you on the station."

There was a pause. "Lambert's got plans. Expansion. He's sending me up north."

"Lambert can go himself and find out what an Enterprise Zone looks like. This is an emergency."

"What are you up to? I don't fancy another duff job. That Tsarina woman made me taxi her and her jumble all the way to Frinton after you sloped off at the airport. I never even got a tip."

"There's a fee," said Archie. "Handsome."

They met in the unheated booking hall of the station. Outside an austral wind cut at their faces.

"You're in trouble," said Nazir getting into the Daimler. "And now I am. Lambert didn't take kindly to the sick uncle excuse. My job's on the line, yours has probably gone. I tell you, the old boy's wigless . . ."

Archie drove them by the promenade where the Bed and Breakfasts looked in need of their annual DIY paint-up in time for the Easter break. He was crumpled, unshaven and oddly formal. "I need help, Nazir."

"You're repeating yourself, old son. Give me the details."

"House-sitting. A couple of weeks, maybe more." Below them, the widow-grey sea slopped round the footings of the embanking wall. "Kitty's gone away and I need an eye kept while I do some errands."

"Handsome, you said?"

"Lavish."

"Immaculate, immaculate," whispered Lambert into his pocket handkerchief. "That's how I thought we kept ourselves in this business, pure as a baby's armpit, until you came along, boy, like some cold-sore infiltrating our parts. Just look at me, I'm ill with it, the worry, the aggravation. How can a man operate when even his health is breaking down from the shock of betrayal?"

For a moment he contemplated the full extent of the handkerchief as though searching for the imprint on St Veronica's pall before stuffing it into his top pocket and rising from behind his desk.

Archie waited for the cup to pass. He knew Lambert of old, but this time the man was evidently *in extremis*.

"I used to have respect. My own front door. Why didn't you pay heed, young Renshawe? You set off jousting at the world, thinking you could unseat wickedness in a matter of days. But a week is more than enough to entrap the unwary."

"What the devil are you driving at, Farncombe? You forced me into the Moscow job, remember?"

"I'm still driving all right, boy. I'm driving *out*!"

Behind Archie there was a click-clack of heels across the polished boards. He turned. The man at his back could have been Lambert's younger brother: slim, sandy-haired, the same infantine old-man's face.

"Let me introduce you," said Lambert. "Adam Crombie. In future he's deputed to do the necessary instead of you, Archibald."

"The sack?"

"The push, Renshawe. Your cards, dismissal, discharge, the whole bloody works. But none of this will go down on paper, you understand," the old man went on sweetly. "You shall have the most excellent testimonials from me. In Adam's words, 'a simple matter of rationalisation'!"

"What he means," said the new man in a nasal south-east Essex accent, "is that he won't put up with wallies like you any longer. Debt-collecting, foreigners – you don't know the first thing about any of it." Crombie sat on the corner of the desk fingering the back loop of his high-gloss rancher's boots. "That 'cello woman, for instance. I would have wiped the floor with her. Now look where she's landed us."

Archie stared straight at Lambert. "Where has she landed us?"

Lambert avoided his eye. "Someone got wind we were over-extended, boy. Adam reckons she's been putting the story about. Or someone has."

"We?"

The old man shifted in his seat. "Well, me, then. A little investment of mine went wrong."

"How wrong?"

"Two hundred and fifty thousand."

Archie whistled.

"Squeezed me, didn't they?" Lambert shouted. "Cut off my line of credit. A lovely development. Sixteen top-class units in a country-house conversion – park, all landscaped. Then someone bribes the builder to abscond with the first-stage payment before laying a brick. That was my liquidity up the spout. I tried fourteen banks to raise the necessary but word had got round and I had to settle for their offer."

"Whose offer?"

"Our new employers, young Renshawe, that's whose. They've

instructed me to terminate your contract. From now on we service a single large account – theirs. No more county court enforcement orders. This is the big time. But none of this is news to you, is it, boy? You knew about it all along, didn't you?"

"I don't believe I'm hearing this, Farncombe."

Lambert's tone suddenly lost its edge. "You mean it wasn't you?"

Archie shook his head.

"Told you, Lambert," Crombie said. "He wouldn't have had the bottle. Remember what the confidential print-out said about him? 'Excellent with small accounts requiring the personal touch but insufficiently adaptable for re-training in the broad-based strategy required for large recoveries.' Verbatim. Like I said, a wally." He smoothed down the fish-tail end of his violet tie between the lapels of his club blazer. "Too soft, see."

Archie ignored him. "If it wasn't me, who did roll you up, Lambert?"

The old man seemed to lose heart. "I don't know, boy, I don't know. Things have gone wrong ever since that professor came on to our books. I picked you special for that job, Archie. You'd have told me, boy, wouldn't you, if you'd done something indelicate?"

Archie thought of Kitty, nude, on the gravy-coloured bed. "Of course I would, Lambert, of course I would."

After Archie had pocketed his redundancy cheque Crombie brought in a bottle and they had a couple of apple brandies apiece. Archie fiddled with the envelope in his inside pocket. "It was that bloody Tremayne, wasn't it?"

"What was?"

"That did the dirty on Lambert and me. I recognise the style. Buying people, paying them off."

"Right in one," said Crombie.

Lambert sat silent contemplating his glass.

"The bastard's ruined me," said Archie.

"And me," said Lambert.

"And terrified the Slater woman. Someone broke into her house. He even tried to gas us."

Crombie grinned. "North Sea, was it?"

"It's not funny, not when it happens to you. And you can bet your life he'll be on to you, too."

Lambert re-corked the Calvados. "The boy's right," he said. "Adam – we need to get our heads together. What are we going to do about this bugger Tremayne?"

*   *   *

That first day Edith Slater did as she had done for twenty years and was to do at exactly the same time throughout Kitty's stay: at the last stroke of noon she unlocked the cold cupboard between her kitchen and scullery and brought out a litre bottle of Gordon's Export Gin, an earthenware jug of Italian vermouth and a bowl of unstoned black olives.

"I do think that a woman who lives alone ought to make an effort. It isn't easy and one needs all the help one can get."

In the drawing-room which smelled of yeast and furniture polish Kitty felt deliciously safe. The gin drew her out. She was struck by Edith's paintings. She thought they were quite beautiful.

"You are very beautiful, Kitty. Will you sit for me?"

And Kitty did in the clear mornings while Edith painted, gently woolgathering before the gin.

"You must feel so desolate, my dear. He said you had had a breakdown. Can you remember?"

At first it seemed enormously important to Kitty that she should not forget anything about Archie that last day. But after a while she could not remember his face clearly. Instead she remembered the set of his shoulders and the cut of his hair. But not until the third day could she bring herself to talk about him. When she began, her whole body shook.

"He has gone," was all she said. Edith had waited, tactfully, until nothing more came, then mixed the drinks and talked about the garden while the girl wandered the room, glass in hand.

There was a grand piano and a record player for old seventy-eights. Cards edged the looking-glass over the chimney-piece, invitations to previews, flowershows, parochial church meetings, mostly out of date. Kitty said to herself, one day we do this, another we do that. How inevitable her existence unfolds. Calendrical. Chronic. Like the gin.

Not since that first time in the seaside dusk when Archie had touched her had Kitty felt so warm and secure. Klavdia had guessed. *Take him and keep him before someone else does. They don't grow on trees.*

Klavdia's vulgarity had caused her to shout back in protest, but Klavdia was always right about such matters, and when Archie had brought her to the horrible house in London he shared with another woman, she had been so distraught and ashamed at the thought of losing him that she had wept. Since then she had continued to weep in spite of what had happened between them. And she thought that she wept because if he had been here he, too, would have wept because he was like her – a victim. Slater had said that was why he married her: to save her. Alone she would have thought to avoid being sacrificed by sacrificing herself first, and after Slater's death she had tried by walling herself up with what remained of him, but she could not put herself to sleep. There was no escape.

"Do you know very much about this Mr Renshawe, my dear?" Edith asked one day. They were in the kitchen, a dark hemi-spherical place where queer pans hung from hooks like blunt surgical instruments.

How could she explain to this quiet lady who made appointments to visit fruit and vegetable shows, that after he had lain with her on her husband's bed she only knew how lost she was before he knew her; and that she believed in fate? What good would it have done Slater's sister to say, I have been weak and foolish and abominable in the face of your brother's death but the thought of the days becoming weeks and my still being without him, this young Mr Renshawe, is turning me sick?

"Almost nothing," she said. "Not very much at all."

"After dinner," said Edith, "I must show you the family album."

Over coffee Kitty obediently went through the pictures. Some had curly guillotined edges the colour of meerschaum. The oldest: Slater leading a pony, Edith on a swing. Then, amongst a group of university people, his first wife and another woman in a broad-brimmed straw hat.

24

"Good heavens." Helen screwed up her eyes against the poor focus of the Box Brownie snap. "I know that woman. When I was an undergraduate we used to joke about her: better off enjoying life and getting a third than ending up like poor old Vera Stacpoole."

"She's Slutskaya now," said Archie.

"I'm not surprised. Always a Slutskaya, our Vera. Couldn't avoid it. In the make-up, you know, though I must say she looks almost human in that hat."

Unsure of himself ever since the lodge porter had brought him to the door of Helen's rooms, Archie remained on his feet, waiting for an invitation to be seated while Helen paced to and fro, tapping her teeth with a pencil.

"God, she was affected! Still the same, apparently, twenty years after, and she was already an old dear then. Are you sure it was her you met on your Soviet jaunt?"

Archie nodded at the photograph. "She's worn well. Recognisably the same person, even without the hat."

"Well, well, there's a thing, the less ourselves we become as the years pass. By now I would have expected her to look like Pol Pot in a frock. Approachable, you said?"

"That varied and seemed to depend on her mood."

"Capricious as always. Yes, that was Vera. In our adolescent vulgarity we girls put it down to an unhappy love affair but, whatever had happened, the poor dear had quite let herself go. I remember she used to appear at tutorials in different-coloured stockings."

Helen's knack for casual brutality reminded Archie that he always ought to have been glad when he awoke and found that her head wasn't still nestling his on the pillow. Twenty years on and she hadn't forgotten the stockings.

"Try the sling-back," she said, noting his discomfort. And while Archie tested out an institutional dowel-and-hessian arrangement she stretched out on a wide, low divan which doubled as a bed. Between them was a table, even lower than the divan on to which Helen flung Vera's photograph. Archie stared at an almanack on the wall behind her with a view of lushly dark college gardens in which two crinolined ladies sat taking tea.

"I know what you're thinking."

She didn't. She never had. She certainly wasn't going to begin now. "How very unlike old Helen all this."

Her, in fact, to a T. Real opulence would have fitted her like a glove, but there was sufficient here to tempt her into brazenness. She heaved an exaggerated sigh. "Three terms only – two here, one abroad, but all found while you're in residence. So what do you think of your clever girl enmarbled in her hall – if we can so term College's subvention of modern architecture?"

Archie enjoyed the depth of the two-storeyed room. Above his head twin balconies jutted out from Helen's sleeping quarters across banks of plants reaching into a high space where steel beams angled to the glass frontage which fell sheer to the unkempt bank of the river. "You're a fortunate lady. I only wish you'd told me before."

"And you'd have paid me a visit?"

No, he would have been alerted sooner to what she said she couldn't find in their relationship, the absence of which she couldn't define, but which had turned out to be what she'd played all her life for: not passion, not even love, simply a congenial place to live, status, and free lunches thrown in.

"I was doing you a favour, Archie. Being cruel to be kind. You might have tried to hang on when we both knew it was finished long before I was awarded this little joy-ride. Besides, I wasn't in the mood for candour. Oxford can be like that, tempting you to throw off the old for the new. But despair not, old cock, it's only a visiting research fellowship after all, so I'll soon be back in London. By the way – out of pure academic interest – how did you track me down?"

Perhaps she knew him better than he was prepared to admit. Her physical presence, the simplicity of her smock frock, the piling of dark hair at the crown of her head were familiarly enticing. "Wasn't difficult. I made enquiries at the Museum. I ought to have let you know I was coming up here to see you, but when Kitty's –" She looked away as though suddenly disparaged by his mention of the name – "Kitty's letter arrived with these pictures of Vera I knew I had to see you at once. I tried phoning but there was no answer."

It was bound to be spontaneous. Any warning, he knew, and she would have taken pleasure in turning him down. But now he had reached her on commission from Kitty, as it were, Helen was indifferent to him in a new way.

"Well, you're looking bright-eyed enough in spite of the Soviet *angst*. Rather slimmer but it suits you. I'd say foreign travel has obviously loosened your stays, darling. A pity you never let *me* make off with you but I suppose Florence and Siena can't compete with Something-or-other-old-Grad. Obviously La Slutskii reckons she found her spiritual home there. So what's Vera doing for the cause these days?"

"She's a pensioner now. Retired. Living in a village near Moscow."

"Sounds heavenly. From manor house to mud hut."

"A sort of cottage, actually." Archie was slightly nettled. "Nothing fancy but decent enough. Nice outlook. Quiet. You know."

"Don't tell me, the Karl Marx Eveningtide Home where she gardens and makes hats."

"Not exactly. Her social life is still quite extensive."

That Vera saw a lot of people, a great deal of some people, everything of a very choice few, Archie kept to himself, but for some reason Helen seemed to find the idea of Vera's retirement very funny and laughed so much that Archie, feeling excluded, got up and began to explore the rest of the ground floor. Under the balconies he found a smart kitchenette. On a little draining-board lay five of his Endymion Road cups.

Helen's laughter was trickling away. She swung her legs off the divan and leant in his direction. "I'm being inhospitable – I expect you'd like a drink after your journey, but it had better be tea, since you're such an abstemious soul."

"I'm afraid I can't stay, Nell. Someone's waiting for me downstairs."

"You are the limit, Archie, don't tell me it's that Russian female who sent the photographs?"

"Of course not. It's one of my colleagues. He's called Crombie."

"You mean you've brought a crummy little bailiff with you, into an Oxford college? Lord God, Archie, where's your self-respect?"

"I wanted your help. I won't outstay my welcome. You can pretend we're insurance men, if you like. I only really care about the pictures."

As he turned to her the lining of his jacket caught the brass handle of a Turkish coffee-pot which fell to the tiles with a crash.

"When you've *quite* finished, Archie," she called from the divan, photographs in hand. "Don't you think we'd better parcel up these little mementoes of yesteryear's intelligentsia?"

She chattered on with the same old affectionate contempt which had once given him an odd sense of security. "What possessed you, anyway, bringing them to me when the right contacts in London wouldn't have given a hoot about identifying these has-beens?"

"OK, OK, I know I shouldn't have wanted to see you. I didn't think I did at first." Her heavy eyebrows contracted in that typical way he knew he was going to mourn. "I suppose I wanted an objective view."

"Plus insights – from one in the know?"

"That, too, yes."

She fanned out the photographs on the table and craned back to peer at them longsightedly. "My problem, Archie, dear love, is distinct lack of curiosity about these specimens. They're extinct types, throwbacks to another age which looked East for solutions to the mess they'd made of themselves. You know, like extras in the Chinese opera, what was it – in the East the Red Dawn rises – something of that sort. Stalin-groupies, golden lads and lasses who discovered social-engineering was better than sex. All monied, of course, and awash with faith in the perfectability of man."

Archie crossed to the divan and stood behind her. "Is *he* there?"

"Who?"

"Oliver Slater?"

She pointed. "Of course, see, there, at the back – the one with the leonine head of hair – that's Oliver Slater. Blond then, but quite white when I knew him. Still a great mane, though, and my, was he proud of it. God knows when it was taken. Post-war – late forties?"

This time Archie sat next to her on the divan, so close he could feel the line of her thigh. Vera and Slater had been snapped under a tree. Away from them, deeper, almost concealed within the summer foliage was another figure, tall, more elegantly dressed than his picnic companions. In his hand a glass. Archie fingered the white blur of the man's flowing cravat. "And him?"

Helen took the photograph and blew a kiss at the face. "Acolytes – remember?"

Vaguely, vaguely, but less vaguely than the pose – reticent and inviting, yet oddly severe. "Yes?"

"Yes, yes, Tremayne, that was him, then. He's changed."

"No," said Archie. "He hasn't changed."

Helen shifted away to rummage in her handbag for cigarettes. "Then you've met?"

"Only the one brief encounter."

"Enough?"

"More than enough but I keep getting demands from him for a repeat." He strolled over to the window where a triple row of bookshelves cut across the run of glass. Along the top shelf stood a magenta porcelain bird, a blue horse and a pair of crystal Venetian fish.

She took another cigarette and lit it. "I'm a rather distinguished academic, in case you hadn't noticed, making my way in a highly competitive man's world. I oughtn't to have let myself go on about the wretched Vera when all the poor old dear found out about men was that her type could be even more condescending than yours."

The attack was factitious, she knew, but once launched she was relentless. Harder now? Unhappier, perhaps?

"All right, Nell, all right. But I did spend a lot of time on you when you were still on the way up. Did Vera go in for affairs?"

"Preferably unconsummated. Nothing so gross as the physical for Vera Stacpoole, I'd have thought. She seems to have preferred men who'd never get down to it – not with a woman, at any rate. Tremayne was right up her street. Very fastidious, he'd faint at the merest whiff of nail-varnish. No, with Evelyn it would have been heart sighing to heart, nothing unhygienic."

Archie wondered if this were her present situation. To judge by the dark half-moons under her eyes, she might herself be suffering the kind of art-historical wooing Tremayne had inflicted on Vera. "Tell me about him," he said.

"Certainly not, it's indecent. You'll be examining me for love-bites next."

"Don't play the fool, Nell. You know I mean Tremayne."

But her lower lip quivered. The mistake was genuine. In the old days she would have enjoyed giving him literally a blow-by-blow account of who did what to whom, and how. Then it had been a prelude, a sexual aperitif, now it might pain him and that would be even more pleasurable to her. Vexed at his apparent indifference, she took the rebuff as a pretext to air her sophistication about the rarified world in which she was at one breath with Stacpoole, Slater and Tremayne, far beyond the reach of a common interloper like A. Renshawe Esq.

"You couldn't begin to understand such a man, because he isn't a man at all – not in your sense of the word. Remember Peter Pan?"

Archie did, with distaste.

She nodded. "Exactly. Tremayne is one of the Lost Boys, a whole generation that loved secrets and soulmates to share them with. No family, no experience of love, simply intimacy with a clique, one which went adventuring politically and sexually. But where in dear dull old England could they find the real smack of discipline?" Helen brought her hand down on the divan with a karate chop. "That kind of spice is exotic. Asiatic, even, so they turned their pilgrimage Eastwards, as I said before, and rediscovered the stern father in Lenin, Stalin, the real gruff old Daddies who stood for no nonsense. Those people in your antique snaps, darling, they had fallen in love with the objective forces of history, or so they thought. Until one day it turns out that Daddy is Captain Hook after all and they're on the sea-end of his gangplank. Only Vera and Tremayne made the final leap. She went over completely, went native, if you like. He stuck it out back here."

"Why, if she'd gone already?"

"They weren't *sleeping* together. She was an errand girl. Besides, it was more use to his Soviet employers in England . . ."

"His *what*?"

"Good God, I thought you said you knew about him, Archie. The man was a traitor. Still is, I imagine. Some kind of fucking gentleman spy."

This revelation about Tremayne did not enhance Archie's frame of mind. "What about the Russian girl, Lambert, the rest of the troupers in this farce?"

"Oh, them," Helen said contemptuously. "They're just being strung along."

He believed her. He knew nothing except that he believed her and because he did only Tremayne was left in the frame. Only him and the old woman with the Red Masque of Death lipstick. "And Vera?"

"Well, she was always rather grand, even after her breakdown. Rich, too, though in my day she lived over a betting shop in King's Cross and kept a kind of bohemian open house. Tremayne used to go to her parties. He loved slumming – a bit like Slater with Slater's woman."

"Wife."

"Lady, then. Tart. Heroine. The widow, victim of the victim."

Archie had been bracing himself for just such an outburst of spite. Down below a man and a boy were kneeling at the riverside. The man was having difficulty in baiting the boy's rod. The afternoon sun had shifted behind them, pricking through the leaves in thorns of white light.

Helen laughed her vulgar laugh. "You've gone all slushy, Renshawe, slushy and intense. What is it this time – spiritual union?"

Archie remained at the window. "When you start acting like this, Helen, I wonder what I saw in you in the first place."

She kicked off her shoes and lit another cigarette. "All right, all right, I'm a sarcastic bitch but that kind of soulful female brings out the worst in me. Being interestingly miserable does wonders for some women. You've never looked at me in the way you do whenever *her* name crops up."

The man placed the boy's hands along the rod and sat back on his heels. Archie turned to her but said nothing. She looked bad.

"Don't go," she said very softly. "Tell me about her, the Slater woman."

He remained at the window, glad that his seriousness had evidently roused her, afraid for himself and for Kitty, wanting and not wanting to be open in front of this woman who had always, somehow, been an intruder in his life.

"You never knew her; if you had you wouldn't have given a straw for my chances. And neither did I until we discovered together that her old Russian boyfriend was a brute and a liar and the husband was worse. The queer thing is, I'm not sure if I even find her ordinarily attractive. She's timid and soft on the surface but underneath very strong. I don't know if I like the combination. Since Slater died her friends have said and done things that would have driven a normal person wild but she seems just to accept them without a word, and you feel stupid, caring about what's been done. With a woman like that I can't tell if she's fooling them, herself, or me; there's no way of knowing."

Outside the boy and his father were laughing. Helen came across the room and took Archie's hands in hers. "That's her technique, darling, hadn't you realised? Frogs into princesses."

He remembered Borka's search for the right word – magician? wizard? witch? "You don't know her."

"I don't need to know her, I know you. You're the same. You've never really believed that the world is as it is, and can become no other thing. And from what you've told me, neither does she. Try it like this: a vulnerable, rather scatty *ingenue* – a Russian, conjuring for a livelihood, for heaven's sake – meets an apparently dear old boy who sweeps her off her feet to a new country, new life, and before she knows where she is – pouf, whizz-bang, he's dead. Then investigations, detectives, sinister gentlemen-callers. Quite a home from home. Can she believe it? Did it happen? Did she ever really leave? Old friends abandon her, new ones pop up insinuating that all is not as it seems. So who can she trust, your wretched little newly-wed whose entire past has been expropriated and handed over to you for in-depth analysis? By now she's off her head, and all you can offer is emotional counselling. What are you going to do, Archie, magic her past away with a second proposal of marriage?'

"Why not?"

"Don't you know anything about women? She's damaged goods already, do you want to destroy her and yourself?"

"She says she loves me."

"Oh, my God, this I'm not hearing . . ."

"What's so weird? You did – once."

"I'm beginning to understand. It's that job, it's rotted you. Of course, of course, she's rich, now, isn't she? Now the husband's out of the way?"

He snatched away his hands. "You don't really mean that."

Father and son were departing across the flooded meadow, swinging an empty haversack between them.

By the time Archie came down Crombie had read all the notices on the board and was doing a soft-shoe shuffle on the tiles of the glazed portico. "What kept you?"

"Business," said Archie.

Outside Crombie stared up at the building. Against the glisten of silvered blinds his green corduroys looked baggy and homespun. "Get off," he said. "Students' place, isn't it? No money in students unless you're Barclays Bank." He pointed to a girl lying on a sofa chewing gum in a long empty room. "Ever watch that *University Challenge* where they ask them what they're reading?" As they passed Crombie's shadow fell across the tinted glass. The girl looked up and smiled. He paused to right the set of his lapels. "*Penthouse*, that's what she's reading. I saw her. Students, I ask you, who needs them? That porter chap had a cheek, too. Asked me not to smoke. Smoke? I said, I don't smoke and I don't read pornography either, but he kept staring at me like I didn't belong in his fish-tank hostel, so I told him, my colleague has an appointment up there, with one of the lady teachers . . ."

"Fellows."

Crombie winked at the girl who blew back a gum-pink bubble between thick half-open lips. "Something you'll never be, will you, darling?" he called back from the gates. "Not a feller."

Insisting on a detour rather than going straight back to the car, Crombie led him through the vehicles massed in the municipal car park before turning right into the main road.

On Magdalen Bridge they looked down into the brown water. A tramp passed them, took a seat on the wooden bench nearby and pulling a clean white handkerchief from his bundle, blew his nose very carefully. "Money," said Crombie when they reached Magdalen Tower. "The place crackles with it. Even the beggars can afford a break."

"Just keep an eye out, will you?" The day was bright and cold and Archie felt glad to have left Helen behind.

At Longwall Street they waited for the lights. "An eye out?" repeated Crombie. "An eye out for what?"

Archie felt embarrassed. The man wasn't a serious human being.

How could you confide to him that you had this feeling that some very serious person had marked you out for attention?

"People," he said.

Crombie looked back towards the gargoyles along the steep frontage of Magdalen. "What people?"

"Not our kind of people."

"That's my kind," said Crombie, squaring his shoulders and increasing pace. "Always one step ahead of your kind of people. If I had any information worth having nobody would need to kill me for it – I'd tell them straightaway at the first sign of violence. That's Lambert's rule, and it's a good one."

"Is that a fact?"

"That's a fact, old-school-tie. Lambert again: 'a constituent of reality'. That's a fact. You can stub you toe on them, facts. Now what facts can you assemble about these mysterious people who're supposed to be on your trail?"

Archie told him: Moscow; Clacton; the gas. "And there was a break-in at my place last night. The landlord's given me a week's notice. Oh, God, Adam, I'm fed up with this job. I used to enjoy it once, beetling around on expenses, flannelling people into paying their dues. Now I curse the day I ever set foot on the Slater threshold."

Kitty sat in the window-seat and looked down on the trees shading Edith's garden. The light was good. Edith began to paint.

"Forget yourself, Kitty. Don't pose, dear."

From the top-floor studio Kitty could see as far as the dark of Ashdown Forest. "Today I am nervous," she said. "Yesterday Archie tells me by telephone the photographs are important. Don't believe me, Edith, but I think he is always right."

"Look towards me. Now a little to the left."

Kitty tried to relax and keep the angle of view. On the palette Edith's brush hand was quivering perceptibly as she worked up a flesh tint. "Is it important to you, dear, that he should always be right?"

"Of course," murmured the girl, her lips tight from the pose. "He is a man loving his work and his work is nothing if some people say to others his work is not good."

Edith cheated the tremor by taking up her brush. "What people, Kitty? Oliver's people? Do you really think poor Oliver's friends would dream of harming a young man's reputation?"

Kitty had not intended to alarm her sister-in-law who naturally still believed that her brother had been an honourable man. And, at times, during the last few days, listening to his sister reminisce, Kitty had agreed. Not loving, not decent, not good. But he had made her rich. Honourable, then, in act if not thought. She squeezed her hands together between her knees. "Oh, Edith, I did not tell you before, but a bad person made lies about Oliver. Archie looks for him now to find the truth. Soon we shall know."

Her head to one side Edith took the measure of the portrait along the blade of her palette-knife. Suddenly, as if inspired, she scraped away Kitty's freshly-painted eyes. "Sometimes the things of the body are better interred with the body, wouldn't you say?"

Kitty did not reply because she did not understand. Talk of Archie had excited her. She imagined him pulling up the collar of his rain-coat, going around London, Oxford, Clacton to follow dangerous, sinister people, and thinking, this is ridiculous, the Russian girl is ridiculous but beautiful, and will have my children. And inside her head she heard his complaints, very clearly, about her and Slater, and she knew that he would continue to follow and complain until he had brought the story of her husband back to her, dead and alive.

She shifted right at Edith's nod. Edith thinks I am deranged by grief and infatuation but only Archie knows me. I was right to send him those pictures. The man in the picture who was not Slater, he will help him to discern the buried truth.

25

I f only Archie had said once that she looked pretty she wouldn't have minded that the bleak morning sun must be showing her up. But when he launched straightaway into a long complicated story Kitty felt that in spite of all the care she had taken the night before, her hair was out of condition, her frock too formal for a day by the sea, and the scuffed heels of her Soviet court shoes gave the lie to any attempt at elegance.

As their cable car twirled in planetary equipoise to the slow motions of the big wheel the breeze played at her uneven fringe disrupting her view. He went on talking, pink-cheeked, earnest, his spectacles glinting against the white foreshore below. First in England, then in Russia, Vera had known Slater who knew another woman called Helen who had never been to Russia but was someone distinguished at Oxford, and knew everyone. On and on he went, until her head was whirling round like the cable seat and she had become so confused that it was impossible to concentrate on anything except her appearance.

The pier had been his idea. A nice day, a stroll, a chat. He had hardly paused for breath since collecting her from Edith's early that morning. In the car it was the house: there'd been changes; he hoped she would approve. Then a new man, Adam, someone who would take turns with Nazir.

What for?

Why, for her protection of course – remember the gas?

The case?

The case was progressing. A few developments while she'd been at Edith's, but they would keep. Until now.

Kitty shivered in the April sun. Pah! Little boys' games! Yesterday had gone in a fever of anticipation: will he have changed? Will I? Will we remember together the flat brown bed? Now she simply wished she had brought a coat.

Today the first kiss had been the only one. On her cheek. And when she allowed her disappointment to show, he stared back gravely like a regretful parent, but made no further move.

The work on the house was not yet finished, she must understand. *Damn understandingness.* "Yes. Of course. I see." He was taking her for granted.

The builders . . .

I hate the builders. Kiss me again, kiss me properly. In the car she had tried to take his hand. *I don't care about anything until I touch you. Let me. Touch me back.*

He had smiled at her, empty-eyed, and did not relax his grip on the gear lever. Now it seemed an age since she had desired him so passionately.

The wheel started downwards. "Archie, I do not like this machine. Let us return to Slater's house, Archie, please."

"Stop behaving like a child, Kitty. You know I can't stay. I've work to do. You made the work – with *this*." From his jacket pocket he produced the sheaf of photographs which she had posted from Edith's.

In reply she merely edged her face closer to his, dreading a repetition of his incomprehensible stories about Slater and all those old people who ought to be dead. She wanted to be reminded of how it had been that first day in the brown bedroom, but these horrible old people kept pressing between her and this man and she felt the coldness of death upon them, stilling her heart. The blast of the mechanical organ music came nearer and with it the smash of heavy breakers on the wooden piles of the cat-walk. Suddenly she was shouting. "You don't love me, bloody man! You are English! You have me so afterwards you can feel guilty as hell. After even one kiss you Englishmen are guilty. You have the women, then think of death!"

He made to put his arm round her but she pushed him away. To make himself heard above the noise he had to shout back. "God above, woman, do you think I go round making love to all my female clients?" When the chairs swayed down to a halt at the bottom her head was drooped back and her breath came so harsh that he almost lifted her out, afraid she might faint, kissing her high on the cheekbone. "Of course I love you, of course, of course . . ."

"Poor kid," said the man operating the wheel lever. "No head for heights. Ought to have more sense, mate, taking nervy ladies for this kind of ride." Between the crude slats of the pierway Archie saw the green-meat lustre of seawater and felt sick.

By the space-age amusement arcade Kitty dug her nails into his wrist and said, "Be nice to me."

"I'm sorry, I'm doing my best but this is hardly the place, and I've got a lot on my mind. Try to see it from my point of view."

But she dashed away to the exit before he could finish. A huge black man in a Batman sweatshirt was asking for her ticket when he caught up. "You want to come back, darling, you need it."

"I never go back," Kitty exclaimed, twisting round in the gateway and pointing at Archie. "You know him?"

The black man shrugged.

"I tell you," she continued. "He pretends to love a woman but he is a liar. After, he leaves her."

The black man looked Archie up and down dispassionately. "That so? I got my own love life, lady. If he wants to go back he needs a ticket. You both need tickets."

Beyond the turnstiles a clockwork Pierrot gyrated inside a glass booth, stopping every so often to let loose a mechanical "Hahahaha".

"We've had enough for one day," said Archie. "We're not going back."

"Suit yourself," said the bouncer and unlocked the gate. As he did so Kitty placed her arm on his and gave a wild shout. "I tell the world – this man." She turned to Archie. "This man is treating me wrong, over and over again he is treating me bad." It sounded like a dirge from some old blues ballad.

Eventually Archie got away from onlookers, half-dragging her across the forecourt, past the padlocked Champagne Bar, the police van, and between the plastic foldaway café tables to a more open spot where a number of people lingered in the morning chill, apparently unable to decide to eat, drink, try the beach or simply call it a day and go home. Kitty leant against the wall of a shuttered beach hut.

"OK, OK, I say I am sorry. I expect things. I am disappointed. So I get exhausted, tired. I get tired, waiting. I look like old woman already and maybe I die waiting for you to start wanting me or not."

A middle-aged couple in blue and white reversible anoraks went by chattering brightly on their way up the cobbled slipway to the cliff steps. Kitty watched. They looked so deep in companionship that she felt shut away from all possibility in life, on this barren foreshore where the current of sea air was penetrating her summer frock.

"Not that again, please," he said. "I can't make you out. I mean, can't you stop exaggerating for once in your life? This all began because I helped you out of one difficulty without realising you'd manufacture others until I don't know where they'll end. I'm fond of you, all right. I probably love you, but I'm hardly the first lover you've had, am I? There was dear old Pymka Floribunda, remember?"

"Ach, Florinskii, I damn his soul." To Archie's amazement and relief she spat at the wall timbers, not at him.

"I daresay, but how do you think that makes *me* feel? Especially now you've started on in the same vein, and in public."

By the time they reached Kitty's street a rumbling sound was coming from under the radiator-end of the Daimler. Outside the gate Archie released the bonnet-catch.

"This noise, Archie. It is an omen."

Back here again, she felt sick from fear and shame.

At first the house looked exactly the same as before, but when she saw it was not because someone had painted the porch-columns cream and there were brown and cream blinds instead of net over the front windows, she felt even more afraid.

"It was an omen," she repeated as Archie helped her out of the car.

"The power-steering cable. It's developed a leak. That's the end of our transport for a while."

Two figures were waiting at the side door. She only recognised one. "Nazir! Nazir!" He at least was unchanged. Noticing that the grandfather clock in the hall had stopped at a quarter to four she felt that the Yucca tree was to blame because its spiky green leaves cast shadows across the one place in the house where there had always been light.

The man called Adam showed her round her own house. On the tiled floor of the kitchen his shoes looked too big to belong to his feet. He introduced the new machines. "Programmable automatic with integral drive, fridge freezer, convector, microwave with browning facility, cordless iron, multi-function food processor. Every mod con the busy housewife requires." He was nibbling a biscuit from a fibre-glass tray on which tea-things had been arranged. "All part of the service. Like a cuppa?" The tea tasted as bitter as wine.

Upstairs smelt of fresh paint and carpet shampoo. A heavy double door bisected the long corridor. At the far end the marital bedroom had been transformed by *mille-fleurs* wallpaper and ivory paintwork which matched the new bed-hangings. All that remained was Slater's old wardrobe. Inside, his clothing was untouched.

"Renshawe drew the line at that," said Crombie. "Sentimental value."

"Give it to Oxford," said Kitty.

Crombie fingered the suit linings. "'Bradbury, Venables and Hookham'," he read from a label below the inside collar of a three-piece suit in clerical grey, "'Gentlemen's Outfitters Oxford'. Think they'd take them back?"

Archie appeared in the doorway, a black plastic bin liner over one shoulder, the tea-tray in his hands. "Stop playing the fool, Adam. *Oxfam*. You know what she means."

"Off with the old and on with the new. Yes, I know what she means." Crombie began to unhook Slater's clothes from the hanging rail, muttering under his breath, "We'll soon have you to rights, Miss. Don't be scared, Miss, Renshawe's on the job, sorting you out a treat. This time tomorrow you won't know yourself."

Archie set down the tray next to a sheaf of irises on the gilt bedside cabinet. "No time to put them in water. We weren't expecting you . . ." He paused, embarrassed, his fingers stiff amidst the tea-cups. "Well, not . . ."

"So soon?" Kitty flicked back the hinged lid of the silver teapot and peered inside.

"Too right." Crombie clumped past with his overfilled bag. "It's not yet safe. We've the mortice deadlocks to change, front and back, never mind sorting the jumble. You've no idea what a proper home-coming entails."

When he had gone Kitty sat down. "Archie, I do not like this Adam man. Not even his tea. His tea is horrible. This is his tea?"

In the distance Nazir was calling to Adam while he tinkered with the car. His voice sounded fleering.

"The renovations cost a pretty penny, I'm afraid. Do you want to go through the accounts now?"

"Later Archie, not now. Archie. Please, now, will you do something I want?"

He put away the big loose-leaf file of tenders and receipts. "Now?"

"Now," she said again, after a very deep breath. "Lock the door and close this new blind."

"But it's mid-afternoon."

"Now."

He shut out the feather-white sea. When he turned the thin little frock was already over her head. "For heaven's sake, Kitty, anybody may waltz in."

"The door," she said from the dark.

Downstairs Nazir was moving from room to room calling out Archie's name. Against the backdrop of the bed her body spread larger than life.

"There isn't time . . ."

She caught at his hair. "Again, again . . . again . . ."

The shouting came nearer.

"Stop. I must stop."

"Not. Not. Not."

Then she screamed. "Archie," she said afterwards. "Is this how it will be always?"

After a long while the shouting stopped and they heard the scuffle of footsteps deep in the body of the house.

"Are you not cold?" she asked simply as if nothing had taken place.

"I'm not anything," he said. "I'm nothing at all."

"But you are mine?"

"That's the dreadful thing, can't you understand?"

She could not understand.

"I've no job, no money, nowhere to live. Even my car's a write-off."

"I have home, money, everything – can this be bad?"

"Yes, it can, because it's not mine."

"And it is not mine." Her hands were at his throat, loosening then tightening the knot of his tie. "It is Slater's. I lose my country, you lose your job. So now I think he owes us his money, this dead old man."

Bored with take-aways after their first week's stay in Kitty's house, the three men had drawn up a kitchen rota. This evening it was Crombie's turn to cook. While he busied himself at the microwave Kitty sat at the corner of the new kitchen table and led the conversation: "You make very nice couple," she said to Nazir who was passing round Polaroids of himself and Klavdia in the Starlight Room of the Moscow hotel.

"Like food additives, the chemicals they use in those instants," said Crombie, inserting his casserole into the mouth of the oven, "makes people seem listless, I always think. Mind you, the thought of setting up house in Southall with Nasruddin Husain's female relations is enough to give any girl the pip. They'll never take to her, mark my words. Clash of cultures, see?" He grimaced at the panel and pressed the touch screen to high.

Kitty knew he meant her, not Klavdia. Was he the only one or did they all think that here in her newly Westernised kitchen, feet planted as firmly as Crombie's on the antique Dutch tiles which Archie had chosen especially with her in mind, she was out of place completely, clashing with them like her salad bowls and cheeseboards from Moscow ranged along the solid Victorian overmantel above the oh-so-English hateful Aga she had never learned to light?

"Take no notice," Nazir murmured to his photographs. "He's

eaten up with envy. Listen, what if I got on the airlines? I could stopover in Moscow and see her weekends."

Never let them out of your sight, Klavdia used to say. But how did you keep a man in view, day and night? Kitty scratched the high-gloss photograph showing them together, with Dymka, all cat-eyed from flashlight. "Are you marrying this girl, Nazir?"

Archie began to stab at the loaves of Ukrainian rye with the point of his salad knife while Nazir stared at the picture, one wing of his stiff white collar sticking out like the ear of a raffish terrier. Everyone, except Crombie, seemed embarrassed at the question.

"Tchah! Of course he isn't. The man's like me, a bigot. The only difference being that I'm an original whereas he comes from an ancient line of bigots."

"Watch your step, Adam," Archie called out. "And stop making trouble. It's not easy for him or anyone, making that kind of move."

Not for him, or for her, or for me, or anyone at all, thought Kitty, whom chance has so randomly placed in this half-and-half world.

Throughout Adam's Colombian *café filtré* and *babas au rhum*, Kitty's anxieties multiplied. "Archie, you are careless, they follow you, there is danger. Why have you not told me before? Stay, I need you, do not go next morning."

"It's all in the mind," said Crombie from the sink where he had begun to do the dishes. "He's been seeing things since that day in Oxford. Nobody's after him. No need to fuss about tomorrow – I'll nursemaid him for you."

The idea of another long journey in Crombie's company was too much for Archie. He shook his head. "No, no, you'll be wanted here with Nazir, to look after Kitty. Besides, now the Daimler's out of commission I'll be going up by train."

Crombie hated trains. "Hire a car."

"At this hour of the night?"

An argument followed until Kitty intervened. The men appeared reproachful.

"You never said Professor Slater had a car. You never mentioned it, not to me," said Nazir.

"Yes, yes, remember – your first time here in the dark winter? You gave me petrol bill. Of course he has his car, but I don't care because I cannot drive."

Archie imagined an Austin Seven rusting in one of the Gothic outhouses. "Where is it, then, this car?"

"Behind the Ivanhoe Guest House," explained Nazir. "There's a lock-up next to the septic tank."

"Eight months in the damp?" Crombie wrung out his dishcloth.

"Not a chance. You'll need jump leads to get her started. Anyway, Renshawe's not insured . . ."

Kitty had tried to put the car out of her mind since Slater's death.

"England is beautiful," she had said. Where the car stood that summer the heath was so thick with gorse that she could not open the door and they had to picnic there on the green seats which smelt of limes and rock-salt. Then she had never even thought about being happy or sad, or about anything at all that was different from how she felt then.

"You are beautiful," Slater had answered. "Nobody can see us. Be immodest. Let us make love now."

It was a semi-automatic Lanchester in British Racing Green. They jacked her off the axle-stands and re-inflated the tyres. After swapping batteries with his Daimler, Archie cranked her with the handle and she fired on the third swing. While the engine was running Nazir checked inside and out. From under the spare tyre in the back he dug out a straw hamper and five empty bottles of Mateus Rosé. On the dashboard lay a pair of dark glasses and an appointment book which he passed out. Kitty watched as Archie flicked through the gold-edged pages. She knew what was there.

"*Christmas at Edith's. Katya, Katya. First New Year***Godmersham***the orchard***Patrixbourne, Wingham, Posling, Fields of wheat.*"

A whole winter and summer, place upon place, star after star.

"I am cold," she whispered.

"*Poor little kid.*" Klavdia's voice came again, bell-like across the thrum of the pistons. "*You look as if you've seen a ghost. Keep them apart. Never go back. Buck up and keep your past out of his hair.*"

"You're crying, Kitty," said Archie. "What on earth's the matter?"

She wanted to say that it was too long ago for anything that mattered then to matter now, but his eyes had that kindly look from before, unknowing and honest, as though he were on the point of seeing into her but had turned away before the realisation.

"What a beauty," shouted Nazir from the car. "Wish she were mine."

Before parting they came down together into the brightly lit hall. Everything was as it had been on the night they first met. The clock ticked. The Yucca had gone, the khaki roller-blinds which Crombie had fitted over the stained-glass panel. Even the batwings of Slater's unfurled umbrella still sagged from the hatstand.

Archie took the brown, leatherbound appointment book out of his pocket. "I shall hand this over to Tremayne tomorrow. Then he will burn it and that will be the last rite between us and him, and him and your Slater. Is that what you want?"

"Of course." She noticed for the first time how his hair was thinning. "What else do I want?"

"This?"

It was a photograph of them together. Slater in white tie, Kitty *décolletée*, looking angry. "I remember Oxford," she said. "The Queen's College, Oxford. A ball. That was how it was once. He was a fraud. We were both frauds, Archie."

He said nothing. On the kitchen table were documents from Slater's car. Here, where the light was cooler, she wanted to touch the bare patch high in his red hair but she did not because he was now going away and nothing further from her would be effective.

"You take his car?"

"I do," he said briskly, and kissed her above the eyes.

Then he would come back because the car was not his? "Then, I will wait for you. You will come back?"

"I expect so." He felt slightly irked at her reasoning. "I expect so," he repeated. "Sometime. Sometime after tomorrow."

26

O n the first floor Tremayne was standing alone among the oval tables, green-shaded lamps and bays of books, his back towards the tall library windows.

"You should have come to me sooner."

He sat down at the table nearest the window. No gin, no invitation to be seated. "Well?"

Archie said, "I had a few loose ends to tie up."

"Very loose, I imagine." On the street an ice-cream van blared out its jingle and a woman laughed. Tremayne was drumming his fingers on the scarlet leather table-top. "Presumably you have, nevertheless, reached some conclusion?"

Archie leant forward to present the cardboard folder containing his report, then stepped back, preserving the distance between them.

"Time presses. I would prefer a verbal presentation, Mr Renshawe."

Archie was ready for this and started well, but his calm, efficient manner seemed to irritate Tremayne who stopped him short. "Your accent . . . Unconducive at this time of day . . . May I?" And with a noise between a groan and a sigh he snatched up the papers and made a bolt for what looked like part of the library wall, but which turned out, after he had disappeared, to be a door cut into one of the panels and decorated with the same pink and sage stucco motif as the rest of the room.

Like the insult about his accent, the venue had been selected to intimidate, but although he was nervous, this time Archie was surer of his ground and consequently less affected by the grandeur of his surroundings. Twice he strolled the length and breadth of the room, touching the thigh of the nymph on the horribly gilt clock, riffling through the books which faced down at him as solid as bricks.

Time had been chosen as well as place: at four o'clock on a Sunday afternoon, in the absence of secretaries, librarians, switchboard girls, everyone except the bald caretaker who had let him in, Tremayne, Archie guessed, would normally have been alone with his gin.

The fake wall-door swung out. "A word?" He beckoned Archie

in, and spoke wearily but quite at his ease, making no effort to curb the disdain which the presence of this guest evoked in his old-school features. "You must forgive the disorder." He elbowed past a tall secretaire from the drawers of which a cliff-face of papers hung over the flap. "Mrs Kavanagh does her bottoming this time of year. Ignore the turn-out, man, find a seat."

Archie cleared a high stool of books and sat over against his host who spread himself rangily in a broad wing-chair. On the patch of cream carpet between them lay Archie's word-processed sheets.

"The annual festival – Mrs Kavanagh's Christmas – bottoming. Never heard the expression except from her. Irish, I take it?"

"English. It's what inflation's supposed to do – bottom out."

"Ah, very Irish," but before Archie could form a polite smile, the voice had sharpened to a venomous whisper. "Understand this, Renshawe, I deeply resent your interference."

Archie had expected that he would.

"A pity, then, that your perspicuity did not extend to providing me with each and every copy taken of the Slater material. Where, may I ask, is the copy made in the Embassy at your instigation?"

He *was* in touch, then, exactly as Archie had surmised. "I directed it separately with a covering letter."

"Through the ordinary mails?"

"Yes."

Tremayne tilted back. Under the direct light from a single ceiling lamp a touch of colour flared at the high points of his cheeks. "Unbelievably foolish! You realise, of course, that the copy has not arrived, and that furthermore, given the method of transmission – and the nature of the material – it may never arrive?"

"Yes."

Tremayne ground a heel into the spread of papers at his feet. "I find your behaviour quite extraordinary. Not satisfied with prying into matters which were not your concern you appear to have taken pleasure in advertising them to other persons whose business it is to pry even more thoroughly. Tell me, I wish to understand the cast of mind of an individual such as you: do you betray trust because someone offers more money, uses coercion, or has uncovered some nasty little secret in your nasty little life that you would die rather than admit?"

He spoke as one convinced that one or all of these pretexts formed the mainspring of human conduct.

Stretching down from the high stool Archie scooped up his dossier between the edges of his black brogues. Underneath was one of Mrs Kavanagh's buttercup-yellow rubber gloves which he passed over to

Tremayne who absent-mindedly stuffed it into the top pocket of his suit. "No, I could tell you that quite easily and because you wanted to hear it, you'd believe me just as easily. You once said you'd always wanted to be a detective. Well, by nature, you are. All the policemen I know have the same interpretation of human behaviour: wind him up with the right motive and a man'll chatter out why he did it like a pair of clockwork false teeth. No, what I did I did because someone ought to know the truth, and for no reason other than that."

"What is truth?" Tremayne began.

"I read, Sir Evelyn, in spite of my accent. I know what Pilate said. He knew what it was, too. Everyone does."

Tremayne seemed to adapt physically to this new state of affairs by articulating his limbs into an even wider sprawl, and his expression, too, relaxed, reverting to the informal, slightly rueful grin which Archie recalled from their first meeting. "The truth about what?"

"You. Slater and you."

"Oh, dear," sighed Sir Evelyn. "Will this take long? I really do need a drink."

Whether it was because the day was Sunday or Mrs Kavanagh had locked away the gin, or he, in fact, hoped that Archie would cut a long story short, Tremayne made no move to obtain the required drink but continued to listen impassively with only an occasional grunt as he corrected the droop of arm or leg, while his companion gave his version of the reality beyond appearances which, according to Archie, was comprised almost wholly of Sir Evelyn himself.

In the course of a few weeks he had been assaulted, his house (and that of Mrs Slater) burgled, had been dismissed from his job; his employer's business had been swallowed by corporate predators; and now he was in fear of his life. Was it merely coincidence that this trail of disaster began a matter of days after he had accepted an apparently harmless commission on behalf of Sir Evelyn?

Tremayne bore the recital amiably, at the end merely raising his eyebrows. "My dear chap, that's nothing to do with me, nothing at all. As I told you in the beginning, I simply required Slater's research material and you contracted to provide it. Now if you decide to extend the scope of your brief to include shady transactions with credit cards, I'm not surprised you bumped up against the criminal fraternity, but that's your line of country and entirely at your own risk. I must repeat – it has nothing to do with me."

"You wash your hands of it?"

"Oh, quite, old fellow. Pilatesquely – with gusto."

From his inside pocket Archie brought out Slater's appointment book. "I postponed this meeting in case there might be something I had overlooked. But there wasn't – except this."

At the sight of the leatherbound book Tremayne gave a shrug and shifted his gaze to an antique urn from which protruded the violently orange plumes of a feather duster. "Significant?"

"I can't really tell, Sir Evelyn. Largely domestic, I would have thought." (*Christmas at Edith's***The Downs***Patrix-bourne***Hinxhill in the rain***Kitty*) "But there does seem to be a record of Slater's meetings with you prior to his Moscow visit, and a sketchy outline of what he had been required to do."

This was an outright lie. Archie had scanned the book only briefly and in the weekly checklist of appointments Slater's handwriting was so cramped as to be largely unreadable. The truth lay elsewhere, partly in the Moscow diary but more starkly in whatever it was Tremayne had paid Slater to find. It had not taken Archie long to work out that in those jottings, *V – Viki* and *T – Tutu* were simple ciphers for Vera and Tremayne. But, clutching the little book as if it contained the whole story, he launched into an account of what must have happened in those weeks before Slater's final visit to Russia.

Tremayne had paid Slater's research expenses and the premiums on the life insurance for Kitty on one condition: that in return Slater should resume his old acquaintance with Vera and worm his way into her circle. He was told that he had only to record the dotty talk of an eccentric old lady and provide a scholarly, exact transcript which could be appraised at leisure back home in this magnificent library. And while he performed this task he was to have the run of Vera's stable of girls.

What a temptation! In the academic community his sexual voracity had been a byword. Hadn't Slater been the perfect candidate, so excited by vanity and lust that he had neglected to examine Tremayne's commission too closely? Only, once out there, trapped by his own indiscretions, Slater himself became vulnerable. Little by little Tremayne applied the pressure, even threatening his bewildered emissary, pushing him to find something more; something big which Tremayne himself dared not seek out.

"You and Vera Slutskaya go back a long way. You thought she had something in her possession which might damage you. Slater couldn't find it and Vera herself was under suspicion. In the end you were desperate enough to suspect Slater, too. No wonder you were so keen to get me to take Mrs Slater to Moscow. It gave you the opportunity to have Slater's house searched."

Tremayne had wandered over to the window overlooking the back of the house where, a couple of storeys below, a narrow apron of lawn ran between two lines of eighteenth-century domestic outbuildings. "Young man, you have been paid a considerable sum of money for your services. I have heard out your fantastical speculation. Simply take the money and be thankful that I am not so vindictive as to demand its return."

Not so vindictive? He'd left the gas on, hadn't he?

"But that," he indicated Slater's appointment book, "that you may leave."

Archie gave it to him.

Once the little book, the copies of Slater's diary and Archie's own report were joined in Tremayne's safekeeping there would be nothing left between the old man and himself. Nothing except an assertion, "I am not so vindictive". It was the debtor's plea reversed – a promise not to pay – and Archie did not believe it. Tremayne's indifference angered him, that and his virtual certainty that he had guessed the story right. But – what else? What if Helen's scenario were truer than even she had realised and Tremayne was still operating?

"You packed Slater and me off, completely in the dark. The only difference being that he had more to lose, knowing the country like he did – knowing you."

"My dear fellow, I was *horrified* at his death. Why else do you think I made the widow such a generous endowment?"

Tremayne walked him down the winding marble staircase to the ground floor. The cripple on the door had gone home leaving his *Mail* open on the desk at the TV pages. At this time of day in the urea-coloured twilight from the high glass dome, the vestibule struck Archie as seedy, forlorn, and he suddenly understood about the gin. What else to turn to in the evening when that great door had been shut on the world?

"Have you ever thought of recommencing your education, Mr Renshawe?" said Tremayne struggling with the locks. "I believe the new universities are anxious to recruit mature students. And financial provision might be arranged."

"That sounds like charity, Sir Evelyn."

"Not at all, not at all. Restitution. Doesn't that have a finer ring?"

"All I want is your guarantee of peace and privacy, for Mrs Slater as well as myself."

"Out of my hands, my dear fellow. I am in no position . . ." He paused, hunching over the final deadlock. "Unless . . ." If shoulders could have emotionalised, the heave of Tremayne's would have made high drama of the concern he was about to express. "Your former employer, of course, an innocent party in all this, will be fully compensated, but you, Mr Renshawe, have proved yourself adept at other kinds of work. Would you wish me to, mmm, take a few soundings on your behalf?"

"That's not a job, Sir Evelyn. It's a calling, and I don't have the sense of vocation. I couldn't live my life under the shadow of martyrdom."

Tremayne cupped a long hand round the edge of the opening door. His smile was not regretful. "Quite," he said, allowing Archie just enough room to pass sideways into the street. "I suffer. I have suffered. Besides, the duties are tedious, and the pay quite ghastly."

As he went through, Tremayne darted out the other hand to touch Archie's shoulder, then quickly withdrew it as though the physical contact had pained him. "I admire your romanticism, Mr Renshawe, very much, but sometimes don't you feel that underneath you're really a bit of a prig?"

In his flat late that night he telephoned Lambert.

"That la-di-da bugger," said the Welshman after hearing Archie's account of his last meeting with Tremayne. "Make you an offer, did he?"

"Two as a matter of fact. Student or spook. Maybe both."

"Simple." The smile was broad in Lambert's voice. "I wouldn't like to think of you footloose in the spycatcher jungle. Too much like your old brothel-creeper line of country. Get some education, Renshawe. Diplomas and certificates never go amiss. You'd be on to a good thing."

"Yes?"

"Yes," Lambert shouted down the line. "Yes, bloody yes!"

There was a brief pause. "Lambert?"

"Yes, boy?"

"Lambert – watch out for me. Let me know if he jumps."

"Leave it to me. One twitch of his scented hanky and I'll be on to you as soon as. Now, what's next on your agenda?"

Archie glanced round the naked room. "I'm moving house. I'll be in touch."

"You're too decent, Renshawe, purblind decent, you know that? Why didn't you ask him to throw in a subsidised mortgage while he was at it?"

After Lambert rang off Archie packed away his table lamps. The only light left was from one sixty watt bulb. He squatted on the floor, picked up the pad of Basildon Bond airmail paper and leaking Soviet ballpoint which Kitty had left behind and began to write.

"My dear Kitty. This is only the second letter I will have written to you, but it may be the last." After that he got stuck. Could he dare write the truth? "Darling. I'm afraid to live with you because I might not be able to live without you." He didn't even know if that was the truth, only that, there and then, under the soulless electric light he felt it might well be so.

No good though – too high-flown. Not him. Straight then – tough but light-hearted. Stoical. "Kit-Kat Miss, we're not out of the wood yet, and I can't take the risk of you being in danger because of me." Cant. He wouldn't have minded as long as they were together. No, the truth was, "You're rich and I'm not . . ."

He began again. "Dearest, After returning your car to Clacton I'm going away and leaving you this note, because although I love you I don't feel . . ."

What? He didn't know what he didn't feel. At all. Adequate to this or any other occasion might just have covered it. The hell with this.

One letter gently preparing the ground was already on its way via Nazir. Did she need another?"

Yet he persisted until his handwriting, normally upright, was slanting forty-five degrees to the horizontal and the Russian ink blued his fingernails. Darling Kitty.

"My darling Kitty, I am not allowed to tell you very much but your late husband died a hero's death while engaged on dangerous government work. I love you very much and hope we shall be together one day, but we must not see each other for a while because there is something dangerous that I must do . . ."

It sounded as if it had been winged out of besieged Lucknow by carrier pigeon but it would have to do. Besides, it was the nearest he'd got to the truth. They were to be apart but he would be close, watching over Mrs Slater in order to get to her before Tremayne's spooks did.

Long into the night he wrote on and on, writing the truth until the letter had become a letter to himself and the truth as clear and compelling as lies.

27

I n the stiff sea-breeze of dawn Archie climbed out of Slater's car and walked the last 200 yards to the house.

His Daimler was parked at the top of the newly laid drive, its boot almost under the Tyrolean porch. To avoid the crunchy gravel, he approached along the narrow strip of lawn skirting the drive-way.

Inside nothing stirred.

The lip of the boot was unlatched, a faint gleam visible through the aperture. Nothing there except his socket set and the Pirelli SP spare with the worn tread. It was then he noticed an interruption to the smooth run of the bodyline. The back nearside door had not been fully clicked to.

About to snap it shut he remembered Nazir. Nazir who couldn't close doors and left lights on. Nazir was supposed to be here with Crombie, keeping watch.

He released his pressure on the thumb-catch and swore: where was the little black-faced swine?

His back was towards the car when he heard the voice.

"Archie, that is you?"

He turned to see the window being quickly wound down.

"You look like seasick man."

However he looked Kitty must have looked worse. He could hardly recognise her. "Have you been out here in my car all night?"

She nodded miserably. Her blue-tinged face was crested with duck-fluff from the leaking eiderdown in which she was bundled. "I try the telephone to you, once, many times. No answer. I am suspicious. I think that you have plans. A plan to leave me. Then I think, you must have the car to leave me. Then I sleep here so you will not disappear without me."

"But didn't you get my letter? Didn't Nazir give it to you?" He pushed in next to her, agitating more feathers which caught at his red cashmere jumper.

She straightened up. Close to, she looked even worse than ever. She'd been crying, crying till her eyelids puffed to slits. "Nazir explained me this letter."

Damn the fellow, he couldn't resist meddling. "Explained you what?"

"That the letter say only one thing: Archie must soon leave you."

"Yes, but didn't he say why?"

"He said because you are stupid, that is why. After, he gives me advice."

I'll bet. He must have loved it.

"So I too write letter."

"And he helped, I suppose."

Kitty put both hands into the longest gash of the quilt and fished out a brown envelope. "I write without help. It is very rude. Listen. I am reading aloud."

Archie fumbled for a bigger share of the eiderdown, relaxed beneath it and shut his eyes.

"'Dear Archie, I walk about tonight and cry because you tell me you will go away. Perhaps for ever. If you go from me I will not be here but in Russia where to die like a dog. You are smoothie . . .'"

Naz.

"'Too clever by half. Bloody woodentop smart-arse, sarcastic wally.'"

Thank you, Naz. In return one day I'll do a girl of yours a favour with some choice Pushtu.

Kitty coughed and scrabbled at her paper. "This is correct?"

"Quite correct, I'd say. Almost native."

Her voice became louder as she resumed. "'Because you think I am stupid and foreign. The floozy . . .'"

"*A* floozy."

"Wrong!" cried Kitty triumphantly. "This is idiom. I hear him, *Ad-ám*, he calls me this: the foreign floozy. OK?"

"OK."

"'I feel you hard like wood.'"

The Woodentop Wood where the Wallies live.

"'Maybe you think I am nothing but I am not your old rubbish. I go home again to my own rubbish.'"

Perfect Adamite idiom. They'd obviously both been lending a hand.

"'Nothing is here for me and when you leave me this is the most wrong thing you do in entire life because I love you, and am loving you still. Yours sincerely, Kitty Slater.'"

Down the road a paper boy pedalled into the rising wind, his orange anorak scudding rearwards. Under the coverlet Archie suddenly experienced a throb of nostalgia for cruel Helen, his adult woman, for whom the pains of separation, like the discoveries of love, were an indefinitely repeatable solace. Once her continued acts of renunciation had bored him; now he craved their excess of feeling. By comparison, Kitty's emotionalism was exotic, stage-struck, always, apparently, contrived. At heart she was a child with a child's longing for a routine which she sensed would be somewhere within reach if only she threw a louder and longer tantrum. Then there was the matter of class. Helen's unpredictability had been so contagious because Archie believed that it was a mark of breeding; intelligence, even. And that a difficult woman was a woman worth having because you never knew where you were with her. Was it his fault that the heart on Kitty's sleeve was not only outsize but bleeding?

After all, he'd written to her, hadn't he? What else could he say?

"Well?" Kitty said after a long silence during which she had folded her letter into a tiny cube before jamming it in the arm-rest ash-tray.

"Well what? I wrote to you, didn't I?"

"You owe me, Archie Renshawe, detective, you owe me explanation."

If he'd had time and inclination, yes, perhaps he did, because she was a grown-up and oughtn't to behave like a child clutching at men as though they were Daddy, come to save her from the wild things with teeth. Attune yourself to the brutality of the beast: do not make confidences which, however welcome, only show you up as inadequate and naïve. And, strict rule, when it's over, don't cling, don't follow or sleep in his car or offer him cash, property or to bear his child.

"In the letter, remember? I gave my explanation in the letter."

She glared at him so fiercely that he shifted away, expecting a blow.

"Ha! I remember. One word, very often: 'incompatible'. I look it up in my dictionary. I remember: 'incapable of being held together'. Nazir says this is your bloody lie because in this house" – she jabbed a finger towards the stunted juniper thrashing in the wind at the foot of the party wall – "we are very well being held together in the bed of my husband. There! Now you remember!"

"That doesn't mean . . . ."

With a rattlesnake shimmy Kitty launched herself across the front seat in a skirr of feathers and wrenched off the driver's mirror. "Look at this woman," she wailed, falling back, but keeping the mirror high between them. "How you did this to her, your dirty trick? You do it because you think she cannot understand her dictionary?"

"Kitty," he said, "not now, love, not now. I'm dog-tired. Will you let me into your house and put me to bed?"

*   *   *

The succession of long warm days broken only by the routine of mealtimes and shopping made Archie lose track of dates.

Most weekends Nazir came to stay. His Russian was coming along steadily and Kitty helped him with his letters to Klavdia. They did this on evenings under the trees by the lawn over sweet sherry and milk chocolate biscuits. During the week Archie continued his work.

A huge wire fence had been installed around the entire Slater house and garden and the drive gates were now controlled by a remote-sensing device in the hallway. Outside, concealed floodlights came on automatically an hour before dusk. Archie had converted a small turret room into a study with a view of the sea, and bought a pair of Zeiss naval binoculars.

"A waste of money," said Nazir late one night after Kitty had gone to bed. "There's nothing to spot except oil-spill from tankers. What else do you expect from the North Sea – a Russian flotilla?"

Archie gave a final polish to the lenses before capping them with cheese cloth. "Neighbourhood Watch. Perhaps I've taken a leaf out of young Sedgewick's book. Basil doesn't trust anything that hails from abroad. He even thinks his mother's restaurant is a threat to the democratic people of Frinton."

"Come off it, Renshawe, you're no stateless émigré on tenterhooks about being shipped back. It's the woman, isn't it? You've put the fear of God into her about something. That's why she's squandered a fortune on crime prevention."

"Better safe than sorry, old chap, as Lambert used to say. Have a drink."

Nazir refused the offer impatiently. "Lambert nothing. Don't try to fob me off. What's going on? This house is a fortress."

Archie perched on the arm of the Chesterfield and sniffed the blood-red sherry. "I'm expecting someone," he smiled. And that was all he said during the time it took to get up, walk to the open window, tip out the drink and come back to the Chesterfield, empty glass in hand.

"Well?"

"Well what?"

"What sort of someone, for heaven's sake?"

"I don't know," Archie said.

"It's living with Kitty that's done it. She thinks people are always trying to climb through the windows. You've gone mad together. I'm supposed to be your friend – why can't you tell me – because I'm not insane, too?"

"All right, I'll explain what I can. I'm expecting a kind of person."

"Ah, now we're getting somewhere. A Russian kind of person."

"The nationality doesn't matter. My kind of person belongs to the nation within the nation. Remember Vera?"

"Only what you told me in Moscow. Mad, too, wasn't she?"

Each time he stayed Nazir noticed the change in Kitty. The alterations to the house seemed to have made it her own at last, and she flustered around with nervous efficiency, learning to make English bread puddings, trying to cut down on smoking, and encouraging Archie to drink a little wine. Now with hair cropped fashionably short, elegant clothes ordered from London and subtler make-up, she was the image of sensual contentment. Even her English had improved but she never spoke it without echoing the desires of the man who had taken over her life. "Archie says . . . Archie wants . . . Archie . . ."

But in his colleague's steady eyes Nazir observed an unfamiliar coolness which jarred with the little woman's bliss.

Yet Archie loved Kitty. He must do. Nazir had often written that in letters to Klavdia, and he never objected.

The August nights were humid. Incapable of sleep Kitty would lie beside the sleeping man and figure the moonlit curtains with the patterned jumble of her past: Death's-head husband clotting the snow, withered into a star on the bulk of her magician's robe which grew little pockets that peeped open to reveal bright-coloured cards hologrammed with winking, hanging men who changed themselves into fluttering doves and brushed the air with their wings.

Slater, my inanimate man, reviving in sight of his marriage bed, jerking on blind strings like a discarded ventriloquist's doll. Archie had even ordered the headstone and seen it erected with suitable decorum.

"I need a man," groaned Mrs Sedgewick. "Otherwise I am ruined. Only a man can save me."

Kitty looked down from the stepladder into the grey and gold zigzags flickering at the crown of Lyudy's roll-mop hair. "*Mi-li-ya*," she sympathised. "And I am so happy."

She was. For one whole hour of this goldy summer morning she had been stapling corn-dollies over the architrave of the wide hall entry with no thought of anything except the warmth of the sun, the smell of new varnish on the door panels and the lady at the church fête who had apologised for the paganness of the corn-dollies, shyly confiding, nevertheless, that they made a woman – what would one say? – *receptive*. Kitty had bought a dozen.

"I need a man like your man," Lyudy went on in English, catching at the mainstay of Kitty's stepladder with one plump hand. "I have misunderstood the Valuable Added Tax. The English customs swine say unless I put in proper manager they will destroy me. Then I shall hang myself."

Archie came in from the kitchen. "Hello, Lyudy, what's all this?"

Kitty caught his eye, tilted back her head and drew a scarlet-ribboned corn-dolly across her throat. Through the open door Archie saw Lyudy's son, Basil, trudging up the drive with his lilac plastic holdall.

"Oh, dear," said Archie. "Family business. Well, don't buy the rope yet, Lyudmilla Sergeyevna. Come into the sitting-room. I'm sure we can sort things out."

The room smelt of French polish from Slater's newly restored bureau. Archie poured half a tumbler of sherry and handed it to the restaurateuse. "What's happened then, dear?" He took his seat next to her on Crombie's Edwardian chaise-longue. "Are the Frintonese off your *Gulbishnik* and *Chicken Chakhokhbili*?"

"Those Aztecs!" cried Mrs Sedgewick. "Instead they ask for pork chops. Do you believe me? They say that unless I goddamn buck up in ideas I shall be out on the street."

Basil came in with a Gilbert and George poster. "Where do you want this, then?" he asked the room at large.

"Vassya, darling, what is to become of you old mother?"

"It's your fault, Ma. You should have listened to me – steak sandwiches, hamburgers, hot dogs, that's what they go for round here. Nobody likes foreign food if it's not American. Now, how about this?" He stood on the desk chair and squared up his poster against the glass-fronted bookcase of the bureau.

Archie gave one sigh which covered both mother and son. His faith in Lyudy Sedgewick's business sense had never recovered since the Tsarina's opening night. "No," he said to the poster before turning to the woman. "No, no. You're exaggerating, I'm sure. Anyway, you can always sell out. There are plenty of Building Societies just aching for a prime site like the Tsarina's."

"But it is my life, this restaurant. Once I was a proud woman. Now my life is killing me, so I humble myself. A partnership, Archie dear."

From above Basil bugled a dirge through the rolled-up poster while his mother flung her arms round the man and cradled her stiff lacquered hair on his pullover. "On paper," she murmured. "Only on paper. You are the man. The man must be in charge."

V

KATYUSHKA'S

Clacton-on-Sea, November

28

One morning in early November Archie was alone in the turret room retouching the plasterwork cornices with a kit from Texas Homecare when the buzzer sounded from the front gate.

After carefully unbattening the final mould, he rinsed his hands in the tool bucket and made his way along the attic corridor, securing the fire doors behind him, and paused at the top of the main staircase.

In the hall young Sedgewick was pointing the nozzle of a fire extinguisher at the front door. He appeared distraught. "What day is it, Mr Renshawe? My digital's on the blink."

"Put that thing down, Basil."

Basil danced around the hallway, waggling his hose at the newly installed intercom which continued to sound with the intermittent honk of a U-boat alarm. Kitty came in from the back sitting-room and stared at the wall panel where a red light flashed on and off in accompaniment to the noise. "*Tishe, Vassya, sevodnya voskresenye.*"

"I knew it," howled Basil, terror in his voice. "I bloody knew it. *Sundays* – no one comes on Sundays. Even the milkman has a rest on Sunday. They've come for me, haven't they? My Mum's sent them."

Before Archie reached the foot of the stairs Kitty had flicked the double switch on the machine killing both alarms. Almost immediately the grille of the audiopanel vibrated from a burst of incomprehensible gabble which drew Nazir from his TV in the half-landing parlour. "That's queer," he said, grinning broadly at the noise in the wall. "I thought it was Sunday."

The disembodied voice suddenly broke up under a barrage of clangs as Basil hurtled at the grille. "I know that language, you can't fool me. I know who you are . . ."

Kitty stood to one side, trembling in the shade of the sunless porch. A wide black car sat at the end of the drive its engine inaudible above the hiss of the remote-control electrics which were slowly parting the gates. She suddenly closed up to Archie, wanting him not to leave her, not to step down into the path of this fat official-looking vehicle, make it stop and have to ask whoever was driving who he was and what business could he possibly have with them?

She had been asleep and while she slept a dream had come about the baby. Out here she still did not feel completely awake and was trying to remember what sex of child her mother had predicted if she slept to the right, when the Mercedes drew alongside. Without waiting for the door to be opened by the uniformed chauffeur, a stocky middle-aged man squeezed out backwards holding above his black head a bouquet of russet carnations. Before the man turned Kitty thought, I cannot be awake. But as he did so, awkwardly, thrusting the cellophaned flowers forward as though in propitiation, a great shout came from behind, breaking her dream, and Nazir pushed to the front with a burst of over-stressed Russian, "*Boris Kirillovich, Borka, zdrastvui, kak dela?*"

"Good God, it's not possible," said Archie. "Kitty, is this one of your tricks?"

She dug her fingers hard into the swell of her waist, alarmed at her own reality in the face of this figure which had materialised from the nightmare of a former existence. "What do you think – I should want to terrify myself by calling up this creature? God in heaven, Archie, what brings him to us? I am so frightened. Hold me, hold me, or I die with this baby."

While they clung together on the steps Nazir continued to greet the visitor with unaffected enthusiasm, clapping him on the shoulder, bearing him round so he could kiss the squabby liverish cheeks, until his few words of Russian ran out and he and Borka fell into relaxed, voluble English.

"Well I'm damned, fancy bumping into you again, and in this of all places. How's the old lady? Any news of Klavdia? Vacation time, is it, or are you on a job? Drug-busting, I bet, international – it's all over the papers, that kind of thing, now it's all different over there . . ."

One prune-stone eye concentrated on the couple at the top of the steps, Borka tacked across the gravel towards them like a burglar fending off an importunate spaniel. "How right! You speak wonderful, Mr Nazir! Well met indeed, my dear . . . A social call, a little business, too, as you say – on the side. I wish to buy English setter . . . pointer . . . retriever . . . You know them? And twin-sets for *Mamochka*."

Eventually gaining the steps, he checked his advance and stretched up his bouquet to Kitty's knee.

"We don't breed dogs," said Archie. "And Harrods is seventy-five miles in the opposite direction. So what can you want with us?"

Borka seized the opportunity to take the next few steps in his stride. "I have told you, Archie, darling friend, this becomes the love of my life. Soon I am retired. Old men need hobbies. All my life I am kept underground – you remember? – offices, places of confinement and what do I yearn for? The open-air life of English huntsman. So Mama says, *Borya*, fetch a London shop dog, a thoroughbred, highly strung, which will love you and only you can calm its nerves."

"That'll cost you," said Nazir brushing up the velvet nap of the policeman's overcoat collar.

"Cost, cost! What is money! I have money for whole flock of dogs!" Confronted by an unmoving Kitty he handed over the carnations to Nazir and felt for his wallet. "See," he shouted, extracting a fat roll of twenty-pound notes. "This is money, money for dogs."

Archie had to let him in because he said he wanted to use the lavatory. At this point, Basil, who, after greeting the policeman's arrival with a single "uh-uh" retreated to the hallstand where he sat on the ledge between the umbrellas biting his nails. "No, he doesn't," he said, accepting from Nazir the bouquet which by now had begun to look rather ragged. "He doesn't need one. None of them needs one. Here," he went on, darting a sneer at Borka's apologetic face and waving his flowers at the garden. "There's bushes outside, *Steppenwolf*. Pretend you're at home. More cover than in bloody Siberia."

But the chauffeur did, too. "Is he Russian as well?" asked the boy.

"English car-hire firm," Borka stated resolutely.

Basil let them past with a show of reluctance.

Afterwards the policeman showed no inclination to follow his driver whom he ushered out to the car with instructions to swab the windscreen and empty the ash-trays. "I may smoke?" he asked Archie.

"I'd rather you didn't. Kitty can't stand the smell in the mornings."

Without appearing to listen Borka put away his cigar case and strolled uninvited into the big front room where Slater's bureau stood in its old place. He made straight for it, poking into the little compartments and caressing the inlay as though he could scarcely credit the existence of such a fine item of furniture in a private house.

By nature deeply polite Archie felt disadvantaged by the familiarity of this unwelcome guest as well as resentful at the disruption of their peaceful Sunday routine. But the best he could manage was a mild rebuke. "This isn't a road-house you know. Why didn't you telephone or something?"

"A fine article," said Borka concluding his inspection and moving across to the mantelpiece. "But of course you are right, dear fellow,

I forget I am in England. Notice is required. I apologise. I am impulsive. A friend tells me about Pierland Kennels in Clacton and I jump into car. Only half-way I remember my friends, they live in this town, they will give me slap-up welcome." He paused, eyes twinkling, quite unapologetic: his stance before the blaze of the gas-fire firm, proprietorial.

Archie was about to retort the obvious when Kitty came in.

"As Mama did for you, Archie, and for you, madame," said Borka with a silky grin. "Or would have done, if you were not that evening otherwise engaged."

She glanced at Archie before raising the oval rosebowl of flowers to its usual position on the mantelshelf. As she withdrew, her hand accidentally touched Borka's shoulder. At the touch her heart missed a beat and her throat seemed to swell as if in a tautening collar.

"How easy he talks, this man," she began in a murmur across the Russian's chest. "He tries to make us guilty because I did not eat with his mother. Why he not warn us, eh? I know him and his kind. Nothing changes – Bolshevism, communism, war communism, co-existence, *détente*, *glasnost*, *perestroika*. See, see, detective, I learn by heart at school every one damn slogan . . ."

Archie strode over and held her close. The front door slammed to with a crash and Basil strolled into the room in green wellingtons. "Still here?" he said, rolling his eyes at the policeman.

"Don't you start," Archie shouted. "There's enough hysteria batting around already. Sit down and shut up. The man's come for some reason that's not the reason he said." Archie found himself vocalising the fluster of his own irritation, fear and outright curiosity. He knew he was not impressing Kitty, let alone the policeman who throughout continued to smile seraphically from one to the other. "Naz! Where's Naz?"

Basil fetched him. "You look as if you all need a drink," said Nazir after a glance at Kitty's staring eyes. He brought in the tray of sherry and snacks which it was his chore to set out every Sunday morning.

"Very nice," exclaimed Borka from the hearth-rug. "Now if I may suggest, we do Agatha Christie in the drawing-room. Each person sit down comfortably and we have a bit of a jaw – OK?"

Everyone agreed except Basil who brooded over his Coca-Cola in the furthest angle of the bay window. "You're a communist, aren't you?" he murmured, his eye on the black Mercedes 300 parked lengthwise to the porch.

Crooking his little finger Borka sipped imperturbably. "Times change. It is difficult to explain to young persons. *Skazhitye menye, pozhaluista imyete govorit po-russkii?*"

The language acted on Basil Sedgewick like snake-venom.

"That's bloody typical. Here you are, thousands of miles from home, licensed to mix with decent people and all you're looking for is other foreigners who you reckon belong to your lot because they understand Russian. I'm sick of it, and look at him." He pulled back the curtain to reveal Borka's chauffeur polishing the Mercedes windscreen. "I bet he's sick of it, too. Call yourself a communist – where's his drink, then? Or has he brought his flask?"

"He gets over-excited in company," Archie explained when Basil had flounced out to the driver with a can of Fosters and a packet of crisps. "A broken home."

The adults reverted to small talk more embarrassed by the detective's unflappable bonhomie than Basil's outburst.

"The doctor says spring," Archie volunteered in reply to Borka's query about Kitty's condition. "We're not married, of course, but, well, nowadays . . ."

Kitty glared, her knuckles white on the arm of her chair. Archie sprinted on wondering when the man was going to stop playing silly buggers and give them the real reason for his extraordinary visit. "My divorce, you see, one has to wait . . ."

". . . Before one steps into the shoes of Professor Slater," said Borka with a sparkling glance at Kitty's figure. "Are they fitting one yet, Mr Renshawe, those shoes?"

The unprovoked malice of this remark brought Kitty to her feet. "Bastard!" she retaliated in their common language. "Why can't you leave us in peace?"

"Oh, Lord, Borka." Nazir interposed himself between hostess and guest. "I ought to have known you two couldn't share an aperitif without provoking an international incident. Look, Archie, how about me driving Kitty down to your Aunt Emily's while you have it out with Borka?"

Before Archie could speak Kitty had resumed her place turning slightly in her seat to face squarely at the fat detective. "Oh, no," she said in English. "I am not ill. I am only pregnant. I shall stand this. Allow him to speak his bloody story about the nice kind Russian police force."

"Go upstairs, dear," pleaded Archie.

But Kitty took Borka on directly, waving aside the protests of her men. "You play cat and mouse: let them think they are safe, in England, in lovely cosy home with pieces of antique. But you know we don't get away so quick from devils who like to set us up, bit by bit. But I am warning you, Satan policeman. My blood is your blood and I am woman with child."

Borka took in the expressions on the faces of the men, evidently not displeased with the effect he had created. "Yes, yes," he murmured soothingly. "Here we have a nice home, very nice, a home where everyone is happy until this inspector calls. He is not clever, first class at Oxford like Oliver Slater, professor, deceased, and he cannot even dream of a nice house by the sea with automobiles and babies to come. Perhaps you need him, this Boris. You and him, Archie, once were chums. Are you not master in this nice home? This fat man, remember, he saved your life. Is this young lady to come between us?"

The reproach was the more insulting to Kitty when Archie instead of brushing it aside, seemed to weigh up its implication.

Borka spoke again. "I bring news from Moscow. A funeral has taken place. Seven weeks ago a lady makes a journey by Metro, *Kropotkinskaya – Biblioteka imyeni Lenina*. One stop. Every Friday she makes this journey. She has studies in the library. But this day she stays on the platform. The crowd leaves and she is still standing."

Kitty knew where. Where they always stood, furthest from the oncoming train, near the indicator which flicks back the seconds remaining between that which has departed and that which is to come. *Your underground is so wonderfully reliable, Mrs Slater.* How long? Two minutes, two forty-five? *Utterly dependable no matter what the time of day.*

"A policeman notices this old lady."

He wants an easy day. He is looking for drunks. A drunk is an excuse to pass half the morning in his snug little billet at the top of the stairs, filling out charge sheets.

"She is too near the edge."

All her life. And now Kitty saw the fat green train rumbling up and the woman looking into the eyes of the guard, and the policeman's face as he realised that between her and him lay a distance outreaching the stars.

"For the driver it was terrible. She was old, this lady, carrying two heavy bags. Her work, she took it everywhere with her – and because of these bags, and because she is not so strong, and at this moment, forgetful . . ."

Wild from the nearness of it, that final unpractiseable moment, she would no more have known how to disencumber herself of the business of life, than how it would feel when the contour of the braking cab impressed itself upon her breast and flung her over, bag and baggage, to be strewn like so much toffee-paper beneath the shining wheels.

Kitty pressed her hands over her ears. "I will not listen," she muttered in Russian. "We try to forget death by looking forward to life, but the smell of death clings to you wherever you go. It is your business, yours alone. You no longer have the right to involve us."

Borka gave Kitty a quizzical glance. "Yekaterina Aleksandrovna says I have no right to tell you who she was, this old lady who died."

"You know she doesn't mean that."

"Ach, so, what does she mean?"

"She means that we already know. For months we've been expecting something to happen. Now it has we're not exactly unprepared."

"I am," said Nazir. "Totally. Nobody tells me anything."

"You didn't know her," said Archie.

Nazir looked to Borka. "Who didn't I know?"

Kitty's throat trembled in a sudden spasm of energy. "They talk about one very old mistress of my old husband. Verochka. You remember her name, but you did not meet her in Moscow."

"Née Stacpoole," Archie said morosely. "The people's friend, an aged intellectual lady who fell for the Soviet Glory Land before the war, but put off her defection until the Brezhnev years."

"So what about her?" Nazir sounded mystified.

"She's dead."

"Good God, Archie old boy, even I've deduced that by now. I'm sorry and all that, but why should it make you and Kitty so miserable?"

"Simple," smiled the fat detective. "Yekaterina Aleksandrovna is angry because he is sad and he hangs his face because he believes he has killed this little old lady."

Kitty was inwardly screaming. No, no, that was not the reason at all. After Slater Vera was alone in a country which could never be her own. After Slater Kitty, too, had been alone, and when you are alone it is very easy to jump because the train has been waiting all your life for this moment to roar out of the tunnel into your face. It is no use weeping even if you are beautiful or old and crazy in the head because you know no one in this foreign place understands you as you once felt you had a right to be understood, so you fall away out of weariness for strangers with whom you had commerce only at the margins of existence.

I know this because I came from there and was saved.

But aloud she said nothing because Nazir was talking. ". . . well, a note, a message . . . That's usually the way with suicides, isn't it –

having the last word? I mean, if there was a letter, Archie here mightn't feel so bad."

Borka produced a narrow strip of paper. "Like this, Mr Nazir?"

"I've no idea, how could I?"

"No more you could, my dear, not being in the business. This," said Borka, "is the last writing of Vera Slutskaya. It is brief, to the point, and English. I shall read: 'NOTHING. I SAID NOTHING.'"

"Is that all?"

"That is all."

"What about her carrier bags, you said they were full of papers, her life's work?"

"Every paper was recovered and examined, seven thousand, three hundred and twenty six separate papers, exactly the size of this paper I hold out to you. Each one has the identical message." Borka placed the strip back into his mottled pocket book. "Nothing," he repeated. "I SAID NOTHING."

Nazir pulled a face. "For heaven's sake, Archie, the old girl was obviously mad. It's nothing anyone *did*."

"Just so," said Borka. "She destroys her academic life's work to make messages . . ." He chopped his fat hands at the air. "So many messages in all the same words. I ask myself – who is she speaking to this way, our mad old girl?"

Kitty broke the silence that followed. "Archie, my sweet, it was not you. Vera was not writing to you."

That was right. Not to him, or for him, so that he would understand, but through him, on behalf of another person who would, and be satisfied in the knowledge.

As if picking up his thoughts Borka reverted to his former ghastly good manners. "And you, dear Archie, are you still pounding detective beat?"

Blinking, as if coming out of a dream, Archie shook his head. "Oh, I gave that up when my employers were bought out. I always told you I wasn't suited to the work. No, Kitty and I are going into the restaurant business."

"Tea-rooms, English," corrected Kitty. "On the promenade for ladies and gentlemen. Tea-cakes, muffins. Very simple."

"Congratulations, young people. I clap for your enterprise. And this unborn child," said Borka with an avuncular glance at Kitty's thickened waist. "You are choosing names?"

"I like boy-girl names myself," said Archie, feeling himself edged out by the mutual constraint which still existed between the detective and the woman.

"A very English child, must it not be, madame? No dark Slavonic shadows on Oliver-Olivia?"

"Evelyn." It was Kitty who had spoken.

Borka gave way to a burst of delighted laughter. "She is priceless, dear Archie, your magician wife-to-be. Everything she touches transforms itself before my very eyes. Evelyn, Evelyn. And they say Russians have no sense of humour!"

In the hallway Kitty reluctantly offered her hand. Borka kissed it on the wristbone and said something which caused her to withdraw, half-closing the door behind her. On the bottom step he turned to take in the vista.

"A sunny day. I do not need to hurry. So show me this English garden, and before going I will tell you why your lady hates me."

Behind the house Archie and the policeman strolled across a well-kept lawn dotted with scarlet bat-wings shedding from the maples.

"She is still our citizen," said Borka. "She may still come to us without harm, and you are the husband, or will soon be, and may come also. With us you will be safe. A sincere offer."

"What do you mean safe? You're in England, remember? We're already safe. We've no plans to move house to Moscow."

Borka lit a cheroot. Field-grey smoke drifted into Basil's Peace roses. "An hour ago you said my reason for my visit was not my real reason. That is God's truth, my dear. Too true. In fact I owe you a favour, Archie darling. Now I shall repay." The Russian felt deep into the left pocket of his mackintosh. "'Swiftly it flies through the air.'" he said. "A motto I saw once on an old painting. 'Swiftly it flies and kills.' A young man sleeps and death is near. You sleep, my beloved friend, in this hazy English garden. Above your head the arrow is whizzing. Very suddenly it will come. Pouf!" He grabbed at the empty air. "Pouf! It will come very soon. The arrow of scandal and ruin and death. And I am sad because it will once more destroy our Professor Slater and our Mrs Slater, and you, and all who belong to you."

"I'm sick of this," said Archie. "I'm sick to death of all this bloody Russian pantomime. Why can't you just go to hell and leave us alone?"

Borka took his hand, girlishly, as if in love and consolation. "A man is left, the man who pays everybody, who paid Slater and his wife and the child within her, and you, and you. Your benefactor."

When Archie tried to withdraw his hand Borka hung on tight. "You think I did not guess, Archie, that you were in his pay? An innocent, just like Slater, a man who did not know what he was searching for, but knew he was afraid because he could not find it."

"You cold-blooded bastard, you knew all along, you read his diary."

"No need, no need. Pictures speak better than words. *Vozmi*." A package the size of a couple of paperbacks. Sugar-paper wrapping from GUM secured by Soviet nylon string. "VHS, Archie. Compatible. The yellow one first. Watch and then discover why you should come home to me."

Archie accepted without reluctance, but in the small of his back came a bright wriggle of pain that made him involuntarily tighten his shoulder. Borka seemed to divine it and caressed the topmost vertebra of the Englishman's spine. "Believe me, my dear," he soothed. "All this and more you could have – houses in town, houses in country, stature, the freedom to breathe." *Christ on the mountain top, the country of heaven on earth.* "Everything, everything."

In his mind Archie pictured the little house near the river beset by earth and sky. "Vera had everything and look what happened to her."

"What is that to you? A compromised woman goes mad from her past. Slutskaya was in danger only from herself. You have no sins to hunt you down."

"There are worse fates. I could finish up a cabaret Englishman with no home to turn to. Like young Basil's mother, weeping gin tears into her borscht while she battles with the VATman. I'm no émigré, Borka."

"Of course you are not. But your wife-to-be, your Katyinka, she is. She hates me because I know that here she cannot be anything else, and therefore can never truly be your wife. Archie, come to us."

Archie almost believed him. He might even have felt grateful had he forgotten that they were in England, and that Borka meant England when he talked about being less safe here than in the country of the mother of his child-to-come.

29

As they strolled in the waning light Archie cut the string with Basil's secateurs. Both boxes were numbered but unlabelled. "This could be Mickey Mouse, for all I know," he said, holding up the yellow one. "Is there a title?"

"Both have only one title, *Victim of Glasnost.*"

"I've seen it already," said Archie. "Channel Four, six months ago. Don't tell me you've come three thousand miles to hand out documentaries."

The lawn sloped down to a makeshift fence separating the garden from a small paddock. Borka gave a throaty chuckle. "It is home-grown entertainment, under the counter. A dirty picture but moral, very moral."

"Be your age, for God's sake, I'm hardly in the market for that kind of stuff."

"Ah, you were, Archie dear. Once, how you were!"

There was a scuffle on the far side of the fence and the heads of a pair of donkeys appeared. "Basil's," said Archie. "We let them graze here in return for him lending a hand with the gardening."

Outside the conservatory Basil was honing his topiary shears on a whetstone. The sight of the boy intent on this innocent task took Archie back to Ben Karpinskii who had loved and trusted Slater who had loved and trusted someone else who had betrayed that love and trust. The cellulose coating of the tape boxes felt suddenly cold in his hand. "All right," he said to the Russian who was twiddling the ears of the larger donkey. "If things get too bad here I'll send a postcard to Moscow."

Basil caught the last word and closed up his shears, looking from one man to the other.

Without warning, Borka swung up his short arms to clasp Archie in tight embrace. "There's a good boy, *golubchik*. You go in now and watch my TV replay and get smart. Then maybe you won't feel like joking."

Basil kept them in view. "I'd watch him, Boss," he called out.

"First they slobber all over you, then they bite. I'd keep my distance – you don't know where he's been."

Alone in the turret room Archie pulled down the roller blind, flicked up the video switch and inserted tape number one. His hands were trembling. A buzz, then a snowstorm of dots, then a room. A grainy monochrome room. An old-fashioned white telephone on a table by a bed. Coats and frocks hung from a picture rail. Dressing-up stuff, elaborate. He remembered Kitty on that bitter cold day in the village.

The camera angle was static. The room. Just the room for what seemed like an age.

Then a woman. When he saw the woman he knew the room. Vera's room. Vera in it. Slightly younger, hair shorter, but Vera frightened, hands clasped, mouth soundlessly working. A silent movie.

Then a man, suddenly, as if from the wings of a stage. Tall, the man, stork-legged elbows breaking the sleeve-line of his English suit. The overlong hair, silverish; the hands, the stoop. Archie knew him, knew him from behind, straight off.

Evie. Tremayne.

Vera went in and out of range, fetching and carrying to the bed. Quite a little pile eventually on the satin quilt: cans of Pepsi and chocolate bars, dozens of shiny parcels done up in starry foil. Tremayne didn't move, simply stood, watching, back to the camera eye. He was evidently waiting. Archie waited, too, watching him wait.

Archie expected a woman. He expected Kitty. But when the man came, between Vera and Tremayne, he knew he ought to have known.

Darkish, darker than in death, eelly as he moved in life, exact, dandified. He bowed, kissed Tremayne, took his arm, gently manoeuvring around so that both men stood eye to eye with the lens hidden in the wall. He knew where it was. He would know. He would be the only one to know. He was in the picture all along, the Georgian, Zhikadze. The pimp.

Tremayne was excited, expectant, looking off camera, away to the invisible door. And it must have been from there that the woman came – a dumpy woman in a black dome-shaped hat. She came into frame leading a child who held a carrier bag. They sat down together on the bed, upright and apart. The child's face was muffled in a scarf which the woman reached out to unwind. It was a male child, blond. Before the hair Archie had recognised the eyes. Solemn, unafraid. It was not that child, the boy left with Zhikadze's body, but the eyes were the same. The same type.

The red London bus. Chocolate. *Gdye dyadushka?*

Zhikadze fell to one knee before the child. From the corner Tremayne passed across toys, hand to hand. A capgun, a popgun, a clockwork fish that waggled its fins. On and on till the parcels were empty and the toys spilled out from the lap of the child.

Zhikadze lit a cigarette and held it between the boy's lips. The boy inhaled, then coughed and his cough caused Tremayne and Zhikadze to smile, so that the boy smiled also. But he was not allowed the presents on the bed until he had kissed Zhikadze. Afterwards, full on the mouth, he kissed Tremayne.

This was the signal for Zhikadze and the women to leave.

Alone with the boy Tremayne began to touch. Under the dark knitted jumper with a pale reindeer on the front, under the white aertex vest, across the naked shoulders within the span of his hands. White on white, insinuating further and further, downwards, all the way.

Archie watched to the end. The end was sudden and brutal; appalling. In the end the child bled. And at the end the silver-haired figure prone on the bed inspected himself and smiled at the blood on himself that had run from between the legs of the child.

Archie wept.

When it was over everything that had led to the final terrible act made perfect sense. Out of fear Vera had procured the child. What could be worse? Tremayne had been worse, that went without saying, went with the looking. But the act, however repulsive, was passionate, compelling. Zhikadze was worst. He must have been colder than death. The hidden camera was his. He would have made copies, distributed copies, sold them, bribed with them. How useful, now, that the order in his country had been so transformed that Tremayne, once an honoured guest whose sexual tastes were to be discreetly indulged, could be himself betrayed, and then employed once again, but this time as a scapegoat for all the characteristic sins of the old corrupt regime.

That was what Borka had on Tremayne: the knowledge that he could destroy him at the flick of a switch. And to applause. Official applause. After the Great Change in the eighties Tremayne must have suspected the possibility all along. That was why Slater was sent out.

Slater had money. Money from Tremayne. Research funds. *Blat.* Bribe-money for anyone who knew anything at all about the tastes of the elderly gentleman from Bloomsbury, to be quiet, to consent to be bought, to have other silences procured. But Tremayne, so familiar to the world of distrust, could trust no one with his secret, not even Slater. So the research was aimless, a futile casting around. Vera's epitaph: *I said nothing*. Hence Slater's: *I knew nothing*.

Lambs to the slaughter, both.

Afterwards, Archie wanted the second film to be over quickly. He steeled himself. The same room, the bakelite telephone, the same wall festooned with cami-knickers and Jaeger-cut suits. But this time a girl on the bed. A blonde. Chubby.

Against the lamplight the silhouette of a man, square-shouldered. He moved into the circle of light. Sixty-ish. A shock of white hair, a beard. Vera stood on the far side of the lamp. She was as Archie remembered, the same butterfly slide clipping back her fringe as she bent over the blonde, unzipping the bodice of the dark frock. Then she flicked up the skirt.

The man fumbled. He looked drunk. Awkward. Vera brought him to the girl with her own hands. The girl fidgeted and began to cry.

At the crucial moment Archie pressed "hold".

The man faced the light. Vera helped him again. Archie leaned closer, pushing "fast forward" then "rewind". Again and again the bearded head ducked up and down. Archie stared. The beard. The beard had once straggled over the collar of the dress-shirt in Kitty's old snapshot.

Slater. Was that him? Really? That stranger, that shadow imprinting itself painfully on to tape? If it was, then he had been a bit of a bungler. Too worried. At the end he was grotesque, like the film. Not blue but black.

Had Kitty ever needed to help him like that? Had he ever failed her as he failed the blonde? Kitty never said and Archie knew she never would. In this, as in so much else, she had been loyal.

Archie set fire to the Slater film in the washbasin of the upstairs lavatory. The stink was so vile that he had to open the window. When the smell had dispersed he removed the headboard of the narrow guest bed in his room and felt for the lever handle of the one purchase not paid for by Kitty out of her late husband's estate.

Chubb safe, fire resistant to one hundred degrees celsius that he had bought with part of his redundancy money. Money from Tremayne. Sweet irony.

He placed video number one on the bottom shelf beside the other insurances: one dozen perfect facsimiles of Oliver Slater's diary, run off the second copy he had made in the Commercial Section of the Embassy that last Moscow day. Single sheets that Nazir had pasted on the back of A4 New Year calendars and mailed home from five different Soviet post offices to members of the tour group: Gavin; two American girls; four Blackburn Jewish boys, and even the elegant fashion-plate who, between arrival and departure, had disappeared completely because, as Archie learned on the way to the airport, she had whiled away all but one of her prescribed Seven Moscow Nights in the bed of Konstantin, a computer hacker in the Baumanskaya District.

Nazir had paperchased round the country in his Deux Chevaux retrieving pages from addressees, all of whom swallowed his story that he was on a sentimental journey to assemble the relics of his blighted love affair: Klavdia's farewell letter, which had to be smuggled out because it contained indiscreet details of their brief liaison.

Down below a window opened and Kitty's childish giggles broke on the air. She was in the kitchen celebrating with Nazir because Borka had gone and everything seemed as safe and cosy again as it had been before. Soon she would call upstairs for Archie to come to lunch.

Tremayne had not intended Slater to die or Kitty to be terrorised or that poor weird Vera should make away with herself. But all of them (Archie included himself) were incidental casualties of Evelyn Tremayne's obsessive fears that someone would expose the truth of his past. Not the spying part – Tremayne must have been an amateur at that as at so many other things.

Slater, Vera, Zhikadze. Bodies staining the snow. And for the wonder that not one was his Archie offered a prayer to Captain Ross who had seconded him in the school boxing ring with shouts to keep his guard high and to lead with his left. The old brute would have been proud to see him now, on his toes, scoring points against the hard men who ran their lives in disregard of the frailties of others. Well, he'd taken their tips and built them into his new life as snug as this fat, grey safe set in the turret-room wall, his Protector Guard against low, amateurish blows.

He understood why Borka had given him the first tape. It was explicit reassurance. Now any threat from Tremayne could be countered by threat. The old man was still powerful, Borka knew that. Was it enough? Borka evidently had his doubts. Otherwise, why the invitation to Moscow? But Archie had already decided: home was home. He would stick it out.

But the second tape, Slater's night with the blonde? It seemed like a typical example of the policeman's malicious humour. Perhaps Borka thought Kitty should actually see the truth about her dead husband. Archie wondered what Kitty's reaction might have been. And how would that have made her feel about Borka? Would she think that at last she could trust him? That she would return, with her child, be secure, put the past behind her? But it was no go with Kitty, Archie knew that. She would never believe that Vera's death was an accident or that Borka's offer might be genuine. And whatever the Russian said or showed, she would also never admit the full truth about Slater. Once, she had given herself to him.

Borka had left after kisses and momentary tears. Sunday resumed with the clatter of pans on the stove and Basil's Japanese organ belling out the trill of a Yakut lullaby at the first pip of the one o'clock news. Archie stood within the curve of the box-sash, looking out over the flattened sea. No wind to raise even a bubble under the still mist welling down to the horizon. A good day for submarines. He fancied their snouts breaking water like fingers through wax.

If the scandal broke, Borka had said, if it needed to break, if either he or Archie had to make it break to keep free and alive, it would come suddenly, like a war, in a rush of fire from the sea. But until that moment they could settle quietly into the Slater fortune bequeathed by their antagonists. Some had already paid for that comfort – life with life; Lambert with his independence; Kitty with Slater; Slater with death. Tremayne would be the last, but one of the first to pay for the end of the old, old, Cold War.

Slater had paid in advance for Renshawe, Kitty, the child. Yet someone must eventually come for the forfeit.

NATALYA LOWNDES

CHEKAGO

'An outstanding debut by an exciting new writer'
Anita Brookner

'What an *extraordinary* novel . . . ovcrall it's the sheer power and
pace of the writing that amazes me . . . wonderful, I adored it'
Margaret Forster

'A uniquely well-informed, vital, sexy story'
Victoria Glendinning

'A first novel of startling originality'
Norman Shrapnel in The Guardian

'Especially acute as a satire of Western illusions about
Mother Russia'
Michael Ignatieff in The Observer

ANGEL IN THE SUN

'The time is 1917–18, the place is a vast estate in south-east
Russia . . . The reckless goings-on in the Great House are an
echo of the collapse of order and authority outside. Natalya
Lowndes has a passion for the country's savage history, as urgent
as a physical sense . . . she is a powerful writer'
Penelope Fitzgerald in the Evening Standard

'A relish for language and for plot; this is storytelling at full tilt'
The Observer

'A feast of a book, marvellously written, and with an authentic
Russian vastness and prolixity . . . the underlying structure is
quite wonderful. Threads which appear to have been spun at
random are skilfully picked up, and woven into a breathtaking
whole, as unforgettable as a vivid dream. Natalya Lowndes has
turned a historical footnote into splendid and original fiction'
The Sunday Times